Innocent as Sin

ALSO BY ELIZABETH LOWELL

The Wrong Hostage

Whirlpool

Always Time to Die

The Secret Sister

The Color of Death

Death Is Forever

Die in Plain Sight

Running Scared

Moving Target

Midnight in Ruby Bayou

Pearl Cove

Jade Island

Amber Beach

Innocent as Sin

Elizabeth Lowell

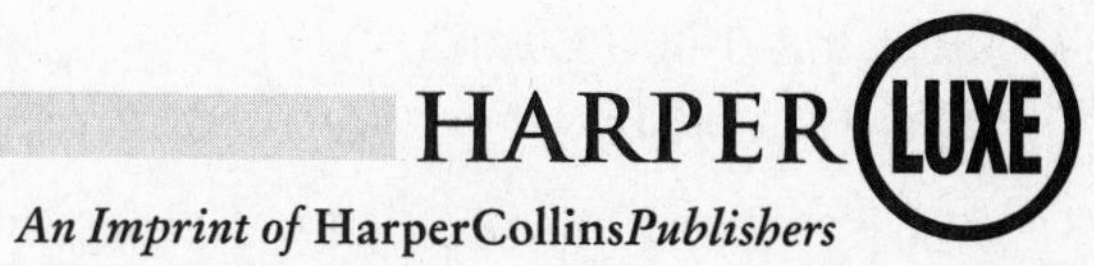

This book is a work of fiction. The characters, incidents, and dialogue are drawn from the author's imagination and are not to be construed as real. Any resemblance to actual events or persons, living or dead, is entirely coincidental.

 For information address HarperCollins Publishers, 10 East 53rd Street, New York, NY 10022.

HarperCollins books may be purchased for educational, business, or sales promotional use. For information please write: Special Markets Department, HarperCollins Publishers, 10 East 53rd Street, New York, NY 10022.

FIRST HARPERLUXE™ EDITION

HarperLuxe is a trademark of HarperCollins Publishers

Library of Congress Cataloging-in-Publication Data is available upon request.

ISBN: 978-0-06-125930-2
ISBN-10: 0-06-125930-6

07 08 09 10 11 ID/RRD 10 9 8 7 6 5 4 3 2 1

For Margaret and Roy
Yeah, sure, you betcha!

Innocent as Sin

1

Africa
Late March

Wearing dirty camouflage gear, boots, and insect repellent, Rand McCree crouched behind the tattered grass blind. His camera's extreme-long-distance lens filled the hole cut in the loosely woven grass. Even though the sun was barely above the eastern horizon, Rand was sweating. He didn't notice it. In the Democratic Republic of Camgeria, whether it was tropical coastland or scrubby interior, men sweated. It was how they knew they were alive.

Through the camera lens Rand watched the rebels—or freedom fighters, depending on your politics—wait next to heavy trucks parked just off the south end of the miserable, barely scraped dirt strip that passed for a runway in this part of Africa.

Next to him, his twin jerked, kicking the AK-47 lying between the two men.

"Settle down," Rand said softly. "The plane will be along eventually."

"Something bit me," Reed muttered.

"Are your shots current?"

"Yeah."

"Then what are you bitching about?"

"I feel like a bush blood bank."

Rand smiled. "You are."

"How did I let you talk me into this?"

"Me? You were the one going on about a lifetime opportunity to get a picture of the most dangerous, mysterious arms trader since—"

"Yeah, yeah," Reed interrupted. "Don't remind me."

"Not more than twice a day."

"More than that. At least twice since—"

"Quiet."

Reed shut up and heard the whining growl of turboprops. He raised his powerful binoculars and began searching the dusty sky in the direction of the sound.

"Got him," he said to his twin. "Coming in at three o'clock, flying low. And I mean low." He whistled softly through his teeth. "That's a ballsy pilot. Or a drunk. His gear is raking leaves."

"Just one of the problems of flying without filing a flight plan." Rand concentrated on getting the unmarked, unlighted Ilyushin Il-4 in focus as it approached the dirt strip. "Keep an eye on the countryside. We don't want to explain what we're doing here."

"Nobody would ask," Reed said. "They'd just shoot us."

"Like I said—"

"He's going straight in," Reed interrupted, excitement in his voice. "You got him?"

"Yeah. Watch that you don't flash sunlight off your binocular lenses."

"Kiss mine. We're going to nail the Siberian's baby-killing ass."

Rand grinned. The thing about having an identical twin was that he was . . . identical. You talked to each other because you could. But it wasn't necessary. He'd do what you'd do in his place.

No thought required.

The plane leaped into focus. No insignia. No numbers. No identifying marks at all.

Surprise, surprise.

Silently Rand went to work.

2

Camgeria
Early morning

The man known only as the Siberian sat behind the copilot and watched the scrubland flash by at eye level on both sides of the plane. At the last possible instant, the Ukrainian pilot lifted the Ilyushin's nose and slammed the metal bird onto the rough dirt runway with the sound of someone whacking a tin coffin with a baseball bat.

The turboprops reversed hard and spooled up, screaming like the undead. The plane bucked and humped on the rough dirt surface. Red dust swirled up from the wheels and the prop wash, sticking to the smears of hydraulic fluid that covered both wings of the aircraft. The first direct rays of the sun turned the smears into blood.

Cargo trucks waited. So did heavily armed men. They hadn't flinched when the plane passed barely five feet above their heads.

Sweating, cursing in two languages, the pilot and copilot wrestled with the controls. Between them, they kept the plane rubber side down in the middle of the narrow strip. Sweat darkened the men's blue coveralls. The aircraft was overloaded and undermaintained, a flying death sentence waiting to be executed.

Any sweat on the Siberian came from the heat slamming into the cockpit from the outside. Compared to what waited behind them on the runway, the shuddering, straining landing of the plane was caviar and toast points.

Halfway down the dirt runway, brakes and reversed props finally won out over momentum. A hundred yards short of the runway's end, the plane sat down heavily on its gear and settled into a more predictable shake, rattle, shimmy, and roll. The pilot cranked the nose wheel and reversed course, beginning the long taxi back to where the men waited.

"Nyet," the Siberian said.

The pilot didn't argue. He might be the number one flyboy, but he knew who owned the plane.

"Keep your engines running but hold this position," the Siberian continued in Russian. He unsnapped the harness that was barely big enough to contain his massive chest. "Make the bastards come to us."

He stood up and leaned forward, watching the trucks and men nearly half a mile away.

"You think it's a trap?" the copilot asked him nervously.

"Life is a trap."

With that he crouched down and looked through the windscreen with binoculars, studying the trucks. After some indecision, their drivers had started up and were heading for the aircraft, trailing streamers of dust. Most of the vehicles were grinding along the edge of the runway, but one of the drivers used the runway itself.

It could be an innocent mistake.

It could be intentional. Lethal.

The Siberian yanked a hand radio from the hip pocket of his white jungle suit. He keyed the microphone and snarled in English, "Tell that idiot to clear the runway, or we'll take off right now."

"Oh, yaasss, b'wana," a voice replied over the radio in singsong English.

"No insolence, Da'ana, or I'll cut your heart out and feed it to those pagans."

The radio popped softly as the man at the other end of the transmission keyed his microphone, acknowledging the command from his boss.

"Stay in the cockpit," the Siberian ordered the pilot in Russian. "Keep the brake set and power on the props."

"What if one of the rebels backs into them?" the pilot asked.

"Haven't you heard? Stupidity is a capital crime."

He turned and growled orders into the cargo area, using serviceable Bulgarian. The Bulgarian loadmaster began undogging the wide double doors just in back of the cockpit.

The Siberian grabbed an Israeli-made submachine gun from beneath the jump seat and headed back into the cargo area. He stood in the open doorway while the first truck arrived and backed into position, its tailgate lined up level with the floor of the plane's cargo area.

Two lean, bare-chested black Africans in tattered camouflage shorts sat in the back of the truck. Beneath their thin butts were burlap bags crammed full of cargo. One of the guards held a Kalashnikov casually in one hand. The other had a Russian-made sniper's rifle slung over his shoulder.

The Siberian switched frequencies, lifted the hand radio to his mouth, and spoke to the rebel commander in French. "I take off in twenty minutes. If you want your merchandise, work fast."

A second truck pulled up beside the first. A gang of sweating black laborers jumped down and mounted the first vehicle. Quickly they boosted heavy burlap bags into the cargo bay and started to scramble aboard the aircraft.

The Siberian made sure they all got a good look at his Uzi. The laborers held out empty hands to show they were unarmed, then began moving the bags forward, stacking them against the bulkhead. When the first truck was empty, the Siberian kicked the bags loaded aboard the plane, found them full and heavy, and stepped aside. The laborers removed five of the twenty heavy wooden crates stowed in the rear of the cargo area and loaded them in the truck.

Within three minutes, the first truck had been unloaded, reloaded, and was pulling out.

The Siberian watched while the first truck drove away and a second backed into position. The two armed guards in cammie shorts stayed in position beside the new load while the laborers repeated their tasks.

Smoking a cigarette, watching the surrounding land, the Siberian prowled back and forth in the cargo bay. The sun was well up over the horizon. The heat of equatorial Africa rose from the ground like an invisible shroud. White Eastern Europeans and black Africans alike sweated and exchanged cargoes without a hitch. No one was new to this game.

As the fourth truck unloaded, the Bulgarian stopped a laborer and used a sheath knife to rip a hole in the heavy burlap bag the man carried. He pried a black stone out of the slit and held it up for the Siberian to inspect.

"What you think? Is it coltan?" the Siberian asked in Bulgarian, one of his six languages.

The loadmaster shrugged. "You tell me."

"It's coltan." He stubbed out his cigarette on the cargo floor and went to the doorway. "They know better than to shit on the Siberian."

Or on his Russian backers.

Not to mention Joao Fouquette, who controlled much of South America's arms trade.

Like the legal world, the illegal world had its shifting alliances, double crosses, armed truces, and brutal wars.

A dusty Toyota pickup with a heavy machine gun mounted in its bed pulled up beside the cargo trucks. A handsome black man in a crisp tan officer's uniform swung out of the cab and approached the loading bay.

"How was your trip?" he asked the Siberian in French.

"Uganda didn't think much of your phony end-user certificates for the Kalashnikovs."

The officer grinned. "That's because the Ugandan defense minister supplied them to me without giving his superiors a cut."

"I thought so. How much did he charge you?"

"Fifty thousand American."

"He must have been feeling guilty. He only tacked on another twenty-five thousand. You'll see it in the transport charges for the next load."

The officer shrugged. "Where are the RPGs?"

The Siberian jerked his thumb toward the rear of the plane. "You'll get them when I've seen the diamonds."

The officer slid one hand into his pants pocket and produced a leather miner's bag. He flipped the bag up to the Siberian, who hefted the bag on his palm, loosened the drawstrings, and spilled the contents into his hand. The morning sun caught on two dozen large rough stones. They were like ragged ice cubes in the heat, gleaming with promise.

"Feels light," the Siberian said.

"They are perfect stones for Antwerp," the officer said, climbing lithely aboard the plane, heading toward the five large wooden crates. "My South African says each will yield several two- and three-carat finished goods."

The Siberian dug a jeweler's loupe out of his trousers and studied the stones. "Perhaps, but documentation will cut into my profit. Even the damned Belgians are demanding paper proof that they are not conflict stones. Nobody wants diamonds with blood on them."

"It washes off diamonds quite easily. I threw in an extra two hundred pounds of coltan to pay for your paperwork."

The Siberian smiled slightly. "The transistor manufacturers of Prague will be pleased."

"So the Czechs are providing you the rifles," the officer said. "Good. Their work is better than that load of Moldavian shit you brought us last time."

"AK-47s aren't all created equal," the Siberian said, smiling thinly. "The price reflects that."

"Show me the grenade launchers."

"Pick one."

The officer pointed to a crate at random.

The Siberian nodded to the loadmaster, who undid the straps that secured the last large crates in place. He frog-walked the selected crate over to the door, laid it down, and pulled a pry bar out of its wall mount. Very quickly the crate gave up its secrets.

Six shoulder launchers rested in their recessed rack. The loadmaster dragged a smaller crate forward and opened it. Inside were twelve grenades, packed warheads up.

The black officer picked up one of the launchers and inspected it. Then he selected one of the grenades, walked to the open doorway, and held the weapons up for his men to see. He shouted something in a tribal dialect. All the Siberian could understand was Uhuru, which was a tribal name for part of Camgeria.

Fifty men cheered. The guard with the Kalashnikov pointed his weapon in the air and fired wildly.

The Siberian came and stood in the doorway beside the rebel officer. He looked out at the ragtag army and smiled. His own spies in their midst and in the camps of the Camgerian forces told him that the rebels were close to toppling one of the most stable of the countries among the oil-rich, tribally divided lands lying along Africa's western coast. If the rebels won, there would be prolonged and brutal tribal warfare.

And oil concessions for the Siberian who brought guns to the winning side.

He turned a mental page in his account book and began formulating the final stage of his plan to move from trading illegal arms in the field to trading oil from the safety of America. Now that the rebels had received fresh stocks of Soviet-era arms, the Democratic Republic of Camgeria would need better weapons. The Siberian would supply them.

And make many, many millions of American dollars, plus connections with and favors from the present African regime. The latter would buy him what money alone couldn't—a place at the international oil-trading table.

Blood didn't stick to oil.

A glint of light caught his eye. The flash came from a rocky hill about three hundred yards off the runway.

Instantly he stepped back into the dark interior of the plane. It would be like the rebels to try and make off with the arms, the coltan, and the diamonds. Or perhaps the Camgerian government had discovered he was selling to both sides of its little war.

In the shadows of the aircraft's cargo hold, the Siberian lifted his binoculars and studied the spot where he'd seen the flash of light.

Like everything else away from the tropical coast, the hill was covered by scrub and dust. He could make out what might be a sniper's keep and thought he could see men inside. But he couldn't be sure he wasn't seeing his own paranoia in the moving wind shadows. The binoculars were inferior Moldavian goods.

Impatiently he turned toward the guard who had the sniper rifle. With both voice and gestures, the Siberian said, "Give it to me."

The man hesitated until his officer barked a command. Reluctantly the guard handed over the rifle.

Still concealed by the shadows inside the plane, the Siberian rested the weapon on a crate and studied the hillside. The telescopic sight brought details into sharp focus.

There were two men. White. Both faces were hidden—one by a camera with a very long-range lens, the other by field glasses.

Then the man with the camera ducked down into the blind. Through the light grass screen across the front of the blind, the Siberian could see that he was reloading the camera. Film, not digital.

Russian curses echoed in the plane. The cameraman had at least one exposed roll of the Siberian overseeing the unloading, the rebel officer inspecting arms, the diamonds and coltan, the rebel brandishing weapons that were being delivered in contravention of African Union and United Nations arms embargoes, in the face of world opinion and all civilized standards. And those would be the headlines if the photographs were ever published.

It would ruin him. He'd live out his life in the stinking hell of Libya's "freedom."

He stared through the rifle's telescopic sight. "Is the weapon accurate?" he asked.

The officer translated.

The guard grinned, nodded, and answered.

"He has it zeroed in at two hundred and fifty yards," the officer translated.

"Excellent," the Siberian said.

He changed his aiming point to compensate for the differences in range and for the fact that he was firing uphill. He would wound one. The other would try to save his comrade.

And both would be his.

Slowly the Siberian's finger took up slack on the trigger.

The spotter moved slightly. For a timeless instant the Siberian and the spotter were frozen in each other's sights.

As the last of the slack in the trigger vanished, the spotter threw himself on the cameraman and shoved him away. The shot echoed. Birds shrieked and leaped for the sky.

Dust leaped from the spotter's cammie shirt, followed instantly by blood.

When the Siberian worked the bolt to reload, it was rough, gritty. The scope jerked. By the time he reacquired the grass blind, both men were gone. Cursing, he fired several times. Then he stepped into the doorway and stabbed toward the hill with his finger.

"Spies," he shouted. "Kill them!"

The officer yelled at his army. As the rebels turned toward the hillside, two men broke cover and began scrambling over the crest of the hill. The rebels fired, but the men were too far away for accuracy.

The Siberian lifted the rifle to his shoulder and fired two more shots without any real hope. A sniper's rifle wasn't much good on moving targets. Disgusted, he slammed the rifle onto the crate.

While the rebels watched, the wounded man fell.

Finally!

Before the Siberian could bring the sniper rifle to bear again, the cameraman bent over, picked up his wounded comrade, pulled him into a fireman's carry, and vanished over the crest of the hill.

"Strong," the Siberian said, surprised. "Very strong."

And very unexpected.

He gestured at the staring rebels. "Go after them, shitheads!"

The officer translated and the rebels ran toward the hill. Before they were halfway, an engine started on the other side of the hill. Moments later dust rose from the tires of a fleeing Land Rover.

The Siberian looked at the officer, who shrugged and said, "There is a track over there that leads to three roads. The Camgerian army controls two of them."

Unease crawled through the Siberian's belly. He had been very careful in his violent climb to the top of a violent profession. No one had ever captured his face on film.

"Prepare to take off," he shouted into the cockpit.

The pitch of the engines increased.

"Get those men," he told the rebel officer. "Bring me their film and I'll give you two artillery pieces and a helicopter gunship. Do you understand?"

The officer grinned. If the Siberian would pay a million at first offer, he'd pay more on the second. "I'll get the film. Then we'll negotiate."

The aircraft doors slammed shut as the plane accelerated down the dirt strip, scattering rebels like dust.

3

Five years later

Near Phoenix, Arizona
Late March
Thursday
8:30 A.M. MST

Kayla Shaw walked out of the little adobe house and put the last of her mementos into the Ford Explorer. It wasn't much of a load, really. Some photos, her grandmother's prize bridle, her mother's barrel-racing trophies, her father's favorite hunting rifle. Small things rich with memories. After work, she'd come back and pack up her clothes.

Technically the place was hers to use for another month, but it felt melancholy to be a tenant rather than an owner.

As Kayla found a safe spot for the small, unframed landscape painting she carried, she remembered her excitement at discovering the piece in a garage sale. It had been just after her parents had died, when she'd been making the difficult adjustment from beloved child to adult orphan. Something in the painting of a predawn forest had whispered to her of time and loneliness and the faintly shimmering hope of a sunrise that might be more imagined than real. When she'd turned the painting over and seen "Maybe the Dawn" written on the back, she'd known she would buy it.

She touched the name slashed in the lower left of the painting. "R. McCree." The artist had helped her through a bad time. She'd been looking for his—or her—paintings ever since, but hadn't found any.

Leaning against the cool metal frame of the vehicle's door, she glanced around at the ten acres of Dry Valley Ranch that had been her home for her whole life. The adobe walls of the house were the dusty color that came of age and Arizona weather. Sun had turned the timber fence of the corral a lovely shade of gray. The lean-to barn looked lonesome and enduring, like a windmill at a remote cattle tank—like the windmill that still supplied water to the house and corrals.

Ten acres of memories.

Sadness curled around her with the cool morning breeze. She hoped the new owner would love Dry Valley as she and her parents had. She hoped, but she didn't know. She'd sold the ranch to someone she'd never met, never seen, and knew only through his agent.

"Change, change, change," she said, pushing her dark hair away from her eyes. "Hello, good-bye, hello to something new. And good-bye, always good-bye."

Despite her lingering sorrow, Kayla knew that selling the little ranch was the right thing to do. The grazing leases on federal lands had lapsed long ago. Without the leases, there was no way to make a living. Even one cow would starve on Dry Valley's ten acres. The ranch was a tiny piece of desert at the farthest fringe of Phoenix's urban sprawl. The house was as spare as the land and needed expensive repairs. Yet taxes had steadily risen as the county assessor reappraised the ground for its potential, instead of its reality.

Good-bye, ranch.

Hello, career in private banking.

Too bad she really wasn't happy in her work. But every request she'd made to transfer out of private banking had been met with a polite, firm refusal.

It was enough to make a girl think of hitting the road.

I'm not a girl. I'm an adult. Lots of people don't like their jobs, but they suck it up and get the job done anyway.

"Think of tomorrow as going to another continent," Kayla told herself. "Everything fresh and undiscovered."

The thought of distant horizons made her restless. Her job as a private banker was demanding, often fascinating, but it didn't ease her wanderlust.

Okay, so don't think about new continents and of years backpacking around the globe. I'm an adult now, with an adult's responsibilities.

Grow up.

Kayla slid into the driver's seat, made sure that the pile of escrow documents she'd signed earlier wouldn't spill off the passenger seat, and admired the check clipped to the big folder. As a private banker she'd handled much larger checks, but none of them had been her own. Her clients' money was just that—theirs, not hers. If she thought of their money at all, it was simply as numbers to be moved from one place to the next.

The check clipped to the folder was hers—$246,407.

Exactly.

Without meaning to, she looked at the battered backpack stuffed into the passenger foot well.

I could go anywhere in the world.

Until the money ran out. Then I'd have nothing.

Grow up.

It was a good chunk of money, but Phoenix's red-hot housing market would gobble it up and not even burp.

Looking away from the backpack, Kayla started the vehicle. She hoped her next real estate deal would be as clean and easy as this one had been. On the real estate agent's advice, she'd offered the ranch at a high price, "looking for the market."

She'd found it, at full price.

The buyer's agent had handled the transaction with the dispatch of the lawyer he was. She'd gotten her price, subtracted the closing costs and rent for the next month, and driven to the ranch to begin packing.

Today she'd have her own money to deposit in her American Southwest account. It wasn't the answer to all her problems, but it was a financial security she'd never had before.

Maybe that security would help her to deal with Elena Bertone, the most demanding client in the history of the demanding world of private banking.

4

Phoenix, Arizona
Thursday
8:40 A.M. MST

Andre Bertone shifted his weight, making the expensive leather chair creak. Few office chairs were built well enough to accommodate the barrel-chested bulk of a man who stood six foot three inches and weighed two hundred and eighty pounds, most of it muscle. The satellite phone he held to his ear looked almost dainty against his hand.

The musical accents of Brazilian Portuguese spilled out of the decoder and into Bertone's ear. Despite the beauty of the language, what was being said made a red flush crawl up Bertone's face. There were very few people in the world who could call him to task. Joao Fouquette was one of them.

For now.

"Naturally, you are impatient to—" Bertone cut in.

Fouquette kept talking. "—more than a quarter of a billion dollars American must be laundered to pay for the arms. The money is coming in from France, Liechtenstein, and Dubai. I counted on you to—"

"And I've never let you down," Bertone interrupted. "Relax, my friend. All is well." *Besides, asshole, half of it is my own money.*

A big gamble, but Bertone hadn't gotten where he was by being timid.

"All is *not* well," Fouquette insisted. "Neto hired St. Kilda Consulting."

"What? I thought Neto was ours."

"He was until he found out who we really backed in the revolution five years ago."

Bertone shrugged. Allies were people you hadn't screwed yet, and peace was bad for business. "I assume that's why he refused to extend the oil contracts with us."

Fouquette didn't bother to respond to the obvious. "There will be a rise in oil prices soon. We want to sell Camgeria's output at the new level. We've moved up the timetable for revolution. Do your connections have the arms we need?"

"As soon as they see the money, we see the arms. Arms are easy to find. The only problem comes in transportation and distribution." That was Bertone's area of experience. He'd seen the choke points in the arms trade, bought planes and pilots, and got very rich transporting cargoes no one else would touch.

"Whatever you do, don't use the old laundry," Fouquette said. "St. Kilda is probably watching LuDoc, waiting to pounce."

"LuDoc is dead."

Fouquette laughed. "So you finally discovered how much he was skimming."

All Bertone said was, "I have been developing a new conduit. A true naïf."

"You have a day to transform your naïf into a whore. The arms exchange must be completed immediately."

"What? You gave me four weeks to—"

"Complain to Neto," Fouquette cut in. "He's the bastard who brought in St. Kilda. I have to move the money fast and get the arms to Neto's enemies faster."

"When will you have all the money transferred to me?" Bertone said.

"As soon as you set up an account, each participant has agreed to put in his share within forty-eight hours."

"By Saturday?" Bertone grunted. "I can't guarantee weekend bank—"

"Don't tell me your problems," Fouquette said over the complaint. "Since he has become president, my sponsor has lost all patience. Get that account set up immediately."

"Perhaps Brazil needs a new president. It could be arranged, yes?"

"Not soon enough. If the arms aren't on the way to overthrow Neto's New Camgerian Republic very quickly, I'm out of a job. And you, my Siberian friend, you are dead."

5

Manhattan
Thursday
12:15 P.M. EST

Former ambassador James B. Steele rolled into the conference room on the fifty-seventh floor of the UBS Building as if he owned the television network headquartered there. He was fifteen minutes late and he didn't apologize. He had more to bring to this meeting than the five people he'd kept waiting.

"Good afternoon," Steele said to everyone and no one.

He guided the electric wheelchair over to the rosewood conference table. An overstuffed leather armchair blocked him from taking his place.

"Oops. Okay, I'll get that," Ted Martin said quickly.

"Thank you."

The field producer had been Steele's principal UBS contact for the past two months of research and negotiations. As Martin scrambled to shove the armchair aside, Steele rolled forward. His position put him opposite the most important man in the room, Howard Prosser, executive producer of *The World in One Hour.*

Steele greeted Prosser and nodded to the most famous face at the table, Brent Thomas. Being the best-looking guy in a war zone drew a television audience, but Steele had seen his own war zones. They hadn't been nearly as pretty as Thomas, who was one of the network's hottest correspondents. And the most ambitious. Fortunately for Steele's plans, Thomas was as smart as he was camera-ready.

"Deb Carroll is our senior researcher," Martin said, gesturing toward a woman who hadn't attended any of the previous meetings. "She'll be in charge of fact-checking all material before it hits the air."

Steele nodded. "I'll look forward to your questions."

Carroll's smile said she doubted it.

"Stanley Carson is our corporate counsel," Prosser said. "He insisted on attending the meeting."

Steele's eyebrows, nearly black despite his silver hair, lifted. "You're wasting your time, Mr. Carson. Truth is an absolute defense against both libel and slander."

"We prefer to forestall suits rather than defend them."

"St. Kilda Consulting has no such aversion to conflicts, legal or otherwise," Steele said pleasantly. "Mr. Thomas may be a pretty face, but he's not stupid. He has documented the leads we gave him very carefully, as I'm sure Ms. Carroll will discover."

"I ran up thousands of miles on some of the worst airplanes that ever got off the ground," Thomas said, his trained voice a mixture of rue and enthusiasm. "All to track down those former rebel commanders you recommended. Great tape on all of them, great interviews. It puts human faces to the arms traffic. That's why Mr. Prosser is thinking about giving us the whole hour for the piece."

Prosser grimaced. "The final decision hasn't been made to air the segment, short or long. There are crucial elements missing, including an interview with our subject, Mr. Bertone."

Steele shook his head slightly. "When we're certain of his location, we'll tell you, so that Thomas and a camera crew can confront him. But Andre Bertone won't give you an interview. It isn't in the man's nature."

Prosser grinned. "No problem. Our audience sees silence as an admission of guilt."

"Hold it," Carson said. "Before I allow this network to air an attack on a man who is an extremely wealthy businessman—and a United Nations diplomat, according to Thomas—I want to see proof."

Steele already knew about Bertone's diplomatic credentials, but he was surprised they did. He looked at Thomas.

"Nice work," Steele said. "If you ever want to leave television, come see me at St. Kilda."

"Actually, St. Kilda Consulting is what we wanted to talk about today," Prosser said quickly. "We're a little, um, concerned about some aspects of your organization—"

"And how your company's rather unsavory international reputation might impact ours," Carson cut in. "There are reports spreading in the European press that St. Kilda Consulting is a private army that hires itself out to the highest bidder. This network can't afford to associate itself with mercenaries. Period. That sentiment comes all the way down from the sixty-first floor."

Steele looked at the researcher, who was examining her nail polish with great interest. "So you read *Le Figaro*," he said to her in French.

Surprised, she put hands over the folder in front of her almost protectively.

"I assume you brought the article," Steele said, switching to English.

After a moment the researcher shrugged, opened the folder, and said, "It's one of Europe's leading newspapers, not some rag."

"Pass the article around," Steele said. "Everyone should see what is being used in an effort to discredit St. Kilda Consulting."

She slid the single sheet of paper toward Prosser, a copy of the article. He picked it up and looked at it. "I don't read French," he said.

"The pertinent section is about halfway down," Steele said, taking the paper from him, "between the two typographic devices this particular gossip columnist uses to break up items in his screed. Correct my translation if you wish, Ms. Carroll."

She pulled a second copy of the article from the folder and read while Steele translated.

" 'The American-based mercenary security organization St. Kilda Consulting, a group well known for collecting extortionate fees from private clients all over the world, is expanding its activities into central Africa, according to well-placed intelligence sources.

" 'It is reported that the group, which outwardly operates as an independent investigative and security consulting firm, has been retained to cripple legitimate commercial intercourse between various French firms and customers in the French sphere of influence in Africa, which includes several countries on both sides of the equator.

" 'It is not known if St. Kilda's efforts are endorsed or perhaps even secretly sponsored by American interests or even the government itself, but various international investigators are pursuing all leads.' "

Steele glanced toward the researcher and waited.

"That's an honest translation," she said, faintly surprised.

"That's not how this article was represented to me," Carson said. "It may be a respected newspaper, but this is a gossip column, not an investigative piece."

Carroll went back to looking at her nails.

"The correspondent is a well-regarded journalist," Steele said, "although that designation has different meanings in different places. He has excellent sources in the French political and security establishment, which is why his attack is so interesting. He has no particular reason to run the item, no news hook, as I believe you in the business call it. He's just throwing mud."

Prosser winced.

Martin began to relax.

Carroll decided that she'd redo her nails in bloodred.

"The attack on St. Kilda," Steele said, "most likely comes from one of France's largest energy companies. The company is seeking oil concessions all over Africa. In the past, the company has paid for such concessions with guns, bullets, aircraft, even machetes like the one that was used so many years ago to chop off John Neto's hand."

"Wait a minute," Brent Thomas broke in. "You're saying that some French oil company is pulling strings behind the scenes, trading guns for oil with one hand and planting rumors with respected and influential journalists with the other?"

"Yes."

"That's either crazy or the best damned news story I ever heard."

"It's both," Steele said.

Carson leaned forward. "All I care about is Andre Bertone. He's the man we're putting in the UBS spotlight. He's the one who'll sue our balls off if he doesn't like what we say."

"Bertone is the cutout for the oil company," Steele said. "If you're a multibillion-dollar multinational corporation with direct political connections, you don't openly buy planeloads of guns and then hand them over to rebels who in return will give you multiyear oil concessions when they come to power."

Carson started taking notes.

"Andre Bertone is brokering the deal for the oil company," Steele continued. "He used to be an ordinary middleman. Rebel groups would siphon barge loads of oil out of transnational pipelines and trade them to Bertone for cases of assault rifles. From there he bought planes and pilots. Now he's an international energy broker who, if Neto is overthrown, will control millions of barrels of potential Camgerian production, which he'll sell to the French for a long-term profit of a billion dollars."

Everyone sat up straighter.

"Billion?" Prosser asked. "As in a thousand million dollars?"

"Profit after bribes and kickbacks are paid, yes," Steele said. "That's why some very powerful and influential people in Paris are unhappy. They don't want St. Kilda to interfere in a revolution that will enrich them so well."

"You can prove this, I suppose," Carson said skeptically.

"Not at all, Counselor," Steele said, "which is why I advise you not to include any of this in your program. These kinds of charges are made only in intelligence briefings and later, much later, in history books. But that doesn't matter."

"It does to me," Carson said.

"Why? All your station has to prove is that Andre Bertone is, or has been, an international arms dealer, a 'merchant of death,' as Mr. Thomas calls him. Your reporter has already laid the groundwork for the story. Now I'm offering you the centerpiece for that program."

Steele reached into the leather saddlebag that hung beside his wheelchair and pulled out a heavy manila folder. He sent it sliding down the sleek table. The folder came to rest directly in front of Prosser.

The executive producer hesitated, then opened the folder. Inside were computer copies of color photographs. They had about the same resolution as pictures printed on the inside pages of a newspaper. The first photo showed a burly Caucasian man in a white safari suit standing in the doorway of a transport aircraft on a dirt strip somewhere in a scrubland. The man was scowling directly into the lens.

"Bertone?" Prosser asked.

"Yes," Steele said.

"Deb, you have our only photo of the guy. Is this him?" He shoved the first print over to the researcher, who produced another file from her leather folio.

"It could be," she said. "This shot isn't much cleaner than the one we have."

"St. Kilda's photo was taken from a blind near a dirt strip in what was then the endless civil war/ethnic cleansing of the King's Republic of Uhuru and is now the New Democracy of Camgeria," Steele said. "The photo is five years old."

"Okay, our photo is a decade old," Martin said. "In truth, we aren't even sure it's Bertone. It's a possible rather than a probable ID. A pal of mine down in Langley got the photo for me. He said there was one positive ID photo taken five years ago, but he couldn't get it for me. Looks like this could be the one."

Steele knew it was.

Prosser was already sorting down through the other prints. Each one of them told a story—the loading of bags of contraband and the unloading of what were clearly cases of weapons.

Then he flipped over a picture showing Bertone with a long sniper's rifle in his hands, staring through the scope.

"Mother," he said, startled. "Looks like he was scoping the photographer."

"He was," Steele said. "Notice that his hand isn't on the trigger."

"Still, glad it wasn't me." Prosser blew out a breath. "These will make a great photomontage, if we can authenticate them."

"Look at the last photo."

Prosser turned over the last one. Everyone at the table except Steele crowded around to look over his shoulder.

Bertone was somewhat shadowed inside the aircraft, but it was clear that he had shifted from watching to acting. His finger was on the trigger.

"He fired a few seconds later," Steele said. "A good young man died."

Prosser blew out another breath. "Shit."

"Pictures are easy to fake," Carson said. "Remember the CBS National Guard memos."

Steele laughed out loud. "Those were badly done counterfeits. No intelligence agency would have bought them and no self-respecting journalist should have."

"The point is—" Carson began.

"Photographic prints can be doctored, particularly in this day of digitization," Steele interrupted. "The prints I brought are computer reproductions. I have the original prints in my safe."

"Talk to me about negatives," Prosser said. "You can screw with prints, but negatives are real hard to fake convincingly."

"When and if UBS agrees to my terms," Steele said, lying with the ease of the diplomat he'd once been, "I'll produce the negatives. I'll also see that you get an on-camera interview with the photographer."

"You told us he was killed," Carroll said.

"I said someone was killed. It was the spotter. The man who snapped the photos is still alive."

Martin grinned. "Okay! When can we have the interview?"

Steele looked at his cell phone. No messages. *Damn it, Faroe, is it too much to ask for you to check in occasionally?* "In the next forty-eight hours. But first you must agree to the terms."

"Nobody edits my stuff," Martin said.

"I wouldn't care to," Steele said distinctly. "But if it comes to filming any St. Kilda employees, you will disguise their faces, and in some cases their voices. This isn't negotiable."

Prosser grimaced. "But—"

"Not negotiable," Steele repeated. "Martin has known that from the beginning. And before you think about screwing me or my employees, think about what St. Kilda Consulting is: a good friend, a bad enemy."

Prosser looked irritated but didn't argue. "What's in this for you?"

"Journalists rarely inquire as to the motivations of a good source," Steele said evenly. "Gift horses and such. All that journalistic ethics requires of you is the belief that my information is valid. It is."

"We'll be checking," Prosser said, looking at Carroll. "You can count on it."

Steele smiled. "I do."

Prosser drummed his fingers on the table and looked past Steele, thinking hard. "What we have now is maybe a ten-minute segment, maybe less," he said finally. "We need more."

"Bertone's backers are getting restless," Steele said. "The window of opportunity is closing. You're either in or you're out. No more meetings."

"Okay. If we got some modern pictures of Bertone, here in the States," Martin said quickly, "stuff from the inside, it would juice up the segment. Otherwise, people won't believe philanthropist Bertone was once a murderous gun smuggler."

Steele sighed and gave in. "The Bertones are having a big party at their Pleasure Valley house on Saturday, plein air artists in some abominable contest. Would that do?"

"If Bertone is in the pics, okay," Martin said. "And we need some idea of how Bertone is getting around our banking laws. The kind of money you've talked about can't be moved around legally without leaving a trail."

Steele's pale eyes narrowed. If Kayla Shaw talked to save her own neck, she'd give them her boss. . . . "We'll do our best."

Martin looked at Prosser.

"You've got a deal," Prosser said.

"Okay!" Martin said.

6

Pleasure Valley, Arizona
Friday
10:31 A.M. MST

Kayla Shaw drove quickly up to the gate of Elena and Andre Bertone's Tuscan-style estate. The five-acre building site for Castillo del Cielo had been blasted out of dry, rocky hills less than two years ago. Now the acres were green and white, lush and expensive. Glass, art tiles, and copper gleamed among columns of imported Italian marble.

She suspected that beneath the marble was good old Arizona stucco.

According to bank records, the Bertones had paid more than five million dollars for the land. They had spent another ten million on construction of the house, guest casita, staff quarters, pools, gardens, and a guarded gate at the bottom of the hill. They even had a heliport out beyond the pool, complete with a racy little helicopter tied down and waiting for the royal whim.

The people who served the royal whims weren't all directly employed. The Bertones had more than $125 million on deposit with American Southwest, which entitled them to an unusual level of service. Kayla paid bills for the Bertones, she moved money among their many accounts, she covered overdrafts and shortfalls, and she made house calls to Castillo del Cielo to pick up deposits and drop off receipts.

In short, she was a gofer. It wasn't what she'd thought banking was all about, especially private banking, but it paid the bills.

As she waited for the guard to come out of his "shack" and buzz her through the gate, she looked at the tumbling, glistening wall of the water feature next to the guard building. Castillo del Cielo's annual water bill for squad-sized showers, epic water features, and three swimming pools was almost as big as the escrow check in Kayla's purse. As a desert girl that kind of extravagance made her uneasy, but the child in her delighted in the play of sunlight and dancing water, and the scent of water in the desert.

Even if it was tainted with chlorine.

She glanced through her open window at the guard shack, where a young man stood listening patiently to the phone held against his ear. Jimmy Hamm had been working for the Bertones for two months. He was a young, chatty former minor-league ballplayer who stared at her legs every chance he got.

She wondered if he'd be so flirty if he knew she made out the employment checks Elena signed.

"Mrs. B. says you can go up, but please hurry," Hamm said, coming out of the shack and smiling at Kayla. "Are you late? You're never late."

Kayla glanced at the clock on the dashboard. "Nope."

"She's been edgy," Hamm said, leaning against the Explorer's door. "The old man is back."

"Mr. Bertone?"

"He got in late Thursday night. At least I think that was him in the back of the limo. Never seen him to swear to it." Hamm leaned close and whispered, "Never seen him in daylight, either. You think he's a vampire?"

Kayla rolled her eyes. "He's a globe-trotting businessman."

"Yeah? What business? Drugs?"

"Drugs?" She laughed and shook her head. "Switch to decaf, Jimmy. Mr. Bertone trades in oil and other natural resources. Now open the gate before you make me late."

Reluctantly Hamm stepped back from the Explorer. He leaned inside the guard-shack door and triggered the gate mechanism.

Kayla shifted into gear and rolled through, both amused and irritated by Hamm's persistent interest in her and his employers. She could handle the smiling come-ons, but the Bertones put a high value on their physical and fiscal privacy. Wealthy families were targets for everyone from civic and political fund-raisers to thieves and kidnappers. The wealthy kept the world at bay with gates and security cameras and a thick layer of servants, lawyers, and bankers.

In the Bertones' shoes, she would have done the same. Especially as they had three young children to protect from the world's predators.

Mentally going over the final details of the Bertones' big art party tomorrow, Kayla pulled into the car park behind the five-car garage. She turned off the engine and automatically gathered her leather valise and purse. She hesitated, put the escrow envelope in the valise, and headed for the back of the house, where Elena had her office. Along the way Kayla waved to the Brazilian chauffeur, Antonio, who was washing a massive black Hummer. Head-high lilies bloomed along the flagstone path to the house. Everything looked and smelled green.

Money green.

"Down here," Elena called.

Kayla swerved without breaking rhythm. Apparently Elena was on the terrace between the Olympic-size pool and the children's splash pool.

"You're late," Elena said. "But I saved you some brunch."

Kayla slid onto a chair beneath the sunshade and dropped her leather bag on the flagstone.

"I'm a minute off, by my clock," she said cheerfully, "and you can blame that on your gate guard, who keeps trying to charm me out of my tiny little mind every time I come by."

"Of course he does." Elena gave her the million-candle-power smile of the international beauty queen she'd once been. "You're an attractive young thing who makes a good living and he's a former athlete who doesn't like working for his bread and butter."

The cool social calculation in the words was pure Elena. She was a stunningly beautiful woman whose figure had only been improved by having three children. She was shrewd, opinionated, socially ambitious, and arrogant in the way that only a gorgeous woman with a few hundred million in the bank could be.

In the quiet of her own mind, Kayla admitted that she would never like Elena, didn't really trust her, but was fascinated by her just the same.

Then there was the fact that Elena was a loving mother to three energetic, utterly confident children. Raised just short of the Brazilian slums herself, Elena had a gut-deep understanding of the difference between poverty and wealth, family and standing alone against the world. The children were home-schooled, as the public schools in America simply weren't equipped to handle kidnap targets.

No matter what Kayla might think of Elena as a person, she respected her client's dedication to her children.

"Where are the kids?" Kayla asked.

She looked around the grounds, half expecting to see Miranda or Xavier or Jonathan peering out from behind one of the marble columns in front of the pool house. In truth, she visited Elena more often than business required because she enjoyed the children.

"I asked Maria to keep them in the house for a few minutes, while we conduct my business," Elena said.

Oooookay, Kayla thought. *No small talk.*

"What do you need?" she asked, pulling out a small digital recorder. Elena's directives rarely came in twos or threes.

"Several things." Elena lowered her chin and looked at Kayla over the top of her sexy Italian sunglasses. "Are the finances all in order for the Desert Art Week?"

"I don't know about the rest of the festival, but everything is ready for your event. I wish we could call it something besides 'The Fast Draw.'" Kayla kept her voice neutral, but it was an effort. *If I was a self-respecting painter, I'd sharpen the end of a brush and fall on it before I entered that contest. I don't care if first prize is twenty-five grand. There's something belittling about the whole thing.*

Elena shrugged. "I didn't choose the name. I simply supplied the money and the place. The arts are very important."

Especially for the socially ambitious, Kayla thought sourly. Social climbing was one of Elena's less charming traits.

Hey, if you'd been raised next door to a slum, you'd want to be accepted by the high and mighty, too, Kayla told herself. *You're just jealous of her looks.*

They're worth being jealous of.

With an effort Kayla dragged her mind back to the Fast Draw event, which was part of an annual art festival conducted to raise funds for the Scottsdale Desert Museum. Thirty landscape painters had been invited to paint the same subject in a two-hour timed contest.

This year the Bertones had made quite an impression by offering their estate as the painting site and promising to purchase the top three canvases. Then they had doubled the total prize money to fifty thousand.

The local press had gone gaga. Not only was Elena Bertone ravishing and intelligent and a sublime hostess, she was incredibly generous too. Definitely the best thing to happen to Scottsdale since reliable tap water.

"The Fast Draw is the name they've used for years," Elena continued. "I'm not ready to change that tradition yet. Have you done everything I required?"

Kayla didn't have to check her notes. The Bertones were far and away her most important client. The fact that her boss, Steve Foley, had given the Bertones exclusively to her a few months ago still amazed her. Maybe he'd guessed that she was mentally packing up and heading out for greener employment pastures.

"The funds are all in the prize account," Kayla said. "I've arranged for a commercial sign painter to do the presentation checks so that they'll show up in the press photos."

"Good." Elena made no secret of the fact that she wanted her face and discreetly presented cleavage on the society pages at least once a week. "The caterer has given me a price of two hundred dollars a head for the Fast Draw party, but he demands a cashier's check before he serves a single canapé."

He must have worked for the superrich before, Kayla thought. People who spent lavishly didn't always pay on time. In fact, they rarely did. "If you want to pay the wine bills and the rest of the party expenses when you pay the caterer, you'll have to top up the entertainment account. I can pull it from the household account as usual."

Elena removed her sunglasses and looked at Kayla like she was interviewing for a job rather than already an employee. "No."

The tone and the cool appraisal in the wide brown eyes made Kayla's neck tingle.

"Deposit this in the entertainment account," Elena said, taking a cream-colored vellum envelope from beneath her plate. "It should settle all bills."

Kayla took the envelope. The heavy paper flap wasn't sealed. She lifted it and removed a single handwritten check. It was drawn on a foreign bank she'd never heard of. Her eyes widened.

"Twenty-two million dollars," she said. "Holy—there must be some mistake. Even you couldn't spend that much on a party."

"Your job isn't to judge my expenditures." Elena's voice was as cold as her eyes. Her faint exotic accent deepened. "Your job is to deposit and withdraw money at my desire."

Kayla's stomach knotted. The words *compliant and complicit* were part of any private banker's training. *Compliant and complicit bankers* were no longer legally immune from the implications of their acts. Or as Kayla thought of it: Launder money and go to jail.

"I'll be glad to deposit this check in any account you specify," Kayla said, "but, as I'm not familiar with the bank the check is drawn on, I'm required by federal government regulations to ask a few questions."

"Questions?" Elena's expression hardened. "You're a banker, not a police official."

Kayla sighed. It wasn't the first time one of her clients had bristled at being questioned. It wouldn't be the last.

But the law was the law.

"Look, I'm not wild about the rules, but I can't change them," Kayla said briskly. "If I don't follow the rules, American Southwest's compliance department will be all over me like dust on the desert and I'll lose my job."

"It's too late to worry about your job," Andre Bertone said behind Kayla. "Worry about your freedom instead."

7

North of Seattle
Friday
9:36 A.M. PST

Rand McCree dabbed at the yellow paint he had just drooled onto the dark green oilskin of his Barbour coat.

"Hell," he muttered without conviction.

It wasn't the first time he'd splashed oil paints on himself. It wouldn't be the last. There was a vivid stain across the shoulders of one of his favorite shirts that looked like a Jackson Pollock abstract. He'd acquired it when the wind blew a wet canvas off the easel and slammed it into his back while he was peeing against a nearby tree. Just one of the hazards of painting outdoors rather than in a studio.

Once he and Reed had laughed about their spattered wardrobes. Not any more.

Don't go there, Rand told himself. *Reed is dead and I'm not. Life's a bitch and she's always in heat.*

All I can do is what he asked me to—paint and live enough for both of us.

He rammed the easel into the wet, cold earth. The meadow at the edge of the old Douglas fir forest had been a favorite subject for three generations of McCrees—grandmother, mother, and twins. The daffodils his grandmother and mother had planted in the meadow had grown from a clump of sunshine to a golden glory the size of an Olympic swimming pool. Wind, cold, and rain were the flowers' favorite weather. The coastal Pacific Northwest provided plenty of all three.

With a pencil Rand sketched a few lines on the white grounding of the fresh canvas. First was a waving line a third of the way down from the top to establish the horizon, then another line a few inches lower to show the edge of the cliff. That left three-fifths of the canvas for the meadow and the windblown shout of yellow that was daffodils.

He looked at the proportions and realized he needed an element on one side of the picture to force the viewer's eye across the meadow, out over the water, and on up toward the sky, which would be the intense light blue that only came after an early-morning spring rain.

With the pencil he moved a fir tree thirty yards across the meadow, creating the effect he needed. That was the joy of the canvas. It let imagination and artistic necessity rule over a world that was full of brutal, unchanging, and often ugly reality.

Before Rand could finish mixing the daffodil colors on his palette, he heard the faint, nasty snarl of a small helicopter. With the eye of a hunter he scanned the horizon off to the east, in the direction of Seattle. The aircraft came in low over the water, rose a hundred feet as it approached the island, and headed straight for him.

Rand held his breath, weightless as the wind, feeling himself spinning away. He'd seen helicopter strafing runs before. The last one had been while Reed lay wounded on the floor of a St. Kilda helo. They'd taken off just as another helo strafed them. Rand got lucky with an AK-47, bringing down the attacking helo as it went by on its second strafing run.

But he'd been lucky too late. Bullets had stitched through Reed, leaving him bleeding from too many wounds. Dying.

Dead.

Get a grip, Rand told himself fiercely. *That was five years ago. Nobody gave a damn but me.*

The helo slowed its approach but came straight in. Fifty yards away it flared and settled onto the meadow

Rand had been painting. The little craft's landing skids crushed daffodils as well as grass.

Rand waited, willing himself to breathe again.

The side door popped open. A tall, lean man in blue jeans and a Gore-Tex windbreaker stepped out.

Though Rand had walked out of St. Kilda Consulting five years ago, he still had friends there. He recognized Joe Faroe instantly—Faroe, who had come close to dying last year in a shoot-out with a drug lord on the Mexican border.

Reflexively Faroe ducked his head, avoiding the helicopter's rotor. As he did, he realized he was walking on the perfume of crushed flowers.

"Sorry, Rand," Faroe said when he was close. "Hope we didn't kill any of them."

"So do I."

"I suppose if I offered to shake your hand, you'd clock me."

"Now there's a thought." Then Rand shrugged and forced the tension clamping around his neck and shoulders to loosen. He associated Faroe with Reed's death, which wasn't precisely fair.

But it was real.

"You're wasting my daylight," Rand said roughly. "I don't want to talk about old times; they weren't much fun. I don't want to get drunk with you; I don't get drunk anymore. And I sure as hell don't want to re-up with St. Kilda Consulting. I've lost my taste for useless adventures in feral cities and failed states. So just climb back in that helo and disappear."

Faroe rubbed his neck and hid a grin. "Grace was right. I should have brought her. You wouldn't be rude to a pregnant woman."

Rand looked at the horizon. He'd liked Faroe once. What happened to Reed hadn't been Faroe's fault. They'd all been consenting adults. With a muttered curse he combed his fingers through his wild mane of hair, yanked the watch cap back into place, and practiced being civilized.

Because rude or civil, hot or cold, Faroe wouldn't leave until he was good and ready.

"Heard you'd been wounded and got yourself a wife and a kid," Rand said.

"Marriage was a lot less painful."

Rand almost smiled. "Heard she's a judge."

"You have good ears. But Grace resigned. Now she has all of her brains and expertise and no federal bureaucracy cramping her."

"She's good for you," Rand said, surprising both of them. "The last time you came after me, we ended up brawling."

Faroe smiled like a choirboy. "Yeah, she's knocked off some of my rough edges."

Rand gave the other man a long look. “You’ve still got plenty to go.”

“Makes your heart warm, doesn’t it.”

Shaking his head, Rand gave in. “What do you want?”

“St. Kilda has found the Siberian.”

Rand went completely still. Then his heart slammed and his senses sharpened to the point of pain, the hunter fully in control for the first time in years. He’d searched long and hard for his twin’s murderer, only to be frustrated by failed states and stonewalled by his own government.

“You’re certain?” Rand asked.

“Very. You still have the negatives?”

“Yes.”

Faroe waited.

Rand started gathering up his painting supplies. “My cabin is just through the trees. We’ll talk there.”

8

Pleasure Valley
Friday
10:37 A.M. MST

Kayla Shaw let the silence expand as she looked at the Bertones. She was a ranch girl, born and raised. She rode, she shot, she killed her own snakes with the little folding knife she always carried.

But she had a cold feeling that Bertone was way beyond her varmint-killing skills.

It's too late to worry about your job. Worry about your freedom instead.

And with that, Bertone had pocketed her little recorder.

She hadn't asked for it back. She knew she wouldn't get it.

"I do believe that's as silent as I've ever heard our little banker be," Bertone said after a time, smiling at his wife.

Elena's smile was meant to comfort Kayla.

It didn't.

"There's no need to be frightened," Elena said casually. She tapped the heavy letter-size envelope that Kayla had dropped. "This is a great opportunity for you. Every woman needs her own independent means. This is how you'll become free."

Silently Kayla watched the Bertones. She sensed that the less she said, the less she'd sink into the quicksand that suddenly had appeared beneath her feet.

Andre sat down next to Kayla and laid a large, plain brown envelope on the white linen tablecloth.

"You become free," Bertone said, "or you lose your freedom. The choice is yours."

Kayla swallowed and hoped her voice sounded less frightened than she was. "What choice?"

"Quite simple. You're a felon."

"What?"

"Whether you suffer or avoid the consequences of being a felon," Bertone continued, "is your choice."

"I haven't done anything," Kayla said.

Bertone smiled. It wasn't a gesture of reassurance. "You concealed the origins of five million dollars in dirty money."

Unable to force any more words from her throat, Kayla could only shake her head.

"Trust me," he said, laughing at the irony. "The money was dirty. You laundered it. According to your ridiculous government, that's worth up to ten years in federal prison."

"All I've done is provide you and your wife with routine banking services," Kayla said hoarsely.

Bertone stroked his fingers over the brown envelope. "You opened several accounts at American Southwest for my lovely wife's art-oriented activities, correct?"

Adrenaline rushed through Kayla, thawing the ice in her throat, her gut. "That's what I'm paid to do—open accounts."

"And you've accepted numerous deposits from our Aruba and Barbados banks to replenish those accounts," Bertone said.

"Only when Elena had unusually large bills." Kayla looked at Elena. The woman was sipping coffee and thumbing through the society pages.

"Don't forget the Russian paintings I bought for Andre's birthday a few months ago," Elena said without looking up. "The sum was several millions of dollars. Five, in fact."

"You paid what the gallery charged," Kayla said. "Way too much, in my opinion, but I'm not an art appraiser."

"Was the source of the money used for payment well documented?" Bertone asked idly.

But his eyes weren't idle. They were the eyes of a predator that had just pounced.

Adrenaline and ice fought for control of Kayla. She had expedited the birthday transfer on Elena's assurances that she would provide the supporting documentation for the transaction as soon as the paintings cleared customs.

Now Kayla knew why Elena had been "too busy" to gather documentation.

"I see you begin to understand," Bertone said. "You established accounts and funded them without a clear idea of the source of the funds."

"It's a technical violation," Kayla said tightly. "Hardly worth a fine, much less a jail sentence."

"There have been several such technical violations over the past few months," Elena said. "Coffee, Andre?"

"Thank you." He glanced back at Kayla. "When those violations are added up, they make a disturbing pattern of complicit and compliant banking practices. Your practices, Kayla."

Adrenaline urged her to flee.

Her brain overruled.

She had been and was under strong pressure from the bank to keep the Bertone account happy. She'd cut a few modest corners to do so, knowing that Steve Foley, the head of the private banking division, would strip naked, jump on a pogo stick, and sing "I Am Woman, Hear Me Roar" to keep Andre Bertone's millions under deposit.

Can't fight.

Can't flee.

Think, she told herself savagely. *There's no other choice.*

Bertone sipped coffee noisily, all but straining it through his modest mustache.

Kayla turned to Elena. "Is this what I get for trying to be helpful?"

"No," Bertone said before his wife could answer, "this is what you get." He picked up the brown envelope and offered it to Kayla.

She looked at it like it was a snake.

"Go ahead," Bertone said almost gently. "The damage is already done."

"This is a fine opportunity," Elena said, her voice impatient. "Don't be such a ninny."

Kayla took the big envelope. She knew her hands trembled, but there was nothing she could do about it. She pulled out a sheaf of documents and fanned rapidly through them.

Escrow instructions.

Quit-claim.

My signature.

Bertone's signature in the margin.

Realization came. "You're the one who bought my ranch."

"Exactly," Bertone said. "I paid you an outrageous price for a few acres of sand and a dull, worn-out house. No matter what the Phoenix Chamber of Commerce claims, it will be many years before development comes to those dismal acres. Who would expect an international businessman like me to pay so much for so little?"

Kayla's stomach slid down her backbone. No one would believe it. She certainly didn't.

Not anymore.

Bertone ticked off points on his fingers. "You opened accounts, you moved money without proper documentation, you never even asked for copies of my passport and my wife's."

Kayla wanted to argue. She couldn't. Taken alone, nothing she'd done would cause a problem.

Taken together . . .

"I see you understand," Bertone said, saluting her with his coffee cup. "To a nasty, suspicious mind, the sale of your ranch would look like payment for the illegal services you rendered."

9

North of Seattle
Friday
9:39 A.M. PST

Silently Rand McCree put the nearly bare canvas into a cubbyhole and propped his folded easel in the corner of the old cedar cabin that served as his studio. He hoped that the ordinary chores would help him get a better handle on the emotions caused by Faroe's arrival.

St. Kilda has found the Siberian.

Five years hadn't taken the edge off Rand's rage at holding his identical twin in his arms and watching life fade from his eyes, hearing the last ragged breath, feeling the utter slackness of death.

It should have been me.

But it hadn't been.

Rand looked at a large, violently energetic painting that nearly filled one wall of the studio. It was a stormy seascape titled *Lucky Too Late.* He'd created the painting in a drunken rage, a savage good-bye to the hope of a better past.

Live for both of us.

Yet Rand hadn't been living. He'd been hiding in booze and the quest for vengeance. Now he both lived and hid in painting.

And waited for a chance at vengeance.

"Hell of a painting," Faroe said, admiring it. "I never saw any of your art before. You won't embarrass yourself at the Fast Draw."

"The Fast Draw? What's that, a pistol contest?"

Faroe laughed. "That's what I thought when I first heard the name."

"How does that connect with the Siberian?" Rand asked bluntly.

"Money."

"One way or another, it's always about money."

"The Siberian made about a half-billion dollars selling arms to both sides of every war he could find," Faroe said, "plus a lot more wars that he started to keep his business humming."

Rand looked from the painting to Faroe. "Keep talking."

"After your brother died, Steele quietly, patiently, started picking apart the Siberian's cover. It took a long time. The man had six identities that we discovered, but every time we got to his last known place, he was gone."

"I know."

Faroe nodded, not surprised. He'd suspected that Rand was always there, a half step behind, as patient in his own predatory way as Steele.

"After the CIA blew off your photos," Faroe said, "you dogged St. Kilda like a bad reputation. In between you came to the Pacific Northwest and started painting again."

"Tell me something I don't know."

"The Siberian is a cashiered KGB operator with diplomatic credentials from Libya who speaks six languages and has a brain that would make Albert Einstein envious."

"Well, that would explain the way he ran us around in circles," Rand said.

"Yeah, he's one bright boy. He bought about half the small arms in what used to be the Soviet Union, bought the planes and pilots to transport them, and resold the arms at a huge profit to private armies and irregular militias all over the African continent. South America, too, but his real specialty is Africa. He made half a billion dollars ramping up the violence between nations, states, tribes, and villages. Without him Africa would have more stable governments and a lot less human suffering."

Rand gave him a sideways look. "Spare me the sermon. I don't lead with my idealism anymore. Just give me an address and the Siberian is dead."

"That could be a problem."

"Why?"

"You might have changed, but St. Kilda hasn't," Faroe said. "We don't hire out as assassins."

"No problem. I'm not part of St. Kilda anymore."

"You will be if you want that address."

For a time there was only the sound of the wind bending trees and flowers with equal ease.

Rand looked at the scar on Faroe's head. "I suppose you got that in the International Court of Justice."

"No. And I didn't get it whacking Hector Rivas Osuna from a sniper's blind. He could have given up anytime. He didn't. I survived. He didn't."

"If Steele didn't want the Siberian dead, why did he track him down?"

"Steele gets downright mean when someone kills one of his employees. In any case, he has dossiers on every international crook and politician and corporation that he might have to work for or against."

"So you have a client."

Faroe nodded. "The client isn't interested in extralegal termination. He wants to find the Siberian's money and seize it before the bastard can start another lovely, enriching African war."

"So you've become some sort of glorified international assets tracker?" Rand asked in disbelief.

"Without money, dictators and crime bosses and other bad guys are about as dangerous as an unloaded gun."

"Put them in the ground and they're about as dangerous as a wet dream," Rand shot back.

Faroe laughed. "I'm going to love watching you tangle with Grace."

"You haven't told me what you want me to do."

"Paint a landscape in two hours on an estate in beautiful, overpriced Pleasure Valley, Arizona."

"That's it?"

"Pretty much."

Rand measured Faroe. "What else?"

"You still good with a camera?" Faroe asked.

"I gave it up five years ago. Besides, you said you wanted a painter."

"I need an operator with your looks and skills."

"Looks?" Rand laughed curtly. "Since when?"

"Since Grace assured me that even with face fur, you're the best looking of the available operators. Elena likes handsome men. And we're hoping a certain ABS banker will too."

"One of us isn't making any sense."

"Are you in or out?" Faroe asked.

"What does this have to do with the Siberian?"

Faroe waited.

"Will it lead me to the Siberian?" Rand demanded.

"Yes."

"I'm in."

10

Pleasure Valley
Friday
10:41 A.M. MST

To buy herself time to think about the dimensions of the cage the Bertones had put her in, Kayla had been going through the escrow documents again. Very slowly.

Twice.

Still her heart was beating too fast, her skin felt clammy, and her muscles were pudding.

Thank God I'm wearing sunglasses. Without them I'd look like a jacklighted doe.

When in doubt, brazen it out.

"Mr. Bertone . . ." she began. Then she said, "Since we seem to be in business together, shall I call you Andre?"

Bertone looked surprised, then vaguely annoyed.

Kayla forced herself to smile. "So what's this all about, Andre? What do you want from me that I haven't been giving you?"

Silently Bertone measured her. Then he turned to Elena. "She has spirit."

"So does a horse." Elena folded up the paper. "That's why we ride with quirts and spurs."

The sound of young, excited voices came from the direction of the house. The back door slammed.

Elena pushed to her feet. "I should have known Maria couldn't control the children for more than a few minutes. She doesn't understand that they must play as well as be quiet, so they test her always. Miranda, especially, ties the silly woman in knots."

With that, Elena walked quickly toward the house. The gems in her sandal straps shot sparks of color with each step.

"Elena told you what she wants," Bertone said.

"A new nanny?" Kayla showed him two rows of white teeth. "Sorry, but that's beyond my expertise."

Bertone's gray eyes narrowed. He tapped his index finger on the creamy envelope that carried his wife's gold letterhead. "Deposit this check immediately into Elena's entertainment account. There will be more coming. Bigger checks. Be prepared to transfer the money from her account to an overseas account as soon as the bank opens on Monday morning." He smiled. "After that, no more special services will be required of you. We'll forget that we ever had this little talk."

Kayla traced the edge of the heavy silver knife that lay alongside her plate. Dull. Like her brain. "I assume you expect me to ignore the regulations that would require me to make sure the money was legitimately obtained."

"If you wish to stay out of jail, yes." Bertone made a sound of disdain. "Your government is very strange. First it tries to make policemen out of bankers. Then business realities force bankers to become criminals. It would be amusing if it weren't so annoying."

Kayla stretched her lips into a grim smile. "You're aware of the fact that I'm only a junior officer at American Southwest Bank. I hope the checks you give me won't be large."

"You've accepted Elena's deposits in the past."

"There's always the chance of a close internal audit, especially with a check this size," she said, looking at Elena's envelope. "Twenty million is a lot of money, even to a bank."

Bertone frowned. "Audit? Is that controlled by your boss?"

"No. It's an entirely different department."

He stared at her, looking for the telltale signs of lies. Unfortunately he didn't see any. "I haven't heard of this."

"Don't feel bad. Learning the ins and outs of banking regulations takes years, and then the regs change overnight." As Kayla spoke, she tried the edge of the heavy silver knife with her thumb again. Still dull as a baseball bat. "I could probably finesse the Treasury regs that require an SAR, but American Southwest is small enough that multimillions in new deposits to an old account will ring alarms all over the place."

"SAR." He said it like a curse.

"Suspicious Activity Report," she translated sweetly. "We have to file a report with the feds whenever we encounter unusual activity in an account. And I believe your request would qualify as unusual if not outright suspicious."

"You're insolent."

"I'm blunt," Kayla said. "The more you know about what I can and can't do, the less chance there is of a big misunderstanding. Who knows, we just might find we have a lot in common. Profitable things."

Elena came back toward them, sandals sparkling. Behind her there was nothing but silence.

Bertone turned to his wife. "You said your banker was a naïf."

"I said she was polite, sweet, and bright."

"I'm flattered," Kayla lied. "Nobody has called me sweet since I told my third-grade teacher to go screw the principal. I work for the bank, but I regard myself as an independent entrepreneur. And so does the bank."

Bertone and Elena exchanged glances. Then he lit one of the Cuban cigars he'd taken up with his most recent identity change. He missed cigarettes, but it was a small sacrifice for freedom. In any case, there were so few places left in the land of the free and home of the brave where a man was free to smoke anything but fish.

"Go on," he said, blowing out a stream of fragrant smoke.

Kayla forced herself to pick up the check she'd rather burn. "Entrepreneurs can be difficult, but they're more useful than clerks. For example, a young bank officer with an entrepreneurial streak might remember that she'd handled transactions from the Bertone accounts at the Bank of Aruba in the past."

"But of course," Elena said impatiently. "You've handled many of—"

Kayla talked over her. "That would mean this entrepreneurial bank officer could say to her bosses that the customer had an established record of legitimate dealings with American Southwest and that the deal was what is called 'normal and expected.' That's the important language, 'normal and expected.' "

Bertone watched her through narrowed eyes.

"Of course," Kayla said, "if somebody challenged the transaction at some later time, the ambitious bank officer would have to say she'd been mistaken about the previous banking relationship. So sorry, my bad, but everyone makes honest mistakes, right?"

For the space of a long, savoring draw on the cigar, Bertone was silent. Then he said, "Wouldn't such a mistake get the young entrepreneur fired?"

"It might," Kayla agreed, "or she might get a raise for bagging millions in new deposits. Banks love big new deposits, so long as they come with plausible explanations. That's the whole fallacy of these 'know-your-customer' regulations. They're really a way the banks can clean their own skirts. Plausible deniability, in political terms."

Kayla flashed a cold, cynical smile, hoping that her clenched teeth didn't show. What she was saying was half true. The other half was that the lowest employee on the banking food chain was the one who got fired and went to jail when *normal and expected* became *unusual and suspicious* in the federal government's 20/20 hindsight.

Like the countless ways to interpret income tax law, the gray areas in banking law were often decided in court.

"In other words, all of this was quite unnecessary," Kayla said. "I'm okay with a direct approach."

"Refreshing," Bertone said.

"Realistic." She dug into her leather valise and came up with the escrow check for the Dry Valley acres. "Let's start over. I'll give you back your money, you can reconvey my ranch, and we'll proceed with the other transactions on a much more friendly basis."

Bertone looked at the check Kayla held out, then at his wife.

"Perhaps we've underestimated your little banker," he said. "She seems more pragmatic than you suggested."

Elena poured her husband more coffee. "I told you she was bright."

When Bertone looked thoughtful, Kayla allowed herself to hope. Then he smiled coldly and shook his head.

"Keep the check," he said. "I've learned that the best relationships are based on motivation. In any case, the escrow company assured me that the sale would be recorded by now."

Beautiful, Kayla thought bitterly. *Whether or not I cash that check, I'm well and truly screwed.* But all she said aloud was, "I see you've done this before."

Bertone's cigar hesitated on the way to his mouth. Then he smiled. "Elena was right. You're intelligent. But I'm surprised. You act like you've been down this road before."

"It's called the primrose path." Kayla wanted to run, so she forced herself to stand and look down at both of them. "A girl knows she's being seduced a long time before she feels the hand on her thigh." She glanced at her unused coffee cup and plate. "Thanks for brunch."

She turned away.

"One minute," Bertone said, his voice like a whip. He picked up the Aruban bank draft and held it out to her. "Deposit this immediately. And I mean immediately."

With cold fingers Kayla took the check. There was no other choice. Not right now. Maybe not ever.

She was trapped, helpless.

For the first time in her life Kayla understood, really understood, why people killed.

"Be sure you're on time for the Fast Draw tomorrow," Elena said. "It's necessary for you to be there. And what is necessary to us, you will do."

"I can't tell you how much I'm looking forward to it." Kayla turned and headed for the parking area.

Bertone drew thoughtfully on his cigar, settled back in his chair, and watched Kayla walk away. She wasn't in Elena's class, but she was an interesting female all the same.

"She's not what I expected," he said quietly.

"She came to heel quickly enough."

He smiled. "I particularly liked the way she tried to turn the tables on us by hinting that she could be bought. That was deliciously inventive of her."

"Do you think she meant it?"

"It doesn't matter. Gabriel will follow her. Her desk, cell, and home phones are tapped. If she is foolish enough to go to the feds, Gabriel will stop her."

"I don't like having her run around free," Elena said.

Bertone sighed. It wasn't the first time the subject had come up. "After the Fast Draw event, I'll give her to Gabriel, but only if he promises to keep her alive until the final transfer is made."

Elena looked thoughtful. She tapped her peach-colored fingernails on the surface of the table. "That leaves too much time before we physically control her. It's still dangerous."

"Money always is. That's why we have so much and others have so little. We risk." He touched the frown lines between her dark brown eyes. "Don't worry, beautiful one. As soon as Kayla transfers all the funds, Gabriel will silence her, the rebels will have the arms to overthrow Camgeria, and the oil concessions will be mine. Then you will dine with presidents and prime ministers as you desire."

But first I will kill Joao Fouquette.

Money was useful, but there was nothing more valuable than power.

11

North of Seattle
Friday
9:44 A.M. PST

Andre Bertone," Rand said, handing Faroe a mug of black tea. "You're sure?"

"As sure as anyone can be in this business," Faroe said. "He's kept the identity for five years. Something of a record for him."

"Sounds more French than Russian. Possibly Argentine."

"It's the name on his UN passport. He was Nicolas Gregori, aka the Siberian, when he killed Reed. Two weeks later Andre Bertone appeared with a cover story that went back to his mother's milk."

"Busy boy." Rand poured his own tea.

"Oh, yeah. Bertone started out life as Victor Krout, a Siberian-born Russian. He was trained in the usual black arts at KGB U in Moscow. He speaks six languages, flies helos and airplanes, and practices tradecraft like a deep-cover agent."

"Is he?"

"Doubt it," Faroe said, yawning and stretching. "The Russians want Bertone's ass. Something about unpaid taxes."

"Bet it's more like unpaid kickbacks."

Faroe shrugged. "In some countries, kickbacks are just another name for taxes."

"What's a former KGB agent doing with a United Nations passport?"

"Ask Libya. Money and guns is my guess."

"The creds must come in handy for a globe-trotting international gunrunner," Rand said.

"Supposedly he's not a gunrunner anymore," Faroe said. "Now he has a bunch of shell companies and old friends standing between him and the obvious dirty stuff. The new and improved Andre Bertone is a respected and respectable international commodities broker. Oil, coltan, diamonds, timber, whatever one African backwater wants to sell and some first-world country wants to buy."

Sipping at the strong, murky tea he loved, Rand paced over to the window and stared out. The bright interval of sun had passed. The sky was slate gray and the wind had increased, whipping the daffodils and turning the unsecured rotor of the waiting helicopter.

Faroe fought back another yawn. He'd been pulling twenty-hour days over Bertone.

"I want to read everything you have on him," Rand said.

"Okay, with the usual reservations."

"The ones that require me to cut out my tongue before talking, my fingers before typing, and my eyes before seeing?" Rand asked dryly.

"You remember. I'm touched."

"Who's the client?"

"An African nation that used the Siberian, got double-crossed, discovered it after the fact, and double-crossed the oil cartel Bertone fronts for in retaliation. Now the cartel is trying to start a civil war so that they'll get oil concessions from the new government. If the oil-backed rebels get enough arms, they'll win. But they won't get arms if they don't get the money to pay."

"You're giving me a headache."

"Get used to it," Faroe said.

"Do you trust your Camgerian interface?"

Faroe's smile was slow and cold. "You haven't lost a step, have you?"

"I lost a twin. Does that count?" Rand made an abrupt gesture. "Who's the interface?"

"A man called John Neto. He was born in Africa and educated at the London School of Economics. Someday he's going to run that oil-rich little country. Right now he's head of the Camgerian national intelligence service—all three employees. He has a fine jugular instinct and the patience of a leopard. Best of all, he hates the ground Bertone walks on. He's been tracking him for years."

"So why does this Neto need St. Kilda?"

"The U.S. government won't cooperate with him."

"Gee, that sounds familiar," Rand said. "So they stonewalled him same as they did me?"

"Yeah. And then they told Neto that he couldn't come to the U.S. and present evidence against Andre Bertone."

"Why?"

" 'Not in the interests of the U.S. at this time.' Visa denied."

Rand made a disgusted sound. "Same shit, different year." He took a swallow of hot, bitter, aromatic tea. "So St. Kilda has suddenly become an agent for a foreign power? Even if it's a tiny African nation that has had more names in twenty years than Andre Bertone, it's still a little dicey, isn't it?"

"Only if we're pursuing another nation's political interests. We aren't."

"Could have fooled me."

"Neto's government has issued a murder warrant for Krout, aka Bertone, which makes this a criminal inquiry," Faroe said.

"Steele is skating on a thin edge."

"Actually it's Grace, and she assured us it's a defensible position. She also assured us that we'd all be a lot happier if we nailed Bertone in such a way that no one would want to make a federal case of it."

Rand thought about it, whistled, and said, "That's some woman you married."

Faroe grinned the grin of a well-satisfied male.

Sun fought to pierce the clouds, failed, and sulked. Rand watched the small skirmish overhead and thought hard. "What do you want from me?"

"You're the one man we know who has seen the Siberian close enough to identify him. If you can verify that Bertone is the Siberian by another name, St. Kilda can chip away at his UN creds. At least that's what the brains of the outfit both say."

"Both?"

"Steele and Grace."

"Steele actually listens to her?" Rand asked.

"At the top of his lungs. And vice versa. It's quite a show." Faroe looked at his watch. "Ready to meet Neto?"

"I thought he was denied a visa."

"Here, but not in Victoria, B.C."

The wind gusted around the cabin. The branches of a fir tree tapped against the glass. It sounded hauntingly like Morse code from a prisoner.

Me.

That's what I've become. Prisoner of the past.

"What the hell," Rand said, shrugging. "I need to go to Murchie's anyway. I'm running out of tea."

"If it goes well in Canada, we're heading straight to Phoenix. Steele doesn't like what he's hearing on the Brazilian grapevine. Neither do I. We could be working on a much shorter clock than Neto believed. Pack your painting gear along with whatever else you think you need," Faroe said.

"I thought the St. Kilda adage was 'Pack your weapons and live out of Wal-Mart.' "

"They don't have the kind of professional painting gear you'll need if you go to the Fast Draw in Phoenix."

"Big if."

"Humor me."

"The last time I did, Reed died."

"Wrong," Faroe said calmly. "I humored Reed and let him follow you around Africa with a rifle. You never had a sense of humor worth mentioning."

Rand almost snarled, almost smiled. "I'll need dossiers on this Elena, whoever she is."

"Bertone's wife."

"And the ASB banker, whatever he, she, or it is."

"She. Kayla Shaw. My computer's on the helo. You can read dossiers while we fly to Victoria. Get a move on. The film crew will be getting restless."

Rand blinked. "Film crew? Are they part of the Fast Draw contest?"

"Hell of an idea. I'll work on it."

"What does painting have to do with Bertone?"

"It's all on my computer."

"Which is on the helo, which is heading for B.C."

Faroe punched Rand's shoulder lightly. "You listen good."

"Too bad I don't obey worth a damn."

"We'll work on that."

12

Phoenix
Friday
12:12 P.M. MST

Kayla was tempted to drive past the freeway turnoff again, but she made herself go to American Southwest Bank instead. More than an hour of roaming Phoenix's ninety-mile-an-hour freeways was all the time she could afford to work off her anger and fear. She pulled into the employee-of-the-month parking space in front of the glistening steel and copper-colored glass building that housed American Southwest.

"What bullshit," she said, turning off the engine. "What complete and utter bullshit."

For the past three weeks she'd enjoyed using the parking space. It wasn't the gold star in her file that she cared about, it was the chance to walk a quarter mile less in the heels all women employees were required to wear.

And that's bullshit, too. If heels are so necessary, why don't men wear the damn things?

She'd take a suit and tie over pantyhose and heels any day.

"No worries," she told herself as she got out of the car. "After I talk with Steve Foley, I won't have to rub up against American Southwest dress codes."

Or any other business kind.

Wonder how I'll look in prison orange.

She slammed the car door. The explosive sound was so satisfying she opened the door and slammed it again. Harder.

Okay, tantrum over.

Now think.

Because thinking is the only thing that will keep me out of bright orange. And I look really lame in orange.

She'd always assumed that people who went to prison had it coming. What really burned her was that she hadn't done anything wrong. Her real estate deal was entirely legal. Any other landowner would have been blameless.

But she was an employee of American Southwest Bank who had, at best, engaged in an unusual private transaction with a very important client. That was a firing offense.

She could live with that.

It was the idea of going to prison for laundering money that spiked her blood pressure.

Automatically she went through the discreet metal detectors, nodded to the guard, and used her electronic passkey on the elevator. Her office wasn't on the top floor, but Steve Foley's was. If neckties and ever-shining shoes bothered him, he didn't show it. He dressed for success, talked for it, breathed for it.

He was the youngest vice president in the bank's history. He'd been at the bank a year less than Kayla, decades less than many of the other women in her department, yet he'd leapfrogged over them and into the corner office with the ease of a handsome, charming young executive bound for greatness.

It hadn't hurt that his father was a member of the bank's board of directors.

Kayla still wasn't sure if she was more annoyed by the implicit sexism or the explicit nepotism in his rapid promotions. She *was* sure that she'd never cared for Foley, had passed up his offers for a social relationship with bland professional smiles, and had worked hard for every tiny raise she got.

Now she had to tell him she'd screwed up. She wondered if he'd be sympathetic or happy to see her on her knees. Her gut said that sympathy was a long shot.

She found Foley behind a clean walnut desk that was decorated with a seldom-used pen set, a never-used baseball autographed by a Diamondbacks reliever who had since been traded to Kansas City, and a booster's award plaque from the National Rifle Association. Pretty typical of an Arizona executive. He glanced in her direction as she entered and closed the door behind her.

"Hey, Kayla." He flashed a smile perfect enough to be a news anchor's. "How's the best-looking banker in Phoenix?"

Kayla ignored both the smile and the personal remark. "Do you have a few minutes to talk?"

Foley glanced at the closed door. "That's what I'm here for." He gestured to the client chair across the desk from him. "What's wrong?"

"I'm not certain yet," she said, which was half true. "I just had a meeting with a client. He asked me to deposit a big check for him."

"Well, that's what banks are for, isn't it?" He pointed to the chair. "Sit."

She was tempted to keep on standing, but she sat down, carefully keeping her knees together, a feat that particular chair made nearly impossible. No doubt that was why Foley had chosen it.

"This is an unusually big check," Kayla said.

"How big?" Foley asked without looking away from her long legs.

"Twenty-two million dollars."

He focused on her face. "Not bad, Kayla. Not bad at all. You should be dancing, not frowning. Unless there's some difficulty with the check?"

"It's drawn on a Caribbean bank by one of our best clients, Andre Bertone."

"He's good for a lot more than twenty-two million," Foley said, rocking back in his swivel chair. "So what's the problem?"

"I thought I should run it by you before I cashed the check," she said carefully. "I've never heard of the bank the check is drawn on, and I've never seen this account in Mr. Bertone's records. When I tried to do some fundamental due diligence, Andre and Elena both told me where the money came from was none of my business."

Foley sighed and shook his head. "Most of our wealthy clients just don't understand our obligations under the Patriot Act. I assume you explained everything to him."

"Of course."

"And?"

"He went postal," Kayla said.

"I don't understand."

"First, he tried what amounted to blackmail. Very cleverly done, but still blackmail."

Foley's mouth opened. He shook his head sharply, then picked up his desk pen. "Explain."

"Remember that land I own out toward Wickenburg?"

"Sure do. Did you decide to sell it like I advised?"

Kayla told herself that Foley didn't mean to sound patronizing. And if she repeated it often enough, she might believe it. "The deal just closed this morning."

"Good. Small ranches are sentimental holes in all but the wealthiest purses. You don't have a big one. What'd you get for it?"

"Twenty-five thousand an acre."

"Yowsa," Foley said, fiddling with the pen. "That's a great price. Did you go with Charlotte Welmann?"

Kayla nodded. She'd taken Foley's recommendation because she didn't know any local Realtors and hadn't wanted the hassle of selling Dry Valley by herself. "Charlotte started with a high price because she wasn't sure what the market would be." Kayla grimaced. "The place sold in a day."

"Huh. Guess you should have asked more."

"That's what she said."

"Who bought it?"

"Charlotte told me the buyer was an out-of-town investor who was quietly buying up ground for a large development. I was required to sign a confidentiality agreement, promising not to reveal the sale. The buyer's agent said his client was worried that other landowners would hear about my sale and start jacking up their prices."

Foley nodded. "That's pretty standard. So what does all this have to do with your, ah, blackmail problem?"

"About an hour after I signed the agreement and picked up the escrow check, I learned the identity of the buyer. Andre Bertone."

Foley's blond eyebrows lifted. "Well, that's a little weird, but I don't see—"

Kayla cut across his words. "Bertone told me if I didn't deposit his twenty-two-million-dollar check without questions, he'd see that I got in trouble with the bank and the federal government over the Dry Valley sale."

Reaching into her valise, she pulled out the check and shoved it across the desk to her boss. Then she rubbed her fingers over her skirt, trying to remove even the feel of the transaction.

Foley picked up the check and looked at it silently. It appeared to be just what she'd said it was.

Twenty-two million bucks.

"Okay, let me get this straight," he said finally. "You think that one of our best clients spent a quarter of a million dollars on a scheme to compromise you, and potentially the bank as well."

She nodded. Foley might be a pretty boy, but he was a damned shrewd banker.

He looked at the check again. "Have you verified that the funds are present in the account?"

Kayla shook her head. "I didn't want to do anything that looked like I was agreeing to Bertone's demands. That seemed to me like a one-way ticket to federal prison."

Thoughtfully Foley slid the check in small circles on the polished surface of the desk. Then he pushed the check back to her. "If this all happened the way you say it did, you've done nothing wrong. The bank will back you two hundred percent."

She let out a long breath she hadn't been aware of holding. "I can't tell you how glad I am to hear that."

"Be serious, Kayla." He leaned forward and grinned. "I always take care of the people who take care of me."

The remark made her uneasy, but she let it pass. She didn't like a lot of what Foley said. "So what do we do—call the FBI?"

He leaned back. "No. That's the last thing we do. The Bertones have been very good customers of American

Southwest. This may all be some extraordinary coincidence, or, more likely, a cascade of misunderstandings. Andre is an international financial force. This may simply be the way they do business in his banking circles. We need to explore a little more, find out exactly what's going on. If we don't like what we find, we'll file an SAR."

"But—"

"So process this check," he said, pushing it back to her, "just to keep Andre happy, while I figure out exactly what we ought to do."

Kayla's stomach felt hollow. "Isn't that a bit risky?" *Especially for me.*

"Not if we can figure a way of covering the transaction for the moment. Is this an account you've handled before?"

"I told you that it wasn't. If I'd qualified this account previously, there wouldn't be any question about the transaction."

He frowned, looking at the check again. Twenty-two million. "Yeah, I guess you did mention that. So we can't clean it up that way."

Clean it up? Kayla asked silently. *I don't like the sound of that. But then, I haven't liked the sound of anything since Elena handed me that check.*

The light on one of Foley's telephones blinked, alerting him to an incoming call. He ignored it.

"What we need to do is find a way of carrying the transaction on our books that won't put us at risk but will buy us a little time," he said. He looked at the check again. "Bank of Aruba, Sugar Sands branch . . . Wait a minute, wait a minute."

He spun his high-backed executive chair and addressed the flat screen of his desktop computer. His fingers moved rapidly over the keyboard, drilling down through pages and documents.

"There," he said. "I knew I remembered that name. They have a correspondent banking relation with us. They've had it for some months now. That will make things much easier."

Some of the tension seeped out of Kayla.

The light still blinked on the desk phone.

Foley turned back to her. "Here's what we do. You call the Aruba bank. Make sure Andre has the money in the account, then put a hold on the funds and tell them you intend to run the draft through their correspondent account."

Kayla hesitated. "I don't know nearly as much as you do about international banking and correspondent accounts, but is it legal? Who's responsible for knowing the customer?"

Foley kicked back in his chair. "Not us, for damn sure. Our correspondent, aka the Bank of Aruba,

Sugar Sands branch, is on the spot for due diligence."

She looked as doubtful as she felt. "You're certain?" *It's my ass on the line.*

"Standard operating procedure," he said. "If anybody challenges us, we simply say we assumed the Aruba bank had done their own due diligence on the account before they let Andre start writing checks of this size."

"Would it fly?" Kayla asked bluntly.

The telephone light stopped blinking.

"It's defensible, which is all that matters. By the way, I really like how you wrinkle your nose when you're thinking hard."

She barely heard the personal remark. She was focused on legalities. "But pushing it off on the Aruba bank is just a bookkeeping trick, almost under the heading of 'the dog ate my due diligence.' How does it get me off the hook?"

Foley laughed. "Sweetie, the bank business is all about bookkeeping tricks. The government makes unenforceable antibusiness regs, and the lawyers find ways around them. Correspondent accounts are a legal superhighway. Nobody ever checks the correspondent accounts, not inside the bank and not at Treasury. Everybody is clean and everybody is happy."

Kayla wished she was happy about what she was hearing, but she wasn't. If the feds came down on her, she wanted something more solid than a "defensible" position to shield her.

The telephone light started blinking again, double time. Urgent.

"So move the money and let me take care of the rest," Foley said. "And if Andre comes up with any more big checks, do the same thing. I'll keep you posted, but don't get impatient. It will take time to do the background work and walk it up the line to Operations."

"You're asking me to move millions of dollars of uncertain origin into the U.S. banking system," Kayla said. "That's called laundering."

"Not so long as I put a hold on the money."

"What?"

"I'll lock down the correspondent account."

"How will that help?" she asked.

"It will be pretty much like the money never left Aruba. Then, after we investigate and find out that everything is kosher, we release the funds and let Andre Bertone do what he wants."

"But what if things aren't kosher?" she asked.

The phone light blinked rapidly.

"I know what I'm doing," Foley said. "Follow my instructions and I'll take full responsibility."

"But—" *My name will still be on the bottom line.*

"Unless you have a better solution?" Foley asked impatiently.

Kayla didn't. She just didn't like his.

"Cash the check. I'll put the rest of it in motion," Foley said.

He turned his back on her and reached for the phone.

13

Victoria, B.C.
Friday
12:15 P.M. PST

Rand McCree looked around John Neto's suite in disbelief. There were TV cameras, lights, a makeup artist, a hair stylist, a continuity person with a clipboard and a frown, the telegenic Brent Thomas with an earnest yet horrified expression on his face, and a black man with a steel-tipped forearm prosthesis talking about war atrocities.

Everything but a dancing pig.

He turned on Faroe. "You didn't say anything about a media circus."

"Interview, not a circus," Faroe said. "*The World in One Hour* is high-class crap."

"Quiet!" someone called out.

Quietly Rand raised a middle finger. Then he leaned close and murmured in Faroe's ear. "Just thought I'd let you know—from what I've read so far, Kayla Shaw isn't good for it."

"Not a crook?"

"Not likely. Read between the lines of her dossier. Backpacked all over the world. Younger sister has a Ph.D. in tropical diseases, married to a doctor, both working for Doctors without Borders. Close family until the parents died. Kayla doesn't gamble, get drunk, do drugs, or hump along the casual sex circuit. Smart, middle-class, hardworking. Somehow Bertone twisted her. It's how he does business."

"I'll keep it in mind," Faroe said. "You keep in mind that most white-collar crooks don't start out to end up felons."

"You really think she's a crook?" Rand asked.

"I'm partial to the Mexican justice system—guilty until proven innocent. Grace feels like you do, if it matters."

Rand shrugged. Nothing mattered but getting close enough to Bertone to kill him.

But he really hated to see an innocent ground to bits by transnational criminals and governments that were rarely better than they had to be to survive.

"Take a break," called someone.

Ted Martin hurried over to Faroe.

"Okay, is this him?" Martin asked, jerking a thumb at Rand. "The photog you told me about?"

"Yeah."

"Okay, but he'll have to wait. We're just getting into it with Neto. Awesome stuff. That pink half-arm on his plum-black body says it all."

Rand stared at the man wearing jeans and a silk sweatshirt, rhapsodizing about a black man whose forearm had been hacked off with a machete and replaced by a white man's prosthesis. Then Rand looked at Faroe and said, "I'll wait until hell freezes solid."

"Okay, can you at least comb him out before we put him on camera?" Martin asked over his shoulder as he hurried back to Neto. "I'll send over Freddie. She could make a woolly mammoth look good."

Faroe snickered.

Rand said something under his breath and ignored both men. He found an empty chair, booted up Faroe's computer, and began reading. Neto's interview made an odd counterpart to the dossiers that clicked by beneath Rand's fingertips. The Scots-accented English that Neto spoke reminded Rand of his grandfather.

"How did you come to be in MI-5?" Thomas asked Neto.

"I was born in Africa, raised there long enough to see the beginnings of the troubles, back when the militias had only machetes." He raised his artificial hand. "We escaped and made it to Scotland, Glasgow. Strange and wonderful people, the Scots. I came to love their bluntness and pragmatism. That is one of the reasons I sought out St. Kilda Consulting. The island of St. Kilda is—or was—to Scotland what Scotland was to the rest of England, a last frontier."

"Have you met Ambassador Steele?" Thomas asked. "His grandfather was the last man to leave St. Kilda when the British forced evacuation of the population and turned the island into a bird sanctuary."

"The ambassador and I have had several long conversations," Neto said, "all in Scots Gaelic. He is one of the few people I have ever met who speaks the mother tongue."

Rand paused in his reading. The world was a very odd place when a black man speaking Scots Gaelic—who was also a former British intelligence officer—was presently chief of intelligence of a small African country that was besieged by transnational criminals from Russia, Brazil, Europe, and the UAE. And this man was being interviewed for American TV in a room in British Columbia, Canada, about a murderous Siberian gunrunner presently living the high life of a socialite in Phoenix, Arizona.

Reed would have laughed his ass off.

Rand didn't. A small world wasn't necessarily a good thing, but it sure was real. Whining about it wouldn't do anything except waste breath.

"It was during those conversations that the ambassador provided me with information about the man who is today known as Andre Bertone," Neto said. "He is the one feeding arms to Uhuru rebels who want to unseat the established government of Camgeria. Thus far they have not been successful, though they have continued to try for many years."

"What do the rebels want?" Thomas asked, keeping his face straight despite the inane question. This was a softball interview, designed to make the subject look good, not the reporter.

"What all barbarians want—conquest, blood, power, wealth. They would replace a thriving black democracy with a dictatorship of violence. All this in the name of righting tribal wrongs that go back hundreds and hundreds of years. I do not want our women and children to be raped and slaughtered in the name of old arguments or new genocides."

"What are you doing to prevent it?"

Neto bowed slightly toward Thomas. "I speak to everyone who will listen about the greed and evil of arms dealers such as Andre Bertone."

"The merchant of death."

"Yes. He is the one who sold arms to the rebels five years ago. He, or his employees, seek to send hundreds of millions of American dollars in arms to the rebels today. The people funding the rebels are not Camgerians. They are not even Africans."

"Who are they?" Thomas asked.

Rand didn't need to hear the answer. It was all there in the files on Joe Faroe's computer. He went back to looking at various pictures of Kayla Shaw. Driver's license. Employee of the month. Yoga classes three times a week. Regular health-club workouts. Horseback riding. Hiking. Passport up to date. Gave regularly to the SPCA. A stack of long-distance surveillance photos and a few shot so close to her that the photographer must have been within reach.

Probably Jimmy "Handsome" Hamm with a lapel camera, Rand decided. He'd already read about the St. Kilda employee striking out in his attempts to get Kayla Shaw's confidence.

If he can't do it, why does Faroe's wife think I can?

There wasn't any answer in the photos. Good or bad, all the pictures showed a dark-haired, light-eyed young woman whose cheekbones suggested Scandinavian blood and whose smile was hard to resist. She wasn't Hollywood gorgeous, but she had a kind of energy and intelligence that intrigued him.

". . . talking about a huge amount of money," Thomas said.

"Over two hundred and twenty-five million dollars American," Neto agreed.

Rand whistled silently and looked up from the computer. Faroe hadn't been real definite about the money involved.

"Where would rebels find that kind of cash?" Thomas asked.

"Barter, not cash." Neto leaned back in his chair and massaged his right forearm just above the prosthesis.

"With what?"

"Blood diamonds, stolen oil, coltan—"

"What is coltan?" Thomas asked.

Rand went back to reading. Unlike the future TV audience, Rand already knew more than he wanted to about the "black stone" that was the basis of modern electronics.

Yet he couldn't help listening to the events that had caused his brother's death.

"Coltan is mucked out of the ground by independent miners, rebels, and men with legitimate Camgerian licenses," Neto said. "There was a time in the 1980s and 1990s when coltan was worth nearly as much as solid native copper and was much easier to find. The rebels who confronted the Camgerian government five years ago used coltan to finance the purchase of arms. They bartered sacks full of it for AK-47s."

Rand saw the words as a series of pictures, vivid as only a flashback could be.

Bulging gunny sacks lined up along the dirt runway.

Sweating black rebels unloading wooden crates of high-tech death.

A Russian turboprop.

The Siberian.

Blood.

Reed's blood.

Everywhere.

"The guns were stolen or purchased in Eastern Europe, from Soviet, Bulgarian, and Ukrainian arms depots," Neto said. "Then they were flown south to equatorial Africa and traded for coltan, which could be easily monetized in the world market."

"Monetized?" Thomas asked right on cue.

"Sweat and blood and coltan turned into hard currency," Neto explained. "Victor Krout, now called Andre Bertone, was one of the leading forces in this illegal trade. He used his ties to the Russian military-industrial establishment to organize what had been random smuggling into a coordinated, very profitable business. I estimate he made one hundred and fifty million dollars over the ten years he was active in the illegal arms trade. Much of that money was wrung from the blood and bones of Camgerians. I will get it back on their behalf. With that money we will dig village wells and vaccinate children, build schools and clinics and hospitals. For millions of Camgerians, that money is the difference between continuing stability and the atrocities of war."

"Can you retrieve that money legally, under international law?" Thomas asked.

Rand's mouth flattened. If international law worked reliably, St. Kilda would be out of business. Transnational criminals weren't stupid. Bertone was nothing short of brilliant. Courtroom proof was hard to find when everyone who stepped forward was murdered.

And that was what Krout/Bertone did.

"Yes, we will prevail," Neto said, "but it will be difficult. Bertone, as he is known today, has long since put his disreputable past behind him. Using money gained from bringing war where peace had been, he has become a very wealthy oil broker, a middleman between renegade African regimes and rebel armies on one side and some of the world's leading oil companies on the other. Bertone has a whole list of former arms clients who are tied to him—rebels who used his weapons to overthrow governments and governments who used Bertone's arms to suppress rebellions."

"You're saying that money, rather than any kind of idealism or politics, motivated Bertone in the arms trade," Thomas said.

"Idealism?" Neto laughed bitterly. "Bertone could not find it in the dictionary. Yet, or perhaps because of that, he has many powerful allies in Africa, Russia, Brazil, France, and even the United States. That is why you had to come to Canada to talk to me. My request for a U.S. visa was turned down."

Rand waited for the next, obvious question: Why would the U.S. refuse Neto entrance?

Instead, Thomas went back to the sexier, safer, far more visual subject of arms, diamonds, oil, and violence. Rand could practically see the montage of film clips that would be used to help the viewer understand that Bertone's profits could be measured in suffering as well as dollars.

Faroe gestured to Rand.

Rand closed the computer and walked to the suite's small dining area, where a portable fax had been set up. "Scrambled?" he asked Faroe softly.

"What do you think?"

"Like eggs at a buffet."

Faroe looked at his watch. The fax began spitting out papers. He handed them to Rand and waited for the explosion.

"Application accepted?" Rand asked in a rising voice. "Invitation included? Frigging parking permit? You mean there really is such a dumb-ass thing as the Fast Draw?"

"Sure is. And now you're a part of it. Come on. Grace is waiting for us in Phoenix. She has more papers for you to sign."

"What?"

"Employment contract."

Rand shook his head sharply. "If my word isn't good enough—"

"Your protection as well as ours," Faroe cut in. "If you're employed, you can claim confidentiality if the feds question you."

"Try it again, in English."

"I knew you'd ask, so I had her write it down." Faroe reached into a hip pocket and drew out a file card the size of his palm. "She said, and I quote, 'American law gives us some cover on the basis of trade secrecy, but only if Rand signs an employee confidentiality contract. Otherwise he would have no plausible basis for refusing to answer FBI questions.' "

Rand blinked. "Was that English?"

"Good as it gets. The original thing was two pages long."

Rand looked at the St. Kilda Consulting contract and read quickly. His only comment was, " 'Employed for a time to be mutually agreed upon.' "

"That's my Grace." Faroe handed the other man a pen.

For a moment Rand hesitated, remembering Reed's bloody death and the smiling life of Kayla Shaw. He hadn't been able to save Reed. Maybe he could help her.

More likely not.

Rand took the pen anyway.

"Welcome back," Faroe said.

"Tell me that in a few days."

Faroe took the signed contract and nodded to a woman who had been waiting across the room. Freddie walked toward them briskly, scissors and comb in hand.

Grinning, Faroe did a fast fade.

14

Phoenix
Friday
7:10 P.M. MST

Impatiently Bertone tapped his fingers against his polished desk. Joao Fouquette might demand that everyone jump through hoops for him, but he took forever to answer his private satellite phone. Knowing the Brazilian's lifestyle, he was probably enjoying a long, leisurely meal with his mistress and was reluctant to focus on business.

Finally Fouquette answered, his voice rough, almost breathless. "Speak."

"The account has been set up at our Aruban bank."

"It took long enough."

"It went more quickly than you had any right to expect, and you know it," Bertone said.

In the background Bertone heard a woman's voice say, "Joao, my soul, you promised me no business. It is my name day."

"I've sent all the information to your coded e-mail," Bertone said over the sound of Fouquette soothing his mistress.

"Expect the transfers within forty-eight hours," Fouquette said almost absently.

"But of course," Bertone said. "I've alerted the men to begin gathering the cargo at the Ukrainian warehouse. When the full payment is transferred, the cargo will be flown immediately to Camgeria."

"Joao," said a pouting voice. "I am cold without you."

Fouquette broke the satellite connection.

Bertone set the unit aside, picked up a scrambled cell phone, and punched speed dial. Gabriel answered immediately.

"All is well?" Bertone asked.

"Ver' quiet. She visit a taqueria and now drives back to her little ranch. Such a hot woman need a man."

"Business first."

Gabriel sighed. "*Sí.* It is a long time I wait."

"Death is a lot longer. Keep it in your pants until I give you the signal."

"And if she goes sideways on you?"

"Bring her to me immediately."

"Alive?"

"If possible. If not, stupidity is a capital crime."

15

Phoenix
Saturday
2:30 P.M. MST

Kayla sat at her desk and wanted to scream. The American Southwest Bank building was pretty much deserted. The only sound she'd heard in hours was the elevator opening and closing while guards or cleaners made their rounds. Everyone was off to enjoy the weekend.

Except her.

Damn it, Foley, where are you?

She hadn't seen her boss for twenty-four hours. As far as she could tell, Foley had left work shortly after he'd talked to her.

Cash the check. I'll put the rest of it in motion.

She had.

Had he?

Anxiety crawled over her like needles, first hot and then cold.

As she'd already done countless times already, she clicked on her e-mail icon. The answer hadn't changed.

Nothing new from her boss.

Almost desperately she opened the last e-mail from Foley, the one from yesterday.

Relax, Kayla. I'm working on it.

"Okay, great," she said under her breath. "But how hard can it be to consult with the corporate counsel and compliance department? Even if you have to bring in the rest of the high-powered executives, it shouldn't take a whole day. Everyone is in town. I checked. So where the hell is my boss?"

She took several long, slow, deep breaths, willing her nerves to settle. Foley might be slick as snot, but he wasn't a fool. Neither were his bosses. They would understand that she was innocent.

Wouldn't they?

She closed her eyes and gripped her desk until her fingers ached. She was the lowest creature on this particular food chain. If anyone was eaten, it would be her.

God, how could this have happened?

Silently she rehearsed the facts she'd have to retell over and over again before this mess was cleared up. And while she did, she prayed she wouldn't have to give her frail explanations to some cold-eyed federal agent.

Part of her wanted to grab her backpack and passport and get on a plane.

Part of her wanted to scream.

Most of her wanted to kill Bertone and dance at his funeral.

Automatically she checked her phone for voice mails, hoping that one from Foley would be there, telling her everything had been handled.

Nothing.

She checked her e-mails again.

Nothing.

Grimly she stared at the screen.

This is all a bad dream, right? It isn't real.

It can't be.

She typed her way into the bank's master database. With shaking fingers she called up the Bank of Aruba correspondent account she had established at Foley's instruction. The screen flashed into focus, then blinked, as if updating itself.

Forty-five million, five hundred thousand dollars.

Air left her lungs in a rush. "That can't be. The check was only for twenty-two million."

With a growing sense of sickness, she scanned down to the banker's code authorizing the second deposit.

It was hers.

No! I didn't make a second deposit.

She refreshed the screen once, twice, three times. Nothing changed except the speed of her heartbeat.

Not a bad dream after all.

Just a bad reality.

Someone was using her bank code to make unauthorized deposits into the Aruban correspondent account that she had created.

Damn it, Foley. You said you would help.

She hit her e-mail button one last time.

Nothing new.

And there was nothing she could do about it right now except trust Foley to get off his ass while she went to the Fast Draw paint-off and smiled so that her picture could be taken with her equally smiling blackmailers.

16

Castillo del Cielo
Saturday
5:30 P.M. MST

The tape securing the recorder to the small of Rand's back itched like fire ants. The nearly invisible wire that served as a microphone tweaked his chest hair when he moved a certain way.

"Stop scratching. It blows out the microphone."

Faroe's voice came from the earphones of the fake iPod that Rand wore. When the Bertones had turned down an offer from *The World in One Hour* to film the contest as a human interest piece, Faroe had wired Rand for sound and given him a special camera. It had been prepared by St. Kilda technicians and was capable of shooting through the compound lens, as any other camera would.

But this particular camera came equipped with another internal hard drive and lens. The second lens took its images through a pinhole disguised as a USB cable port on the side of the camera and sent the results to a memory stick. The second camera's field of view was at precisely ninety degrees to the normal lens.

All Rand had to do to take photos from the second lens was to depress a disguised second shutter release and remember to keep his finger away from the USB port.

"Damn wire is plucking me bald," Rand said under his breath.

"Wait until I pull off the tape—you'll scream like a girl. You see Bertone yet?"

"No, but his wife is all over the place like a rash."

"Don't scratch her either."

Rand laughed silently. Faroe's acid comments were the only thing amusing about the Fast Draw. As far as Rand was concerned, the contest was an absurd pursuit for adults who lived in a world overflowing with violence. The fact that the party was paid for by the man who had armed most of the African continent just added to the absurdity.

But at least Rand was used to painting in the field. He was a plein air artist in the original sense of the word. Not every invited artist at the party was. After the invention of good color film, many painters chose to work from photos rather than from field studies. The fact that someone painted excellent landscapes didn't mean that he or she routinely worked outside of a studio with its good lighting, controlled weather, and endless supplies.

The thirty artists were all painting some aspect of the Bertone estate, all within the same two-hour period. They were surrounded by more than three hundred members of Arizona's movers and shakers. The women wore "resort" clothes, the kind that cost thousands of dollars and were accessorized by sandals, purses, sunglasses, and jewelry from every country that catered to the world of European fashion. French champagne and Phoenix gossip fueled the party.

Rand scanned the crowds of expensively dressed socialites and wondered how many of them knew the truth of Balzac's epigram: Behind every great fortune is a crime.

He sketched in a few lines for the pool, the pool house, and the concrete deck that provided the best view of the Phoenix landscape. For a few more moments he assessed the slanting, golden light. Then he decided it was time to quit sketching and start painting. He set aside the pencil and chose tubes of oil from his small worktable, squeezing and mixing colors quickly on his palette.

"See Bertone yet?"

"Shut up, I'm working," Rand muttered.

"So am I."

He painted quickly. And he hoped his disgust didn't show behind his ruthlessly trimmed beard and newly collar-length hair. The sage green shirt Grace had presented him with was exactly the color of his eyes—or so she said. The old jeans and boots he wore were splattered with oils.

Soon the new shirt would be, too.

"Ah, he's painting at last," said a woman, her voice carrying clearly above the party's chatter.

Rand ignored the woman, who was wearing black silk jeans and blouse and massive Native American jewelry.

"I told you so," another woman said. "Elena assured me that he's a fine young painter."

"R. McCree. Never heard of him."

"You don't do the Pacific Northwest art scene."

"Why would I?" the first woman asked. "And why is he painting all alone over here? The others are all over there, with that spectacular view of the valley. Castle of Heaven might be a trite name, but it sure fits the view."

Rand hoped the women would leave and plague the other artists. Then he shut out the chatter and concentrated on the piece of the estate he'd chosen to paint. Both the spy and the artist in him was pleased with his choice—a vantage point overlooking Castillo del Cielo's grounds.

"One of those women is really rude," Faroe said.

"You should know," Rand muttered.

Painting in a controlled fury of creation, he ignored Faroe and the sweat that dried on his skin almost as soon as it appeared. Phoenix already had one foot into the searing summer that defined its landscape and the lives of its citizens. The pouring afternoon light picked out every line and curve of the land like "star lighting" in an old black-and-white movie.

That kind of light was the artist's best friend.

And worst enemy.

Because the desert light itself was so different from the cool, diffuse light of the Pacific Northwest, Rand had decided against doing a pure landscape. It would take time to master the subtleties of desert light. He didn't have time.

So he was counting on the vanity of Elena Bertone, who was one of the three judges. According to St. Kilda's dossier on her, she'd overseen the details of Castillo del Cielo's design with an intensity that had driven the architect to drink. Literally. Castillo del Cielo was Elena's, and she loved it like a child.

So he would paint her baby.

A smart choice, but not an easy one for him. He'd never before painted a subject he didn't enjoy. Like the party, to him the estate was . . . wrong. It had been hammered onto a site blasted from rock and cactus. The gem blue of the pools and the diamond glitter of huge water features fought with the sun-ravaged hills and spare shapes of cactus on the unbuildable ridgelines around the estate. The house itself was in the Tuscan style, calling upon a past that simply didn't exist on this side of the Atlantic.

Wrong.

And very expensive.

"Why didn't Bertone just take out a billboard advertising his gross worth?" Faroe asked. *"And I mean gross."*

"Quit reading my mind." The words didn't go beyond Rand's collar, which was far enough.

"I was eavesdropping on that irritating woman. Wonder if her man of the moment gags her before he screws her."

"Go away."

"Find Bertone."

"Quit chewing on me because Hamm couldn't get a photo of Bertone," Rand said. "I've taken enough color photos of the estate for twelve coffee-table books."

"Bertone never goes to the parts of his estate that are monitored by closed-circuit security TVs. He's one crafty bastard. That's why we're paying you an outrageous amount to play with oils and trick cameras."

"I'd have done it for free," Rand said, painting fiercely, trying not to remember the twin who had died in his arms, taking too much of Rand with him.

"Your job isn't to avenge Reed. Remember that."

Rand didn't answer.

17

Castillo del Cielo
Saturday
5:35 P.M. MST

Kayla Shaw stood off to one side of the pool, searching the crowd for Steve Foley. Surely he would at least put in an appearance at the premier event of the bank's premier private clients. Surely he'd tell her to relax, it was taken care of, she was safe.

Surely she was being paranoid.

The grim lines around her mouth were out of place in the beautiful, slanting light. The sun was still hot, but coolness seeped up from the ground itself, a reminder that winter wasn't completely gone. Or maybe it was just her nerves, the paranoid part of her screaming *Get out! Run! Hide!*

Kayla pulled her black linen jacket closer around her. The rich teal of her silk blouse glowed in the light, as did the black pearl earring studs that were her parents' last birthday present to her. Her body all but vibrated with tension as she scanned the thirty artists slapping paint on canvas as if their lives depended on it.

Foley was nowhere to be found.

What am I going to do?

The question rang in her mind like a frantic heartbeat.

Don't think about it. All you can do right now is play nice so that the Bertones don't get suspicious.

But if—

Don't think about it. Not now.

But—

Not now!

"Are you enjoying yourself?" asked Bertone's voice right at her elbow.

Kayla jumped sideways, startled that he'd been able to slide in so close without her knowing it.

He grasped her arm and pulled her back from the edge of the pool.

"Nervous, are we?" he asked.

"I always jump when somebody sneaks up on me," Kayla said. "What about you?"

"Sneak?" He laughed and didn't release her arm. "*Ma petite,* I weigh in excess of two hundred pounds and am over forty. I could not sneak if my life depended on it. Are you sure you aren't nervous?"

"Should I be?" she answered, pulling away from his grasp.

"I suppose it's rather like bridal jitters. But then, you hinted this wasn't your first time on the, ah, 'primrose path.' "

Kayla set her teeth and didn't say anything.

Bertone caught her chin with his strong hand. Slowly, almost gently, he forced her to look him in the eye.

Anger.

She was furious.

"Are you truly that much an innocent?" Bertone asked. "Have I really misread you that badly? You do understand how things are done in the real world, don't you?"

"Yes." She stepped back, freeing herself. "As profitably as possible."

His eyebrows rose. "Ah, so you feel underpaid."

She shrugged tightly.

"You interest me," he said.

She stiffened as Bertone's glance ran up and down her body like hands. She had deliberately dressed plainly in a linen trouser suit and a silk top cut just low enough to show the rose tattoo on her collarbone. But the way he was looking at her made her feel like she'd been stripped to her skimpy underwear and doused with cold water.

"Did the second wire transfer post to the new account?" Bertone's voice was once again neutral.

Kayla wanted to sigh with relief. "Yes."

Then realization hit and the ground jerked beneath her feet. She hadn't spoken with the Bertones since the first deposit, yet somehow Bertone already knew not only that the correspondent account was open but that a second deposit had been made.

Her desire to talk to Steve Foley took on a keener, more bitter edge.

Bertone or the feds, the devil or the deep blue sea. Take your pick, you lucky girl.

None of the above.

There has to be a third choice. It's up to me to find it.

Real quick.

"There will be more transfers today and tomorrow," Bertone said. "Bigger amounts. Quite sizable, actually."

She drew a shallow breath, then another, forcing herself to meet his eyes. When she spoke, her voice was calm despite the panic twisting her stomach. "In this country, banks aren't open on the weekend. I'm not even sure the Fedwire operates."

"It does."

She shrugged tightly. "Then the money will transfer, but it won't be posted to the account until Monday. In other words, no matter when you transfer it, the money won't be available for withdrawal until Monday."

"As early as possible on Monday," Bertone said, his voice like a whip.

"Of course," she said through her teeth.

He looked at her again, hair to toes and back up, lingering in all the expected places.

"I meant what I said earlier, *ma petite.* Your future is in your hands. If you wish more profit, you must give more."

"I always take care of my clients' money."

"I wasn't talking about my money."

Kayla's stomach turned over. "How does your wife feel about . . . extra service?"

"Elena is a woman of the world. She knows the difference between wife and paramour."

"Just as you know the difference between husband and gigolo?" Kayla retorted before she could think better of it.

Bertone surprised her by throwing back his head and laughing. "Yes, you do interest me. It has been a long time since anyone has. There is a little garden behind the garage. After you give the prize check to the most earnest dabbler, you will go to the garden. I will come and discuss with you gigolos and paramours."

Said the spider to the fly.

But this time Kayla guarded her tongue. The last thing she wanted to do was "interest" Bertone any more.

18

Castillo del Cielo
Saturday
5:40 P.M. MST

You see Bertone yet?" Faroe's voice came from the earbuds Rand wore.

"Shut up," he said beneath his breath. "Painting while holding my nose is hard work. Needs all my concentration."

"Take a break. Look around."

"In a minute."

Rand squeezed a long bead of ocher onto his palette and mixed in a touch of black and a touch of crimson. To his eye, the color of the stone walls of the Bertone house was offensive.

"Brindleshit," he muttered.

"Excuse me?" Faroe said.

"The color of the house."

With that Rand shut out the world and concentrated on creating a color that was close to that of the house, yet more pleasing against the natural desert backdrop. It took time, but then he found the right color, the right balance of weight and light, and the painting began to condense in front of his eyes. This was his favorite part of his work, when he vanished and only the canvas lived.

When he finally stepped back to view his progress, the scent of cinnamon and vanilla curled above the pungency of his oils. The perfume alone told him that a woman was standing behind him. Close. If she hadn't moved away quickly, he'd have bumped into her.

Without looking at her, he waited for her to speak.

She didn't.

Curious, he glanced over his shoulder—and into Kayla Shaw's ice-blue eyes. His first thought was that the surveillance photos hadn't done her justice. There were shadows and light, haunting sadness and laughter, heat and cold, a whole universe of possibilities in her fiercely intelligent eyes.

He felt like he'd been sucker-punched.

"What are you thinking?" he asked.

"I'm thinking where the hell is Bertone?" Faroe shot back.

Rand pulled out the earbuds and put them in his pocket with the butchered iPod.

Kayla looked from the painting to the man. Somehow she expected artists to be short or slight or old or shy or . . . unthreatening. This man wasn't any of those things. Tall, long-limbed, wide-shouldered, powerful, with gray-green eyes that could etch steel.

"I think," she said, "that it's too bad the subject isn't worthy of the artist."

Rand almost smiled, almost swore. She'd seen right through him, knew he thought the Bertone estate was a screaming paean to bad taste.

"I'm not quite sure what that means," he lied.

She smiled, softening the lines of tension around her mouth. "I think you do. But don't worry. Elena will love your work. You make her look good."

What's a woman like Kayla doing in a place like this?

But instead of asking the age-old question, Rand used a palette knife to blend some of the fresh oil paint, then applied a few dabs to the canvas. He squinted to measure the effect.

"It's called artistic license," Rand said without turning around. "If you don't want the filter of the artist's vision, use a camera."

"Flattery is Elena's meat and drink. You've read your hosts beautifully."

He continued to work, still with his back to his critic, still with the scent of cinnamon in his lungs, in his blood. "You say that like it's a bad thing."

"No. I'm just jealous. If I had that kind of instant insight into people . . ." Kayla shrugged. "It would be useful." *Understatement of the year. Maybe the decade.* "At the very least, I'd be rich."

Rand gave in to temptation and glanced briefly at Kayla. She was turned half away from him. If you didn't look in her eyes, she seemed younger than he knew she was. Her body was athletic, fit, attractive, and so tightly strung she all but vibrated. Tan skin, black linen, and a scoop-neck silk blouse that just revealed a small rose tattoo on her collarbone.

He wanted to lick it.

This is one hell of a bad time to get a boner.

But there it was. Her dossier had intrigued him, his dreams had been hot, and her reality was even hotter.

Cursing silently, he focused on the canvas and said, "I thought everybody here was rich."

"Some of us are hired help. We get to drink the champagne, but first we have to dance attendance." Kayla hoped the artist didn't hear the bitterness in her voice.

"Yeah, I bet the Bertones have cast-iron whims," Rand said casually. "At least she does. I haven't seen him. Is he here tonight?"

"Yes." She knew her voice was too curt, but she couldn't do anything about it. Bertone flat-out scared her. "I've seen a painting before . . ."

"Of course."

Her laugh was as tight as her body. "No, I mean a painting like this."

"Same subject?"

"It has nothing to do with the subject."

There was silence, the soft sound of paint spreading on canvas, and then, "Meaning?"

"I'm not saying this very well," Kayla said. "There's something . . . the way you see light. No, the way you paint it. Alive and powerful, defining the ridgeline and the fountain and even the wild rosebushes around the helipad beyond the pool. I've seen that kind of light before." She laughed suddenly. "I bought one of your paintings at a garage sale. R. McCree, right?"

R. McCree. The name rang in Rand's mind. *Does she have one of Reed's paintings?*

"That's right," he said. "Rand McCree." He certainly wasn't going to raise the issue of his murdered twin with the killer's banker.

"I don't remember you being on the program."

"I'm a late entry," he said easily, but he was careful not to look at her. He'd seen more beautiful women, but none of them had the ability to blow his concentration to hell like she did.

With a feeling close to awe, Kayla watched Rand bring the canvas to life. The result was beautiful but not at all mild. A very masculine kind of beauty. Intense. Edgy. Riveting.

Like him.

"Garage sale, huh?" Rand said. "Which painting?"

"'Maybe the Dawn' is written across the back, along with a date." Then she said quickly, "Garage sale sounds awful. It was really an estate sale."

"I feel a lot better," he said dryly. "But I'm sorry to know that Mrs. Braceley is dead. She hoped she'd live to be one hundred if she got away from the Pacific Northwest's cold rain."

A woman's artfully modulated laughter rose above the sound of the fountain. Elena Bertone, responding to something a gorgeous young man had said to her.

"My hostess," Rand said. "See a lot of her in the society pages. Haven't seen a picture of him, though."

"He's a very private man. This is only the second event he's attended. Elena is the public face of the Bertones."

"So this is a really special occasion."

"Yeah. I'm betting that Elena expects this shindig to cement her position on the board of directors of the Plein-Air Museum."

"That's important to her?" Rand asked.

"One way or another," Kayla said absently, watching Rand work, "Elena has put out several million dollars in the name of Phoenix art, so yes, it must be important to her. Not to mention how she twisted arms and called in favors so that most of the important socialites and half the politicians in the West are here."

Then Kayla heard her words and cringed. Private bankers shouldn't gossip about their clients. It was a fast way to get fired.

"Forget I said that," she said quickly. "I was paying attention to your art rather than my tongue."

"Forget you said what? I didn't hear a thing," he said.

He heard her long breath of relief and almost smiled. He didn't blame her for being nervous. Bertone might not be called the Siberian anymore, but beneath the designer suits, he was still a very nasty piece of work. Anyone gossiping about him would have a short future on his payroll.

And maybe a short future, period.

Under the pretext of viewing the canvas from another angle, Rand turned sideways, coming closer to her. Cinnamon and vanilla. Sunshine and just plain woman. Her dark brown hair was streaked by the sun or a very expensive colorist. Ice-blue eyes, minimum makeup, and that damned tempting rose tattoo.

I hope you're as innocent as I believe you are, Rand thought grimly. *But innocent or not, we're stuck with each other.*

Maybe we should just lie back and enjoy.

"Your hands look too big, too rough, for an artist," Kayla said without thinking.

They fit real well around a man's neck. And that was something Rand didn't plan on telling her. "They come in . . . handy."

She groaned at the pun.

He grinned.

Curious, she studied him rather than the canvas. He was dressed in black jeans with generous paint smears, a loose-fitting shirt the precise color of his eyes—except for the paint blobs—and soft black leather boots that bore random decorations in paint. Despite the evidence of the canvas and his paint-smeared clothing, he just didn't seem to fit the artist mold. Or maybe it was just that some of the darkness he saw so clearly within light was also inside him.

"You aren't from around here, are you?" she asked. Then said quickly, "Sorry, you have a bad effect on my tongue."

He gave her a sideways glance that picked up her heartbeat. "Sounds promising."

She hoped that the color climbing up her face would be written off as sun flush rather than foot-in-mouth blush.

"I spend most of my time in the Pacific Northwest," he said, turning back to the canvas. "Have you lived here long?"

"Born and bred a Zonie," she said.

"How'd you end up working for the Bertones?"

"I don't. Not exactly. I'm their banker. I work for American Southwest Bank in Scottsdale. At least for now," she added, then wished she hadn't.

The earlier meeting with Bertone had rattled her more than she'd realized.

Or else R. McCree did. It wasn't often she found a man with the body of a linebacker and the edgy soul of an artist.

"Sounds like you're jonesing for another job," Rand said.

"Everybody needs a new challenge from time to time," she said. "I'm thinking about a career change."

"You don't like banking?"

For the first time Kayla realized that she didn't. Not anymore. "It's always about money, and money doesn't always bring out the best in people."

"Artists don't know much about money," he said.

"You know enough to paint yourself into a lather over a faux canvas that might be worth first, second, or third prize, when you ought to be somewhere else painting something worthwhile." Then she blew out a breath. "Sorry, I didn't mean that the way it came out."

Rand doubted that. But then, he felt the same way. "It's called putting bread and beans on the table."

"And it's always just a question of what you'll do to keep from starving to death, right?" she asked with false brightness.

"Pretty much. Speaking of starving, what are you doing afterward?" He glanced at her in time to catch her startled expression. "What's the matter? Hasn't a man ever asked you out for dinner?"

"Not five minutes after I first met him, and not ten minutes after somebody else asked me to meet him in a few hours."

"I'm too late? Please tell me I'm not too late," Rand said lightly.

It was easy to flirt with her, maybe too easy. Maybe she was playing him instead of vice versa.

Problem was, he didn't feel like playing at all.

"I kind of have another commitment," Kayla said.

The look on her face said she didn't want it.

"Can you break it?"

"I'm thinking about doing just that."

"So I'm not entirely out of the running," Rand said.

"Why do I feel hunted?"

"My technique must need work." Rand turned to smile over his shoulder at her.

And saw the one man in the world whose neck he wanted between his hands.

19

Castillo del Cielo
Saturday
5:51 P.M. MST

"Who's that?" Rand forced himself to ask.

Kayla looked over her shoulder, saw Bertone and another man striding toward her. The men were having an animated but not angry conversation.

"The tall, burly guy on the right is Andre Bertone," she said quietly. "On the left is Don Cowley."

"Ah, Mr. Bertone, the mysterious host," Rand said, hoping his voice didn't reflect the adrenaline hammering through his body, bringing him to fight-or-flight alert. "Should I know the dude with him?"

"He's a political consultant for statewide and national congressional candidates."

"Big man, huh?"

"Very big." What she didn't say was that Cowley was an American Southwest private banking client whose political business had made him very wealthy. Anyone who wanted to go anywhere in state politics had to get his blessing first. "A real mover and shaker."

Bertone and Cowley stopped long enough to shake hands. Cowley said something that made Bertone laugh. The deep, rich sound punched through the background noise of the party.

As soon as Cowley turned away, Bertone's expression changed. He frowned like a man making a decision he wasn't entirely happy about. Then, sensing he was being watched, he looked toward Kayla. Immediately he started striding up the flagstone steps to where she stood.

Rand turned around and started painting again. It was all he trusted himself to do. The microphone taped to his chest still itched, but he didn't care. Undoubtedly Faroe had heard that Bertone was present. Rand didn't need a bud in his ear to know that Faroe was holding his breath for a photo op.

The special camera seemed to be burning a hole in Rand's backpack. Quickly he sorted through reasons he could use to take out the camera and aim it away from Bertone.

None of the excuses flew.

Give it time. The night is young.

And Reed will never get any older.

Ignoring the artist, Bertone said to Kayla, "Do you know the man I was just talking to?"

"I've seen Mr. Cowley at the bank."

"I just agreed to help several of his candidates in the primary election. I want you to process the checks I write to him. I want to be certain the accounting is . . . appropriate."

Kayla's mouth thinned. "I always account for funds that pass through the bank, Mr. Bertone. If you require something extra, you'll have to be more specific in your requests."

Silently Rand whistled. *The lady is pissed. Foolish, too. I wouldn't take on that Siberian tiger with only a rose tattoo to protect me.*

Bertone stared at her a long moment.

She forced herself to meet his eyes.

He glanced past her to the man working at the easel. "We'll discuss this—and other things—later tonight."

"I'm not feeling well," she said. "Some other time would be better for me."

"Not for me, Kayla. Mr. Foley assured me you were willing to discuss banking business at my convenience."

"Business, yes."

Bertone looked almost amused. "Then it will be strictly business, if that's what you wish."

"It is."

"Elena will serve us coffee in the garden at seven tonight."

"Elena?" Kayla smiled with relief at not having to meet Bertone alone. "That's fine. Seven."

Bertone smiled slightly. As he turned away, he glanced at the painting on the easel. He walked toward it, looking with real interest. He examined the unfinished canvas before he stared directly at the artist.

Despite the adrenaline spiking through Rand's blood, he met Bertone's eyes calmly. Rand had wondered for five years how good a look the Siberian had gotten through his sniper's scope, if he'd seen the face of the man he'd murdered—the face of the man's identical twin.

It was why Rand had refused to shave or cut his hair short. Five years ago both he and his twin had been bare-cheeked and military-clipped.

Bertone stared for several seconds, pale eyes narrowed. Then he looked back at the painting. "Very nice. Quite good, actually. But you should get back to work if you want to win my wife's little contest. Time is running out."

Rand forced himself to smile. Obviously the sniper's scope hadn't been as clear as the camera lens. Or the cheek fur was a good enough disguise.

Or Bertone had killed so many men he didn't remember all the faces.

"Glad you like the painting," Rand said easily, "because I'm just plain staggered by the subject."

Kayla suspected he was telling only the polite half of the truth. It was a social skill she was still working hard to acquire.

"Is my employee distracting you?" Bertone asked, glancing at Kayla. "I can have her removed."

"Not on my account," Rand said. "She's a savage critic and I'm a closet masochist. Perfect match."

"Then I will leave you to your pain and pleasure," Bertone said. He looked at Kayla. "Until after the contest, *ma petite*."

Rand watched his brother's murderer walk away. When he glanced at Kayla, her face was pale.

"That was a pleasant little chat," he said.

She looked at him in disbelief.

"Irony," he said quickly. "You look like you just stepped on a snake. If I heard what I think I heard, you can haul him up on sexual harassment charges."

She made a sound that wasn't quite a laugh and not quite a curse. "Waste of time. Thousands of women would line up to be harassed by him."

"You aren't one of them."

"So does that make me picky or stupid?"

"You're a long way from stupid. May I call you Kayla?"

"Anything but *ma petite.*"

"Okay, beautiful."

She surprised both of them by laughing. "Thanks, handsome. I was feeling . . . smudged."

Rand reached out to touch her cheek, saw his paint-spattered fingers, and wiped them on his jeans. Kayla Shaw was a little too attractive and maybe a lot too vulnerable.

But she was the tool he'd been given to use.

20

Castillo del Cielo
Saturday
6:10 P.M. MST

From the corner of his eyes Rand saw that Bertone had finally stopped circulating. Now he was making nice with the people standing near his wife.

"Okay," Rand said, sticking a brush in a jar of turpentine. "Take me to my hostess."

"You're done?" Kayla asked, startled.

Close enough for this farce. But all he said aloud was, "It's a field study. Any rough edges are looked at as virtues, not flaws."

"And if you schmooze the hostess enough—"

"Yeah," he interrupted. "She might forgive the flaws. So introduce me to her."

Kayla hesitated.

"What?" he asked.

"I'm trying to decide whether your honesty is appalling or appealing."

Rand gave her a smile that was all sharp edges. "Think about it while I talk to her." He reached into his backpack and pulled out a camera.

"What's that for?" Kayla asked.

"I'm hoping to do a portrait of Elena Bertone, Arizona art maven. Sort of a companion to the field study."

"You really are trying to flatter your way into winning, aren't you?"

Rand had a momentary flashback of Reed's dying eyes. "Whatever works."

"Appalling."

"What?"

"I've decided. Your honesty is appalling."

"So is starving. Unlike Renaissance Italy, America doesn't have patrons to support the purity of an artist's soul. Rat-infested garrets are overrated."

"Why don't you try cutting off your ear?" Kayla asked coolly. "That seemed to put van Gogh on the fast track."

"Do you really think I'd look better that way? If so, I'd consider it."

She put her hands on her hips. "You're maddening."

"I'm serious."

"You mean you'd cut off your ear if I told you to?"

"No, I said I'd consider it. What do you think?"

Not knowing whether to throw up her hands or laugh, Kayla looked first at Rand's left ear and then at his right. "Leave them be. They're a decent enough pair."

His glance dropped from her eyes to her lips and all the way to her toes. "You have a decent pair, too," he said.

"You're outrageous."

"I compliment your eyes and you call me outrageous?"

She opened her mouth.

He looked hopeful.

"Right," she said. "I'm taking you to Elena."

Rand would rather have stayed with Kayla, but staying wouldn't get the job done. Automatically he checked his camera again, making certain the memory stick was secure, the lens clean, and his fingers nowhere near the USB outlet.

"Ready to go," he said, taking Kayla's arm.

Kayla looked over to where Elena laughed and drank champagne with several politicians. Then she saw Bertone. "Don't point that camera at your host."

"Wouldn't dream of it. He'd break the lens."

"I mean it," she said quickly. "He goes postal if someone tries to take his picture. He nearly ripped the face off a photographer at a Christmas fund-raiser. Then he exposed the film and gave the photographer a thousand for the insult."

Rand didn't doubt it. "No problem. I'll be very careful to keep this pointed away from him."

At exactly ninety degrees.

Kayla led Rand through the packed crowds on the patio to a beautifully landscaped fountain area that was discreetly roped off as a VIP reception area. Rand looked around, sizing up the backdrop.

The last rays of the sun sparkled on the three-tiered waterfall and on the trays of champagne glasses filled with golden wine. Elena Bertone, perfectly turned out and ravishing in a lime-green suit that fit her lush body like a silk stocking, was chatting and laughing with a circle of men and the few women brave enough to compete with an international beauty queen.

Behind Elena and to one side, Andre Bertone stood smoking a fat hand-rolled cigar. He was listening to a balding suit who might have been a lawyer or a political aide. Or both.

Elena was an accomplished actress, which made her a fine hostess. She was animated, vibrant, gracious. She could carry on three conversations at once and still be fully aware of everything going on outside her inner circle. When she saw Kayla approaching, Elena smoothly left the group she was with and walked toward her banker.

"What is it?" Elena asked.

"Elena, this is Rand McCree, one of your artists. He'd like to do a quick portrait of you to go with his canvas of the beautiful home you designed. Rand, Mrs. Bertone."

"A pleasure," Rand said.

And wished it was.

Elena inspected him from boots to hairline and liked what she saw in between. She flashed her perfect smile as she offered her hand.

"I know how much in demand you are," Rand said as he took her elegant hand and shook it once, formally. "If I could just snap a couple of pictures, profile and full face, I can download them to my computer and paint from them."

Elena glanced in the direction of her husband, who either hadn't noticed the good-looking artist approach her or didn't care.

"I told Rand that Mr. Bertone dislikes being photographed," Kayla said. "He'll make certain that your husband's privacy isn't invaded."

Rand made it a point to turn his shoulder toward Bertone as he asked Elena, "Would you mind giving me a few moments?"

Elena checked the nearby people. All of them were engaged, no one was looking lost, and the staff was circulating with an endless, expensive river of champagne and canapés.

"Artists call this time of day sweet light," Rand said. "It only lasts a few moments. It makes your skin glow like amber."

"You flatter me."

"The camera won't lie, Mrs. Bertone. You glow." It was the truth, but that didn't make Rand like himself any better.

Get over it. You'd do a lot worse than suck up to a murderer's wife to get your hands on Reed's killer.

Kayla listened to the flattery and wanted to hurl, even though what Rand said was accurate—probably because of it. Elena did look like a goddess in the slanting light.

But does he have to drool?

He's an artist. Of course he admires beauty.

Elena touched Rand's shoulder, felt strength, and smiled. "Kayla, be a dear and tell Andre what's going on so he won't worry. I don't want another scene like the one at the Christmas fund-raiser."

Kayla wanted to point out that Rand couldn't take a photo while the subject was rubbing up against him. Instead, she turned sharply and walked the ten feet to Bertone.

With the speed of a professional photographer, Rand took a few insurance shots of the lovely Elena. She posed and projected for the camera like the model and actress she had once been.

"You're a natural," he said, adjusting focus and depth of field. "The camera loves you."

And vice versa.

But Rand wasn't going to bite the hand that was allowing him to line up Andre Bertone in the second lens.

"You could have made millions with that face and those gorgeous cat eyes," Rand said, working quickly through the major lens. "Now, just a few more with the fountain in the backdrop and the light on your face."

"Do I really want that?" she asked. "Women over twenty run like Andre if a cameraman catches them in sunlight."

"You have nothing to worry about," Rand said. "Now let me try a couple from this side."

He switched position, carefully keeping his primary lens aimed at Elena and getting a perfect full-face shot of Andre Bertone with his hidden lens. Bertone was watching him intently, alert for the instant the camera swung his way.

Rand held the camera up for long seconds, appearing to adjust the focusing ring, but actually holding down the second shutter release on the hidden lens. By the time he lowered the camera, he had twenty separate photos of Andre Bertone on his memory stick.

"Thanks so much for your indulgence, Mrs. Bertone," Rand said. "I'll try to do your beauty justice, but oils are a poor substitute for skin that glows like yours."

Elena's laugh was soft and sexy. "You're a brash rascal, aren't you?"

"You have no idea," Rand said, flashing his teeth. "How else would an artist get away with asking thousands of dollars for thirty dollars' worth of paint and canvas?"

Before he looked toward Kayla—and Bertone—Rand lowered the camera, capped the visible lens, and pointed it at the ground like it was the muzzle of a pistol. He sensed Bertone watching every motion until the camera vanished inside the backpack once more.

Only then did Rand glance up to Kayla.

Bertone was still staring at him.

For an instant Rand was afraid that Bertone had finally recognized him. Then Bertone nodded, his head moving more than an inch but less than two. He went back to his conversation.

Rand casually waved his thanks to Kayla and headed back to his easel. As he walked, he put one of the earbuds back in.

"Got it. Twenty times."

"Sounds like you damn near got Elena in the sheets, you silver-tongued devil."

Rand scratched his shirt over the microphone head, making Faroe's ears ring.

21

Castillo del Cielo
Saturday
6:45 P.M. MST

Reluctantly Kayla approached the broad flagstone terrace that stepped down to the gardens, forming a natural stage. Three canvases were set up along one side. Three artists waited to see who got the big check and who got a fiscal pat on the head.

Deliberately Kayla didn't look at Reed. The fact that his canvas was hands down the best of the lot just made her angrier.

That doesn't mean he'll win. What do I know about art?

The only good news was that Andre Bertone had vanished. The terrace was blazing with photographers' lights. The awarding of the checks would be recorded for the pages of the local papers and the glossy lifestyle magazines that catered to Phoenix socialites.

Kayla took her place a few steps out of the spotlight. With every breath of wind, the ridiculously large presentation checks she clutched threatened to pull her off balance. At center stage Elena announced the Fast Draw winners.

Rand McCree came in third.

Arizona artists came in first and second.

Elena wasn't stupid. She understood her audience very well, and the need to flatter local pride.

Kayla didn't know which disgusted her more—Elena's socially correct choices, Rand's unblushing use of flattery to get ahead, or the recognition that Kayla herself did something similar every time she dealt with clients she didn't particularly like.

I'm not as bad as Rand or Elena.

Not as successful, either.

With a muttered word she shifted the awkward checks under one arm and grabbed champagne from a passing tray to toast the winners. If nothing else, maybe the alcohol would take the bitter taste out of her mouth. As she took several fast swallows, she was honest enough to admit that she was attracted to Rand and disgusted enough to wish she wasn't. He was a charmer and a user.

She was glad he came in third.

Yeah. Like I'm little Ms. Perfection. I'd love to have him looking at me the way he does Elena.

But it would take more than a makeover at the local Nordstrom to have that happen.

Be grateful. I've got enough trouble without tripping over that handsome artist's big feet.

She finished the champagne in time to set the glass and her purse on a table near the stage, straighten her jacket, and sort the checks she was going to give to Elena.

With a professional smile rigidly in place, Kayla stepped into the lights. Elena handed out the third- and second-place checks quickly, then lingered to have her picture taken with the first-prize winner.

"Looks like local interest trumps flattery," Kayla said under her breath to Rand. "Welcome to political science as practiced on the ground."

Rand ignored the brittle edge in her voice and words. "Where do you want to go for dinner?"

"I've lost my appetite."

As Kayla stepped back, her heel caught in one of the electrical cables that fed the photographers' lights. With a catlike movement Rand caught and righted her.

Holy hell, he's fast, she thought, startled.

And strong.

"I haven't," he said.

"What?"

"Lost my appetite."

She looked into his gray-green eyes and forgot to breathe.

He wanted her.

"Dinner is optional," he said softly, releasing her.

Before she could think of anything to say, Elena broke away from the winner and stood close to Rand. Very close.

"I want to commission a larger, more finished portrait of the Castle of Heaven," Elena said in a husky voice. "Please stay. Once the dancing begins, we can talk."

Rand didn't need an earbud to know what Faroe would say. "You flatter me, Mrs. Bertone."

"Elena, please." She flashed that million-watt smile and put her hand on his bare forearm.

"Elena." Rand smiled. "I'll be glad to stay for the rest of the party."

Kayla wondered if she was the only one who noticed the difference in Rand's eyes when he looked at his hostess. He enjoyed Elena's beauty, but he didn't want her.

Is he picky or stupid? Because he sure isn't blind.

And he sure isn't stupid.

Kayla told herself not to be flattered.

She was anyway.

Elena squeezed Rand's arm and glided out to her guests, jeweled sandals flashing in the bright lights.

"What the hell do I do with this?" Rand asked Kayla, flicking the huge check with a paint-splashed fingernail. "Paper a wall?"

"Cash it at the issuing bank on Monday."

"American Southwest? Where's that?"

"Try MapQuest."

"I'd rather try you."

Kayla stared at him. He meant it.

Or at least he looked like he did.

How can I tell what's true and what's false in a man who had Elena Bertone eating out of his hand with just an easy smile and some deep-voiced flattery?

"Aren't you afraid that Elena will discover her new lapdog is jonesing for another lap?" Kayla asked, irritated and curious at once.

"Even lapdogs have teeth." Rand showed her a double row of his. "I just know when to bite and when to shut up and wag."

"Wagging draws the better paycheck. But there are more important things than money."

"Easy for a banker to say." Rand spoke through clenched teeth. "You have no idea what's at stake." *And*

I'm a fool for caring what she thinks of me. This isn't about a bonehead with a boner.

This is about Reed.

Kayla looked at her wristwatch. Almost seven. She picked up the purse she'd left on a table next to the stage. "See you around."

"What about dinner?"

"Enjoy it. I'm busy."

She walked off and didn't look back.

Grimly Rand shouldered his backpack, screwed in an earbud, and listened to Faroe's laughter.

"Relax," Faroe's voice whispered. *"They only spit like that when they're interested in a man."*

"Screw you."

"Jimmy will bump into you at your car. Literally. Pass him the memory stick."

"When?"

"Five minutes."

"I'm supposed to stay around."

"So pass it and go back. I want that stick off the estate ASAP. Where's Bertone?"

"He took off when the photographers appeared."

"Keep looking. I don't trust him behind you."

Neither did Rand. He looked for Bertone and finally found the big man back in the shadows, lighting a cigar, well away from the area where photographers were allowed.

Bertone was watching Kayla's progress across the party into the shadows at the back of the estate. When she disappeared, he turned and looked up at the second story of the Castle of Heaven. A thin man leaned on the balcony rail, watching the party.

Watching Bertone.

Rand had noticed the man before and assumed he was one of the many bodyguards who circulated every minute of every hour, protecting the Bertone family.

Bertone took a deep pull on his fresh cigar until its ember glowed like a stoplight. Once. Twice. Three times. Four. Then he dropped the cigar and crushed it out beneath his heel.

Immediately the thin man vanished into the house. He reappeared a few moments later at the back of the house, heading in the same direction Kayla had. In his left hand he carried a small duffel.

Bertone lit another cigar and walked back to the party. In moments he was talking with a group of people.

Rand looked at his watch. Seven o'clock.

Yet neither Elena nor Bertone was headed to the garden for a private chat with their private banker.

Only the thin man was.

"Houston," Rand said softly to his collar, "we've got a problem."

22

Castillo del Cielo
Saturday
7:00 P.M. MST

Kayla strode down the lighted path, wishing her shoes flashed and sparkled rather than being dark and banker-perfect. The wishing didn't stop with her shoes. The rest of her was depressingly banker-perfect, too. Except on the inside. On the inside she was jittery, irritated, fretting and pulling at the bit like a green-broke bronc.

Freedom.

She could taste it.

She just couldn't live it anymore.

Grow up, she told herself impatiently.

I did. I don't like it.

Working with Bertone and the glittering Elena was too high a price to pay for being an adult.

Where's my backpack when I really need it?

The path ended in a head-high wooden gate next to the wall of the seven-car garage. The motion-sensor light mounted on the corner of the garage came on as she approached. Hidden speakers breathed out faint music from the party.

The garden walls were covered by fast-growing flowering vines whose twisted stems were almost as thick as her wrists. The fragrance was like a caress in the dry air. The padlock on the gate was open, hanging crookedly behind the latch. The wrought-iron latch lifted smoothly, almost silently. She hesitated, then stepped into the Bertones' refuge from the rest of the world.

It felt like a flower-lined trap.

With a whisper of metal on metal, the gate shut behind her. The sound made her jump. She pushed at the gate, reassuring herself that the padlock hadn't somehow leaped up and closed itself over the latch, locking her behind high walls.

The gate opened instantly.

With a relieved sigh, Kayla turned back to the garden. It was as beautiful as hard work and money could make it. Roses and gardenias, flowering vines and palms as graceful as dancers, heady fragrance and inviting stillness. The walkways were monitored by motion sensors so that every few steps she took lit up a new vision of artfully arranged plants. A fountain sang softly in the darkness ahead, drowning out the murmur of music from concealed speakers.

As she walked toward the fountain, more lights came on, making the water shimmer with life and possibilities. The gentle music of water soothed her nerves, as it was meant to do. Desert cultures realized how people became starved for the liquid promise of water.

Lights went out behind her, making her nerves jump. The motion sensors were on short timers. She felt like running around the garden, setting off all the landscaping lights.

Or just running, period, right out the gate and into her car.

Kayla fought with the impulse, telling herself that she was jumping at shadows. She'd met other bank clients in public parks and private homes, behind guarded doors and in skyboxes at sporting events, in parking lots after hours and at restaurants after ordinary diners were sent home. She shouldn't be nervous about meeting the Bertones in their garden while a party chattered on a few hundred feet away.

Well within screaming distance.

She just wished that Bertone wasn't a crook. But then, he wasn't the only ruthless man in the private-banking world. He was simply the one who was her client.

Big honking deal, she told herself roughly. *Settle down. Even the lapdog artist has real teeth.*

She'd seen them a few minutes ago, when Rand watched Andre Bertone walk away from them. Rand's words echoed in her mind: *You have no idea what's at stake.*

Hardly the reassurance she needed.

Hardly the words of a foot-licking lapdog.

Uneasiness crawled over Kayla. She couldn't just stand and wait for the Bertones to schmooze their way through the guests and down to the garden. Impatiently she paced the flagstones, light blooming softly in front of her and then fading behind her into scented darkness.

Disturbed by her passage, a canyon wren sang from the flowering vines growing thickly on the far garden wall. After a few moments the bird settled into an irritable kind of silence.

She looked at her watch. Seven after seven.

Overhead a billion stars glittered through the ambient radiance of the city night. She considered counting them to pass the time.

The hell with this. I'm not waiting around like some kind of goat staked out for the tiger's gloating pleasure.

As she turned toward the wooden gate, the lights went out. The metal-on-metal sound of the gate's padlock closing came like a gunshot.

Silence.

Then came the soft whine of hinges moving, a hidden garden door opening. The wren shrieked and exploded into the night, flying as rapidly as Kayla's wild heartbeat. Her eyes struggled to adjust to the darkness.

A figure stepped from behind the vines into the faint radiance cast by a wall of pale flowers. The man was too thin to be Andre Bertone, too thin to be anyone Kayla recognized. He pulled the door shut behind him and stood motionless, letting his own eyes adjust to the faint light.

Kayla shrank back into a dark alcove, grateful she'd worn a black linen suit. Part of her waited to hear him call her name and tell her the Bertones had decided to delay the meeting.

The rest of her fought not to scream.

The man didn't call out. Instead he prowled the garden like a skeletal ghost, poking at the tallest bushes.

He's looking for me.

Kayla opened her mouth to scream for help, but before she could, rock music from the party crashed over the garden like thunder. Someone had ramped up the garden's sound system to the point of pain.

If she screamed, the only one who would hear her was the man stalking her.

Slowly she put her hand in her purse and pulled out the LadyBug she used for opening envelopes and pulling staples. At three inches long, the little folding knife wasn't much of a weapon, but it was better than fingernails and teeth.

She hoped.

23

Castillo del Cielo
Saturday
7:07 P.M. MST

Rand broke into a run as soon as he saw the lights go out by the garage.

"Where's Jimmy?" he asked. "The lights just went out."

"I'm driving toward the garage. He's bringing an ATV from the back. He's in uniform, so don't— What the hell is that?"

"Music."

"Sounds like a train wreck."

"Louder than a scream," Rand said roughly. He hurdled some plants to straighten out the meandering walkway.

"Not good."

All Rand said was, "Light a fire and get there!"

"Limos are cluttering up the drive."

"Put it in low range and make your own road," Rand snarled. "Is the garden wall set to stun?"

A pause while Faroe radioed Hamm, then Faroe said, *"Not electrified."*

"Thank you, God."

"You're welcome."

Rand hit the gate at a run, grabbed the top, and vaulted over. The backpack caught on vines, pulling him off balance. He landed hard, went to his knees, and scrambled upright again.

"Talk to me."

Rand didn't answer. He didn't know where his enemy was, but he was certain an enemy was there, waiting in the scented darkness.

"Two minutes to backup."

When Rand spotted the thin figure against a bank of pale flowers, he knew Kayla didn't have two minutes. He shucked his backpack, reached in, and pulled out a wicked folding knife. He opened it with a flick of his thumb. His other hand held a big, dark flashlight.

"One bogey," he murmured. "I'm going in."

"Wait for backup."

Rand ignored his boss and shouted, "Kayla, stay hidden!"

Kayla heard Rand, but couldn't see him. All she could see was the thin man coming closer to her with each step. She would rather have run, but she was cornered. Grimly she held on to her little knife and waited. She'd only get one swipe at the man. She wanted it to count.

Light speared out, pinning the thin man's face in its blinding beam. He flinched and covered his eyes. He was wearing thin black leather gloves. Metal flashed in his hand.

A knife, not a gun.

Kayla didn't wait for a better chance. She sprang out of cover and ran in the direction Rand's voice had come from.

Rand turned off the light, opened his eyes, and went down the pathway with the gliding strides of a hunter.

The thin man went into a knife fighter's crouch. Rand kept on coming. The man saw the gleam of metal in Rand's hand, the length of his opponent's arms, and decided to fight another day. He spun and ran.

Rand took off after him. Before he could gain any ground, the thin man scrambled up the vines, went over the fence, and vanished. Rand thought about going after him, but didn't want to leave Kayla alone. No doubt Bertone had more than one killer on the payroll.

The screaming feedback from the speakers went silent.

"Jimmy killed the speakers. What's your status?"

"One bogey over the fence, west side of garden. Can Jimmy get him?"

"He's on the east, but he'll try. How's Kayla?"

Rand switched on the flashlight and ran it over Kayla. Pale, trembling a little, breathing hard. "No blood." Then he smiled slightly. "Nice knife, honey. Just big enough to get the job done. You can put it away now."

Kayla looked at the knife in his hand.

He folded it with a swift motion and put it in his pocket. "See? Totally harmless."

She gave him a look of disbelief, but she folded her knife.

And waited.

"Jimmy says the bogey is gone. Poof."

"Probably went home to Poppa," Rand said.

Kayla started to say something, realized he wasn't talking to her, and shut up.

"What?" Faroe asked.

"He's Bertone's. I saw the pass-off when Bertone sent him after Kayla."

"What a sweet cluster this has become."

"Ya think?"

The lights in the garden came on again.

"It's Hamm," a voice called out. "I'm coming in."

Kayla flinched and opened her knife again.

"Easy," Rand said, grabbing her wrist. "Hamm is on the side of the angels."

"He works for Bertone."

She yanked back suddenly, trying to free her wrist. Rand didn't let go. Kayla went still, waiting for a chance to run.

Again.

24

Castillo del Cielo
Saturday
7:09 P.M. MST

"Move slow," Rand said clearly. "Kayla's still on edge. She thinks you're one of the bad guys. But don't get all teary about it. She doesn't trust me either, and I just saved her life." He looked at her, smiled slightly. "You can say 'Thank you.' Really, I won't faint."

Kayla slanted him a glance that told him how not funny he was.

"We're on the same side," Rand said. "What other proof do you need?"

She looked at his hand clamped around her wrist. "I don't trust either of you. I'm not sure I trust anybody in this."

"Finally, she understands," Rand said. "Too late, but hey, better late than dead, right?"

His eyes were as hard as his voice, as bitter as his words. Instantly her adrenaline flashed into anger.

"How do I know the skinny dude wasn't after you?" she shot back. "He didn't say a word, didn't call out to me, nothing. Hell, he might have just been smelling the flowers."

"With a seven-inch blade in his hand?" Rand made a disgusted sound. "I take back what I said about you understanding."

Hamm trotted up, dogged by motion sensor lights. "You okay, babe?" he asked Kayla.

"I'm not a babe," she said through clenched teeth.

"Adrenaline," Rand said to Hamm. "Never can tell how it will hit someone. Right now, Kayla is channeling her inner bitch."

"Quit yapping and get her the hell out of that garden trap," Faroe said impatiently.

He must have said the same to Hamm, because the guard touched his ear and looked hard at Rand. "The Man says to get moving. She's not safe here anymore."

Kayla looked from Rand's earpiece to Hamm's. His wasn't an iPod, but apparently they were talking to the same person. The Man, whoever that was.

She was terrified that it was Bertone.

"Let's go," Rand said.

"I'm not going anyplace, not with you and not with him," Kayla said. "For all I know it's Bertone whispering in your ear."

Rand pulled out his earpiece and screwed it into Kayla's ear. "Say hello, Joe. The lady thinks you're Bertone."

"Christ Jesus, I should have left you painting flowers in the rain," Faroe snarled. *"Now get your ass out of there."*

Kayla blinked. "He's not a happy camper."

"That's our Joe," Rand said, taking back the earpiece.

"You're burning a lot of bridges, McCree. If she's Bertone's stalking horse, I'll kill you myself."

"Oh, yeah, talk dirty to me, you know it turns me on," Rand said. Then, to Kayla, "Have you ever seen our skinny pal before?"

"No."

"Would you recognize him if you saw him again? As in a mug shot?"

"Are you a cop?" Kayla asked, startled.

"No. Would you?"

"You're the one who jacklighted him," she said.

"I kept my eyes closed so I wouldn't lose night vision."

"Yes, I'd recognize him." She shivered and stopped trying to free herself from Rand's grasp. "I think he dropped something before he climbed the wall."

"He was carrying a small duffel when I saw him head for the garden," Rand said. "He didn't have it when he went over the top."

Hamm clicked on a flashlight and ran its beam along the base of the west wall. The spear of light picked out a dark, shapeless blob.

"Get it," Rand said to Hamm. Then, to Kayla, "What did the guy look like?"

"He was dark, mestizo," Kayla said, "not much taller than me, really thin but ropy, too, like he'd put on all the muscle he could. I've never seen him before."

"Bertone has. He sent him after you."

"There's no reason for him to," Kayla said bitterly. "He's the blackmailer, not me."

Hamm trotted up with the small bag. "You're gonna love this."

He tossed the bag to Rand, who caught it without letting go of Kayla. "What is it?"

"A handy-dandy kidnap kit," Hamm said. He looked at Kayla and shook his head. "You were lucky, babe."

"Christ. Get her out of there NOW," Faroe snarled. *"Bertone has a lot of thugs working for him."*

Rand looked at his hand on Kayla's wrist. "You going to run if I let go, *ma petite*?"

"Go to hell."

"Been there. Not worth a rerun."

Rand waited.

Kayla looked at him for a long moment. Nothing about him made her nerves curdle the way they did when Bertone was near. And Rand had indeed been ready, willing, and frighteningly able to fight for her.

Some artist.

Hey, you wanted a third option, Kayla told herself bitterly. *Looks like Rand is it.*

Oh, lucky, lucky me.

"I won't run," she said. *For now.*

"Then let's get out of here."

Rand dropped her wrist and started walking quickly toward the wooden gate. As he walked, he rummaged in the duffel. His hand reappeared holding a small black pistol with a silencer screwed on, ready to go.

"Sweet." Rand smiled rather fiercely. "Bet it's stone-cold, too. Thanks, Bertone. I'll put your gift to good use." He shoved it in his waistband at the small of his back, right next to the taped area that was chewing on him.

"Was that a silencer?" Kayla asked, hurrying after Rand.

"Sure was. Skinny is quite the dude. He came ready to party. Duct tape, handcuffs, a black cloth people sack."

"He wanted to kidnap you," Hamm said matter-of-factly. "Sack you up and take off."

"How can you be sure?" Kayla asked, dazed.

"If he'd wanted to kill you," Rand said, touching the new gun at his back, "you'd be dead. A professional gun trumps an amateur knife every time."

She stared at him as he held the gate open for her, then looked away and slowly shook her head. "This is so not happening. Not to me. I backpacked through guerrilla territories and dope smugglers and pythons and never once was in real danger. Now I'm a banker and I'm—" Her voice broke and she shook her head again.

Rand tossed the bag to Hamm. "Give this to the tech guys. They won't find any prints because he was wearing gloves, but we might as well do it by the numbers."

"Got it."

"Joe," Rand said to his collar, "I'm either staying with her or bringing her in. Which is it?"

"Bloody hell. Bring her in. If she goes sideways on us—"

"Yeah, yeah, my ass is potato salad. Just remember who sweet-talked me into coming back."

"If I find the bastard, I'll kill him."

Rand laughed, surprising himself. "Yesterday I would have helped you."

"But not today?"

Rand found himself looking at Kayla. "Not today." The same fingers that had handled the deadly gun tipped her chin gently up toward him. "I can't explain here. No time and no place to hide. Let me take you to a place where there's time and safety."

She just stared at him.

"I promise I won't lie to you, ever," Rand said. "Ask me anything you want. If I can't answer, I'll tell you why. In return, you'll be honest with me. Deal?"

She was silent, then, "You are an artist, right? You didn't just make that part up?"

He smiled slightly. "You saw me paint. You have one of my paintings."

"I don't trust what I've seen." Her voice was weary and wary. Then she looked at him again, trying to read his eyes. "Who are you working for?"

"St. Kilda Consulting."

"Shit Marie," Hamm said, shaking his head. "When you take a burn, you take a big one. Faroe's going to go right through the earphones and give you a Colombian necktie."

Rand ignored him, pulled the camera out of his backpack, and gave it to Hamm. The memory stick went with it. "Don't lose this."

"Ten-four."

"Anything else?" Rand asked Kayla.

"I have to go back to my ranch for a few things. Will you let me?"

"If I go with you."

"Son of a bitch! You bring her right to the motel."

"But it will be dangerous," Rand said calmly. "Your ranch is the second place they'll look for you."

"What's the first?"

"The apartment you just rented and haven't had time to really move into."

Kayla digested the fact that he knew a lot more about her than he should. "I'll be quick at the ranch. Take a back road."

"Don't even—"

"Shut up, Joe," Rand said. "It's not that big a risk."

"The hell—"

Rand talked over Faroe. "It will take Bertone time to reorganize. Besides, you wouldn't want her little babies to starve, would you?"

"Her what?"

Rand didn't answer.

25

Castillo del Cielo
Saturday
7:25 P.M. MST

Not many people could make Gabriel Navarro uneasy, but Andre Bertone did. It wasn't just Bertone's burly body, his height, his wealth, that made Gabriel wary. It was a killer's knowledge that he was in the presence of a better killer.

And Gabriel had pissed that better killer off.

Elena's laughter wasn't helping. "Oh, my. Tell me again how a little mouse of a banker defeated one of the best—"

"Enough." Bertone cut across his wife's amusement. "Who came to Kayla's aid?"

Gabriel shrugged and stubbed out his cigarette in a crystal ashtray. Then he crossed his legs and looked at Bertone. "Tall dude. Moved good. Like a fighter, you know?"

Elena snickered and said mockingly, "But of course. We have so many warriors in Pleasure Valley."

"What did he look like?" Bertone asked.

"I told you. Tall."

"Mexican, white, black, mestizo?" Bertone asked impatiently. "Young, old?"

"Like I said. The dude blew out my eyes with his flashlight. Didn't see shit 'cept for a big knife. Moved like he could use it. You said no killing, so I booked."

Bertone said something in Russian and lit his cigar.

Elena sighed and opened the French doors to air out the smoke. With every step her sandals flashed wealth and impatience.

Gabriel watched her without seeming to. If she'd been anyone else's woman, he would have tried to put his hands on her.

But she was Bertone's.

"You're sure he called out Kayla's name?" Bertone asked.

"Yes."

"Find her," Bertone said.

Gabriel stood up. "Catch or kill?"

Bertone's eyes narrowed. The intelligence and instincts that had gotten him from the frozen gutters of Siberia to Arizona's Pleasure Valley were twitching. Right now, Kayla knew more about who had saved her than he did.

Knowledge was a weapon.

"Catch," Bertone said curtly.

He could always kill her later.

26

Beyond Phoenix
Saturday
8:04 P.M. MST

"Slow down," Kayla said to Rand.

He looked sideways at her. After she'd gotten in the car and given him directions to Dry Valley, she hadn't said a word.

"I thought you were asleep," he said.

"Just thinking." *Trying to get used to the impossible. Failing. Trying again. And again.* "There's a deep dip up ahead, a desert wash that runs wall-to-wall in the monsoons. If you don't slow down, you'll—"

The suspension on the SUV bottomed out as Rand crested a little rise and dropped into the arroyo she was describing.

Kayla grabbed the overhead handrail and grunted at the impact, then again when the vehicle crested the rise on the far side. She felt weightless in the second before the body of the car slammed down again.

"About that dip," Kayla said through her teeth. "There are others. If you don't listen to me, what's the point of having me along?"

Rand lifted his foot, dropped back to a more reasonable speed, and smiled slightly. "Still channeling your inner bitch?"

"Listen, macho man. I don't do any better with the 'You Tarzan, me Jane' bullshit than I do with the toe-licking lapdog. And I figured out real quick in the garden that the lapdog was an act."

"What about Tarzan?"

"I'll get back to you on that."

"When?" Rand asked.

"When I'm damn good and ready."

He gave her another sideways glance. She was stiff, clutching the handrail with one hand and bracing herself on the console with the other.

"Still scared?" he asked gently.

Her mouth flattened as she stared at the night racing by on either side of the headlights. "I don't like handcuffs. They freaked me out more than the silencer on the gun did."

"Rather be shot than bound, huh? Me too."

She blew a little breath out of her nose. "Listen, Tarzan. A woman living alone in this world is considered fair game. Smart women know it. Dumb women end up handcuffed one way or another."

"My name is Rand," he said patiently. "You can call me McCree if Rand is too friendly for you. Unless you want to be called Jane?"

She almost smiled. "Okay, McCree."

"As for being fair game, everybody in the world is fair game for a guy like Bertone."

"So you do know him," she said.

Gunfire stitching through the helo.

Reed bleeding, sighing.

Dying.

"We'd never met face-to-face until tonight, but yeah, I know a lot about him."

"And me."

"And you," Rand agreed. "You can read my dossier if you like."

She blinked. "Will it tell me why you wanted to slit Bertone's throat?"

"I'd better buff my acting skills. I didn't think I gave myself away."

"Only once, the last time he turned his back on you."

Silence filled the car.

Kayla waited.

"Yes, I know Bertone well enough to want him dead," Rand said. "But that makes me one of about a million potential assassins."

"Why? Because he's rich?"

"Because he's evil."

She drew in a deep breath. "Interesting choice of words."

"It's the twenty-first century," Rand said calmly, steering the SUV through another steep dip. "People are free to talk about evil rather than bad childhoods, which most people have without turning into murderers. The Siberian started poor, but so do billions of people. They don't end up like him."

"Siberian? Bertone? He's Russian?"

Rand nodded.

"That explains it," she said.

"Explains what? No country has a corner on evil. I'll match some American-grown thugs against Bertone any minute of any hour."

"It explains his accent. His English is grammatically perfect, almost without accent, but there is a heaviness to it that you only get in Slavic tongues."

"The dossier didn't mention you were a linguist," Rand said.

"I traveled a lot, right after college, after my parents died."

"Did you like it?" he asked, because that part of her dossier had been blank except for passport entries, the coming and going of a world traveler.

"Like it? No. I loved it. I hit every continent except Antarctica. I was looking for a job that would let me save the world. Turns out the world didn't want to be saved."

Rand's smile was a knife-edge of white. "True fact."

"Then gringos became everybody's favorite target," she said without bitterness, "so I hung up my backpack and got a job close to home."

"Smart. Your experience should make it easier."

"Make what easier?" she asked.

"I'd hate to try and explain this transnational clusterfuck to someone who'd never been farther than Kansas."

Rand turned right at the country intersection.

"Are the hummingbirds actually in my dossier?" Kayla asked after a moment. "My babies, as you called them."

He laughed. "St. Kilda is nothing if not thorough. Those kinds of details are how you discover where someone is likely to surface next. Helps to reaquire the target. You love those flying beggars, which means you'll show up to feed them, at least for the rest of the month you occupy the ranch."

"Any other time of the year, I'd let those little flying pigs pollinate cactus, but right now it's migration time. They count on me to get to Montana. One of my neighbors loves the birds, too. She's agreed to start feeding them next week. Until then, it's on my karma."

Rand couldn't help liking Kayla better for caring about something that brought her no obvious return. "What species do you have?"

"Oh, I've got them all right now, broadtails and Anna's and Costa's and even some rufous."

"The rufous aren't headed for Montana. They summer by the thousands north of Seattle. In a few weeks they'll be showing up on my doorstep."

"You feed hummers?" she asked.

"I even paint them. Or try to. They're as fast as they are fierce."

Kayla knew it was crazy, but she trusted Rand more because he shared her love of those flying bits of life.

Then he killed the headlights and her throat closed.

Trust was overrated.

27

Dry Valley
Saturday
8:08 P.M. MST

"What are you doing?" Kayla asked tightly.

"Going in stealth mode."

She gave him a disbelieving look. "We're miles from the ranch."

"Light shows a long way in the desert. I'd rather see someone before he sees me."

She let out a ragged breath. After a few moments, she got the rhythm of driving in the dark. It helped that the night wasn't absolutely black. Once her eyes adjusted, the starlight was surprisingly bright, throwing ghostly shadows. The dirt road was a pale ribbon unwinding through the darker plants of the Sonoran Desert.

The longer she went without artificial light, the more she saw. Features of the landscape became distinct; subtle divisions between rock and plant and shadow became clear.

"I used to ride at night," she said finally. "I loved it. Nobody was trying to kidnap me then. But I see things even more clearly now."

"Amazing how a little fear sharpens the senses. You ran straight for me in the garden, like a cat."

"I hadn't thought of it that way. I was too busy being scared silly."

"You weren't silly," he said. "You had your best weapon and were ready to defend yourself no matter what the odds. That's all anyone can do."

She was silent for a moment, then let out a long sigh. "Thanks, Rand. I needed that. I felt so damned helpless."

Rand remembered holding Reed, seeing death take life from his eyes. "I've been there. Helpless and screaming inside."

"You sure didn't look helpless tonight."

"Different time, different place. Next time, next place—" He shrugged. "Who knows?"

What she could see of his face told her the same thing his voice did. He meant every word.

Not Tarzan, yodeling through the jungle on waves of testosterone.

Not a lapdog.

Altogether intriguing.

The SUV popped over a rocky ridgeline and started down into Dry Valley. In the distance, a light burned. As they came closer, the single yard light in a fixture on a power pole next to the ranch house outlined every detail around the small house.

"No cars," Rand said. "No trucks. But then, I'd put my wheels out of sight and wait inside."

"I don't like the sound of that. Do you really think someone's inside my—Bertone's—house?"

"Probably not. But why regret not doing what's smart?"

He drove slowly into the yard between the corral and the low-roofed ranch house. The cone of light from the single bulb fell across a post that was mounted with three swinging arms, each about a foot long. At the end of each arm there was a hummingbird feeder with a clear plastic barrel and red plastic base.

"You still have a key to the door?" Rand asked.

"I never lock it."

"You live alone and you don't lock up?"

She shrugged. "Mom and Dad never did. There's a deadbolt on the inside I can use if I'm home."

"The last of the innocents," he said softly. "After I get out, crawl over to the driver's side. Don't open the door. If you see anyone but me, hit the horn and drive like a bat out of hell to the Royal Palms. Ask for Joe Faroe."

"What about you?"

Instead of answering, Rand lowered the window and listened.

Above the sound of the engine came a rush of wind, the rub of dry plants against each other, the call of a song-dog wishing for the moon. Rand listened as the coyote called again.

Nothing answered.

"Put your hands over the dome light," he said.

She stared for a moment, then put her palms squarely over the SUV's interior light. Her hands glowed red when he opened the door. Quickly, quietly, he shut the door behind him and disappeared into the shadows beside the corral and barn.

Kayla scrambled across to the driver's seat and watched the ghost that was Rand. He used every bit of darkness and landscape to break up his outline against the pale dirt and star-blazing sky. Slowly he circled toward the back of the house.

And vanished.

When he disappeared, she felt a sudden isolation. She was in a place that was utterly familiar to her. And utterly *un*familiar, because a stranger was in the shadows of her childhood home looking for other strangers carrying bags holding handcuffs and duct tape and silenced guns.

I don't know who advised people to believe three impossible things a day, but I'm working on it.

Don't work, she told herself. *Just accept.*

Treat this like a foreign country. I don't need to understand everything at once. I used to be good at that, at letting go, at not getting hung up on differences to the point that I couldn't enjoy a new place.

Now I'm in a new place.

Accept it.

Rand appeared at the other end of the ranch house. The silenced gun gleamed dully in his hand. He tested the front door, found it unlocked, and pushed it wide open. Then he waited, listening. After a few moments he went inside.

Kayla waited, listening, breath held. She flinched and let out an explosive breath when a light turned on inside the house. Other lights came on. Rand reappeared on the porch and walked to the SUV. The gun was nowhere in sight.

"Shut it down," he said. "We're alone."

She turned off the engine and got out of the car, walking into a familiar, foreign land.

He took her arm with his left hand. It was an impersonal gesture, a means of guiding her, yet Kayla was aware of his touch immediately, intensely. Then she saw that his right hand never strayed far from the gun at the small of his back.

"I thought you said we're alone." She looked pointedly at his right hand.

"I'm ninety-seven percent sure. The gun's for the other three percent."

"Are you certain you aren't a federal cop?" she asked.

"Would you feel better if I was?"

"No."

He stopped by the front door. "Interesting. Why?"

"I saw Bertone talking to some of the most powerful politicians in the state tonight. I've seen thousands and thousands of dollars in campaign donations flow from the Bertones to national politicians all over the States."

"So?"

"So right now I don't trust anyone who draws a public paycheck. Call me a cynic."

"I'd call you a realist. Money is just another word for power."

Rand suspected that Faroe could name every politician who'd taken Bertone's money, but Rand would ask Faroe just to be certain.

Bertone's political allies were Kayla's enemies.

"Anything look out of place to you?" Rand asked when Kayla walked into the house.

She glanced around. "Considering that I've been packing up stuff, no."

She walked into the bedroom.

He followed.

"You're neater than I am," Rand said, looking around the room. "Or did you pack up all the little things already?"

"No. But too much clutter is like a traffic jam—it makes me edgy."

An open book lay facedown on the bedside table. Rand picked up the paperback. The Lonely Planet guide *Australia and New Zealand on a Shoestring*. She'd been reading about the high lake and glacier country of South Island.

"Is this where you were going to go to ground?" he asked, gesturing with the book.

"Up until yesterday, all I had was itchy feet."

"And now?"

"I itch everywhere."

He almost smiled. "Smart."

"Uncomfortable."

"You get used to it."

"I'd rather go to Queenstown and stop itching."

He gave her a sideways glance and saw that she was looking wistfully at the picture of glaciers and lakes.

"You mentioned blackmail," Rand said.

"I did?"

"Back in the garden. You said Bertone was the blackmailer, not you. What did you mean?"

"Guess my dossier wasn't quite complete," she said.

He closed the book and turned to her.

"Thursday I sold the ranch," she said. "Got a really great price, never met the buyer."

"Bertone."

"How did you know?"

"I know Bertone."

"Well, thanks to him," she said bitterly, "now I look like a down-and-dirty banker."

"Figures."

"You believe me?"

"It fits with the rest of your dossier," Rand said. "You're too clean to volunteer for the kind of mud bath Bertone needs. He had to have a twist on you. Why didn't you go to the feds?"

"Bertone has a lot more traction with the feds than I do. I didn't want to bet my freedom on a he-said-she-said slanging match. Maybe I should have. But I couldn't get enthusiastic about my chances of winning, so I looked for another way out."

"Find one?"

She looked him straight in the eye. "I don't know."

Kayla turned and walked out of the bedroom. The kitchen area was the center of the small ranch house. With the ease of long familiarity she pulled out several stockpots, dumped in sugar and hot water, and put the pots on the gas stove. Each burner came on with a soft *whump.*

She stared at the flames.

"What do you think?" she asked finally. "Should I go to the feds?"

Rand thought of Neto being refused a visa—*not in U.S. interests*—and of the politicians sucking up expensive champagne at the Bertones' paint-off. "As a last resort, maybe."

"What about running?"

He shook his head slowly. "You don't have enough money to hide for the next fifty years."

"That's what I figured. Then I went to my boss."

"Which one?"

"Steve Foley."

Another name to run by St. Kilda's research department. "And?"

"I can talk about what happened to me, my personal finances. I can't talk about my clients. I could get fired."

"There are worse things. Handcuffs, for instance."

Kayla flinched. "I have a responsibility to my clients and my bank."

"That's what Bertone is counting on. A sweet little bird who's terrified of singing outside the choir."

She set her jaw, stirred each pot, and watched bubbles rise.

"So Bertone is leaning on you to do something illegal with his money, using the bank," Rand said after a time. "It's called laundering, and the feds hate it. Right so far?"

Kayla didn't bother to deny the obvious.

Or confirm it.

"What's your stake in this?" she asked him.

He hesitated.

"No lies," she said. "Remember?"

Silence stretched in the kitchen as Rand watched Kayla stir sugar syrup until it came to a boil. When she turned off the burners beneath the pots, he went to the refrigerator and pulled out a bucket of ice cubes.

"What are you doing?" she asked.

He shoveled ice cubes into one of the pots until the syrup was cool.

"We don't have all night to wait," he said as he tested the syrup. "You don't want a silly hummer to burn its tongue, do you? You have to dilute the syrup anyway."

He tested the solution. Getting there. A few more cubes and it wouldn't be a threat to the tender tongue of any hummingbird desperately clinging to a perch at the edge of the yard light.

Kayla tilted her head and looked at him like a curious cat. "I was going to pull out my big feeders, but even the biggest will be cool long before morning."

Rand nodded. "That's fine, but right now there's a very hungry little guy needing to be fed. He's waiting on a perch, hoping for a miracle to pull his feathered ass out of a crack."

"At this time of night?" she asked, startled. "Hummingbirds shut down at sunset."

"Unless they're having a tough time on migration. Then they push too hard. The lucky ones find a yard feeder. The unlucky ones starve to death. Where are the feeders you want to use?"

"Cupboard behind you."

She watched him take out a clean half-gallon feeder and fill it with cool, diluted syrup. Every movement was efficient, practiced. He might not be answering the question she'd asked, but he sure hadn't lied about knowing how to feed hummingbirds.

"You've done this a lot," she said.

"At the height of the season, I go through more than five pounds of sugar a day."

"Holy hell. You must be feeding hundreds and hundreds of the flying pigs."

"Easily. May and June are the big months. The birds are pretty well gone by the end of July."

"And they're all rufous?" she asked, trying to imagine what it would be like to see clouds of flying bronze jewels feeding at once, flashing their crimson gorgets to warn off others.

"Nearly all my birds are rufous. Nasty little heathens," he said, smiling slightly, "but damn beautiful. They remind me that no matter how pretty, life is always a battle."

Kayla waited until Rand had topped off the last feeder with cool syrup before she asked, "Are you going to answer my question about why you're helping me?"

"Like you, not everything I know is mine to tell." Rand screwed the feeding platform in place. "You already know the most important things."

"Which are?"

"I want you alive and Bertone dead."

28

Dry Valley
Saturday
8:20 P.M. MST

While they hung the feeders in the shelter of the ranch house porch, Kayla was silent, thinking about what Rand had said. Even before she stepped back from the first feeder, a hummingbird appeared on it. Ignoring the humans, he drank and drank and drank. After a few minutes of resting, the bird shook himself, fluffed his feathers, but stayed clamped to the perch.

"He'll drink at least once more," Rand said quietly, "then he'll head on out into the desert and bed down in a safer place."

"I've never seen a hummer come in at night like that."

"He'd have taken on a bobcat for that nectar. Being desperate does that to you." He glanced at his watch. "Time to go."

"You're sure I can't go to my apartment?" Kayla asked. "The only packing boxes of clothes I left at the ranch are full of jeans and such."

"Jeans are good."

She followed him back into the bedroom, where she'd stacked full boxes for her next trip to the new apartment.

"Which one?" he asked.

"One? But—"

"One."

"Hell."

"Don't worry. There are a lot of Wal-Marts in Phoenix."

She rolled her eyes and picked up the box she'd marked RANCH CLOTHES. "Oh, well, this *is* Arizona, famous for casual wear." She gave him a sidelong look. "Isn't it?"

"Are you asking me where you're going from here?" Rand said, taking the box from her.

"Clever of you to notice."

"Phoenix," Rand said.

"Royal Palms?"

"Yes."

"Joe Faroe?" she asked.

"Among others."

She followed Rand out to the car, then confronted him before he loaded the box into the SUV. "And I'm supposed to take all this on faith."

"I wasn't the dude waiting for you with handcuffs and duct tape."

Kayla closed her eyes. All she saw was the handcuffs, scuffed from horrible use, and thick duct tape to force back her screams. "Point taken. But that still doesn't tell me why you helped me."

"I want you."

Her eyes snapped open. "Well, that's blunt."

"You wanted honesty. You got it." *Half the truth, anyway. The rest isn't mine to tell.*

She stepped aside. "Be careful what you ask for, is that it?"

"Pretty much." He tossed the box in back and started to get in the driver's seat.

"McCree, this is my car. It says so down at the DMV."

"Your point?"

"I drive."

"Have you been trained in high-speed evasion?"

She stared at him, then turned and got into the passenger side. The door slammed behind her. Hard.

"The thing about choices," Rand said as he drove out of the ranch yard, "is that they're never as clear as they seem when you make them."

It didn't take Kayla long to get to the bottom line. "What do you know that I should and don't?"

"Nobody's motives are pure. Nobody's."

"Including you?"

"Yes."

"St. Kilda Consulting?" Kayla pressed.

"It's a human organization made up of people whose motives aren't one-hundred-percent angelic."

"Joe Faroe?"

"He's nobody's angel."

"Like Bertone," Kayla said.

"No. Faroe is a hard son of a bitch, but he's honorable. Bertone is slime on cesspool walls."

"What if I don't want to go to Royal Palms? Do I have a choice?"

"You have the same choice you had in the garden before I showed up."

"Fight and die." She made a low sound. "You really know how to sweet-talk a girl."

"You're a woman."

"Doesn't mean I don't like sweet talk," she retorted.

"Every time I call you beautiful, or touch you, you stiffen up like I burned you."

She shrugged. "You did."

In the dashboard lights, Rand's expression shifted. "Talk about blunt."

"Being hunted by a kidnapper does that to me."

"Frees your inner bitch?"

"That, too," Kayla said, smiling. "But mostly it reminds me that my next breath is a gift, not a guarantee."

Rand's mouth thinned as he thought of Reed. "Amen. Amazing how knowing, really *knowing,* the fragility of life makes choices easier. 'If I don't do this, will I go to my grave regretting it?' is the only question that matters."

The first thing Kayla thought was how she would feel if she didn't pursue the heat she felt between herself and Rand.

It's been too long since a man made me curious, edgy, aware of every difference between male and female.

Girl, your timing sucks.

"So you count regrets in terms of things you haven't done," she said.

"Always."

"Is that why you work for St. Kilda instead of painting full-time?"

"My time at St. Kilda could be real short," was all Rand said.

"Why do I get the feeling that you aren't entirely happy working for St. Kilda?"

"Because I'm not." His voice didn't encourage more questions.

She asked anyway. "Then why are you with them?"

"They made me an offer I couldn't refuse."

"They threatened you?" she asked, startled.

Rand's fingers tightened around the wheel as the SUV sped through the darkness, pushing a cone of light ahead. A desert night and sweeping light that Reed would never see.

"My reasons for being with St. Kilda are personal, private, and have no bearing on your decision," he said.

"Which decision?"

"To go or not to go to Royal Palms," he said sardonically.

"Whither thou goest," she said, her tone equally biting.

He gave a crack of laughter. Then he realized how long it had been since he had laughed. "I like you, Kayla Shaw."

"Same back, Rand McCree. Well, most of the time."

He was tempted to ask about the rest of the time, but he didn't. "Liking you wasn't part of the plan."

"What plan?"

"Despite its lack of perfection, St. Kilda Consulting is a necessary organization in today's world of transnational crime, failed and failing states, feral cities, and the just plain savage places in between. All the places where duly appointed and lawful governments are just short of useless, and corrupt governments thrive."

She turned and looked at him. "Is that an answer or an evasion?"

"Yes. If you go to Royal Palms, and if Grace and Joe like what they see of you, they'll want you to sign up with St. Kilda Consulting. If you don't feel that grateful, you can leave."

"And if I don't go with St. Kilda, I get to choose between Bertone and the feds." *Or trust my boss, Steve Foley, to bail me out.* She grimaced. *Not in this lifetime.* "All in all, I'd rather see what St. Kilda has to offer. Assuming that they'll let me walk away if I don't like what I see?"

"No handcuffs or duct tape, guaranteed," Rand said. "All they'll ask is that you don't mention anything about St. Kilda to Bertone or to your bank."

"I won't. What about the feds?"

"Let's just hope the question never comes up."

"St. Kilda is publicity-shy?" Kayla asked.

"That, too. Mostly it's the fact that we work where U.S. agencies can't or won't work. All the shades of gray that don't fit into ten-second sound bites and political slogans. We've made friends. We've made enemies. Working for St. Kilda carries baggage. Some of it is dangerous. Most of it is just irritating."

When he looked at Kayla to see how she was taking his words, she surprised him.

She smiled.

"You make St. Kilda Consulting sound like hummingbirds," she said, "at war with one another and the rest of the world."

"Close enough," Rand said, and he smiled in return.

"What would you do if you were me?"

"Run like hell for the nearest exit."

The light from the dashboard made his eyes look hard, almost silver.

"Interesting," Kayla said. "Why haven't you?"

"My motives have no bearing on your decision, remember?"

"Whew. Talk about honest." Her voice said *brutally honest.*

Silence grew.

Rand hissed a word under his breath. "Look, I can't make the decision for you. You have to make it because you're the one who has to live with the results."

"Like you."

"Just like me. Your own devils, your own hell." *Chosen very carefully by you.*

"What about angels and heaven?" she asked.

"Hasn't come up on my radar."

"Never?"

"I only knew it when it was gone."

Too late.

29

Phoenix
Saturday
9:10 P.M. MST

Is this car registered in your name?" Rand asked.

Kayla blinked. It had been a long time since he'd spoken. "Yes."

There was silence again while he eased the Explorer into traffic on southbound Interstate 17, heading deep into the Phoenix metro area. Without warning he cut across lanes, accelerated, cut across more lanes, slowed down, and watched the mirrors.

Nobody had speeded, slowed, changed lanes, or done anything to tickle his suspicions.

"Then we'll have to get rid of it," Rand said.

She stared at him. "My car? I can't afford another one."

"You don't have to. But from here on out, you've dropped off the scope of your everyday life. You won't go to your new apartment. You won't go to the ranch. You won't drive your car. You won't talk on your cell phone."

"Tell me you're kidding."

Silence.

A lot of it.

"You aren't kidding." She sighed. "Is all this really necessary?"

"Bertone wants you. You want him to get you?"

She shuddered.

"That's what I thought," Rand said. "Remember the handcuffs. It will help you stay focused."

"You can be a cold bastard," she said.

"It can be a cold world."

"I didn't mean that as a slam," she said. "It just—surprised me. Then I remember your painting and know I shouldn't be surprised. You'll do whatever it takes to get the job done. Were you always that way?"

"No."

Rand turned off the freeway onto Scottsdale Road and headed south on Resort Row. Four minutes later, he drove through the impressive entrance of the Royal Palms.

"St. Kilda Consulting must have a lot of money," Kayla said.

He didn't answer.

A few minutes later he drove into a small parking area reserved for a cluster of three resort bungalows. A man stepped out of the shadows. He carried a flashlight big enough to light up the Explorer's interior. After a look in the cargo area, he snapped off the light and walked over to open Kayla's door.

"Good evening," he said. "They're waiting for you in Bungalow One."

He was polite, crisp, and terribly British.

Rand got out and pitched the keys to the guard. "Dump this at one of Scottsdale Air Park's long-term lots. I want anybody interested in Kayla to think she could have jumped a private jet and disappeared."

"Right, Mac," the guard replied. "I'll bring the ticket to you, Miss Shaw. You can pick the car up when it's safe."

"Thanks." She looked at Rand. "When will it be safe?"

When Bertone's dead.

But all Rand said was, "You'll know."

He guided her down the soft, sandy path toward the lighted bungalow, then up the short stairway that led across the central patio to the first bungalow's door. Rand raised his hand to knock, then stopped.

"Last chance," he said, looking straight into her eyes. "There's a Gulfstream executive jet at Scottsdale

Air Park. You could be in Cabo San Lucas in two hours. You'd be safe."

"Forever?" she asked.

"Nobody's safe forever. But you would be safe until we get a choke hold on Bertone."

Kayla took a deep breath and stared off into the night. Beyond the soft lights from the bungalows, she could just make out the rolling landforms of a green, manicured golf course that ran out to the edge of the desert. Calm, peaceful, normal in the faint glow of city lights and starlight. She shook her head.

"What does that mean?" Rand asked.

"It looks so ordinary out there."

"Death is damned ordinary."

She made a sound that might have been laughter. "You're one of a kind, McCree. A real sweet-talking man. You're just trying to make this sound irresistible to me, aren't you?"

He shrugged. "If it all goes from sugar to shit, I don't want you standing there, watching me with a surprised look on your face."

Like Reed, dying.

"Lead on, McCree," Kayla said.

30

Royal Palms
Saturday
9:15 P.M. MST

The last thing Kayla expected to find in the bungalow was a man and a pregnant woman quizzing a good-looking teenage boy about the Krebs cycle. She gave Rand a look.

He gave it back.

"Right down the rabbit hole," she said under her breath.

"You expected sweaty, muscular men with real short hair cleaning guns and sharpening knives?" he asked dryly. "The mean-looking dude is Joe Faroe. The beautiful rapier—"

Grace snorted. "I'm pregnant, McCree."

"—*mind* is Grace Faroe," Rand said without missing a beat. "The lanky bottomless pit with computer attachments is Lane, their son. Meet Kayla Shaw, the banker Andre Bertone tried to kidnap."

"That's my cue," Lane said, coming to his feet. "Pleased to meet you and I'm gone."

"Go online and get a better explanation of the Krebs cycle," Faroe said to Lane's retreating back. "The textbook they gave you is lame."

Lane waved and vanished through a bedroom door.

Grace smiled and held out her hand to Kayla. "Ignore Joe. He's a little new to the teaching game. He thinks glucose metabolism is something exotic and inscrutable."

"OIL RIG," Kayla answered.

Grace blinked.

"Oxidation Is Loss, Reduction Is Gain," Kayla explained. "There's more, but that's all I remember from my advanced-placement biology class."

"Did you hear that, Lane?" Faroe asked the bedroom door.

"OIL RIG," came faintly from behind the door, followed by train-wreck music.

Faroe grinned.

Grace shook her head. "Sorry, we're home-schooling the heathen."

"Beats having him kidnapped again," Faroe said. "Coffee? Wine? Beer? Cheese and crackers? Peanut butter?"

"Bring it on," Rand said. "The canapés wore off hours ago." He looked at Kayla. "What about you?"

"Lane was kidnapped?" Kayla asked, shocked.

"We got him back," Faroe said. His voice said it hadn't been easy.

"A very powerful Mexican drug lord was killed in the process," Grace said. "Joe is still at considerable risk."

"So are you," Faroe said from the kitchen area. "So is Lane. I wish Mary the Markswoman had had a chance to drop that *cabrón*'s nephew."

Grace gave her husband a slicing, sideways look. "I didn't hear that."

"Hear what?" Faroe asked blandly.

Kayla glanced at Rand. "Even paranoids have real enemies, right?"

"Nonparanoids, too. They're just too dumb to know it."

"I don't know how much McCree has told you about St. Kilda Consulting," Grace began, giving Rand a hard look for saying anything at all without permission.

"Enough that I know you aren't owned by politicians," Kayla said. "And don't want to be."

Grace gave Kayla a considering look. "You're not as innocent as you look."

"I might have been two days ago." Kayla shrugged. "Even sin was innocent once. The rest is timing and opportunity."

Faroe's surprisingly warm laughter rolled out of the kitchen area. "Innocent as sin, huh? McCree, you brought us a keeper."

Rand smiled and touched Kayla's dark hair so lightly she wondered if she'd felt it at all. "She grows on you."

"So now I'm fungus," Kayla said. "McCree, you really need to kiss the Blarney stone. Twice."

Faroe brought out plates of crackers, cold cuts, cheeses, and fruit from a high-end deli. "Start on this. I'll bring some drinks."

"I'll get them," Grace said.

"Amada," Faroe said, "sit down. You're on your feet too much."

"It's a miracle I got through the first pregnancy without you," Grace said under her breath. But she sat down, sighed with pleasure, and put her feet up on the coffee table.

"Where's the nondisclosure agreement, Judge?" Rand asked. "Or don't you have it ready?"

"It's ready," Grace said. "Is she?"

They looked at Kayla.

"I'll know after I've read it," she said. "Or do you expect me to sign something blind?"

"St. Kilda wouldn't want to work with anyone stupid enough to sign before reading," Grace said.

She picked a sheet of paper from the end table. Rand took the paper before she could give it to Kayla. He read it quickly, nodded, and handed it to Kayla.

"This is legal lite," Grace explained, "but it will give protection to you and St. Kilda Consulting if the feds come calling."

Kayla read the document quickly.

> I, Kayla Shaw, do agree to discuss certain matters involving myself and Andre Bertone, as well as other matters arising from an investigation by St. Kilda Consulting. I do so freely and without duress.
>
> I hereby promise not to disclose the nature of these discussions with subject Bertone or with any other persons not involved in St. Kilda Consulting's investigation. I promise not to disclose St. Kilda Consulting's proprietary information to any person not approved by one of the principals of the organization, namely James Steele, Joe Faroe, or Grace Silva Faroe.
>
> In return, St. Kilda Consulting and its representatives agree not to disclose my cooperation with

> them. Under terms of this agreement, I accept the payment of one United States silver dollar and other valuable considerations.

Like saving my life? Kayla thought.

There was a signature line across the bottom with her name and the date typed beneath.

Faroe handed her a pen and waited while she signed. Then he gave her the silver dollar.

The coin felt heavy in Kayla's hand, solid, real. She worked with money all the time, but it didn't have substance. Not like this. With an odd smile, she flipped the silver dollar into the air, caught it, and slapped it down on the back of her hand.

Heads.

Whatever that meant.

"Now what?" she asked.

"Tell us about your relationship with Andre Bertone," Grace said.

31

Outside Phoenix
Saturday
9:25 P.M. MST

BLA-BLAM!

Two shots rang out almost as one.

A second later, *BLA-BLAM* again, the same deadly double-tap, a heavy auto-loading pistol, then again and, after a slightly longer interval, again.

Steve Foley stood in a shooting stance, firing at four silhouette targets that were suspended from clips on wires at ranges from seven to twenty meters. The sharp reports of his gun were muffled. The Arizona Territorial Gun Club's indoor shooting range had earth-buffered concrete block walls that swallowed up echoes and fed back dead air. The clearest sound was the hard metallic clicks as the shooter ejected the magazine and cleared the breech of his weapon.

Even though the club was on the edge of one of America's fastest-growing metro areas, no whisper of gunfire disturbed civilians beyond the building.

Without moving from behind Foley, Andre Bertone inspected the two-shot patterns in the targets.

"Very nice," Bertone said.

"I got a little loose on the long shots." No longer shooting, Foley held his specially balanced and ported Model 1911A Colt pistol with the muzzle in the air. "It's amazing how much a muzzle can wobble in the span between two bullets."

"It wobbles even more if the target has the chance to shoot back," Bertone said. "Or even if the target is merely alive. You've never fired at a living human, have you?"

"That's why I burn two hundred rounds a week. If it all becomes automatic, there's less chance of clutching when it counts."

Foley checked the chamber of the pistol in his hand to make sure it was clear before he closed the slide. The smooth metallic action snapped shut with authority. He put the gun into its nest in an aluminum Halliburton case and snapped the catches on the lid.

Bertone watched with an amusement he didn't bother to conceal. Practice was one thing.

War was quite another.

Foley was dressed in a black special-ops coverall, black boots with soft rubber soles, a black baseball cap without insignia, and sport-shooters amber-colored glasses. He looked more like a member of a police weapons team than a fast-rising banker.

Quickly Foley opened a second metal case and lifted out a bulkier weapon, a German-made nine-millimeter submachine gun with a folding stock and a heavy, cylindrical sound suppressor threaded into its short, matte black barrel. This was Foley's personal favorite weapon, a highly modified and militarized H&K MP5A.

"Sweet, huh?" Foley said, admiring the muted play of light over the weapon.

Bertone didn't answer. He used guns, but he didn't love them any more than he loved toilet paper.

Tools were made to be used.

Men were made to use them.

Smiling, Foley hefted the gun lightly. Because he was a civilian, it was illegal for him to own the silenced submachine gun. For that reason he seldom used it, not even in the shooting house of the most sophisticated firearms club in the gun-proud state of Arizona. Though he was both a member of the Arizona Territorial Gun Club and on its board of directors, normally the club wouldn't have winked at the presence of a weapon whose possession would cost its owner twenty years in federal prison.

But the club was officially closed now, empty but for Foley and Bertone. Foley wasn't going to turn himself in, and neither was Bertone.

"At least you got away from Elena's party in time to shoot," Foley said. "Silver lining and all that."

"I always make time to shoot."

Bertone watched as Foley slid under the spell of the deadly weapon. Some men got off on after-hours strip clubs or motorcycles, extreme boxing or illegal gambling. Foley got off on the shooting house, with its targets and its mock-up hostage rooms. Bertone, a behind-the-scenes owner of the Arizona Territorial Gun Club, was more than happy to ignore violations of federal firearms law by members of the club who could be useful to him.

Like Foley.

The banker pulled the bolt on the weapon, checked to make sure it wasn't loaded, then snapped a twenty-shot magazine into place. The gun suddenly acquired the lethal weight that he loved. Nothing felt as good as holding a loaded weapon.

"May I?" Bertone asked politely, holding out his hands for the weapon.

Reluctantly Foley handed the gun over.

"Thank you," Bertone said when the weapon was finally presented to him.

He knew how unhappy Foley was to part with the gun. That was why Bertone had asked for it. He hefted the gun, slapped the bolt forward skillfully, and lifted the gun to his shoulder, keeping the muzzle pointed downrange and in the clear.

He tested the gun's balance, lowering it and then fitting it back into the firing position. A silencer usually made a weapon awkward, but this one was carefully designed. Much better than the planeloads of Cold War–era Kalashnikovs and Dragunovs that he'd sold over the years.

"How did she get away?" Foley asked, frowning as he watched Bertone handle his weapon with eerie skill.

Without benefit of sights, Bertone aimed at a standard silhouette target fifteen yards away and pulled the trigger.

The loudest sound was the working of the bolt as he fired three separate three-round bursts in quick succession. The soft fluorescent light of the range appeared magically through three tight groupings in the body mass of the target. He pointed the muzzle into the air and stepped back from the firing line.

"One of my security guards was too alert," Bertone said. "He saw her heading into the garden alone, saw the lights go out, and was worried. He interrupted Gabriel before he could secure his target."

"Well, that sucks. We need deniability and Kayla is it. Get her back."

"Gabriel will reaquire her."

Foley moved uneasily. He'd only met Gabriel once. It had been enough. The man's eyes were empty.

Bertone smiled. "Gabriel is adept with many weapons. You would have liked the weapon he was carrying—a silenced Chinese pistol, absolutely untraceable. It's so rare that even the FBI's firearms library collection doesn't have one."

"Why didn't he use it?"

"He didn't have time. When the security guard charged in with a flashlight and a gun, Gabriel went over the fence and worked his way back around to the house."

"Does this guard know where she went?"

"I assume so. He went with her."

"Are you saying that she ran off with this guy?"

Bertone shrugged slightly. "It's possible. Other members of the guard detail say that the two have flirted in the past."

Foley thought of all the times Kayla had brushed him off when he tried to flirt. "I can't believe she'd go for some meaty rent-a-cop. Are you sure that's all there was going on?"

"Jimmy works for a private company that supplies our security under contract. The background check on him was quite thorough. He's just a good-looking ten-dollar-an-hour punk. She's probably screwing him or some other blue-collar stud while we speak."

"Well, hell."

Disgusted by Kayla's lack of taste, Foley threw the MP5A to his shoulder and emptied the rest of the twenty-round magazine into the target. Eleven rounds ripped the paper and disappeared into the downrange berm. Gaping holes opened in and around the silhouette's head.

Bertone watched without real interest. Then he tripped a switch and retrieved the paper target. He inspected the pattern from Foley's angry burst and shook his head.

"You're scattering your shot," Bertone said.

Foley tapped the three holes in the silhouetted head. "That's why machine guns were invented. It may not be real efficient, but it sure as hell gets the job done."

"I've sold tens of millions of bullets," Bertone said, his tone as jaded as his eyes. "I've sold tens of thousands of machine guns to fire them. I can assure you that one well-placed shot is worth a hundred badly aimed bullets."

"Tell it to your pet, Gabriel."

"He already knows."

"But he let her get away. Some hit man he is."

"He was told to acquire, not to kill."

"Why bother with grabbing her and hiding her?" Foley objected. "All it takes is one shot. I mean, Phoenix has plenty of drive-bys. Nobody would pay much attention to a random hit on the street. It would look like an accident. Hell, I could do it myself."

"You don't have what it takes to pull the trigger on a live target."

Behind his amber shooting glasses, Foley's narrowed eyes glared at Bertone.

"Somebody has to do it," Foley said. "If Kayla's still floating around out there, she could bring you down, and me with you."

"You, yes. Not me. I am a citizen of the world. In less than an hour I can be on a plane out of the United States, leaving a dozen lawyers to clean up behind me. Can you?"

Foley still had the gun in his hands, muzzle pointed toward the ceiling. He brought the barrel down slowly, letting the black eye of the muzzle slide past Bertone's mouth. The insult might or might not have been deliberate.

"I thought not," Bertone said, letting his contempt show.

"One way or another, you're vulnerable," Foley said, keeping the muzzle just barely away from Bertone's face.

Bertone pulled back his jacket, exposing the butt of a heavy black pistol that was stuffed into his belt without a holster. With smooth, easy motions he pulled the gun, pointed it at the spot between Foley's eyes, and slipped the safety.

Foley acted out of reflex, bringing the silenced muzzle of the MP5A to bear on Bertone's midsection. His finger curled around the trigger.

Too late Foley remembered the open bolt, the empty magazine.

Bertone smiled thinly. "Tell me again how equally vulnerable we are."

The silenced muzzle wavered, then sagged. Foley tried to focus on something other than the open eye of death staring at him.

"Fine," Foley said angrily. "As usual you have the upper hand. What's your plan?"

Bertone lowered the pistol, engaged the safety, and slipped the weapon back into his belt.

"We must find Kayla," Bertone said matter-of-factly. "I sent a man to the apartment she rented. No one was there. He went to the ranch she just sold. No one was there."

"Beautiful," Foley said sarcastically.

"She's a young woman of limited means and less imagination. She's probably still somewhere in Phoenix. Call in any markers you may have with the personnel department or whatever it's called nowadays."

"Human Resources," Foley said. "It's the weekend, but I can get to her files. I have remote access to the corporate computer."

"Find out whatever you can, her extracurricular activities, friends, boyfriends. We will find her."

"And then what?"

"Give her to Gabriel, of course."

"She doesn't have a boyfriend," Foley said. "At least, none has ever picked her up at work or taken her out to lunch. She has some friends in the private bank division. I can get you a list of names."

"Call them yourself," Bertone said.

"I don't think it would be a good idea for me to be too closely—"

"You're already in over your head," Bertone cut in. "Unless you want to take the responsibility for my correspondent account, find Kayla Shaw."

32

Royal Palms
Saturday
9:35 P.M. MST

Then Steve Foley," Kayla said to Grace, "told me to open a correspondent account with the transmitting overseas bank and deposit Bertone's check while Steve went to the CEO for advice on the Bertone account."

"Did you?" Grace asked.

"Yes."

"When?"

"Friday."

"What did the bank's CEO say?" Faroe asked.

"I haven't heard from Foley. Not one damn word." The look on Kayla's face said she was scared.

And angry.

"How long does it usually take for Mr. Foley to reach the CEO?" Grace asked.

"A phone call. At most, maybe an hour or two of phone tag. Foley is a golden boy at the bank."

Grace nodded, sipped lemonade, and said, "Tell me more about this correspondent account. How is it different from an ordinary account?"

Rand chewed a mouthful of cold cuts and listened. Grace had been a federal judge. She knew how to cut to the heart of the matter, but she could do it without pain if she liked the person.

So far, she'd been kid-gentle with Kayla.

He didn't know if that was good or bad. All he knew was that he'd warned Kayla. After that, the choices she made were hers. She was a woman fully grown.

And his palms itched for the feel of her skin.

"I'm no expert on correspondent accounts," Kayla said slowly. "My expertise is domestic rather than international banking."

Grace waited.

"Usually," Kayla said, "correspondent accounts are arranged on a bank-to-bank basis. Someone on the sixth floor had to walk me through the process."

"Why did your boss ask you to do something out of your usual area?" Faroe asked.

"Steve said that using a correspondent account would subject our bank to slightly different rules. In effect, it would shift responsibility for knowing about the customer's background from us to the transmitting institution. We could cash Bertone's check and still . . ." Kayla's mouth flattened.

"Have a defensible position if the feds came calling?" Grace suggested.

"That's my take," Kayla agreed. "But I'm small change in the banking world. What I see might not be what I think I see."

"I think you have excellent vision," Grace said.

"Whatever. The account worked. Too well, if you ask me."

"Meaning?" Faroe said.

Kayla's slender hand became a fist around the silver dollar. "When I checked the account yesterday afternoon, it had almost doubled since I deposited the first check."

Grace and Faroe looked at each other.

"How much money are we talking about?" Grace asked.

Kayla hesitated, then opened her palm. The silver dollar gleamed. "I'm not sure our 'prenup' covers information that specific."

Grace laughed.

"How about if we tell you?" Faroe said.

"Excuse me?" Kayla said.

Faroe went to the table that held the scrambled fax machine. He flipped through papers until he found what he wanted. "According to our figures, Bertone has transferred two separate sums to your bank. The transmitting bank was the Bank of Aruba on the island of Aruba. Total deposits were slightly less than forty-two million bucks, U.S."

Kayla swallowed hard, then nodded. "I guess you wasted your silver dollar. You don't need me."

All Grace said was, "Is that money still on deposit at your bank?"

"Last time I checked."

"Do you expect more deposits in the future?"

Kayla hesitated, then sighed. "Yes. Bertone said he'd make more, and quickly."

"When did that conversation take place?" Grace asked.

"Earlier this evening, just before—" Her voice broke at the memory of the shadow man, the garden, the knife.

"Just before he tried to have you removed from the scene," Grace said.

"Just before he tried to have her killed," Rand muttered.

"I like her version better," Kayla said.

"Putting lipstick on a pig doesn't change the oink factor," Faroe said.

Kayla made a tight sound that could have been laughter.

Faroe lowered himself to the couch next to Grace and asked, "On the paperwork that went into creating that new correspondent account, who is the responsible bank employee?"

Kayla closed her eyes. When she opened them, Faroe was watching her with something close to compassion.

"Me," she said bleakly. "My name is on the account. Everything will come back on me. God, I'm so screwed."

Faroe glanced at Grace. Both of them looked at the corner of the room, where a very discreet security camera recorded everything that happened.

The fax whined and spit out sheets of paper.

Faroe got up and retrieved them. He nodded to Grace. Then he turned to Kayla.

"If you'd disappeared tonight, like you were supposed to," Faroe said, "you'd have gone down for money laundering when that bank account was flagged by an auditor."

"But you didn't disappear," Grace said. "You didn't hop a plane for Ecuador or Uruguay. You're still here, still alive. If you let us, we'll make sure your side of the story gets told."

"I could get on a soapbox and sing arias for a grand jury," Kayla said bitterly, "but that wouldn't change the fact that it's my word against my golden-boy boss. Guess who comes out on the losing end of that scenario?"

"You're right, Rand," Faroe said. "She isn't as innocent as she looks. And thank God for it."

"Does that mean she's off your short list of suspects?" Rand asked.

"His what?" Kayla asked.

"My shit list," Faroe said. "We had to decide if you were a sacrificial lamb or a crooked banker taking bribes to launder millions of dollars in dirty money."

Kayla looked from Faroe to Rand.

"I disagreed all along," Rand said. "I knew the Siberian—Bertone. No one like you would have willingly gotten in bed with him."

"What you've told us meshes perfectly with what we already knew," Grace said.

"And your mental attitude is solid," said Faroe. "There aren't many young women—or men, for that matter—who could keep level with what's happened in the last forty-eight hours."

Kayla lifted her eyebrows.

And waited.

Grace smiled.

Faroe said something under his breath. Then he met Kayla's cool eyes. "We need you to get inside this mess and shut Bertone down."

Kayla flipped the silver dollar. "I thought this covered it."

"That's a bikini. You need a Mustang survival suit."

"What does a survival suit cost?"

"Sign on with St. Kilda Consulting."

"Told you," Rand said.

Faroe ignored him. "We'll give you cover, employment, and pay that equals the risk. It's the same agreement we sign with all our operators."

"If you sign on with St. Kilda," Grace said, "I doubt that American Southwest Bank would ever employ you again."

Kayla laughed abruptly. "Ya think?"

"But part of the deal is that St. Kilda would make sure you had legal coverage for any trouble the bank might want to make," Grace finished. "Your choice, Kayla."

"The bank is the least of my worries," Kayla said. "Andre Bertone isn't. What about him?"

Faroe gave an odd, elegant, exaggerated shrug, the kind Kayla had seen Mexican businessmen make in the middle of negotiations. It was sign language for *Que sera, sera.*

What will be, will be.

"We'll do everything we can to ensure your safety," Grace said.

"As long as it doesn't interfere with the assignment," Rand pointed out coldly.

"Back up," Faroe said to him. "Kayla isn't stupid. She knows she's at risk." He handed her the papers he'd just pulled out of the fax. "The ambassador agrees. If you want to work for St. Kilda Consulting, we're yours."

"Can you bring Bertone down?" Kayla asked.

"With you, I'm betting yes. Without you . . ." Faroe shrugged again.

Kayla looked at Rand.

He shoved his hands into his pockets and waited.

"So this was a recruitment from the instant I saw you at the party," she said to Rand. "You were told to hook me and reel me in so St. Kilda could look me over, decide if they trusted me."

"I never lied to you," Rand said.

"And if I don't sign up?"

"We'll give you a safe house while we go after Bertone," Faroe said.

"But without me, you won't have as good a chance of getting him."

Faroe nodded.

Oh, well, I guess I never really was cut out to be a banker anyway, Kayla thought. She read the fax pages quickly, then more slowly. With a rather grim smile, she took the pen Faroe offered her.

Move over, Alice. I'm coming down the rabbit hole.

She signed and handed the pen back to him.

"You can keep the silver dollar," Faroe said to her.

"I was planning to."

33

Royal Palms
Saturday
9:50 P.M. MST

Faroe shoved an unlabeled DVD into the TV player, handed the controller to Kayla, pointed to the pause button, and said, "Grace and I have to go wrestle with the Krebs cycle. Knock on the door if you have any questions Rand can't answer."

As Faroe and Grace left the room, a Scots-accented voice came from the TV speakers.

"My name is John Neto. I am an intelligence official employed by the government of Camgeria. My small country is in the heart of the conflict zone of equatorial West Africa."

The screen showed a montage of beautiful seacoast, vivid green jungles, wild scrubland, and slender, very dark people who looked into the camera with indifference or hostility.

"I've been there," Kayla said. "I spent a week trying to get a bus to Niger."

"There aren't any roads from there to Niger," Rand said.

"Yeah, well, I didn't speak the language. It took me a week to give up and take a Russian-made passenger plane flown by the most drunken pilot who ever got off the ground. Landing in Niger was . . . an experience."

"What did you think of Camgeria?"

"Amazing. Appalling. Yet so vivid in spite of the poverty. Smiles everywhere. Kids laughing."

"Have you seen it lately?"

"I read the papers and surf the Net," Kayla said.

And even if she hadn't, the images on the TV in front of her would have told her all she needed to know. Photos, headlines, web site content from Camgeria and other West African nations.

Armed insurrections, genocides, and refugee camps, all played against a backdrop of green and blue. And red.

Blood.

Agony.

Death.

Whoever had put the DVD together was a master of the PowerPoint presentation. Kayla felt herself drawn back to her youth, to a time when her world was wide open, when optimism was the rule rather than the exception, when all possibilities were equal. Camgeria had been a kind of paradise then. Now it was a kind of hell.

Maimed children.

Starving babies.

Mothers with empty eyes and breasts.

"God, such misery," Kayla said. "What happened?"

"Andre Bertone."

The TV showed a still color photo of a white man standing in the middle of a group of black men. Behind them was a dirt landing strip.

"East Camgeria?" she asked.

"You have a good eye."

"I spent a lot of time trying to get out of there," she said dryly.

A large twin-engine transport plane whose tail numbers had been painted over crouched on the dirt strip, props turning, dirt and grit flying. Shirtless black men carried off armloads of assault rifles from the cargo hold of the aircraft. In the foreground, another group of laborers stacked heavy, lumpy burlap bags.

"Coltan," Rand said before Kayla could ask. "It's vital for modern electronics. There's been a worldwide shortage of coltan for the last decade. Each of those bags holds fifty kilos. That would make them worth about five thousand dollars apiece."

Kayla stopped counting bags on the screen when she passed a quarter million dollars.

The camera zoomed in on the white man.

"That's Bertone!" Kayla said.

"Aka the Siberian," Rand agreed.

Bertone was wearing a white expedition suit he'd sweated through at the arms and back. Red dust clung to the wet places. He was smiling.

"Like a vulture at a carcass," Rand said.

"When I was backpacking, we called Bertone's costume a 'bwana suit.' He looks like he was born for it."

"A gunrunner in a bwana suit. As far as I know, this is the only photo that shows the Siberian in action."

"Why do you call him the Siberian?"

"A few years ago Bertone, aka Victor Krout, aka a lot of other names, was one of the most successful arms merchants in the world. He imported a quarter million small arms, twenty million rounds of ammunition, at least a million antipersonnel land mines, fifty thousand heavy machine guns, give or take, and numerous military vehicles, including at least a hundred armored personnel carriers and twenty decommissioned Soviet assault helicopters. All of it was used to attack native villages in four separate African countries."

"That's how he made his money? Running guns?" Kayla asked. "According to what he told the bank, he's an oil broker."

"He is, now. Before that he was the gasoline that turned centuries of smoldering ethnic and tribal conflict into a hellfire that killed thousands of innocent people. They're dead because Bertone poured a flood of modern military weapons into primitive tribal politics."

Rand started to say something more, then let John Neto's voice talk over the savage images.

"My people have been killing one another for a long time, yes, but Bertone and his ilk made it possible to murder with ruthless modern efficiency. The losses were horrifying. We were a primitive people delivered into the hands of modern warfare, warfare driven by gunrunning opportunists like Andre Bertone."

Kayla hit the pause button. "I thought diamonds were the bloody item of barter."

"Bertone took whatever was offered—exotic hardwoods, illegal ivory, minerals. His favorite was bargeloads of oil siphoned from government pipelines by rebel thieves." Rand smiled thinly. "He is one smart son of a bitch. When other arms runners demanded cash, he pioneered the barter economy. Really widened the killing field."

Before yesterday, Kayla wouldn't have believed it. Arms dealing in the upper crust of Phoenix? No way. That sort of thing was reserved for third-world outlaws.

She hit a button on the controller and continued her unhappy education.

"Bertone has a genius for turning a profit on a transaction with one group of combatants, then reinvesting that profit in more arms, which are then sold to the first customer's enemies."

The picture on the screen changed. No longer a voice-over, the camera pulled back to reveal Brent Thomas and John Neto.

"Yet today," Thomas said, *"Andre Bertone has UN diplomatic credentials and is a respected international oil dealer."*

"Yes. Enough money buys respectability. As we speak, Bertone is an intermediary for shiploads of Eastern European weapons that will be paid for with long-term oil concessions the Camgerian rebels will grant to oil companies owned by Brazil and France. Even your own government deals with Bertone for oil." Neto smiled thinly. *"Like gold or diamonds or dollars, oil can be laundered to hide its source. Andre Bertone is brilliant at just that. Oil-hungry governments, or*

governments wishing to arm the enemy of their enemy, are willing to overlook Camgerian deaths. We are a pawn in the larger global game.

"And we are being sacrificed."

More images of butchery, starvation, disease; vultures thick on the ground.

Kayla didn't want to believe it, didn't want to think she lived in a world where war was a commodity like any other.

And worse, that she'd handled blood money for the bloodiest butcher of all.

Rand grabbed the controller just before it dropped to the floor. He paused the DVD. "You okay?"

"No," she said. "I feel sick. Dirty."

"Bertone will do that to anyone with any decency in them."

She thought of the glitz and glamour of the Fast Draw, canapés paid for in children's blood, politicians paid for the same way, everyone lining up like cattle to be serviced by the merchant of death. It had happened only hours ago, hours that felt like days, months.

Another life she had lived in another time.

And now she had hit the bottom of the rabbit hole hard enough to break her soul.

Rand saw the tears streaming down Kayla's face and wanted to swear. Only the decent felt another's pain.

Only the decent could be corrupted. Only the decent could be made to feel dirty.

He didn't think about smart or stupid, should or shouldn't. He just gathered her into his arms, tucked her face against his shoulder, and held her. The hot silence of her tears reached him as nothing had since Reed's death.

"It's not your fault," he said, stroking her hair, kissing her eyelids gently, tasting her tears. "None of this is your fault."

"I helped him." Her voice was as bleak as her tears.

"You didn't know."

"I do now."

"I'm sorry," Rand said.

"It's not your fault."

"Isn't it?" he asked against her hair. "I brought you to St. Kilda."

"It's not St. Kilda's fault. They're just the messenger."

"Yeah, well, we all know what happens to messengers."

She smiled sadly at him, sighed, and took the controller back. But when she moved to separate from him, he held her close.

"I'm okay now," she said.

"I'm not."

She didn't know whether to laugh or cry some more. So she leaned against him and started the DVD again.

"How can you stop it?" Thomas asked seriously. *"You're a very small nation whose supposed allies are very close to Andre Bertone."*

"Camgeria and some of the other small African nations victimized by Bertone have come together to establish the West African Regional Tribunal."

"How will that help?"

"The tribunal is an investigatory body that is accumulating evidence against Bertone and his ilk. We will prove that the peoples of West Africa have been victimized by some of the most unscrupulous men on the face of the earth. Then world opinion will force that money to be returned to the people from whose blood and bone it was squeezed."

"That sounds like a huge job."

"It is. Interviews like this are just the beginning. We need help. We need friends. We need people who haven't been purchased by Andre Bertone."

The DVD ended with the stylized logo of the channel.

Kayla let out a long sigh, relieved that no more images of suffering would be burned into her conscience. "How did I miss this show? I'm a fan of *The World in One Hour.*"

"This segment is still in production," Rand said, tossing the controller aside. "It won't air at all unless we get more evidence against Andre Bertone."

"More? What I saw was devastating. Bwana-suited gunrunner becomes Phoenix socialite and benefactor to state, national, and international politicians."

"You and the guy who took that picture are the only ones on earth who can link Bertone to the bwana suit."

"You're kidding."

Rand looked at her.

"You're not," she said quickly. "I knew that. I just didn't want to know it."

She swiped the back of her hand against her eyelashes, taking the last of her tears, wondering if she'd really felt Rand's lips moving so gently over her skin.

"Pictures are powerful, but they can be Photoshopped," he said. "Anybody who saw President Bush supposedly giving the world the Roman salute knows all about digitizing photos."

She started to object, then sighed. "And the first thing Bertone's lawyers would scream is Photoshop."

"Yeah."

"So even if *The World in One Hour* airs that show, Bertone will still have deniability." Kayla's mouth turned down. "Like my bank, shifting the responsibility somewhere else."

"That's where you could help."

"How? After what Bertone did to me, I'm already compromised. And my boss. Let's not forget the golden bastard."

"I'd rather bury him," Rand said under his breath.

"What?"

"Your reputation will survive if *The World in One Hour* beats Bertone's lawyers to the press."

"Big if."

"Not as big as it was before you signed on with St. Kilda."

"How so?"

"Easy. Under the charter of the West African Regional Tribunal, Neto can seize any money, anywhere, that's connected to illegal activities. But first he has to know exactly where said dirty money is."

She got it. "Cue Bertone's private banker."

"Bingo."

34

Phoenix
Saturday
10:01 P.M. MST

The Jumping Cholla bar on Indian School Road was as close to home as it got for Gabriel Navarro. The taste of beer was mother's milk. Tequila was the sting of his father's hand across his mouth. The smoky air was a familiar blanket. Taverns, cantinas, blue-collar bars in white-trash neighborhoods, they were all places where men were men and any women present ran from soft hookers to hard pros.

When Gabriel had been a kid, men in his knee-breaking line of work had to hang out in beer bars and strip clubs and sports joints. If he was a regular, he could give clients the phone number and know that the bartender would put his calls through or take a message.

For a price.

Cell phones had really cut into a bartender's income. With his own phone, Gabriel was never more than a ring away from his clients, no bartender required. But he still liked to hang with his Phoenix homies in the bars north of downtown and west of Central Avenue. Despite his slight, ropy build, he didn't have to fight every night or every week to prove himself. The thought made him smile.

Here, everyone knows that Gabriel Navarro is a stone-cold motherfucker.

It had been three years since he'd killed anyone in the Jumping Cholla, and that hadn't been done to polish his reputation. The dude had needed to die. Gabriel had taken care of it.

The mixed clientele of the bar—Indian, Indio, Mexican, the odd gringo—reflected his own heritage. He could drink here and shoot eight-ball with the cross-eyed Cajun from Baton Rouge for a hundred bucks a game and nobody bothered him. Well, the bar girl asked every half hour if he wanted another schooner, but she always came close enough for him to grab her ass, so it wasn't really a hardship.

The last thing Gabriel expected to see as he chalked his cue stick was Andre Bertone walking in through the open back door.

Ay, chingón! *He has my cell number. What is he doing here?*

Immediately Bertone stepped into the shadows and stopped to size up the bar. He didn't have to take a deep breath to know what kind of place he was in. The mixed odors of tobacco, beer, male sweat, and a urinal more often missed than hit were familiar. By comparison to places he'd been in around the world, the Jumping Cholla was almost upscale. At least someone had tried to cover the urinal's stink with a pungent disinfectant.

Even if the bar hadn't been relatively genteel, Bertone wouldn't have worried. Once he'd delivered a million-dollar cash bribe to an African defense minister in a place far worse than this. Another time he'd shot to death a Bulgarian helicopter pilot who had hijacked a load of rocket-propelled grenades. Another time it was a knife and a fool who had tried to step on Bertone's shoes. Never had any of the bar patrons tried to stop Bertone.

If he decided that Gabriel had lied to him about the girl's escape, no one would stop the death Gabriel deserved.

The bartender spotted Bertone and made him as *wrong.*

Bertone almost smiled. Maybe it was his white silk shirt open at the throat, his heavy silk slacks, and his thousand-dollar loafers. Or a haircut that cost more than most men in the place cleared in a week.

With a sound like a pistol shot, the bartender slammed the heavy glass he'd been polishing on the bar.

Heads raised, looking first at the bartender, then in the direction of his eyes.

Gabriel didn't look up from the shot he was setting up at the pool table. "*Bienvenido* my house, *esso*," he called out in sliding, slurred English. "I thoug' I see you soon. But no here, *esso.* You 'ave good sources."

"I found you once a long time ago, Gabriel. After I have found you once, I can always find you again."

With that Bertone turned away and walked back through the door into the deeply shadowed parking lot.

To the surprise of every man in the room except himself, Gabriel racked his cue and walked toward the back door.

The Cajun had hair the color of chili colorado and a rough voice. "Hey, bro, you forfeitin'?"

"It's a draw, asshole," Gabriel said without looking back.

The Cajun didn't argue.

Gabriel found Bertone leaning against the gleaming black flank of his bulletproof Humvee, puffing on a cigar he'd just lit. A gold-plated Zippo gleamed in his thick fingers.

"Tell me what really happened," Bertone said.

"Like I told you," Gabriel said, shrugging. "Bitch had a knife. She opened it with one hand, like maybe she knew how to use it. You tell me no blood, so I hadda think. Then the fuckin' guard turned on the light. I figure I wait for a better time."

Bertone puffed on the cigar and watched Gabriel through the smoke. The man wasn't smart, he wasn't worldly; a primitive, really.

But a useful, ruthless one.

"So you climbed the wall and came back to the main house," Bertone said.

"Guard had a gun. If I don't book on out of there, he make a big noise you no like with all those fancy guests around."

"What happened to your gun and the rest of the gear?"

Gabriel's mouth opened, then closed without a word. He lit his own cigarette with a match scratched across the butt of his jeans.

"I got my own gun," he said finally. "I can use rope when I find her again."

"If you find her, you cretin." Bertone's voice was a lash.

"I know Phoenix. You watch the airport. I find her."

"You lost your gun, tape, and handcuffs. If she found them, she'll run to the police. If the guard found them, he didn't mention it to me, probably because I haven't seen the guard since Kayla disappeared."

Despite the cold fury of Bertone's voice, Gabriel forced himself to shrug. "You want I find the dude?"

"His name is Jimmy Hamm," Bertone said, stuffing a sheet of paper in Gabriel's hand. "This is his employment application form. It has his last known address. Find him. The girl may be with him. If she is, kill them both."

Gabriel shook out the sheet of paper and frowned.

"You do know how to read, don't you?" Bertone snarled.

"Yeah. Sure. Got my GED, no sweat." But some of the words were puzzling just the same.

Knives were much easier to use.

Bertone pushed into Gabriel's personal space. It was a silent threat. Both men knew it.

Gabriel took it.

Bertone slapped an envelope against Gabriel's chest. "Here are copies of the records in Kayla Shaw's employment file and the files of her closest friends at the bank. Don't bother to check her ranch or apartment again. She's not that stupid. Concentrate on the friends. Look for her car near their driveways, see if there are any signs of her inside their houses."

"Shit, man. I prowl a banker's house in the middle of the night and the cops come screaming."

"Use some of your homeboys," Bertone said, jerking his head toward the bar. "If they're surviving out of the joint, they must be good on the prowl."

He tossed a round cylinder into the air.

Faster than a cat, Gabriel's hand flashed out to catch the roll of fifty-dollar bills.

"Bring her to me," Bertone said.

"Breathing?"

Bertone opened the driver's door of the Humvee and looked across it at Gabriel.

"Find her, kill her, and bring me proof of death."

The door slammed and the big engine fired up. Bertone backed out quickly, then flipped on the bright headlights, spearing Gabriel. Bertone held that position for a few moments, making the hit man feel exposed, vulnerable.

"Chigna tu madre, cabrón," Gabriel said under his breath. "But maybe you don' even have a mother."

The Humvee rushed off into the night, leaving Gabriel standing alone with papers in one hand and a roll of fifties in the other. He stuffed Jimmy Hamm's address into the envelope, stashed it under his shirt, and went back into the Jumping Cholla.

Smiles flashed through the smoke when he started spreading money around.

35

Royal Palms
Saturday
10:40 P.M. MST

Kayla shook her head sharply.

How did I get myself into this?

Just when she thought her life couldn't get any more bizarre, she found herself getting dusted with face powder for an interview with a famous name she'd seen only on the news. He'd be the handsome star in suit and tie.

She'd be the talking silhouette.

A well-powdered one.

And her voice would be disguised.

Probably sounds like a frog on speed.

Ted Martin, who had been introduced to her as the field producer for the show, came over just as the woman called Freddie switched from powder to comb and scissors.

"Don't waste your time," Ted said to the woman. "She'll be backlit and shadowed."

"So was the dude," Freddie said without backing up. "If I hadn't trimmed him up, he'd have looked like a gorilla in silhouette."

Kayla wondered who "the dude" was. Then she glanced at Rand. He had a freshly barbered look.

"Him?" she asked Freddie, pointing toward Rand with her chin.

"Him. I took off about a foot of fur."

Kayla snickered.

"You have good hair," Freddie said. "Just need a brush and some gel so that nothing sticks out. If you weren't going in stealth mode, I'd put some more cold packs on your eyes. Crying is hell on 'em."

Martin made an impatient sound. "We're ready."

"I'm not," Freddie said. "And tell Mr. Gorgeous his nose is shiny."

"Do you know what overtime costs?"

"I know what I'm charging and I know what I'm doing. Get out of my face and let me work."

"How long?"

"Long enough for you to go over it once more with her."

Martin gave in and turned to Kayla. "Okay, no need to be nervous. This is only a fast interview so we have something for the files if the story breaks early. We can cut and paste and retake, redo the whole thing, whatever we need to so that you look good. Okay?"

Kayla didn't nod—Freddie was waving her scissors again.

"We'll feed you questions about Bertone, you answer, you get fed more, you answer more. Don't worry if you show that you're upset by what's happened to you," Martin added. "The more emotion, the better. Okay?"

"Not for her eyes," Freddie muttered as she worked gel into Kayla's hair.

"Get their hearts and their minds will follow," Martin shot back.

"Cry for the cameras?" Kayla asked.

"Okay, that'd be good."

"I'm not an actress."

"Yeah, I figured that out real fast," Martin said. Then to Freddie, "Two minutes or we'll start with you in the picture."

"I'll paint a happy face on my butt and moon you." Freddie winked at Kayla.

Martin walked over to where Faroe and Rand stood talking.

"Okay," Martin said. "What do you have new?"

"It's only been an hour since we briefed you," Faroe said. "You'll be the second to know if more comes in."

"I'd rather be the first."

Faroe wanted to roll his eyes like a girl.

Rand coughed instead of laughing. Then he looked at Kayla—and looked again. Something Freddie had done had transformed Kayla's hair from a sleek professional 'do to a wind-blown innocence that made her look about seventeen.

"You're good," he said to Freddie. "Too bad it will be wasted in silhouette."

"The hair won't be," Freddie said. "You watch."

Rand watched.

And learned.

He'd always known that news shows were as much staging—emotion—as news, but he hadn't really *known* until he saw the result when Kayla was put into the chair and backlit just enough to show her slender silhouette.

The innocent hair came through like a halo.

"Really good," Rand said, saluting Freddie.

"Quiet," Martin snapped.

Rand listened while Thomas joked Kayla out of her nerves, made her forget the camera, and led her through the small steps that had taken her right off the cliff of complicity.

"Oh, yes," Kayla said, "I was very pleased when my boss gave me the Bertones as my special clients."

"Special?" Martin asked. "How so?"

"I was their interface with the private banking arm of American Southwest. I kept their various accounts—personal and professional—moved money between accounts, that sort of thing. If they wanted anything that had to do with their money, they called me."

"And you found nothing unusual in those accounts?"

"No. They spent more than an average household, of course, but they earned far more than average."

"Didn't you wish you had that kind of money?" Thomas asked, his voice deep, sincere. "I would."

Kayla's teeth gleamed in a brief smile that shone through the shadows veiling her. "Nope. It's hard for people outside the banking business to understand, but when I handle a client's money, it's not real money, like the kind I pay my bills with. A client's money is just numbers I move from one account to another. Numbers, not dollars."

"So you didn't wish you had some of the Bertones' wealth?"

Slowly Kayla shook her head. "I have some money saved for a vacation, some money for retirement, I pay down my credit cards, that sort of thing. Real money. Real life."

Rand almost clapped.

Faroe leaned over and breathed into his ear, "She's good."

Shaking his head, Rand said very softly, "She's real. Thomas is good."

Martin glared at them.

Something in Faroe's jeans vibrated. He patted the pocket and headed back to his bungalow.

Rand wondered what had come unstuck, and where, but he stayed with Kayla even though she didn't need the moral support. He needed to give it. So he listened while Kayla's story and her life unraveled for the education and titillation of news groupies across America.

He barely looked up when Faroe let himself back into the bungalow that had become a stage set for *The World in One Hour.* Faroe went straight to Martin. Papers rustled as Faroe handed them over.

Martin started to complain.

And then he started to read. A minute later his head snapped up. "Okaaaay! Is this solid?"

"Like a rock," Faroe said.

"Christ." Grinning, Martin called over his shoulder. "Cut!"

Lights came on or went off. Everyone in the room looked over at Martin or began talking.

"What's up?" Thomas called over the noise.

"A wet dream come true." Martin walked over and shoved papers into the reporter's hands. "Read this."

Thomas read, then read again. "Is this—"

"Yes," Martin interrupted. "Use it."

Kayla shifted in the uncomfortable chair.

"Don't move," Martin said. "We're just getting to the good stuff."

"I'll take it from the sale of her childhood ranch," Thomas said.

Kayla flinched. She really didn't want to go through it again—the bittersweet, the simply sad, all the childhood memories tangled with adult necessities.

Rand saw the emotions crossing Kayla's expressive face and wanted to interfere. She'd been through the wringer enough. She needed a break before she broke.

"No," Faroe said softly, closing his hand over Rand's arm, holding him.

"Why not?"

"News is emotional, not rational. You know that as well as I do."

"She needs—shit," Rand hissed.

"Shit indeed. We can't change human nature, but we damn well can use it to our advantage."

"I'm sure that comforts Kayla no end."

"Grace made certain Kayla had the bathroom with the big Jacuzzi."

"Oh, well, that makes all the difference," Rand said sarcastically.

"Better than a kick in the ass with a frozen boot."

Martin began snapping out the commands that would once again make the bungalow a TV set. Lights dimmed. Others brightened.

Silence.

Then the sound of Thomas asking how Kayla had felt about selling her childhood home.

Then he asked about how she felt when she had that last breakfast with the Bertones.

How she felt when her boss told her to set up that account.

Emotions, Rand thought bitterly. *Screw the facts. How did you* feel*?*

And it was working. Kayla's voice was more hesitant, more husky, the voice of a woman fighting tears, fighting fear.

Thomas was sympathetic, relentless.

Brilliant.

Eat your heart out, Oprah, Rand thought. *That white boy can pluck heartstrings with the best of them.*

"Were you aware of the source of the money that was deposited in the Aruba account you set up?" Thomas asked.

"When I verified that the funds existed to be transferred to the correspondent account, I spoke to a young woman with a Jamaican kind of accent. She put me through to the president of the bank. His name was Mr. Thronged. He sounded Dutch and was very efficient."

"Mr. Thronged," Thomas said, glancing through the papers Martin had given him. "Did you know that the helpful woman with the lilting accent runs a small store at the north end of the island of Aruba? She makes a hundred dollars a week answering overseas phone calls like yours and putting them through to a retired Dutch banker—a Mr. Thronged—who conducts most of the Bank of Aruba, Sugar Sand branch, business from a phone and fax machine under the bar in his seaside tavern. The capital stock of the bank is all owned by Andre Bertone."

"I—are you sure?"

"Yes. I'm sorry. I can see that you're shocked."

Kayla fought the urge to put her face in her hands and wail. "All I was told was that knowing the source of the funds Bertone was transferring wasn't my problem—that is, my bank's problem. It was the problem of the bank in Aruba."

"Then you weren't aware that Andre Bertone emptied accounts that John Neto had located in Basel and in Liechtenstein, as well as a seventy-million-dollar account at the Bank of Sark in the Channel Islands?"

"No," Kayla said.

And even she wasn't sure whether she was answering a question or simply denying that she could have been so badly fooled.

Thomas tapped his finger on the papers Martin had handed him. "All told, Mr. Neto has traced more than two hundred and thirty million dollars that were wire-transferred into the Caribbean Basin."

"I—no," Kayla said huskily. "My God, no."

"The funds went to a variety of offshore accounts, all of which were shielded by bank secrecy acts in their various jurisdictions. Could Bertone be moving the funds through those secret accounts, then consolidating them in the branch bank of Sugar Sands, in order to funnel them here, into the United States?"

"A quarter of a billion—" Kayla's voice broke. "No. I haven't seen that kind of money."

"You've seen some of it," Martin said gently. "Haven't you?"

"I—"

"The money from arms trafficking, oil-for-food corruption, blood diamonds, ravaged hardwood forests, children starving, children maimed, children raped and dying, you've seen some of that money," Thomas said, his voice a sympathetic rapier slicing down into Kayla's soul. "Haven't you?"

The tears shining on Kayla's shadowed cheeks were her only answer.

"The master correspondent account you set up is nothing but a conduit for dirty money, isn't it?" Thomas asked sadly. "A conduit greased by hush money, bribes, and corrupt employees."

"I'm not one of them," she said hoarsely, her voice breaking. "I'm being set up by Andre Bertone. I didn't know where the money came from, someone tried to kidnap me, and all I did was try to follow the rules." She put her face in her hands. "My God, who will believe me now?"

Thomas let the silence stretch . . . and stretch . . . until the sound technician got the hint and turned up Kayla's mike. Soft, muffled sounds came from behind her hands.

"Cut," Martin said. "First-class work, Brent. That's it for tonight. Okaaay, who's ready for a beer?"

Faroe's grip shifted from Rand's wrist down to the fist he had made.

"Don't clock Martin," Faroe said. "He's on our side."

36

Royal Palms
Saturday
11:55 P.M. MST

Fragrant steam swirled around Kayla's head, making her feel even more like she'd been cut loose from reality and was spinning off into an alternate universe.

Nice try. Doesn't fly. There's only one reality, and I'm stuck up to my lips in it.

Bertone, dirty money, knives, and all the rest.

She nudged the controls. The jets shut off. The water slowly stilled. Fragrant steam still rose around Kayla's head.

Okay, some of my reality isn't bad.

Without meaning to, her thoughts went straight to Rand. When she'd looked up from her televised pity party, he'd been watching her with feral green eyes. The muscles on Faroe's arms had been rigid, as was Rand's fist in the other man's grip. After a few moments Rand had jerked himself free, gone to Kayla, and pulled her into his arms.

Normally she would have resented a man's protective hug, but not that time. She'd hung on to him like the safety line he was.

A very polite safety line.

He'd brought her to the luxurious two-suite bungalow, pointed out the Jacuzzi, and closed the door separating her suite from the shared living area. The door had made a soft, final click as it shut.

Followed by the sound of him going out the front door of the shared area and locking it behind him.

A gentleman.

Both of them knew her defenses were gone. If he'd wanted to make a pass, she'd have jumped to catch it. She was scared, ashamed, wrung out, and in need of comfort.

Well, the Jacuzzi is pretty damned comforting. And it doesn't need to be complimented on its performance.

So she lay there with relaxed muscles and her mind racing like a squirrel on speed.

Screw this. Any more hot water and they'll have to iron me before they put me on camera again.

She fiddled the stopper out with her foot, stood, and wrapped herself in a cushy robe that fell to the top of her toes and fingertips. The living area that separated the two suites was empty.

Kayla told herself she wasn't disappointed.

She went to the built-in bar and decided that whoever had researched her background was thorough—a bottle of Grand Marnier awaited her.

"Now I'm scared. Or I ought to be."

Mostly she was grateful.

She took a few cubes of ice from the bucket, dumped them in a squat whiskey glass, added a little water, and poured a splash of liqueur in on top. Sipping it, she fought the need to pace, to think.

To scream.

None of that will do me any good.

Take Rand's advice.

Relax, damn it!

She turned off the lights, closed the door of her suite behind her, and went to the bungalow's private, walled-in patio, which opened off the shared area. The flagstones underfoot were heated. The air was cool shading into cold. The water dancing in the triple fountains shut out other noises. As her eyes adjusted to darkness, she enjoyed the subtle flash and shift of moonlight over the fountains placed at intervals along the walls.

The front door opened, but the lights stayed off. Her heart hammered, then settled when she recognized Rand's wide-shouldered silhouette walking across the shared living area. She waited for him to knock on her suite door. Instead he bent and started to slide an envelope under the door.

"What are you doing?" she asked.

He straightened and spun toward her so quickly that she flinched. She didn't feel any better when moonlight flashed off the gun in his hand. Before she could blink, he holstered the gun at the small of his back and walked toward the patio.

"You scared the crap out of me," he said.

"Same here. Anyone ever mention that you have fast hands?"

"Once or twice." His smile gleamed. "What are you doing out here in the dark?"

"Trying to relax."

"How's that working for you?"

"Lousy." Ice clinked as she lifted the whiskey glass to her lips.

"I see you found the Grand Marnier."

She saluted him with the glass. "Who do I thank for it?"

"Grace, probably. She's the one who made sure you had the suite with the Jacuzzi." *And the fountains turned on hard enough to thwart eavesdroppers. But still . . .*

"I'll share."

"The Jacuzzi?" he asked, startled and intrigued.

"That, too. But I meant the liqueur." She took another sip. "What's in the envelope?"

"Walking-around money."

She blinked slowly. "Excuse me?"

"Come inside, where we can talk."

Reluctantly she went back inside and slid the patio door shut behind her.

Rand checked the electronic device Faroe had fastened to the door, saw the green status light, locked the door, and went to Kayla.

"Take it," he said, holding out the envelope. "So you don't have to use your credit cards or bank account."

She took the envelope, surprised by its thickness. "Thanks."

"All part of the St. Kilda service. You'd better count it. There should be five grand."

"Five thousand dollars? Are you kidding?"

"No." He reached for the whiskey glass she was waving around. "I'll get you some more."

"What am I supposed to do with that?"

"Drink it."

"The money," she shot back. "Five thousand dollars!"

"It's the standard St. Kilda Consulting advance for an agent in the field. You run out before next week, you have to submit a requisition detailing why you need extra cash."

Usually for bribes, but I don't think she wants to hear about that right now.

"Room and board comes out of this?" Kayla asked.

"Not if you stay here." He headed for the bar.

She hefted the envelope in her hand. "First Bertone buys my land for too much money. Now St. Kilda is giving me a five-thousand-dollar gift, with more to come next week. Gee, I'm beginning to feel . . ."

"Special?"

"Hunted."

"I always knew you were smart." Ice clinked, followed by the soft splash of liqueur. "It's not a bribe, Kayla. Money is a tool. St. Kilda doesn't want an agent to screw up because he or she didn't have the cash for a plane ticket on the run."

"Um," was all she said.

Rand appeared in front of her, holding out the cut-crystal glass. It was half full.

"If I drink all that, I'll crash," she said, eyeing the glass.

"I'll help you."

"Crash?"

"Drink."

"Good idea." She took a healthy sip, cleared her throat twice, and looked at him from beneath dark eyelashes. "Whew. I usually add water."

"Ice melts. Same thing."

"Why didn't I think of that?"

He took the glass from her fingers, sipped, and said, "Sweet. With a bite."

"Better than beer—sour with a bite."

He laughed softly and told himself to turn around and go to his suite and stop thinking about what he shouldn't be thinking about.

Kayla, naked.

"How do you feel about single malt?" he asked.

"Scotch?"

"Yeah."

"Smells better than it tastes."

He laughed. "I had a buddy once who said he wanted to die of Glenmorangie."

"Did he?"

"Still working on it, last I heard."

"You sound like you envy him," Kayla said.

When Rand didn't answer immediately, she realized that he was watching her. Or to be precise, watching the triangle of skin revealed by the robe. Heat that had nothing to do with her recent bath flushed her skin. She shrugged the robe more closely around her.

"I might have envied him, once," Rand said. "I'm older now." *A lot older. Too old to be thinking with my dick.*

But there it was, ready, willing, and begging to think for him.

He turned and headed back to the bar.

"Now what?" she asked, settling into a chair.

"I want more bite."

She was about to offer her teeth on his skin when she heard him crack the seal on a whiskey bottle and pour it into the glass. No ice followed.

Knowing St. Kilda, she bet the brand was single malt, Glenmorangie.

"No ice?" she said. "No water?"

"Neat."

The pungent scent of the single malt rose to her nostrils as he settled in a chair near her.

Rand raised his glass, then looked at her. "What shall we drink to?"

"After today, let's drink to innocence. The few shreds of it left in the world ought to be celebrated."

"To innocence," he said, clinking his glass lightly against hers. "Honored in the absence."

"How did you lose yours?" she asked, sipping.

"The usual way. Backseat of a car."

She choked, let him whack her on the back, and then waved him off. "I wasn't talking about sexual innocence," she said.

"I'm not sure I ever was *that* innocent. I was raised by a half-Tlingit grandmother whose own mother had been stolen as a slave. My father was a commercial salmon fisherman in the San Juans and in Alaska. He was gone half the year. My mother was an artist from Seattle who was gone as much as she was home. From what I saw, it was an open marriage. That's what they're calling it now, right? Not infidelity, or adultery, or cheating, just mutual understanding of needs and being sure not to bring anything home but memories."

The coolness in his voice made Kayla flinch. "That's a fair load of sophistication, or something, for a kid to be exposed to."

"It was home." *And Reed was always there, ready to laugh or fight or hide, whatever was needed.*

Rand sipped his whiskey, letting the smoky fire spread across his tongue. Every nerve in his body was on alert. Every sense honed to a fighting edge. Or fucking. He'd take either right now. Anything to push back the intimacy stealing over him, the scent of the woman next to him, her voice soft in the darkness, her skin pale, inviting.

"Any sibs?" she asked.

"Younger brother. By twelve minutes."

"Identical?"

"Like peas in a pod. Reed always said he was better looking. People always said I was smarter." *They were wrong.*

He let the hot, snarling kiss of scotch spread over his tongue, swallowed, sipped some more. He knew it wouldn't stop the memories, but it might just blunt the sharpest edges.

"Identical twins," Kayla said, grinning. "That must be great."

"It was." Rand let more whiskey bite his tongue, spread fire.

"You don't get along?"

"He's dead."

The fountains laughed liquidly in the silence.

"I'm sorry," Kayla said. "I can't imagine—"

"You don't want to."

She closed her eyes. The neutrality of his voice told her more than any words; his twin's loss was still an open wound on his soul.

Silently Rand watched a feral cat slide from shadow to shadow, hunting rodents in the exclusive resort's carefully tended gardens.

Good hunting, buddy. The world needs less rats.

Kayla knew she should let the subject go. And she knew she wouldn't. Rand interested her in too many ways, on too many levels.

"When?" she asked simply.

"Five years ago. In Africa."

She remembered scraps of information that Faroe had given her. Goose bumps rose along her arms. "The man in the bwana suit?"

"Yeah. Only we knew him as the Siberian. I was the photographer. Reed was the rifle. One of us gave away our position. The Siberian shot Reed, then sent the army after us. I survived. Reed didn't."

He sipped the drink again and was surprised to find it half gone. *Slow down, fool.* He set the drink on a small glass end table and shifted his shoulders. At least the knots were looser. A little.

"That's how St. Kilda got to you," Kayla said. "They dangled a chance to get Bertone."

"Pretty much."

"So St. Kilda hires assassins?"

"No. They want Bertone alive. Dead broke, but not dead."

"What about you?"

"Dead. Period."

37

Royal Palms
Sunday
12:15 A.M. MST

Kayla drew a deep breath, then let it out slowly, telling herself that Rand didn't really mean his words literally.

Knowing that he did.

"When I was in college, my parents died in a small-plane crash in the interior of Alaska," she said finally.

Rand nodded.

"You knew that already," she said. "It was in that damned file."

He nodded again and said, "Just like I know that kind of loss rips out a chunk of your soul that's never replaced."

"You get used to it. The pain." She grimaced and set aside her drink. "That sounded way too close to another pity party. What I meant is that you get past it, you get used to the new reality, and you get on with your life. But then, you already know that."

Not really. I'm still learning.

Then Rand realized that he'd spoken the words aloud. He twirled his glass on the side table set between the two chairs. The faint sound, glass on glass, was impatient. *After Bertone is dead, I'll . . .*

Yeah, fool. What then? Will you finally get your act together? Or will you still feel like you're on the outside of life, looking in?

Half dead and the other half lonely as death.

Kayla's silence finally registered. When he looked at her, he could see unshed tears magnifying her eyes.

"Don't," he said roughly. "It was five years ago."

"Not to you. To you it's here and now and as new as your next heartbeat."

"My problem, not yours."

"Yesterday you'd have been right."

Something in her voice caught him. "And today?" he asked.

"Today I know that I could die between one heartbeat and the next. I *know* it. I don't want to die regretting any more than I have to."

He waited, telling himself that she wasn't saying what he hoped she was.

She put her glass next to his, stood, and held out her hand. "I want you. I believe you want me."

He came to his feet like a hunting cat. "You know I do."

She smiled. "I know you make me feel . . . glittery, hot, different than I've ever felt with a man."

"It's called adrenaline."

"It's called lust. I've never felt it before." She smiled. "I like it."

He pulled her close, licked her lips, tasted tears and liqueur. "So do I." Then, reluctantly, he straightened. "Are you sure?"

One of her hands lifted from his shoulder, smoothed down his chest, and slid over the front of his jeans. "Oh, yeah. I'm sure. And you're interested."

His breath stopped as she stroked him through the denim. The humming sound of pleasure she made as she measured him just about brought him to his knees.

"What do you have on underneath that robe?" he asked roughly.

"Me."

His breath hissed out. "Bedroom. Now."

She looked over at the lounge waiting against the side of the patio.

"No," he said. "Too many guards. The fountains can't drown out the kind of sex I want with you."

"I forgot where I was." She made a ragged sound. "Sorry."

He felt the heat climbing her cheeks and wanted to howl. "So am I. So I'll take a rain check on sex beneath the stars."

Before Kayla could decide on an answer, a sweep of Rand's arms yanked the patio drapes closed.

A night-light glowed like a candle on the bar.

"I'll try to make it good for you," he said against her neck, "but it's been way too long for me."

"For a guy, two hours ago is too long."

He gave a crack of laughter and pulled her closer, tugged at her lapel, and finally had a chance to taste the maddening tattoo that had been playing peek-a-boo with her robe.

"This has been driving me crazy," he said against her skin.

She shivered. "The tattoo?"

"Yeah. I wanted to lick it the first time I saw it."

"Then I'm glad I have two more."

"Where?"

"One follows me everywhere."

"Show me."

Kayla pointed to her left hip.

He licked his lips. "Show me."

"You mean . . ." Her hands went to the bow she'd tied in the robe's sash.

"Yeah. Strip."

"You first."

He toed out of his shoes while his fingers yanked at shirt buttons. It was way too hot in here for clothes anyway.

"Jeans," he said huskily. "I've got something in my pocket."

She rolled her eyes. "I haven't fallen for that one since I was in second grade."

Rand laughed despite the need hammering in his veins. He wanted to think it was because it had been too long since he'd buried himself in a woman, but he didn't believe it. Something about Kayla just flat turned him on.

"Unless you want to go commando," he said, shrugging out of his shirt, "you'd better get in my pocket."

"Commando?"

"Bare." His hands were on his fly. "As in no condom."

Her hands dove into the hip pockets of his jeans. She searched, squeezed. Nothing but hard man muscle.

"You're killing me," he said, watching her smile.

She moved to his front pockets. Searched, squeezed. More hard man muscle. Very hard.

He groaned. "You're a tease. Do it again."

Finally she pulled her hands out of his pockets. Foil packets gleamed. In one impatient motion he pulled off his jeans and underwear and reached for her.

Condoms scattered from her fingers as he stripped her robe off, turned her around, and fastened his mouth on her second tattoo. He bit gently, then not quite gently, felt her shiver.

"I never knew I had a thing for tattoos," he said, "until I saw yours."

"You'll love my third one," she said, her voice husky.

"Where is it?"

She turned, showed him.

He whispered something, bent his head, and licked. Sucked. Nibbled. Sucked harder.

She tried to breathe, but there wasn't enough air in the room. The tension that had been drawing her tight, achingly tight, tighter—suddenly snapped, sent her spinning, crying, heat exploding.

Rand felt her release, tasted it, and shuddered. He barely remembered to sheathe himself in the condom before he sheathed himself in her.

She was everything he'd been afraid she would be.

Perfect.

Tight.

Hot.

For the first time since his twin's death, he let go of hate and allowed himself to live.

38

Royal Palms
Sunday
6:15 A.M. MST

Fully dressed, Rand sat beside the bed and watched Kayla sleep, telling himself how many kinds of fool he was. The problem was that he couldn't decide whether he was a fool for letting himself love her last night or if he was a fool because he wasn't in bed with her now.

I'm sorry, Reed.

When Rand heard his own thought, he was shocked. Was he really feeling guilty because Reed was dead and he was alive?

Got that in one, fool.

He didn't know if it was his own voice or Reed's that pitied him.

After I kill Bertone, then I'll . . .

Then what? Reed would come back from the dead? Rand would be alive again?

I was alive last night.

And guilty as hell for it this morning.

Rand set his teeth and told himself he was a fool.

Big news flash that was.

Sunlight slid through a crack in the drapes and spread across the bed, across Kayla, highlighting the rose tattoo on her collarbone. He'd been with other women since Reed's death, but he'd never felt guilty about it. Why Kayla? What was it about her that made him want . . . too much?

That's easy, bro. She makes you feel alive.

Rand went stiff. *Reed?*

About time, too. I told you to live for both of us. One of us dead is plenty. Kayla is good for you. Don't fuck it up and blame it on me.

Before Rand could move, could think, he realized that Kayla's eyes were open, slowly focusing on him.

"Who was here?" she asked sleepily.

"Just me."

"No. Someone else." She yawned. "Like you, but different." Her eyelashes lowered, stayed down. " 'S too early to get up." She sighed, pulled the covers up over her shoulders.

"Go back to sleep," Rand said softly.

One eye opened. "What about you?"

"If I get in bed, neither one of us will sleep."

"You say that like it's a bad thing. Or are we out of condoms?"

He smiled in spite of himself as he remembered the hours before they fell asleep. "Getting there."

"No wonder they gave you five thousand dollars." She yawned again. "Condoms aren't cheap."

Rand laughed out loud. It felt so good that he did it again.

"Are you laughing at me?" she asked around another yawn.

"No, at me," he said.

He took off his shoes and stretched out next to her on top of the bed. She turned toward him. She smelled of bath oil and sex and sleepy woman. He pulled a bundle of covers and her against his body.

"Go back to sleep," he said against her forehead. "I kept you up too long last night."

"Huh. I thought I was the one keeping you up."

"Sleep, Kayla."

She tried to, but it didn't work. She was awake enough to remember all the reasons she shouldn't be relaxed.

Bertone.

Handcuffs.

Dirty money.

Her name on the bottom line.

"Well, damn," she said against Rand's chin.

"What?" he asked.

"I'm awake."

"Hungry?"

"Yeah."

"I'll call room service."

"Food?" she said, nibbling on his chin, tugging on his beard with her lips.

"Not many calories in a beard," he said dryly.

"Mmmm, the Beard Diet. Works for me. Nibble the pounds away."

"You don't need to lose weight. In fact, some more weight would look good on you."

"More? Yowsa. Now I know I'm in love."

Rand didn't fight the laughter crowding his throat. He just let it go and enjoyed.

She snuggled closer. "Yesterday I felt like I was in a combat zone. Today I feel ten feet tall."

"Life is a combat zone. That's why you have to take love where and when you find it. But I'd forgotten about that until last night. You aren't sorry, are you? I know you're not the one-night-stand type."

"Couldn't prove it by me," she mumbled, flushing.

"I read your file."

"When do I get to read yours?"

"What do you want to know?"

Everything. Nothing in particular. "Is this a one-night stand?" she asked.

"I've been wondering the same thing," he said. "You know, don't you? You knew last night when you held out your hand to me."

"What did I know?"

"I'm going to kill Andre Bertone."

She looked at Rand's eyes, sage green and clear. Cold.

"I knew," she said. "I saw it at the party."

"You didn't let it stop you last night."

It wasn't a question, not quite, but it was close enough that she answered.

"You haven't killed him yet," she said.

"And when I do?"

Silence came, grew, and vanished into a sigh. "I don't know. I'd like to kill Bertone myself. I thought about doing it. A way out of this mess, you know?"

Rand nodded and watched her like a feral cat.

"It wasn't so much a thought," Kayla said, "as a bone-deep desire to wipe him off the face of the earth. For the first time in my life I understood how someone could be driven to kill."

"If you back a mouse into a corner, it will try to rip your throat out. And you're no mouse."

She let out a long breath. "Were you and Reed working for St. Kilda when he died?"

"Sort of. The Camgerian government was paying, but we were hired through St. Kilda, though we didn't know it at the time."

"You were soldiers?"

"As in mercenaries?"

She grimaced. "I guess."

"No. We were hired to train Camgerians to use the kind of arms that would give them a chance against the ivory poachers who were destroying the elephant herds. We were also trying to teach Camgerians management techniques for their game preserves. So officially we were members of an international wildlife conservation group helping the locals to protect and manage their valuable resources. Unofficially . . ." His voice faded.

"What?"

"The poachers were all rebels bent on overthrowing the government. Ivory, oil, coltan, hardwood, whatever would sell, they stole it and got arms in return, AK-47s and RPGs."

"Bertone."

"Krout, the Siberian, Bertone. All the same man."

"So you were training men to fight the rebels."

"In a side-door kind of way, yes. Back then Reed and I were young enough to be idealists and smart enough to know that idealism is a young man's game. We didn't think of ourselves as starry-eyed virgins, but we were." Rand's mouth flattened. "We believed that the good guys always win in the end."

Kayla bit her lip and didn't ask any more.

Rand kept on talking. "We thought we'd seen it all. We hadn't. Somebody once described Africa as a place where anything that can be done by a gun has been done there. Faroe knew that."

"Joe Faroe was over there, too?"

"Through St. Kilda, Faroe was working an operation on behalf of an American NGO, trying to discourage the arms trade. Reed thought Faroe was the greatest man he'd ever known, smart, tough, resourceful. I wasn't quite as charmed. I kept telling Reed that Faroe could get us in trouble."

"Did he?"

"No, hell no. We did it all by ourselves. Our training gig was up, but we both were sick of seeing what the arms trade was doing to Africa. We talked to Faroe. St. Kilda hired us to gather information on Krout/Bertone and his operation. To shut the bastard down."

Kayla's hand touched Rand's cheek, stroked lightly above the soft beard. "It was a job worth doing."

"Intellectually, no argument. But my gut doesn't think that Reed's death was worth it, no matter how many others might have survived because of what we did. His death was goddamned real. The lives he saved . . ." Rand shrugged. "Not real enough."

"So you set out to get proof that the Siberian was a gunrunner," she said, luring Rand away from his bleak thoughts.

"Reed and I figured out the Siberian's smuggling network, his cutouts, who took his bribes. We wrote down the tail numbers on all his planes, documented the arms he was delivering. But none of that was quite enough. We needed solid, undeniable proof to nail the Siberian's ass. Reed got wind of a planeload of arms coming in. We went to the dirt strip, built a blind, and waited."

"Did the plane come?"

"Yeah. The pilot was either certifiable or clanged when he walked. I got it all—the plane, the waiting rebels, the cargo off-loaded, the coltan loaded in return. Even the bag of diamonds passed directly to the Siberian. Then it all went from sugar to shit."

Kayla waited, not sure she wanted to know, but certain she should.

"The sun moves real fast in that part of the world. Either my lens caught it, or Reed's binoculars. The Siberian picked up a sniper's rifle and drilled Reed. I grabbed Reed and an assault rifle and took off for the Rover. I drove us to the helicopter that was waiting. Before we could take off, a rebel helicopter strafed us. I brought it down, but it was too late. Too fucking late. I buried Reed in the savanna he loved." Rand met Kayla's eyes and said, "I'll bury Bertone, too."

"What if you bury yourself?"

"Then Reed won't be alone anymore. Win-win." *At least, it had been until last night.*

"Well, you're honest," Kayla said, shoving the covers aside. "One-night stand it is."

"What are you talking about?"

"You love Reed more than you love your own life." She began dressing with short, sharp motions. "Sorry if I diverted you from your hair-shirt shrine."

"I told you I wouldn't lie to you. Bertone needs killing."

"You aren't a murderer."

"You don't know me very well."

"You don't know yourself very well," she retorted, pulling on a T-shirt. "You don't understand what it will cost you to drop Bertone in cold blood."

"Obviously it will cost me you," Rand said.

"It will cost you *yourself.* But then you don't care about that, do you? You hate yourself for living when Reed didn't."

“Kayla—”

A shadow showed against the bedroom curtains. Rand shot to his feet and lifted the curtain aside just enough to look out.

Three men with drawn pistols were charging the St. Kilda compound from the direction of the golf course. Brakes shrieked as two cars and a pale green van blocked the driveway and parking areas.

“Shit! We’ve got to—” Rand said.

The blare of loudspeakers shut out the rest of his words. “EVERYONE STAY PUT! THIS IS A FEDERAL RAID!”

Rand went through the bungalow at a run, checking that locks and bolts were in place.

“What should we do?” Kayla asked.

“Stay out of sight until we’re told otherwise.”

39

Royal Palms
Sunday
6:25 A.M. MST

"Get that camera crew awake and shooting *now*," Faroe snarled into the telephone.

"Okay, I'm on it," Martin said. "You want us in the open?"

"Whatever it takes to get sound and action."

Faroe hung up and went out the front door, shutting it behind him. He met the raiding party on the front stoop of the bungalow. The lead agent, a heavyset man in a dark green Border Patrol uniform shirt, carried a pistol at high port arms.

"What the hell is this?" Faroe demanded.

The next bungalow's door opened silently. A camera lens poked out the partly open door, as did a directional mike.

The agent saw only the tall, hard-looking man blocking the door of the bungalow he'd been ordered to search.

"Out of the way, sir," the agent said. "We're conducting an immigration employment verification action of this establishment."

Faroe pointed toward the resort's main building. "Well, shit howdy, cowboy, the kitchen is over there and the groundskeeper headquarters are about a quarter mile back the way you came from."

"Stand aside, sir."

"This is a private room," Faroe said distinctly. "Nobody here is undocumented."

"Get out of the way, *sir*," the agent barked, "or you will be subject to arrest."

Behind Faroe the door opened. Grace stood there, tying a red silk robe over the mound of her pregnancy.

"No, he won't step aside, Officer." Her voice had the snap of a judge used to ruling a courtroom—and the cops in it. Her dark eyes went to the officer's name tag. "Agent Morehouse, you're very close to overstepping whatever authority you believe you have."

"Pardon me, ma'am, but who the hell are you to question my authority?"

"My name is Grace Silva Faroe," she said. "I retired six months ago as a federal judge in the Southern District of California. That district includes San Diego, a place where the Border Patrol was and is very active."

"I know what the Southern District is," Morehouse said curtly. "Step aside, both of you. Now."

"Not yet," Grace said, each word distinct. "You need a specific warrant to enter private residences. Under the law, rented hotel rooms have the same privileges and protections as private residences." She held out her hand. "I'll see the warrant, please."

"We have information that a specific individual may be in this bungalow and that said individual is in the country illegally," Morehouse said.

Faroe hadn't budged from his place at the top of the three steps leading to the bungalow. Morehouse couldn't go forward unless he went through Faroe and the pregnant lady.

Agents piled up behind Morehouse.

"Ma'am—" Morehouse began.

"If you had specific information," Grace cut across him calmly, "you should have applied for a warrant. Who is this specific individual, anyway? He must be important." She flicked a glance at the men behind Morehouse. "And dangerous."

With a muttered word, Morehouse pulled a notebook from his hip pocket. Command presence sure wasn't making a dent in the couple in front of him. Maybe a show of cooperation would get the job done.

"The name is John Neto," Morehouse said. "He's a Camgerian alien who, according to our information, entered the country illegally from Victoria, Canada, on a tourist visa."

Faroe and Grace traded looks.

"That's specific information, all right," Grace said. She shut the door and walked two steps to the porch railing, where she looked down at the milling of agents. "And obviously this Neto is an extremely dangerous man. Otherwise the immigration service wouldn't have sent all these men." She looked out at the grounds. "I count eight men in five vehicles. That's a tremendous show of force," she said, turning back to pin Morehouse with cold black eyes, "particularly here in Phoenix, where I'd guess one person in six entered from Mexico without papers."

Morehouse sighed. He'd known the minute he picked up his orders—and enough men for a baseball team—that this assignment stank. Now he had a hard-case male and a pregnant woman in his face before he'd even had two cups of coffee.

"Ma'am, I have my orders. Just stand aside and we'll be in and out real quick."

"Where did these orders come from?" Grace asked.

"The district director," Morehouse said. "Ma'am—"

"At seven o'clock on a Sunday morning?" Grace interrupted.

"He said it was a top Homeland Security priority. Now, if you'd just—"

"Orders? From Washington?" she asked, pitching her voice to carry to the mike next door.

"I don't know," Morehouse said impatiently. "I just take orders."

Faroe made certain that none of his amusement showed. He'd worked with men like Morehouse—decent, steady, unimaginative.

Grace would make pâté out of him.

"I understand, Officer," she said sympathetically. "And we certainly don't want to impede a legitimate federal investigation. If you'd give me a telephone number for the district director, I'll discuss paperwork with him."

Morehouse said something under his breath. "Tell you what, ma'am. We'll come in and check, and you can talk to the director later. It'll be a lot easier that way."

"It might be a lot easier if I signed a permanent waiver of my Fifth Amendment rights," Grace said. "That would hardly be good for America, would it? But never mind about the number. Senator Miller's chief legislative aide is a good friend. I'm sure Jerry will have your director's number."

Morehouse looked at her and knew it was going to be a bad day.

"You aren't getting inside without paperwork," Faroe said. "Court order, warrant, or the phone number. Your choice."

The line of Morehouse's mouth said he wasn't happy.

"Take it from me," Faroe said, "this woman eats badges every day and spits out itty-bitty staples."

Morehouse knew a political impasse when it was shoved down his throat. He told Faroe the phone number. Grace went inside, closing the door behind her.

Faroe peered into the morning sunlight and almost winced. Summer was more than a promise in that Phoenix sun. It was a threat.

"I'm getting a cup of coffee," Faroe said, turning away from Morehouse.

Morehouse grabbed Faroe's arm. "Where do you think you're going?"

"I just told you. You want a cup?" He looked at the agent's belly. "Double cream and sugar, right?"

The agent's fingers dug into Faroe's arm. "You and your lady are impeding federal officers, and I'm getting sick of it. We'll have a little respect around here or somebody's going to jail. Now break out some ID."

"I don't need any."

"You need ID if I say you do," Morehouse snarled. Over his shoulder, he said to one of his men, "Cuff this clown. Sack him up."

"What's the charge?" Faroe asked.

"No ID," Morehouse shot back. "I think you look illegal, and I'm taking you in until I'm sure you're a citizen in good standing."

Faroe's smile was a knife sliding out of a sheath. "I once carried a badge pretty much like yours. Like you, I tried to bootstrap a disagreement with a suspect into an immigration violation."

Unwillingly, Morehouse eased his grip. "So?"

"I knew the guy was a citizen," Faroe said, "just like you know I'm a citizen. I even knew that a citizen is under no affirmative obligation to prove his status, so long as he is already here on U.S. soil. But I went ahead and sacked him up anyway."

"Hooray for you," Morehouse muttered.

"I did a year in federal prison for a civil rights violation," Faroe said pleasantly. "Back off, or you'll do the same."

Morehouse stared at Faroe for a long five-count, then released his arm.

"Friggin' lawyers all over the place," Morehouse said under his breath.

Grace emerged from the bungalow, carrying a cell phone. She held it out to Morehouse.

"It's your boss," she said.

Morehouse looked at the phone like it was a snake, then took it and held it to his ear.

"Yeah, this is Morehouse." He listened, grunted, listened some more, grunted, and sighed. Then he handed the phone back to Grace. "He wants to talk to you again."

Grace held a short, crisp conversation with the bureaucrat at the other end, thanked him, and hung up.

"Will there be anything else, Officer?" she asked pointedly.

"No. Sorry about the bother. Ma'am." Teeth clenched, Morehouse turned and waved his men back to their vehicles.

Thirty seconds later there wasn't an agent in sight.

"Nice job," Faroe said, nuzzling Grace's cheek. "Did you pick up anything useful from the director?"

"He was as confused as Agent Morehouse." She frowned. "He said they were acting on information directly from Washington, but he wouldn't tell me from where inside the Beltway."

"Must have been a hot call to get those boys out at the crack of dawn on a Sunday. Good thing you convinced Neto to stay in B.C."

"Which the agents must have known," Grace said. "Undoubtedly they have someone watching him. Maybe they lost him."

"Or maybe they were after us all along," Faroe said.

"An intelligence-gathering raid?"

"Probably," Faroe said. "They can't get to Neto, so they'll settle for identifying and interrogating the rest of us. How'd you get rid of Morehouse?"

"I told the director he was being used as a political cat's-paw. No enforcement agent ever likes that idea. I also told him not to send anyone back without specific and narrowly defined search warrants."

Faroe grunted. "They might get them."

"They know me, and they know St. Kilda Consulting's lawyers. It will take time." She grimaced. "I should know. I'm still trying to shake a warrant out of a judge to freeze Bertone's accounts."

Faroe looked toward the resort grounds. "Even if it takes time, we're suddenly hotter than a flat rock in July."

"You think they left someone behind?" Grace asked, looking around the grounds.

"I'll bet the place is crawling with plainclothes playing tennis or golf—with long lenses," Faroe said, pulling her inside and locking the door behind them.

"We have to keep Kayla off the federal radar," Grace said tightly. "For whatever reason, the feds are on Bertone's side. If the political pressure is bad enough, Morehouse will be back with paper I can't talk us out of honoring. Kayla will be on the firing line."

Faroe smiled coldly. "They'll have to find her first."

40

Castillo del Cielo
Sunday
6:40 A.M. MST

The child's soft footsteps woke Elena immediately. She slipped out of bed and went to the door. Miranda was in the hallway outside. Tears magnified her big golden eyes.

Elena gathered the weeping child into her arms and rocked slowly. "What's wrong, pet? Did your bad dream come back?"

"Y-yes." The little girl threw her thin arms around Elena's neck and hung on. "Maria s-said I was a b-baby and—"

"Hush, little one. You're a beautiful child and Momma loves you. I understand about bad dreams and night fears. I used to get them myself."

The girl drew a ragged breath. “R-really?”

“Of course. It’s all part of growing up.”

“Oh.” Miranda snuggled against her mother and slowly relaxed. “You smell good. The monsters don’t like things that smell good.”

“Then we shall be certain you wear my perfume when you go to bed.”

The girl smiled.

And stayed wrapped around her mother.

Elena soothed Miranda and mentally rearranged her schedule so that she could fire the useless nanny. Then she had to begin the tiresome process of hiring someone who understood children’s needs.

“Where is my angel?” asked Bertone’s voice from the bedroom.

“You have two angels now.” Elena walked back into the bedroom, carrying the daughter who would soon be too big for her mother to lift.

Irritation flashed across Bertone’s face, followed quickly by resignation. His plans for morning sex had dissolved in Miranda’s tears.

The last thing he’d expected when he married the gorgeous Elena was to find the heart of a good mother beating inside the sex-goddess body. Watching Elena with their children had at first been baffling, then amusing.

Now he was charmed.

"It's time for angels to be in bed," he said, lifting the covers.

Elena and Miranda came to bed as a unit.

Smiling, Bertone stroked Miranda's fine hair and wondered when his contacts in the government would find Kayla Shaw. She was an annoyance. A dangerous one.

And soon, a dead one.

41

Royal Palms
Sunday
7:00 A.M. MST

Okay!" Ted Martin clapped his hands together and laughed. "Okay, that's really fine!"

Rand didn't bother to look at the TV, which had been playing and replaying "film" since the agents left. DVDs didn't wear out, which was a good thing. But Martin had cloned this one, just in case.

"Pregnant woman stands off raiding party." Martin hooted. "Okay! At this rate we're going to get the whole hour, girls and boys. The whole mother-hugging hour!"

"Sound quality is spotty," Thomas said.

"All the better," Martin shot back. "We'll do print at the bottom of the screen, leave the off-center shots, the jigging camera, make the viewer feel like he's right there, watching it go down. Great stuff! Gotta love that red silk robe."

Faroe and Rand exchanged looks and said nothing.

"You going to blank out her face?" Thomas asked.

Martin looked uneasily at Faroe. "I hope not."

"Jury is still out on that," Faroe said.

Martin wanted to argue. He didn't. When Faroe's eyes went narrow, smart people backed off.

"Okay, play it again, Sam," Martin said.

Thomas stared at his producer. "You didn't really say that."

"Just play it, okay?" Martin snapped.

"Right," Thomas said. "You want me to do a voice-over in the background?"

"I'll think about it."

Somebody knocked on the door.

Faroe shot a look at the cameraman, who'd immediately grabbed his small, shoulder-held video camera. "Not unless I give the signal. Got it?"

The man swallowed and set aside the camera. "Got it."

"It's the deliveryman," called a voice from the other side of the door.

Rand went to one of the heavily curtained windows and lifted the cloth just enough to see a slice of the front porch. There was a small electronic device on the window. It put out vibrations that disturbed any attempt at long-distance sound surveillance. There was one such device on every window in all three bungalows. It was doubtful that the feds had put that kind of high-tech equipment in place before they were routed, but Faroe was a paranoid bastard.

It was one of the things Rand really liked about him.

Faroe went to the spy hole. He saw a distorted, barely recognizable Jimmy Hamm, complete with face-shielding sombrero and wraparound sunglasses.

"He's alone," Rand said to Faroe. "Hands full of packages. Where'd he get that hat—Central Casting?"

"He mugged a burro."

Faroe unlocked the door, opened it just enough to let Hamm in, and locked it tight again.

"Should I take Kayla's clothes over to her?" Hamm asked.

"No. There's a blind spot between the two bungalows. She's in here with Grace."

"Blind spot?"

"As in can't be covered by long-distance surveillance," Rand said. "I'll take these to Kayla."

Reluctantly Hamm passed over the purchases he'd made in the gift store—after he woke up the management. "You got a thing going with her?"

Rand gave him a look Faroe would have been proud of.

"Well, dang," Hamm said. "All the interesting ones are taken."

"As long as you remember that, your pretty face will stay intact," Faroe said.

He went to the bedroom door, opened it, and stuck his head in. "If you and Lane are finished trading acronyms about the Krebs cycle, we need you out here."

Kayla glanced up from a textbook thicker than her wrist. "This is hip, highly colored, diagrammed-up-the-wazoo gibberish. They had better texts when I was in school, which was shortly after the dinosaurs went extinct."

"That book was personally approved by every politician in the state of California," Faroe said. "What can I say?"

"A camel is a horse made by a committee," Kayla said, setting aside the book.

"Amen."

Grace came out of the bathroom wearing maternity jeans and a T-shirt advertising the joys of exercising your constitutional right to silence. When she saw Faroe, she said, "I've been thinking."

"Uh-oh," Lane said. "Am I old enough to hear this?"

"No, which is why you're studying in here and we're all going out there." Grace swiped her son's thick hair off his forehead and peered into his eyes. "Maybe the book would make more sense if you could see it."

He rolled his eyes.

"Just a thought." She smiled and let the hair flop back in place. "I can't wait for international soccer stars to cut their hair."

Lane ignored her, but his grin gave him away.

For a moment Kayla wanted to be a student again, with no more worries than the next paper, the next test, the next party. But reality was what it was, and her reality right now was a roomful of relative strangers and a man with sage-green eyes she felt she'd always known.

Don't forget the guy who would like to kill you. He's way too real.

With a shudder, Kayla went to the bungalow's main room. As soon as the door shut behind her, Grace turned to the younger woman.

"Can you monitor Bertone's correspondence account from outside the bank?" Grace asked.

"I'm not authorized for remote access," Kayla said. "That's only for the brass, people at Steve Foley's level and above. Why?"

"If Bertone gets wind of you being with St. Kilda Consulting, he'll pull the deposits out of the account you set up before I can persuade a judge to freeze everything."

"Then we'll have to chase that money all over hell again," Faroe added.

"We don't have time," Martin said, panicked. "That can't happen, okay?"

"Good-bye," Faroe said to the TV crew. "We'll call you if we get anything new."

Martin started to object, looked at Faroe's eyes, and made a round-them-up-and-head-them-out gesture with his hand. Very quickly the bungalow's living area was empty of all but St. Kilda employees.

"Can you freeze the funds in Bertone's account?" Kayla asked.

"We've been working on a judge since we debriefed you," Grace said.

"Problem is, Bertone is real well connected," Faroe said, heading for the little kitchen. "Sit down, *amada,* it's going to be a long day."

Grace slanted him a dark-eyed look, but sat down. He was right. Any day that began with a dawn raid was bound to be a long one.

Kayla frowned. "Bertone mentioned moving a lot of money into the account. Last I heard, it was only at forty million and change. If you freeze the account . . ."

"That's the heart of the problem," Rand said. "St. Kilda is playing high-stakes poker with Bertone. They want him to move all his money into the account before they freeze it. If they freeze it too soon, a lot of money goes missing. Freeze it too late, and it all goes missing. Timing is everything."

"According to the intel I've been getting from Brazil," Faroe said, returning with a cup of coffee, "we have until bank opening Monday morning. After that, Camgeria goes in the shitter."

Kayla closed her eyes briefly and tried not to see snapshots of bloody children. "When you get a temporary restraining order, the bank won't have any choice but to hold all transactions, no matter how many complicit bankers Bertone might have in his pocket."

"Then it becomes a legal battle," Faroe said. "But thanks to Grace, it's a battle we have a chance of winning."

"So you want me to figure out a way to monitor the account so you can freeze the money when it's all in and before it's paid out?" Kayla asked.

"Bingo," Faroe said. "But you're going to have to do it from somewhere else."

"Why?"

"The feds," Rand said.

"But—" she began.

"Now that feds of various stripes are hanging around," Rand cut in, "we need a new place to hide. If one of those feds identifies you, and word gets back to Bertone, Camgeria is up that nasty creek without a paddle."

"Are you telling me that Bertone can get federal agents to do his dirty work for him?" Kayla asked in disbelief.

"You need to understand something about investigators," Faroe said calmly. "The dudes Grace just ran off—and even the FBI agents I'll bet are hiding in the bushes out there—are feeding their findings back to some faceless desk officer in Washington, who is briefing some nameless senior official in the White House or at Langley or wherever."

Faroe took a sip of coffee.

Kayla kept her mouth shut and waited.

"That nameless senior official has an interface with Bertone," Faroe continued. "Maybe Bertone is a major political contributor. Maybe he's become so successful in the oil brokerage business that he can call in favors from somebody in the Energy Department. Maybe Bertone is playing the old boy network left over from his days as a spook. Doesn't matter how he does it. The point is that he can."

"The point is," Grace said to Kayla, "that we have to keep you under wraps in order to keep our assignment viable and you intact."

"Right now," Faroe said, "Bertone's working like a dirty bastard to find you. If he links you to us, he'll have no choice but to eliminate you and St. Kilda Consulting—man, woman, and child."

Kayla looked as horrified as she felt.

"The really bad thing," Faroe added, "is that Bertone's rich enough, powerful enough, and smart enough to get away with it."

Kayla wanted to argue.

She couldn't.

Faroe looked at Rand. "Come with me to the bedroom. I'm loaning you something. The last time I left home without it, I ended up in the hospital."

42

Royal Palms
Sunday
8:05 A.M. MST

Just as Rand finished buttoning up his shirt, Kayla walked out of the bathroom and stalked to the living area of the St. Kilda bungalow. She was covered head to socks, face to fingertips. The sun-protective clothing and very wide-brimmed hat were stylish, colorful, cool on her skin, and concealed her identity quite thoroughly. The wide wraparound sunglasses added a final anonymous touch.

"This is so not me," Kayla said, flicking her fingers against the hat. "Do you have anything in the Stetson line?"

"If I can shave"—*and wear Faroe's body armor*—"you can sport a silly hat," Rand said, cinching the hat under her chin. "Wear it until we lose our tail. Then you can strip and go as naked as my cheeks." He grinned. "I'll look forward to it."

Snickers came from the direction of the kitchen, where Faroe and Grace were eating breakfast.

Kayla rolled her eyes. "This outfit is the kind of thing Elena Bertone would wear to protect her flawless complexion. Mine, in case you hadn't noticed, is already desert leather."

Rand finished zipping her backpack and threw one strap over his shoulder. Then he ducked in under her hat brim and brushed his lips across hers. "I think your skin feels just fine," he said in a low voice. "Now get a move on. You're distracting me."

"Huh." She ran both palms over his face. "All that smooth skin on your face is distracting me. Thank God Freddie left enough hair up top for me to get my fingers into."

Rand gave Kayla a kiss that really distracted her, then dragged her out a patio door.

Kayla wasn't sure what kind of escape vehicle she expected, but what she got wasn't it. She stared.

"Are you kidding?" she asked.

"Think of it as a souped-up golf cart. Gas, not electric. It's an ATV in disguise."

"That's your story and you're stuck with it."

Smiling, Rand tossed her backpack onto the shelf behind the seat where his stuff was, slid onto the bench, and checked the controls. Then he grabbed the Stetson Faroe had stashed on the floorboards and jammed it on his head.

"Get aboard," he said. "Faroe's diversion won't last long."

"He's paranoid," she muttered.

But she got in.

"He's smart. There are probably a dozen feds out in the parking lot, with a dozen surveillance vehicles ready to roll out on our tail. Some will follow Faroe. Some won't. But we've got the fastest ATV on the track."

Or he hoped they did. Faroe was betting the feds didn't have anything better than an electric golf cart out on the course.

"Doesn't this thing have a lap belt?" she asked.

"Use that," Rand said, pointing to a handle firmly bolted to the dashboard in front of the passenger.

"What is it?"

"I've heard it called a lot of things." He grinned and began rolling forward. "My favorites are 'Jesus Bar' and 'Oh Shit Bar.' "

"Why?"

Rand twisted the throttle. The ATV leaped forward, slamming Kayla back into the seat.

"What are you— Oh shit!" Kayla said, grabbing for the bar.

"There you go."

Grinning, Rand cut the wheel hard to the right, shot through a gap in the oleander hedge, and burst into the sunlight on the tenth fairway of the resort's golf course.

The ATV four-wheeler moved so fast that she had to pull the wide brim of the sun hat around her face to keep from strangling on the chin strap. She was completely hidden when a mid-thirties white man dressed in resort clothes stepped out of a stand of bamboo near a water hazard. He carried a camera that was dwarfed by a long telephoto lens. Swearing, the cameraman started banging off pictures as the ATV sped past.

Rand gave him the back of his head and the universal sign of friendship.

"Are you trying to piss them off?" Kayla asked.

"Hey, if the feds are going to stand in the sun and shoot surveillance photos, they should be rewarded. Federal cops are way too used to having things go their way."

"Do all St. Kildans have a bad attitude about authority?" Kayla asked.

"Most of us have had enough authority in our lives to know its limitations. Federal cops still have to learn."

"And you live to teach them," she muttered.

"It's a dirty job—" he began.

"And you love doing it," she interrupted.

"Oh, yeah."

Clenching her teeth, she hung on to the dashboard bar while Rand swerved around a sand trap and shot up over a dune at the far side of the fairway. When she risked a peek over her shoulder through the folds of her hat, she saw that a second man in casual clothes had joined the first fed. He, too, had a fancy camera. He was talking on a cell phone or a radio.

"They aren't chasing us," she said.

"Surveillance teams don't pursue. They radio ahead. Now we pray they don't have anyone positioned on the far side of the golf course."

Rand cut across another fairway before he hit open rolling desert at the eastern edge of Scottsdale. A mile ahead of them lay the concrete piers of the 101 Loop Freeway and a scattering of multistory buildings in new industrial and office parks.

Kayla braced herself and kept a stranglehold on the bar. The ATV was well suited for cross-country desert travel, but it wasn't always comfortable. The wheels raised a thin cloud of grit as Rand slewed around creosote bushes and dodged patches of prickly pear.

"There it is," Rand said, barely missing a rock.

Kayla squinted through her glasses as he skidded onto a narrow dirt track that headed toward civilization again. He twisted the throttle on the ATV. Suddenly they were rushing along at more than thirty miles per hour on a road just bumpy enough to make the ride interesting.

Kayla felt like laughing out loud. When she'd sold the ranch, she hadn't expected to be on an ATV anytime soon. Even though she was used to being the driver, she trusted the man beside her. He had the lanky yet powerful build of a bronc rider. The Stetson added to the aura.

Too bad the ranch is gone. Rand would have looked right at home on it.

Without thinking, she touched the back of Rand's hand on the steering wheel. His fingers lifted, caught hers, squeezed, and released. He slowed the ATV as the road crested a bank and dropped down into a dry wash. He braked, then turned downstream toward an office park that was under construction. The ATV's two-stroke engine screamed with the pleasure of being let off the leash on a brilliant desert morning.

Minutes later they flashed up over another bank and through the open gate of a construction yard. A white Dodge SUV with heavily tinted windows was parked inside the yard. Rand braked to a skidding stop next to the vehicle.

"Backseat," he ordered Kayla.

He snatched the backpack and his laptop computer off the cargo shelf and tossed them into the back of the SUV. Kayla slid into the right rear seat and made a startled sound.

The driver was Jimmy Hamm.

He looked past her, searching for any dust from followers. "You're clean," he said to Rand. Then, "Shit, what happened to the fur?"

"Freddie."

Hamm glanced at Kayla in the rearview mirror and smiled. "Hey, darlin'. Love that take-no-prisoners grin."

With that he put the idling vehicle in gear and accelerated out of the construction yard onto the street.

Kayla dipped her chin, looking over the rims of her sunglasses at the man who had flirted madly with her for the past several months.

"Liar," she said.

He took his eyes off the road for a second and glanced in the mirror at her, surprised. "What? What did I do?"

"You let me think you had the hots for me," Kayla said. "But you were just trying to get inside Andre Bertone's life and his bank accounts."

"Babe, you thought I had the hots for you because it was the truth." He gave her a friendly leer. "That was the easiest cover I ever put on."

Rand turned back from watching their rear and said to Hamm, "Remember what Faroe said about the interesting ones." Rand smiled from the teeth out.

"Well, hell," Hamm muttered. "Kayla, can you ID the dude that made the hard pass at you last night?"

Startled, she looked at Rand.

"In Bertone's garden," Rand said, and this time his smile was real.

She hoped her floppy hat covered her blush.

"Yes," she said to Hamm. "Not that I want to see that cockroach again, but I'd recognize him."

"I did a little nosing around with my colleagues on the security detail," Hamm said. "Then I checked the employee database and came up with a possible name, Gabriel Navarro. He's supposed to be some kind of majordomo of the estate grounds, but nobody remembers seeing him around any of the gardening crews."

"I recognize the name from the employee payroll," Kayla said, "but if Mr. Navarro is a gardener, even the chief cheese, he's really well paid."

"How much?" Rand asked.

"Ten thousand a month."

"I'm betting he plants things in six-foot holes," Rand said.

Images of the handcuffs and the ugly little pistol spiked through Kayla's memories. Gooseflesh rippled. She hated being scared, but she was too smart not to be.

Hamm wheeled onto a westbound on-ramp, merging with light Sunday-morning traffic. "St. Kilda hacked into the employee database at the Castle in the Sky, so we know where Gabriel lives. Faroe hired two private types to stake out Gabriel's house. He's there, but we need Kayla for an eyeball ID."

The last thing Kayla wanted to see again was the face of her nightmare. "Sure. Whatever. Let's get it over with."

"Change into these first," Rand said, dropping jeans, a T-shirt, and a baseball cap on Kayla's lap. Then he looked at the driver. "Handsome, if I catch your eyes in the rearview mirror while she changes, you'll need a new nickname."

Hamm kept his attention on the road. Strictly.

43

Guadalupe, Arizona
Sunday
8:55 a.m. MST

Hamm parked on a dirt side street that had a view across a sandy town square toward two ancient whitewashed churches. If Kayla squinted enough to fuzz out the freeway in the background, she could almost believe she'd been transported five hundred miles south, into the Sonoran Desert of interior Mexico. The bells in the tower of the larger church began ringing, calling the faithful to worship. A knot of dark-skinned, dark-haired young men plodded across the sandy square toward the church.

"That explains something," Kayla said.

"What?" Rand asked.

"The man in the garden—"

"Gabriel Navarro."

"—was Latino but not really Mexican. He was too dark, like mahogany-colored lava."

Rand waited, absently rubbing his shaved cheek. He felt naked. "So?"

"This little town is called Guadalupe," she said. "It was established more than a century ago by Yaqui Indians from northern Mexico, refugees from the Mexican Civil War. The man in the garden was *muy indio*, very dark."

"That means we're going to have a hell of a time getting closer," Hamm said.

"Wrong color?" Rand asked.

"Or something," Hamm said. "The Yaquis are clannish as Gypsies and twice as suspicious. They don't even trust their fellow Mexicans. That's why there are two churches side by side, both Catholic, one for *Mexicanos* and the other for Yaquis."

"Guess we won't be walking around," Rand said.

"Don't have to. We have those local private investigators hanging in the neighborhood, passing themselves off as repo guys from a car dealer. They can work in close to Gabriel's house. We'll stay here and work at a distance."

"Binoculars?" Kayla asked.

"Telephoto camera," Hamm said, passing it over the seat. "Tourists like to hang out here on the weekend, watch the funny locals."

He opened the glove box and dug out a Diamond-back baseball cap that matched the one he was wearing. He tossed it to Rand, who ditched the Stetson, grumbled about being a Mariners fan, but put the cap on anyway.

Hamm's cell phone rang discreetly, the sound of a cardinal chirping. He answered and listened.

"There's something happening at the house," Hamm said. "A van. Driver's a white guy with red hair." Then, into the phone, "Go ahead, slide in a little closer. Guada-lupe is always crawling with repo guys in tow trucks."

Hamm listened some more. Then he relayed more information. "The van says 'Arizona Territorial Gun Club.' "

Kayla said something under her breath.

"What," Rand demanded.

"Steve Foley is a redhead," she said, "and he's a member of that club."

"What kind of place is it?" Rand asked. "Antique weapons and pistols at dawn?"

"More like Rambo's wet dream," Hamm said, flip-ping through his mental files. "High-tech all the way."

"Steve likes to think of himself as a sports shooter," Kayla said, "but here in Arizona, that could mean anything from a nervous grandmother to a Wyatt Earp wannabe."

"You know where the club is?" Rand asked Hamm.

"At the edge of the desert, on tribal land."

"No feds allowed?" Rand asked.

Hamm shrugged. "Every tribe's treaty rights are different. I've never been invited, so I've never been inside the club. Just hearsay from those who have."

"Steve is always talking about the club's 'Tire City' and their close-quarters course, whatever they are."

Hamm and Rand exchanged glances.

Tire City.

The term sent a chill through Rand. Modern urban warriors practiced close-quarters combat in open-roofed buildings with walls constructed of discarded auto tires filled with dirt. He had a mental image of the kind of place Kayla was describing, concrete block buildings, gravel canyons, and indoor labyrinths of movable shooting galleries with overhead observation platforms. Foley's gun club was a fortress in the desert, remote and bristling with firearms.

"What does 'Tire City' mean?" Kayla asked.

"It's slang for simulation bunkers," Rand said. "Close-quarters courses are run-and-shoot ranges. Usually such places are reserved for advanced training in law enforcement or military counterterrorism units." He smiled thinly. "Think of it as a kind of live-fire Disneyland for the well-armed adult."

"That would be Steve," Kayla said.

"Sweet," Rand said.

She shrugged. "As far as gun laws are concerned, Arizona is the last wild frontier. We have an open-carry law."

"Meaning?" Rand asked.

"You can still walk most of our streets with a side-arm, so long as you display it openly. I've seen guys in the Costco parking lot with pistols on their hips."

"Really sweet." Rand smiled grimly. "Hide behind the camera, Kayla." Then, to Hamm, "Get closer to that club van. Go real slow, like a gringo looking for his drug dealer."

Hamm started to object, then remembered Faroe's orders: Rand was the boss.

"There are four males in the carport area," Hamm said, slowly driving closer, "including the redhead from the van. My spotter says they're moving something from the club van to the back of a beat-up, solid-sided blue panel truck."

Hamm made a right and a left. The town square gave way to a tired little subdivision of one-story houses with satellite dishes and swamp coolers on the roof.

"Coming up."

Kayla focused the camera on the sidewalk and made a startled sound.

"What?" Rand said.

"Where's the Oh Shit Bar when I need it?" she said. "That's Steve Foley. Next to him is Gabriel. I don't recognize the other two."

"Slouch down." Rand enforced the command by pulling her facedown into his lap. "Hamm, eyes front when we go by."

"Yessir."

Whatever Kayla said was muffled by Rand's lap.

Hamm passed the house slowly, seeming to pay no attention to it. Rand lounged with his shoulder against the door, largely shielding his face. But he managed a long sideways glance up the driveway and past the gleaming, lipstick-red club van, which was sitting stern to stern with a weary-looking blue Chevrolet delivery van. The Chevy's rear cargo doors didn't match. And one of them had some thin, rectangular patches on it.

"Did you see the weapons?" Hamm asked Rand after they were past.

"Yeah."

"We done?"

"Yeah."

Gradually Hamm picked up his speed.

Rand helped Kayla sit up again.

She swatted at him with her cap. "That's for the mouthful of lap."

He leaned closer and said softly, "You didn't mind last night."

She swatted him again.

"Did you see what they were unloading?" Hamm asked.

"Galil assault rifle," Rand said.

"What?" Hamm asked, looking in the rearview mirror. "You sure?"

"Positive," Rand said. "Bertone was the only one who could get Galils into Africa. I guess he still has good connections. Good enough that he could drop two Galils on Steve Foley to hand over to Gabriel."

"Two?"

"I saw that many. Could be more."

Hamm swore. "Then they just expanded their killing field by about a thousand yards."

"There were what looked like gun slits in one van's back doors," Rand said. "Metal sliders."

"Judas Priest," Hamm muttered. "What next?"

Kayla's cell phone rang, reminding her that she'd forgotten to turn it off. She dragged the phone out of the backpack and glanced at the caller ID window.

She flinched.

"Who is it?" Rand asked.

The cell phone rang again as she showed the ID window to Rand. "Steve Foley."

"Ten to one he's setting you up for Gabriel," Rand said.

Nobody took the bet.

44

Guadalupe
Sunday
9:15 A.M. MST

Kayla stared at the cell phone in her lap. It wasn't ringing any longer.

Foley hadn't left a message.

Hamm closed his cell phone with a distinct click. "The Arizona Territorial Gun Club van is still in Gabriel's driveway."

Rand nodded and listened to Faroe on his own scrambled cell phone. Without taking his glance from Kayla's pale face, Rand asked questions, listened to answers, and made his own requests. When he was certain everything would be in place, he hung up.

"Foley will call again," Rand said. "Bertone has to smoke you out for Gabriel. We have two choices. Stay quiet or use this opportunity to take Gabriel off the board."

And pray like dirty bastards that he doesn't take Kayla out of the game instead.

All in all, Rand would rather have that skinny snake in a cage than loose on the streets with a Galil. He just didn't want Kayla to be the bait. But no matter how he'd argued, Faroe hadn't budged. If Rand revealed himself to Bertone as the one who could ID him with a planeload of arms in Africa, Bertone would get in the wind faster than St. Kilda could follow.

It was Kayla Bertone was looking for.

It was Kayla Bertone expected to find.

Kayla, who sat with her hands clenched around the Stetson he'd taken off. Her fingers had left creases in the hat's creamy surface. She'd overheard enough of what he'd said to know that she was going to be an actress again.

She hated acting.

"Your choice, Kayla," Rand said. "I mean it. If you don't want to talk to Foley, you don't talk. End of subject."

Her cell phone rang again.

Rand waited.

Kayla listened to her gut instinct. *Answer or not?*

The phone rang.

She picked it up but didn't open it.

"If you answer, put it on speakerphone," Rand said quietly.

She changed the setting on the phone and looked at it without answering.

"Hamm, head for that mall we saw from the freeway."

"Chandler Mall?" Hamm asked.

Her phone rang.

"Is it the closest?" Rand asked.

"Yes," Kayla said. "Any final instructions before I answer?"

"Play hard-to-get before you invite him to the Cheesecake Factory at Chandler Mall. Don't tell him about me." Then, to Hamm, "Go."

She opened the phone as the SUV accelerated away from Gabriel's house.

"Hello," she said tightly.

"Hey, Kayla, it's Steve, how's your Sunday going?" Foley's voice was clear, friendly as a salesman.

"Just great," she said, "but I'm breaking a personal rule, talking and driving eighty miles an hour on the 101 Loop. What's up?"

Rand gave her a thumbs-up for the response.

"Well, look," Foley said, "I hate to bother you on a weekend, but something has come up. I have to see you. Can we meet at your ranch?"

Simultaneously, Hamm and Rand gave her a negative head motion. She gave them a *Well, duh* eye roll.

"I'm really jammed up today," she said. "Can't we handle it by phone?"

"Sorry." Foley's voice said he wasn't sorry at all. "It absolutely has to be done in person. That's what being a *personal* banker is all about."

"Hell," Kayla said, just loud enough for Foley to catch. "I'm just really, uh, busy right now. I'm entitled to a private life on the weekends."

"At the expense of your career?"

The whip in Foley's voice would have worried her if she hadn't already written her career off.

"This is bank business?" she asked.

"Why else would your supervisor be giving you a direct order?"

You've given me lots of direct orders, jerkwad, and you usually change your mind a few minutes later. But all Kayla said aloud was, "I'm listening. What's so urgent?"

Rand made a motion with both hands and mouthed, *Draw it out.*

"I certainly hope it doesn't involve the Bertone account," she added.

Her tone was so sweetly reasonable that Rand had to smile—sweet reason had nothing to do with her eyes. They wanted Foley's ass on a platter.

"Actually, it does," Foley said. His tone was less certain, like an actor whose lines had been changed.

"I thought it might," Kayla said gently. "I left the fund-raiser rather quickly last night. I wondered if Andre and Elena would be upset."

"What happened?" Foley asked. "We've been worried about you."

Rand wanted to spit on the floor.

From the twist of Kayla's mouth, she did, too.

"Well, I was kind of upset," she said. "A stranger made a hard pass at me in Bertone's garden."

"Uh—" Steve cleared his throat. "That's awful. Are you okay?"

"Yeah, I'm fine. Somebody happened along at the right moment and wilted the guy's dick."

Rand almost laughed out loud.

"But I was too upset to stay," Kayla said. "I spent the night at a friend's house in Gilbert."

"Someone from the bank?"

"No. No one you know."

"Are you headed to the ranch now?" Foley asked. "I know you've got more stuff to clean out."

Rand shook his head.

"No," Kayla said. "I'm just running some errands."

"Oh. Well, maybe I'll drop by the ranch later, when you're home, and help you out. I hate to think of you being alone after what happened last night. Poor baby. I'm so sorry."

Kayla lifted her middle finger at the phone, but her voice was smooth as she said, "Hang on a sec." She put her hand over the microphone, looked at Rand, and said softly, "Sure you don't want him at the ranch? We could give him and his gun-freak pal a real welcome."

Her smile was hard and predatory. Clearly she liked the idea of ambushing the ambushers.

Concrete hummed beneath the SUV's wheels. Hamm had turned onto the freeway and was speeding away from Guadalupe.

Finally Rand shook his head. "Too many places for a sniper to hit you along the way."

Kayla took her hand off the microphone. "Oops, damn, I'm about to drop in the cell-phone dead zone at Shea. I'll call you right back."

"Who were you talking to?" Foley asked.

"Myself, same as always. Can't break the habit."

"You've lived alone too long, babe. Why don't—"

She punched out and looked at Rand.

"Why can't we just call the cops and have them rig a trap at the ranch?" she asked.

"Faroe is trying, but do you have any idea how much hassle it would be to wire the Maricopa County Sheriff's Office into this situation on a moment's notice?" Rand asked. Then he added in a breathless falsetto, "Oh, Deputy, a very wealthy citizen who also happens to be an international arms smuggler and money launderer is trying to have me killed. He's using a prominent banker, a Yaqui Indian thug with some ugly friends, and illegal automatic weapons he smuggled into the country."

"But St. Kilda—" Kayla began.

"Is working for a foreign country in a gray area of the law. And the attack on you last night was never reported. Explain that away."

"Crap. I feel like Linda Hamilton in *Terminator 2*."

"Get used to it. The first data dump on the Bertones' political activities just came back from St. Kilda's research group. Last year they gave more than $1,700,000 in contributions, half to local politicians and half to national candidates. And that's just the money we've traced so far. Who knows what they've given to elect the local sheriff? Money like that buys a certain amount of clout with local and federal cops."

"St. Kilda found out all that overnight?" Kayla asked, startled.

"The Internet never sleeps and neither does a St. Kilda researcher. But it was no big hacking deal. Legal political contributions are mostly a matter of public record."

"So you're saying we can't count on any help from the authorities?"

"Eventually, yes, they'll trip all over themselves to help us. But not until we have solid evidence against Bertone. A lot of it. If we don't get that, we'll use the outrage after Okay Martin runs the show to twist the politicians, who will then lean on the cops."

Kayla laughed. "Okay. That's Martin's favorite word."

"You noticed. Anyway, we can't count on outside help right now. If nothing else, it's a weekend. Local cops with enough brass to go after Bertone are playing golf."

"Why can't St. Kilda do the job?" Hamm asked.

"If we go looking for a gunfight, ex-judge Grace Silva Faroe will have our balls for breakfast."

Kayla grimaced. "I'd rather eat at Cheesecake Factory, thanks all the same."

"In a booth away from the windows after eleven," Rand said. "Anyone good enough to use a Galil is a sniper who will wait for a sure kill. Last thing he wants is you in a hospital surrounded by cops."

"What if Foley doesn't want to play it my way?" Kayla asked.

"Then tell him you're too busy, you'll see him at work Monday."

"He could fire me on the spot. Then we'd never figure out what he and Bertone are up to."

"Then we lose Bertone and live with it. I won't let you meet Foley in a place we can't control."

"I'm willing to risk it."

"I'm not," Rand said. "Call Foley back."

"But—"

"Call him," Rand interrupted, "or I'll visit him personally and boot this whole bloody act into the crapper where it belongs."

Kayla looked at Rand for a long moment. Shaving off his beard should have made him look softer, more civilized.

It hadn't.

She picked up her cell phone and called Steve Foley.

45

Chandler Mall
Sunday
10:55 A.M. MST

"Yeah," Faroe said into the mike beneath his collar. He had an earbud in each ear. Hamm was one connection. Grace was the other. "Got it. You make any progress with the cops?"

"Finally," Grace said. *"Good thing one of your old Border Patrol buddies is a desk sergeant."*

"Poor sod."

"Hey, Sgt. Masters is drawing a Border Patrol pension while drawing full pay from Phoenix PD. Poor doesn't describe him."

Faroe grunted. "Be ready to patch me through to Masters."

"I live to serve."

He grinned.

Beside him, Lane looked around the parking lot of the huge mall. "Bet they have a cool computer game store here."

"After you pass that test, we'll worry about game stores," Faroe said. Then, into the mike: "No, not you, *amada.* Lane is jonesing for a shopping expedition. And no, I don't see a beat-up delivery van with mismatched cargo doors. Hamm says they haven't left the driveway yet."

"Lane should be studying," Grace said through the earbud.

"All work and no play makes—" Faroe broke off and touched the earbud in his right ear. "Hamm says they're moving. I'm switching over to Rand's frequency." He twisted the dial on one of the iPods in his pocket and said, "Angel on the move."

A scratchy sound came back as acknowledgment.

"Showtime," Faroe said to Lane.

"Is the TV crew going to be here?"

"Yeah, but you better not see them."

Lane grinned like a pirate. "See what?"

46

Chandler Mall
Sunday
11:05 A.M. MST

The Cheesecake Factory brunch crowd had spilled out into the morning sunshine in front of the Chandler Mall. Rand and Kayla sat inside, with Rand between the door and Kayla. Hands in jeans, he leaned one shoulder against the wall, looking like a man listening to his iPod and waiting to be fed.

Kayla glanced at him.

A slight shake of his head was the answer. Then he scratched his neck, reminding her that he was part of other conversations.

"Hamm tells me the van does indeed have metal slides set in at least the left rear door," Faroe said.

"Score one for you. Looks like they're setting up a mobile shooting platform. Two dudes. Two Galils."

Relief went through Rand like rainwater. "Thank God," he said without moving his lips.

"You're welcome."

"You're not God."

"Stop. You'll make me cry. No one has seen Foley's car yet."

Rand flicked his collar in acknowledgment.

"I'm calling in a local cop on a 'hot tip,' but I'd like to have Foley on tape first. And camera."

"Don't wait too long," Rand said through his teeth.

"If Gabriel shakes Hamm, I'm shutting this op down and pulling Kayla. Be ready."

Rand straightened his collar, then bent over Kayla. "Everything's ready for lunch."

"We're an item, right?" She gestured with the electronic paddle that was issued by the restaurant receptionist to signal diners that their table was ready. "I'm all over you like body oil so that Foley can't miss the message?"

Rand smiled slowly. "I'll handle the body oil part. You can concentrate on Foley."

"An undercover item," she mumbled.

"Well, I do recall being under the covers . . ." He nuzzled her neck, then covered the microphone with his fingers. "It wasn't a one-nighter, no matter what you say. Got that?"

She brushed his cheek with the paddle. "Will Foley buy it?"

"Fuck Foley. I'm talking to you."

"You fuck him. He's not my type." She couldn't help smiling. "Okay. I hear you."

"Do you believe me?"

"I want to." She let out a long breath. "Let's table it until this is settled."

He bit her gently. "Or until tonight."

She closed her eyes. "Or until tonight."

"Deal." He nuzzled her again and released the microphone.

She cocked her head at him—Stetson, dark shirt stretched over wide shoulders, narrow hips in close-fitting jeans. Definite drool material, and so not the type of man she'd dated since she "grew up."

"I hope Foley buys it," she said.

"Buys what?"

"Me hitting the sheets with a western studmuffin."

Rand choked. "Studmuffin? Jesus, lady, you—"

"What if Foley recognizes you as the artist from the party?" she interrupted in a low voice.

"Then I shaved and cut my hair because you asked me to. But I doubt that he'll recognize me. He's too full of himself to really look at other people."

"But what if he does?" she insisted.

"You can't control all the elements of an undercover op. You just go with the hand you're dealt."

"Meaning?"

"I'm going to nail Foley's ass to the shooting house wall."

She blinked at the banked fury in Rand's calm voice. "Why? He's not the one trying to kill me."

"No, he's just the one setting you up for the hit. Nothing to worry about at all. He's a real sweet guy."

She rubbed her temples. "I keep hoping it's a bad dream."

Rand's smile slid into a downward curve.

"Well, not all of it was bad," she said, touching his cheek, kissing him softly.

He returned the kiss with interest, then broke reluctantly. "Faroe is around here somewhere. He might have Lane with him for cover—weekend dad takes teenager to the mall. They'll probably work in pretty close, but don't see them."

She nodded.

"There are several other operators around," Rand said, "so if somebody grabs you and whispers 'St. Kilda' in your ear, do whatever they say."

"Anything else?"

"I laid a hundred on the receptionist and told her I'm asking you to marry me over nachos. As soon as we spot Foley, I'll signal her and we'll go to the head of the lunch line. After Foley arrives, be ready to leave the instant I tell you. I don't want you out in the open one second longer than—" He broke off.

Faroe was whispering in his ear.

"Get a table. Foley's here."

47

Chandler Mall
Sunday
11:15 A.M. MST

Steve Foley was wearing pressed black jeans and a white silk golf shirt. His leather boots had sterling silver toe guards. The wide amber sunglasses he wore were the type favored by trap and pistol shooters. The laptop computer case he carried was made of the same soft black leather as his boots, with the same engraved silver accents.

White silk wasn't a good choice for a man wearing a wire. Though loose, the fabric clung to Foley's gym-hardened muscles . . . and the dark shadow of the wire he was wearing on top of them.

"He's wired for sound," Rand murmured to his collar as he leaned close to include Kayla in at least part of the conversation.

"Beautiful," Faroe said. *"Any guesses on the range?"*

"A thousand feet, max. No bulges for a bigger transmitter. He's carrying a laptop, so I suppose he could be wireless."

"We haven't found a reliable way to make that kind of transmission go beyond a building. He could have a bigger transmitter in his jeans."

"No bulges there, for sure."

Faroe laughed. *"I'll tell St. Kilda."*

The hostess showed Foley to the table personally. Her smile said that if he was lacking bulges anywhere, she hadn't noticed.

"Don't you ever take a day off?" Kayla asked.

Foley looked blank.

"Your laptop," Kayla said.

He smiled tightly. "Money never sleeps." His smile faded when he looked at the man beside Kayla.

Rand met Foley's glance with a total lack of interest.

Rude bastard, listening to his iPod while on a date, Foley thought. "Where did you find him?"

"She pulled back the sheet and there I was." Rand's smile was all hard teeth.

Kayla rolled her eyes. "*Jerry,* this is my boss, Steve Foley. Steve, this is Jerry."

Neither man offered to shake hands.

If Foley asked for a last name, Kayla was going to say she and "Jerry" hadn't gotten that far.

Foley slid into the booth opposite the closely pressed couple. Then he winced and shifted slightly.

Rand almost laughed. *Poor bastard. Someone didn't put the wire on right. It's jerking every time he moves.*

"What's up?" Kayla asked, leaning against Rand with the ease of a woman with her lover.

Rand nuzzled her neck and watched Foley's leather laptop case. If the banker started to take anything lethal out of it, Rand would be over the table and around Foley's throat before anyone could blink. That case was wide and deep enough to conceal more than one weapon.

"Sorry to interrupt your Sunday morning, but I need Kayla for a few minutes. Bank business, you understand. Private." Foley's smile was barely civil.

"I'll just put in my other earbud," Rand said, straightening and moving slightly away from Kayla. "Plenty of privacy that way."

"I hate to be rude," Foley said, "but Kayla and I have work to do."

"You're not being rude." Rand grinned. "Kayla's been praising you to the skies. Says you're the world's smartest banker. I've got money to invest. Match made in heaven, right? You just go ahead and conduct your off-hours business while we eat lunch. That way she won't put in for overtime."

Foley stared at the other man.

Rand stared back.

The banker realized that short of physically throwing Kayla's date out of the booth, he wasn't going to get her alone. A scene was the last thing Foley wanted, but he gave in with little grace.

"Lunch." With a grimace, Foley picked up a menu that had more pages than a small weekly.

"Order for me," Rand said to Kayla, running his fingertip over her bottom lip. "You know what I like."

She caught the fingertip in her teeth, nipped, licked, and released. "I sure do," she said in a husky voice.

Foley's eyes narrowed.

"Is Lane old enough to see this?" Faroe's voice asked in Rand's ear. *"We're only a few tables away."*

"Behave, darlin'," Rand said, "or we'll never get rid of—um, get through with business and on to better things."

Kayla ordered steak and eggs for them.

Foley ordered a Bloody Mary.

While the server wrote, Rand looked casually around the restaurant. Faroe and Lane were in place several tables over. They'd been there long enough to have food in front of them. Faroe was drinking coffee with his sandwich while Lane sucked up cola and made his way through a plate of cheeseburgers that were barely bigger than silver dollars. Lane was careful not to look anywhere but at his dad or his food.

The server left, promising Foley the drink in short order.

If there were other St. Kilda operators in the restaurant, Rand didn't recognize them. Nor did he see any of the thugs who'd been gathered around Gabriel in Guadalupe.

A minute later the Bloody Mary appeared in front of Foley. The restaurant made its profit on the bar. As long as someone was drinking, the food would wait.

Foley took a swallow, then another. "Kayla, we really should be alone to talk about the account I have in mind."

"That dude makes a lousy undercover," Faroe murmured in Rand's ear. *"You're supposed to guide the mark, not beat him to death."*

Kayla managed a look of confused innocence. "I don't understand. Is this about the Bertone account?"

"Some aspects of banking involve proprietary information," Foley snapped. "Our clients expect confidentiality. I shouldn't have to explain that to you."

"Then you're here about the Bertone account?" Kayla repeated.

"Yes," Foley said through his teeth.

"Good." Her fingers drummed on the table. "I've got to tell you, I'm not happy about the Bertones. Come Monday, I'm thinking about going to Mal Townsend and asking for reassignment."

Foley looked like someone had handed him a foot-long worm. "What are you talking about? Mal isn't your boss. I am!"

"And Mal is your boss," Kayla said. "You've turned down my requests for reassignment for months. I don't have any choice but to go above you."

Foley straightened in the booth. The Bloody Mary glass met the table's polished surface hard enough to slosh a few drops down the side. "You'd go against my direct order?"

"I said I was thinking about it." She frowned and rubbed her eyes. "I'm spooked by this Bertone situation, and you're not giving me much help."

"What the hell is she doing?" Faroe asked.

Rand scratched his shirt. Hard. It was Kayla's show. He yawned and made a show of putting in the second earbud. Soon he was jiving to an imaginary beat.

Foley glared at Rand. "I really don't want to discuss bank business in front of a total stranger."

Rand had closed his eyes and was humming a tune. Badly. He could still hear the conversation but gave no sign of it.

"Ignore him," Kayla said, shrugging. "Jerry's high-octane in the sheets, but beyond that he's no lightbulb."

Four tables away Faroe almost choked on his coffee.

"Trust me," she said to Foley. "It's not like we're giving Bertone's private banking information to the comptroller of the currency." Then her eyes widened and she looked at her boss like she'd never seen him before.

"Kayla—" Foley began loudly.

"That explains a lot," she said over him. "We're avoiding the normal reporting requirements for large transactions by handling them through a correspondent banking account. Right?"

Rand began snapping his fingers lightly, shoulders swaying to an imaginary beat, hips hitching in time. He opened his eyes long enough to give Kayla a come-and-get-it leer.

Foley's hands fisted. He glared at her through his amber shooter's glasses. His expression said he would love to see her over the sight of a gun. And her boyfriend right after her.

"You don't know what you're saying," Foley said.

"I know that my name is on the bottom line as the one responsible for the Bertone account, that you told me to set it up, and that nowhere are you on record as being responsible for anything to do with Bertone's money."

"Go, sistah!" Faroe said in Rand's ear.

"Oh, yeah, babe," Rand sang huskily. "Lay it down on me."

She kicked him under the table.

He didn't open his eyes.

"I don't have anything to do with Bertone's money," Foley said.

"Bullshit," Kayla said sweetly. "I suppose you didn't recommend a real estate agent to me when I wanted to sell my ranch."

"Well, I, uh, yeah," he said, surprised by the change of subject. "I was just trying to help."

"Who? Thanks to the agent you sent me to, my ranch was instantly sold at a price well above market value to—surprise!—Andre Bertone." Kayla's voice wasn't loud, but it was sarcastic enough to curdle milk.

"Uh . . ." Foley drank more Bloody Mary. It didn't inspire anything but another drink. He signaled the server.

"So now I look like a dirty banker," Kayla said. "You gave me full responsibility for the Bertone account to set me up. You've been planning this for months."

Rand kept his eyes closed. He whisper-sang words to an old blues tune. Hip-hitches kept time.

"Will you tell that idiot to stop twitching?" Foley snarled.

"As soon as you cut me in on a share of the profits from Bertone's correspondent account."

Foley blinked. "A share?"

"As in money. Real money. Half of what you're getting."

"Are you crazy? You can't—" Foley broke off as the server returned with another Bloody Mary. He took a steadying swallow. "You can't prove any of this."

She smiled slowly. "Want me to try?"

Foley wondered how the hell the conversation had gotten out of control. "Look, you misunderstand."

"That was yesterday. Today I'm a lot smarter. Half of what you're getting."

Foley looked at the table. "Listen, babe, you really don't know what you're talking about."

"Then I'm out of time for you," Kayla said, tucking the strap of her purse over her shoulder. "Places to go, things to do, and most of all, *people to talk to.*"

She put her hand around Rand's wrist and tugged.

"Huh?" he said.

She lifted out one earbud and leaned in close. "We're gone."

"Wait!" Foley said.

"For what?" Kayla asked.

"Look, I know how hard you've been working," Foley began. "You're overdue for a raise. Twenty thousand a year, okay?"

"Twenty a year? That's chump change," she said.

But she stopped pushing Rand out of the booth.

He stuffed the second earbud back into place and closed his eyes, mostly because he was afraid to look in Faroe's direction. Both of them would have fallen out of their chairs laughing.

"She's a natural," Faroe said between snickers.

"You're making a lot more than twenty thou a year under the table," Kayla said to Foley.

"I didn't say anything about money under the table, babe. I never said a word about that."

"I see. I threaten to talk out of school and you decide I've earned a raise. Yeah, that'll fly, *babe*."

Foley's lips moved, but nothing came out.

"You're booking a fat, fat profit on Bertone's money coming through the bank," Kayla said. "It will look sweet on your year-end evaluation, so good that your bosses won't go looking for unhappy lumps under the know-your-client carpet. Bet you get performance bonuses. Big ones. You're a director, after all."

Foley took another swallow of his peppery drink, coughed, and cleared his throat.

Rand sang fragments of "Devils and Dust." Springsteen's driving rhythms were echoed in Rand's hips.

"So I want the same percentage of profit from Bertone's account that you get in bonuses," Kayla said. "Somewhere around two million."

Foley removed his glasses, revealing the red eyes of a man who hadn't slept well. He pinched the bridge of his nose and looked around as if expecting someone. "That's impossible," he said finally. "I can't justify a raise like that."

"Make me a vice president, with performance bonuses backdated to a month ago," Kayla said. "Of course, you'll have to clean up that lousy personnel evaluation you gave me two months ago, but I'm sure you're up to it."

Rand forgot the words and just kept humming.

"Hoo-yah," Faroe said. *"She's a pistol!"*

Foley looked like he wanted to bang his head against the booth. "All right. It's a deal."

"What is?" Kayla insisted.

"You'll be a VP and report directly to me. You'll have your choice of offices—"

"Yippee skip," she said.

He ignored her. "Plus the raise."

"Fifty thousand, minimum," Kayla said.

"But—" Foley throttled back his temper. *The hell with it. The bitch won't live to collect a cent.* "Of course."

"I don't expect to get paid the same performance bonus that a director gets," she said reasonably, "but be smart and don't chisel me."

"Don't worry," Foley said through his teeth. "You'll get everything you deserve."

48

Chandler Mall
Sunday
11:28 A.M. MST

Andre Bertone's hands were locked around the wheel of his parked car hard enough to leave dents. They'd been that way since he'd seen Kayla walk into the Cheesecake Factory with a man who looked like a cowboy and moved like a bodyguard.

The headphones he wore kept bringing him news that went from bad to worse. Part of Bertone admired Kayla's brass.

Most of him just wanted to kill her. Then Foley.

Slowly.

What a putz.

But a useful one. Until that changed, Foley would live.

Mother of God, he didn't even ask for Jerry's last name. She could have told him everything!

Not that it mattered. The snipers could kill two as easily as one. It was just that Bertone hated incompetence. He'd killed men simply because they were too stupid to live.

Foley was shaping up to head the Must Die list.

Bertone forced himself to unclamp his fingers from the wheel. No matter how delightful Foley's neck would feel crushed between Bertone's hands, the banker was necessary. It would take time to cultivate another bank, another banker, all the messy details needed to launder money safely.

In the meantime . . .

Bertone punched a number on his speed dial.

"Bueno."

"Nothing good about it," Bertone snarled to Gabriel. "There's a man with the Shaw woman. Tall. Jeans and a black shirt. Cowboy hat. You kill him. Tell Uri to take Kayla."

"Sí."

Bertone hung up and waited for two dead people to walk out of the restaurant.

49

Chandler Mall
Sunday
11:31 A.M. MST

There's been activity in the correspondent account," Kayla said. "Since I'm on record as the account executive, I should know a little bit more about what's happening."

"I've discussed it at length with Andre," Foley said. "He's using the account to finance acquisition of some long-term oil—" He broke off and looked at Rand.

Rand snapped his fingers and mouthed meaningless words.

"Look," Foley said flatly. "You want to know more, get rid of lover boy."

"You're the one who asked me to meet after hours."

Foley's jaw flexed. He slammed his laptop case on the table.

Rand's eyes opened just enough to see into the case as it opened. Nothing more deadly than a computer. Even so, he didn't really relax. Knives were easy to hide.

Hell, given the right incentive, even the dull ones on the table could get the job done. The long forks would get it done faster.

"All I need from you is access to the account," Foley said. "There are some transactions that have to be posted, but I can't gain access through the remote portal. I'm screwing up part of the protocol, I guess."

Because you never bothered to learn how to do it right, suck face, Kayla thought savagely. *You always had one of the "girls" do it for you.*

She smiled. "No problem. I'll do it."

"That's why I rely so much on you," Foley said with a grin as he logged on to the bank web site. Or tried to. He barely managed to keep from smashing his fist on the computer keyboard. "I can get into the account to monitor activity, but when I go to conduct transactions, it says I'm not authorized."

"I'm not authorized for remote access at all," Kayla said. She tilted her head. "Maybe the portal you're using is read-only. Or maybe you need special access to conduct after-hours operations."

He shook his head. "That's not good enough. One of Andre's requirements is that he has access to his money twenty-four/seven. That's what I promised him. He conducts business all over the world, all the time."

Kayla's mouth thinned. *Do you know what kind of shitty business he's conducting?*

"See this?" Foley demanded, slanting the laptop screen toward Kayla. "I can get into the account to read balances, but I can't move sums to other accounts, either within the bank or outside of it."

Through slitted eyes, Rand watched Kayla. She'd gone still, then gooseflesh had broken out on her arms. The restaurant was air-conditioned, but not to the point of chill.

The feral smile on her face sent adrenaline into Rand's blood.

"Let me try something," Kayla said.

She took the laptop and stared at the screen. "Wow, this is awesome, almost like having your own private bank branch on your laptop."

And Bertone had been depositing money right, left, and center. One hundred and eighty-two million, and counting.

Holy hell. War is expensive.

"I see our client has been busy," Kayla said mildly.

Foley looked hard at Kayla's date, but the idiot still had his eyes closed and was swaying and hip-jigging to a tune only he heard. He hadn't even tried to peek at the computer screen.

"I got it that far," Foley said, "but I can't make any transactions inside the account."

Kayla put her fingers on the keyboard and typed for a few seconds. Then she frowned and studied the screen. Gooseflesh rippled again as the simple, beautiful, incredible truth echoed in her mind.

Bertone doesn't control his account.

Foley doesn't.

I do.

She'd been in such a rush to set up the correspondent account that she'd chosen the password for it herself. She'd meant to give it to Bertone at the Fast Draw but had forgotten.

Being blackmailed by a client was distracting as hell.

"I know what part of your problem is," she said. "The portal isn't set up for access to correspondent accounts, only for private-bank checking and savings accounts."

"You mean there's no way to conduct business right now?" Foley's voice was raw.

"Not until the main system comes back online," Kayla said casually. "Even the bank president can't move money from that account until Monday morning at nine." *At least I sure hope that's the case.*

Foley muttered something savage under his breath.

"I'll be glad to take care of the transactions on the account first thing Monday morning," she offered.

He shook his head abruptly. "No. Andre's instructions for the transactions are very detailed. Nine o'clock Monday?"

"Not a minute before. But everything would be posted to the account Monday, anyway, even if you made transfers today. So Andre won't lose any interest or anything. On an account of that size, interest will matter."

Rand started humming "Diamonds and Rust."

Kayla kicked him again under the table.

"You said my portal was only part of the problem." Foley frowned at her. "What's the rest?"

"You don't have the password. Without it, you can't move money out of the account."

Foley shrugged. "Bertone will give it to me."

"He doesn't have it."

Rand went still.

Foley's mouth opened, closed, opened again. "What?"

"Everyone was in such a lather to open the account, I couldn't get through to Bertone for him to choose a password, so I did it. I'm the only one who can move money out of that account."

"Christ Jesus," Faroe breathed in Rand's ear. *"Why didn't she tell us!"*

It took Foley a moment to digest her words. When he did, he spoke through clenched teeth. "What. Is. The. Password."

Subtly Rand gathered himself, ready to jump Foley if he went through with the violence vibrating in his voice. He'd rather belt Foley than twitch to imaginary music any day.

"I don't know the password," Kayla said.

Rand forced himself not to react.

Faroe groaned. *"So near and yet so far."*

"What do you mean, you don't know?" Foley asked.

Kayla yawned and nudged Rand in the ankle. "I use a million passwords, so I write them down in code in my little black book."

"Where's the book?" Foley demanded.

"At Jerry's apartment with my overnight case."

50

Chandler Mall
Sunday
11:33 A.M. MST

Bertone couldn't move, couldn't breathe, could barely think.

Kayla had the password.

Gabriel would kill her the instant she left the restaurant.

Cursing in five languages, Bertone punched Gabriel's number into his cell phone. He tugged one of the earphones out, slammed the cell phone to his ear, and listened to it ring.

And ring.

Foley's voice talked into his other ear. *"Get it. Right now. I'll follow you."*

Kayla's voice declining. *"We've got errands to run. I'll call you with the password as soon as I get it."*

"I want it now!"

"What's the hurry? Even with the password, you can't move anything until Monday morning."

Gabriel's phone was still ringing.

Nobody was answering.

Caught between rage and fear, Bertone willed Gabriel to pick up his cell phone.

"Wake up, Jerry."

And a man's voice. *"You finally through, sweet thing?"*

"Oh, yeah. I'll call you in a few hours, Steve. Enjoy our meals."

Bertone listened to the sounds of Kayla and her boyfriend leaving the booth, walking away, heading for the restaurant door.

Going straight into Gabriel's ambush.

Numbly Bertone sat and waited to hear the shots that might as well be aimed at his own heart.

51

Chandler Mall
Sunday
11:34 A.M. MST

Just as Rand and Kayla passed Faroe's table, he shoved to his feet, bumping against her. He grabbed her arm to steady her.

"Sorry," Faroe said. "Didn't see you."

Then in a voice so soft Rand thought he imagined it, Faroe said in his ear, *"Take her shopping. It's going down now."*

Rand pulled Kayla close. "You okay, sweet thing?"

"Never better, stud."

Faroe's mouth twisted as he fought a smile.

"Remember that naughty little pink thingy you showed me?" Rand said. "I've decided I'm going to buy it for you right now."

He hauled Kayla out the restaurant's side door and onto an escalator headed for the second floor of the shopping mall. He made sure that he was standing between her and any view of the parking lot. He wasn't going to expose her until he was sure Gabriel and the two Galils were out of the game.

"What was that all about?" Kayla asked under her breath.

"Faroe didn't want us in the parking lot right now," Rand said.

The escalator gave him a clear, gliding view of the parking lot in front. The place was alive with squad cars.

"Now that's sweet," Rand said, grinning.

"I can't see."

He leaned aside.

Kayla saw five white Chandler squad cars pulled up at odd angles around the tired-looking Chevrolet van she'd seen in Guadalupe. Officers swarmed around the van, which was parked with its rear cargo door pointed in the direction of the restaurant's front door. Three officers had opened the cargo doors and were leaning in to examine the interior of the van.

Two men were facedown on the asphalt, their hands cuffed behind them.

"Is it—" she began.

"Oh, yeah," he said, glancing around while he appeared to be nuzzling her hair. "Hell's angel was flying too close to the ground. Crash and burn, you bastard."

An officer emerged from the cargo area carrying a lethal-looking long gun with a sniper's scope on it.

"One of the guys on the ground, the skinny one—" she began.

"Yeah," Rand said. "Say buh-bye, darling. He's going down, big-time."

"Is that one of the guns we saw in Guadalupe?" Kayla asked very quietly.

"I'd bet on it." Then, "End of the ride. Watch your step."

She walked off the escalator, but all she could concentrate on was her memory of the parking lot with its silent show-and-tell. "You were right. About the gun slits."

"Sure was."

"Don't sound so cheerful. I was the target, wasn't I."

It wasn't a question.

"It wouldn't surprise me," Rand said. "But if it was Bertone on the other end of Foley's wire, he must have been shitting green lizards."

"Why?"

"Because you, you clever little banker lady, have the key to his millions. If he kills you, he kills himself. But he didn't know that when he pointed his skinny death angel at you and told him to pull the trigger."

Her mouth flattened. "Now what?"

"Tell me you didn't forget Bertone's password."

"I didn't."

He let out a breath. "Good."

"Just because my hips swing when I walk, I'm not stupid. And I sure don't have a little black book of passwords."

"Dang." He smiled slowly. "Here I was getting all hard just thinking about it."

She gave him a look as he hustled her past windows full of things with price tags and blank faces. "Are we going somewhere in particular?"

"No. We're waiting for Bertone to get in touch with his inner password."

"What about my naughty pink thingy?"

"I'll get in touch with that."

52

Chandler Mall
Sunday
11:40 A.M. MST

Lane walked eagerly next to his dad as they strolled toward the gang of squad cars blocking the parking lane in the crowded mall lot.

"This is a classic example of a felony takedown," Faroe said. "Watch and learn."

"Beats hell out of the Krebs cycle," Lane said, peering at the milling officers.

"Gotta watch that adrenaline. It's witchy stuff. Just remember, your mother as a judge has done more to leave the world a better place than she found it than I have hanging with St. Kilda."

"Then why isn't she still a judge?"

"Ask her."

"I did."

"What'd she say?"

"To ask you," Lane said.

"Sometimes good doesn't get the job done. Then St. Kilda does. We're the guys in the gray hats."

"Look at that gun! What kind is that?"

"Ease back," Faroe said quietly. "The cops have things under control, but they're still full of adrenaline and their guns are full of bullets. Give them plenty of room and don't do anything sudden."

One of the cops who was leaning out over the hood of his squad car with a shotgun at the ready glanced up at them and said flatly, "Stay back. This is a crime scene."

Faroe stood with his hands out at his sides, palms open.

Lane imitated him.

The cop nodded.

"I'm just worried about my car, Officer," Faroe said. "I don't want any buckshot holes in it."

"Your car's fine, sir. Just stay back out of the way."

"Yessir," Faroe said.

He drew Lane back behind a red Ford pickup, where they could watch without making anyone nervous.

"The nice thing about Arizona cops," Faroe said, "is they're used to dealing with armed suspects and felony takedowns."

"You mean that open-carry law that Mom is always rolling her eyes over?"

"Yeah. Note how the cops all pulled in from separate directions, but left firing lanes open in case the mopes in the van tried anything. Good technique."

Lane watched the officers unload two heavy-caliber automatic weapons and a half-dozen magazines of ammunition from the van.

"Why didn't the dudes fight back?" he asked. "Look at the firepower they had. Those things are more than a match for shotguns, aren't they?"

"The mopes on the ground are pros, just like the cops," Faroe said.

"How can you tell?"

"They survived a felony takedown."

"Huh?"

Faroe put his hand on Lane's shoulder and continued teaching his son the things that someday might help him to survive when others died.

"Note the jailhouse tattoos and the iron-pile physiques on those cuffed arms," Faroe said. "Pros know when to fight and when to fold. It was folding time. If there are six cops here now, there are eighteen more on the way, and the clowns on the ground want to live to fight another day."

"How did you get them to send six cops in the first place?" Lane asked. "Mom wasn't sure the desk sergeant would respond at all."

"I made sure that the police got two different calls, both with pretty much the same level of detail," Faroe said. "A single call about a Mexican in a van brandishing a long gun might have gotten the dispatcher to send a car or two. That would have tempted the bad guys to try something, which would have been messy but would have kept Gabriel off Kayla."

"Messy was what Mom was afraid of."

Faroe shrugged. He hadn't been thrilled with the odds, but he hadn't had a lot of time for finesse. "I made the first call and she made the second. Both of us specified the vehicle and the kinds of weapons, which brought the threat level way up. Then we had Javier Smith—the tall guy pretending to be a gardener—call the cops and give them a heavily accented tip about a gang hit going down in Chandler Mall."

"Awesome." Lane's eyes were bright with excitement.

"It got the job done. Cops usually do the right thing if they have enough information at the beginning. It's only when they start fumbling around in the dark, hunting rattlesnakes with their bare hands, that things go to hell real quick. Today was one of the good days."

Lane watched as the cuffed men were levered to their feet.

"C'mon," Faroe said. "Recess is over. Time to go back to the Krebs cycle."

53

Chandler Mall
Sunday
11:45 A.M. MST

The instant Foley answered his cell phone, Bertone began talking.

"I'm four rows down from the restaurant's front door. White Toyota rental sedan with California plates. You have three minutes to find me."

Bertone punched out and waited. While he waited, he watched while a former Ukrainian army sniper and his spotter, a Latino gangster named Gabriel, were stuffed into separate squad cars. Bertone wasn't worried about what they would tell the Chandler Police Department. Both men had already proved their ability to shut up many times.

And if they did talk, there were always men in prison who were eager to kill. The Ukrainian knew it. Gabriel knew it.

But the person Bertone really wanted to kill was walking away, laughing with a teenage boy. Bertone didn't recognize the boy, but he recognized Faroe as a man rumored to be a St. Kilda operative.

St. Kilda Consulting, which had been hired several months ago by John Neto to get revenge on Andre Bertone.

It could be simple coincidence.

Bertone wasn't going to bet his life on it.

He was still thinking about the unhappy implications of Faroe's appearance when Steve Foley knocked on the passenger-side window. Bertone hit the unlock button.

Foley took one look at Bertone's face and really wished he could be somewhere else. But he couldn't, so he slid in.

"I didn't hear any shots," Foley said.

"Be grateful. If you had, you'd be dead."

"Listen, I haven't done anything but follow your—"

"Shut it."

Foley swallowed hard. On the way from the restaurant to the car, he'd thought about his own situation. He wanted out.

Alive.

He was just a banker, no more or less honest than his corporate bosses and his wealthy clients required him to be. The money-laundering laws were flexible. They seemed designed more to shield clever bankers than to prevent illegal or immoral financial transactions. But at the same time, the laws provided steep penalties for bankers and banks that got caught sneaking around them.

Kayla had been his cover. As long as she was alive and talking, he was on short time as a free man.

"Did you correct the problem?" Bertone asked coldly.

Foley reached underneath his shirt and ripped out the wire, transmitter, and tiny microphone. "You know I didn't."

"You told me I would have ready access to that account at any moment. Then you told me weekends weren't included. Then you tell me that the account has a password, and you don't know that password. Now tell me why I shouldn't kill you."

"I was wrong about the capability of the remote access system," Foley said quickly. "But I'll take care of it as soon as I get the password from Kayla. The CHIPS transfers to Romania and the Czech Republic will clear immediately. The Russian transfer will take longer. That's just the nature of using SWIFT wires—"

"Your banker's codes and acronyms don't impress me," Bertone cut in. "Do you believe what Kayla told you?"

"Uh, yeah. Sure. She's not all that smart. You heard her try to put the arm on me for more money. She believes she's getting what she wants, so why should she lie to me?"

"Her new boyfriend. Did he have words with a tall man who was with a teenage boy?"

Foley blinked. "Yeah, how did you know?"

"The man is Joe Faroe, probably an agent for St. Kilda Consulting."

"Never heard of them."

"You've never heard of a lot of things that can kill you."

Foley shifted uncomfortably. "So where does Gabriel come into this? I thought he was supposed to take care of Kayla when she left the restaurant."

"The police arrested Gabriel and the Ukrainian before they could get Kayla."

"What?" Foley leaned against the dashboard with one hand like he was dizzy. "How?"

"How doesn't matter. In the end, the police and St. Kilda did you a favor."

Foley looked blank.

"If she had died without giving up the password, I would have taken great pleasure in killing you myself," Bertone said matter-of-factly.

"You've lost me, Andre. You're leaping all over the place."

"A retarded child could lose you. Obviously St. Kilda has a wire into the bank. Is it you?"

"What are you talking about?"

Bertone said something in Russian, then switched back to English. "You're too shallow, so I must assume it is Kayla who talks to St. Kilda."

Shaking his head again, Foley rubbed his hands against the black jeans. He wasn't liking anything he was hearing. None of it made sense.

"Look, I don't know about this St. Kilda, so how did Kayla?" he asked. "I mean, I suppose she could be some kind of undercover, but it doesn't make sense. Hell, nothing does. This isn't my world anymore."

"It is now."

Foley frowned and rubbed his palms rhythmically across his jeans. "You sure the tall guy wasn't a fed? That'd make sense."

"If federal agents have anything going, I will know it as soon as they do," Bertone said. He lit a cigar. "St. Kilda Consulting is private."

"Private? Like private eyes? You've got to be kidding."

"Unfortunately, I am not." He drew hard and exhaled the same way, filling the car with rich smoke.

Foley hit the window button. Nothing happened. He looked at the key, but didn't have enough nerve to reach into Bertone's space to turn on the windows.

"St. Kilda Consulting is very sophisticated and well financed." Bertone blew more smoke and watched Foley squirm. "They have been retained by an African government that is close to being replaced by a rebel insurgency based in a neighboring country."

"Who cares?" Foley muttered. "It's Africa, for chrissake."

"Precisely. Such things happen all the time in that part of the world. Unhappily, this potential target for regime change retained a private military and security company to press its interests on the worldwide stage."

"Expensive."

"A lot cheaper than war, actually. Pity, that. In any case, St. Kilda's efforts have been quite successful. They are the principal reason I felt compelled to enlist you and your bank in my operation."

"Christ," Foley said, putting his face in his hands. "What have you dragged me into—some kind of international spook party? I want out. I want out now!"

"There is nothing I would like better than to remove my money from your bank at the speed of light," Bertone said.

Foley looked relieved.

Bertone kept talking. "Then I would be free to kill you."

Pallor swept over the banker's skin.

"Ah," Bertone said. "I see I have your full attention. Finally. I have more than a hundred million of my own dollars invested in a game whose stakes you cannot imagine. I have enlisted the assistance of government officials in several countries, including your own. I am in quiet contact with international corporations of a size to make your bank's entire worth look meager. No doubt people will die before this business is concluded. I assume you would like to avoid being one of the bodies. Correct?"

Sweat showed on Foley's forehead. "Shit, yes. I'm in over my head, but I've got to keep swimming."

"Good, you are beginning to think like a man," Bertone said.

"As soon as the mainframe comes online at the bank Monday, I'll make sure the money gets transferred. Just tell me where to send it."

Bertone thought for a long moment, smoking, thinking.

"Assumptions," he said quietly. "Assumptions. They are the source of most serious mistakes in life."

"What's that supposed to mean?" Foley asked.

"You have assumed Kayla Shaw told you the truth. We have recently seen that she is not to be trusted. Why should we do so now?"

There was a long silence.

"I take that as agreement," Bertone said.

Foley was glad Bertone's attention had switched to Kayla. "Thinking about it now, she might have been lying," Foley said.

"About what?"

Foley hesitated, thinking fast. "About the reason I couldn't get access. She said it was because correspondent accounts aren't configured for remote access transactions. But how does she know that? She isn't even authorized for remote access."

"You think she was trying to mislead you?"

"Yeah. It's possible."

"To what end?"

"How the hell would I know? Isn't that the whole point of lying—to mislead?"

"Then guess," Bertone said.

"Maybe she was trying to buy time."

"To what purpose?"

"If she's involved with the international PI outfit, or whatever it is, maybe they're planning something down the line."

"Such as?" Bertone questioned, watching the other man closely.

"Uh . . ." Foley rubbed his sweaty palms over his jeans. "The feds often try to freeze accounts when they suspect money laundering. Maybe that's it."

Bertone was motionless but for a long exhalation of smoke. "Interesting. Tell me more."

"It happened one time, about a year ago. DEA and the IRS traced a Mexican drug lord's money to an account in our private bank. The first thing I knew of it was when an IRS enforcement agent walked into my office with an order from a federal judge in Tucson, freezing the account."

"Go on."

"I called the bank's corporate counsel, and he told me I had no choice but to shut down all access to the account. We ended up sitting on about two million bucks for almost three months while the client's attorney fought the order in federal court."

"Did the client win?"

"No, but it turned out pretty well for the bank. We had use of the money and never did have to pay the client interest. In the end, the feds took the money and we got a little smack on the wrist for being sloppy."

"I find my sympathies are with the client. Were it to happen to me, the banker would suffer a great deal more than a smack on the wrist." Bertone's back teeth chewed the end of the cigar.

"Uh, yeah, of course," Foley said hurriedly. "But that case taught me to be careful about whose name is on account documents as the banker. I gave your accounts to Kayla because I didn't want another laundering case tracked back to me."

"So you knew about this possibility, and you didn't mention it to me," Bertone said around the mangled end of the cigar. "You should have told me before I entered into this arrangement with you. I had no idea American Southwest was so careless with the client's money."

"Give me a break," Foley said. "You're a big boy. You ought to know how the business works."

"I conduct 'business' all over the world. My bankers *always* find a way to protect my interests as well as their own. That protection is the job of the banker, first and foremost. I do not hire bankers to be puppets of the local or federal police."

"We protect our clients until we're served with a federal restraining order. Then"—Foley shrugged—"we follow the letter of the law."

Bertone smoked in silence. He had investigated America's money-laundering laws just enough to know how to get around them. The nuances of the laws hadn't mattered then.

They mattered now.

"Are restraining orders like moving money?" Bertone asked. "Can it only occur during normal business hours?"

Foley nodded. "They sure can't just be shoved under the front door of the nearest local branch bank. There are proprieties to be observed, or our lawyers will feed the feds their restraining order and make them eat it."

Bertone stubbed out his cigar. "Then we must be certain the account has been emptied before the FBI and the IRS can act."

"I can't do anything before Monday morning."

"So says Kayla Shaw. You will test her words."

"Look," Foley said wearily. "I've already tried everything I can think of on the remote-access portal."

"Then go to the bank. Try it there."

"But—"

"Call me as soon as you arrive."

All Foley really heard was the chance to escape. He reached for the door handle. "Yeah, sure, whatever."

Just before the door closed, Bertone said clearly, "Do not make the mistake of thinking that Gabriel is the only killer I control."

Foley shut the door and forced himself to walk, not run, away.

54

Chandler Mall
Sunday
11:55 A.M. MST

Rand hung up his cell phone and crowded Kayla into a little alcove behind a towering potted plant.

"Grace can't believe that you just realized you have Bertone by the short and curlies," he said against her ear. "I'm having a tough time myself."

"That's because you're not an honest banker."

"Isn't that an oxymoron?" He *oofed* softly when her elbow met his belly.

"I was an honest banker. That means I never thought of my client's money as, well, accessible to me. Their money was just numbers in a column."

"So when did the lightbulb come on?"

"When I realized I hadn't given the password on Bertone's new account to anyone. You can add money without a password, but you can't subtract it from the account, even as a transfer to another of the client's accounts. I was going to tell Bertone at the party, but I forgot."

"Before or after the handcuffs?"

"About the time Bertone was telling me how he required special service from his bankers."

"Yeah, that'd be downright distracting. But was the rest of what you told Foley the truth?" Rand asked.

"Which part?"

"The one about not being able to move money from a remote access portal."

"I think it's true." She shrugged and nibbled along Rand's chin. "But true or not, Foley won't be able to. When it comes to computers, he doesn't know his butt from butter. He won't be able to do anything until Monday morning."

Rand kissed her hard, then straightened. "I hope that's enough time."

"For what?"

"Grace to get that restraining order on the account."

"Is there a problem?" Kayla asked.

"With bureaucrats, there's always a problem."

55

Scottsdale
Sunday
12:02 P.M. MST

Grace tapped her finger impatiently on the scratched and gouged end table next to the rump-sprung bed.

"Of course I know it's the weekend," she said crisply into the phone. She'd been so informed by a series of underlings until she had finally broken through to the judge's personal underling. "Unfortunately, criminals don't work regular hours."

The person on the other end of the line repeated his unwillingness to disturb an already overworked judge on the judge's birthday.

"As a former judge, I sympathize," she said. "However, as a judge, I wouldn't have minded the few minutes it would take to lock down a money launderer's accounts. I would consider it time well spent."

She closed her eyes and listened to the same unwillingness restated in different, less polite words. Pushing him any harder would just make him angry, which would make him even less helpful later on.

If there was a later on with Bertone's account.

Why do laws work so well against the lawful?

"Thanks, I really appreciate all you've done," Grace lied sincerely. "If anything new breaks on this, I'll call you."

She hung up and said bitterly, "But I don't know quite *what* to call you. Joe will. He's good with those kinds of words."

Pushing herself to her feet, she straightened her T-shirt over the growing mound of her pregnancy and headed for the unbolted doors connecting two of the cheesy motel's even cheesier rooms. The sharp scent of cleaning chemicals tainted the air of every room in the Scottsdale Sun-Up Inn, but Room 203—the one that had been reserved in her name—was rank with old cigarette smoke barely covered by some cheap room perfume that made her nose itch.

Arizona, last bastion of smokers and gunmen, she thought with a grimace.

She glanced around the room. Empty. It had been turned over, with fresh sheets and towels and a quick vacuum, but it was still a tired, threadbare motel room that had been inhabited by years of smokers.

"Joe?" she called out.

No one answered.

Lane was in the second room, nose deep in a textbook. She closed the door behind her, crossed the room, and headed for yet another interior door. When she opened it on her side, she came face-to-face with Faroe. He put his hand around her neck and kissed her thoroughly.

"I hope you aren't planning an assignation," she said, leaning her stomach against him, "because cheap motels and oily bureaucrats don't put me in the mood."

Lane snickered. "La la la, I'm not listening, la la la, I'm not—"

"No luck on the lockdown warrant?" Faroe asked.

"I didn't realize a judge's birthday was a sacred holiday," she said curtly.

"Only to oily bureaucrats." He rubbed her stomach, felt the baby doing backflips, and said, "C'mon. Rand and Kayla just got here."

"Lunch?" Lane asked without looking up.

"I gave you my last candy bar," Faroe said.

"I ate it."

"Then you'll survive for a few more minutes."

Faroe led Grace out of the second motel room and through the unlocked companionway door to a third room. Drawn drapes contributed to the gloom. Officially, this room hadn't been rented. The desk monkey had a fifty-dollar bill and a promise of two more if it stayed that way.

Nobody spoke until Faroe closed and locked the door. "Did the feds tail you?" he asked Rand.

"If they did, I didn't spot them."

"Then they probably didn't follow you."

"Good." Grace went to a chair, lowered herself into it, and sighed. "We left the camera crew at the compound to keep most of the surveillance teams anchored." She stretched her legs out on the cigarette-scarred coffee table. "Explain to me again why we need three rooms?"

"It's a cheap way of confusing the guys with the eyeballs," Faroe said. He slipped off her shoes, sat on the floor, and began rubbing her feet. "They saw you come in two-oh-three, so they'll probably camp all day on two-oh-three, waiting to ID whoever you meet there. Meanwhile, we'll come and go from two-oh-seven all day long, and they'll never figure it out. I hope."

"Hope is good." Grace yawned. "It's all that's keeping me from grabbing someone and squeezing his balls until his eyes cross."

"Oily bureaucrats don't have balls," Faroe said.

"Quiet, you're ruining my fantasy." She looked at Rand. "Joe has already filled me in on your meeting with Foley. Anything to add?"

"Bottom line hasn't changed," Rand said. "Bertone is trying like a dirty beggar to move that money, but so long as the account is protected by Kayla's password, that money is as secure as it would be under a temporary restraining order."

Kayla touched the back of Rand's hand and said, "Not quite. It's secure from the remote access program, but if Steve Foley goes back to the office, he could override my password with his own. If he thinks of it."

"Will he?" Grace asked sharply.

"He's a doofus on the computer, but he's under a lot of pressure right now." Kayla turned her hands palms-up. "He could figure it out, or he could get some computer-literate underling to talk him through it."

"Not good," Faroe said.

"No shit," Rand muttered.

Grace started to push herself to her feet. "I'm going to start chewing a personal underling's ass. We've got to get that warrant *now.*"

Faroe gave her a hand. He knew as well as she did that the chance of getting the warrant in time was melting away like ice on a hot griddle.

"Would St. Kilda get all upset if I moved the money in Bertone's account to one of mine?" Kayla asked.

"Forget it," Rand said instantly. "It's called theft, and you'd do hard time when it's discovered."

She looked at Faroe, then at Grace. "Is that St. Kilda Consulting's official answer?"

"Officially, St. Kilda hasn't heard a word of this," Faroe said. He looked at his wife. "Right?"

"Heard what?" Grace said automatically, but she was frowning as she settled back into the furniture. "Just for the sake of having a Plan B, no matter how unlikely it is to be used, tell me more about steal—moving Bertone's money to an account he can't touch."

"If I—um, whoever wanted to do that would have to go to my office."

"Too dangerous," Rand said flatly. "By now Bertone has probably speed-dialed every hit man in Phoenix."

"Why your office?" Grace asked, ignoring Rand.

"I don't have any kind of remote access," Kayla said. "I have to be at my office computer to, um, work with the account."

"Assuming someone got into your office and had the password," Grace said, "what would happen next?"

"I—someone would transfer the entire proceeds of the Bertone correspondent account to a personal trust fund."

"Can you really move almost two hundred million dollars into your own account?" Faroe asked, astonished.

"Sure. Moving money is what I do all day."

"How long would it take?" Grace asked.

"About three keystrokes," Kayla said.

"Followed by fifty years to life," Rand said roughly.

"But—" Kayla began.

"It's called grand theft," Rand said over her.

Grace sighed. "St. Kilda may push the frontier of law, but we usually leave ourselves a legal defense."

"Or no witnesses," Faroe said.

Grace ignored him. "Among other things, my job is to make sure we run as little risk of prison as possible."

Kayla tried to measure the risk rationally, but she kept seeing images from the DVD, tragedies and deaths that could have been avoided.

Should have been.

"I'll take the risk," she said.

"When you're one-hundred-percent certain of being caught, it's not called *risk*," Rand snarled.

"If the bank catches me—"

"—*when* they catch you," Rand cut in.

"Fine. When they catch me." She turned to Rand. "I'm not stupid."

"Can't prove it by Plan B."

She gave up and faced Grace. "The bank is superconscious of its public image. If St. Kilda Consulting and *The World in One Hour* spread muck all over Andre Bertone, I could end up looking like a brave little bank gofer who averted a tragic and illegal war."

"And if no one can spread enough muck on Bertone?" Rand asked.

"Then I gambled and lost," she said without looking at him. "Shit happens. This is the cleanest way to destroy Andre Bertone."

"No."

Kayla said distinctly, "It's a lot better than your Plan C, which is dumping Bertone in cold blood. You're not that kind of killer."

Faroe looked at Rand. "Plan C?"

Rand didn't say a word.

"Tear up my employment contract with St. Kilda," Kayla said to Faroe. "If I get caught, I don't want to take everyone down with me."

"Then you better tear up my contract while you're at it," Rand said to Faroe. "I'm going with her."

"You can't," she said.

"Watch me."

"I'll watch you as far as the front door of American Southwest Bank. After that, the security department will watch you waiting in the parking lot. No one—repeat no one—who isn't preauthorized gets into the operations area. It's basic security against kidnap and extortion."

Rand let out a long breath and tightened the leash on his temper. Nothing was turning out the way he wanted it to.

Kayla would be at risk.

And he couldn't stop her.

Rand stared at her for a long time, then said, "If anything jumps the wrong way, at any time, I'm going back to Plan C."

"I'll be right behind you," Faroe said. "When finesse doesn't get the job done, there's always brute force."

56

Phoenix
Sunday
1:15 P.M. MST

With a grim kind of pleasure, Kayla pulled into the parking space marked "Employee of the Month" and shut down the engine of the new rental car. Faroe and Rand had both insisted that she drive a "neutral" vehicle. In Phoenix, it didn't get much more neutral than a white SUV.

At the head of the parking lot, a bush covered with red flowers just made for a hummingbird's beak was an explosion of color.

"Enjoy the view," she said to Rand. "Come tomorrow, I bet they revoke my parking privileges."

"Embezzlement," Rand said.

She rolled her eyes.

"That's the word I've been trying to remember," he said. "It's when an employee diverts an employer's money. Losing your gold-star parking space is going to be the least of the fallout."

She reached over and kissed him on the corner of his unsmiling mouth. "I know what I'm doing."

"Good," he shot back. "Then maybe you can explain it to me."

"It's really simple," she said, spacing each word, speaking slowly. "I'm going to shift the money in Bertone's correspondent account into an account at the United Arizona Bank. The account was my grandmother's. I've kept it open, a kind of safety valve. I put my travel funds there."

"Kiss it good-bye."

"Oh, I don't know. Maybe I'll just take it and run." She nuzzled his chin and fanned her eyelashes outrageously. "Would you come with me?"

Rand stared at her for a moment, then gave up and laughed. "Hell, why not? Anywhere but Camgeria. The San Juan Islands in Washington would be good. The worst of winter is over. Maybe the FBI won't look for you on a nameless islet with no electricity."

"Do you mean that?"

He pulled her close for a hard kiss.

When he finally released her, she blew out a deep breath. “Hoo-yah. You mean it.”

“Sure do. You?”

“Oh, yeah.” She reached for her purse on the backseat.

“What in hell—?” he said suddenly.

She turned and looked out the windshield. A dark, strikingly large hummingbird was hovering around the bush directly in front of the car. As the bird turned in the sunlight, its vivid green gorget flashed, setting off the distinct white spot behind its eye.

“Magnificent,” she said. “Wow.”

“Pretty, too.”

“No, that’s its name, the magnificent hummingbird. They’re one of the biggest and rarest, but we see them regularly in Arizona.”

“I wish I could bug him,” Rand said.

“What?”

“It’d be easier to keep an eye on you.”

The bird zoomed off, returned, hovered, zoomed, and vanished.

Rand focused on the glass wall of the ten-story bank building. “Which one is your office?”

“Third floor, third from the corner,” she said, pointing it out. “Foley’s is the corner. Other private bankers are between.”

"No lights on."

"Bankers' hours. Gotta love 'em. No weekends, no holidays."

"Turn your lights on as soon as you get to the office," he said. "Turn them off when you leave. You get five minutes coming, five minutes in the office, and five minutes to get back here. Any longer and I'm kicking over a beehive. Got it?"

"Um, yeah. Five minutes up. Lights on. Five minutes with computer. Lights off. Five minutes back. Or you go postal."

"Believe it."

She looked at him and believed. "Start counting."

He reached for his door at the same time she reached for hers.

"No," she said urgently. "The weekend guards are off-duty Phoenix PD. They're authorized to carry live ammunition. They don't cut slack for anyone, not even sweet young things like me."

He looked at her across the console. "What's my cell number?"

"It's number one on the speed dial Faroe gave me along with the car."

Rand closed his eyes and saw his brother's blood. Everywhere.

"Come back to me, Kayla."

She brushed her hand over his cheek, his lips. Then she grabbed her purse and walked quickly to the bank entrance.

This will work.

It has to.

57

Phoenix
Sunday
1:22 P.M. MST

Kayla slid her employee ID card through the card reader. The latch on the glass door released.

One down.

How many to go?

The guard looked up from his *Guns and Ammo* magazine. He was a Latino with a buzz cut and a gentle leer.

Kayla didn't recognize him.

"What's a pretty thing like you doing working on Sunday?" he asked, laying the magazine aside and reaching for the entry log.

"I'm here to rob the bank," she said cheerfully. "Sunday seemed like a good day."

The guard spun the log and offered a pen so she could sign in. "Need any help?"

"If the bags are too heavy, I'll holler."

"Bet there's a handcart in the janitor's closet," he said, watching her write. "Just let me know."

As Kayla signed in, she saw that she was the first employee to log in since Saturday. She had the run of the place.

Time's a-wasting.

She turned toward the elevator.

"Uh-hummm." The guard cleared his throat.

"Is there something else?" Kayla asked, hesitating.

"You don't know the drill, do you? I need to verify your ID."

She handed over her ID card. "I keep my weekends to myself. But this time . . ." She shrugged. "No help for it."

"I guess it's only executives who put in the long hours."

"Yeah." *On the golf course.*

Something bankers and judges apparently had in common.

The guard compared Kayla's signature to the name on the badge, then consulted an employee directory.

"Private bank. Third floor, right?" he said, handing the badge back.

Kayla nodded.

"Don't go anywhere else."

She blinked. "What?"

"The security chief has issued new regs. He doesn't want anyone wandering after hours. You want to use a bathroom, come back to the lobby."

"Shouldn't be a problem. What I have to do will only take a few minutes."

"Whatever," the guard said, glancing over his shoulder at the elevator status board on the wall behind him. "I can check every floor from here to the roof with closed-circuit television monitors, so just go right to your office and come right back."

"Closed-circuit TV? That must make for some interesting videotapes."

The guard grinned. "I caught one of the vice presidents last weekend. He was polishing the wall of the elevator with his secretary's panties. She was still wearing them."

"Too much information. Way too much information."

"It's just for your protection, *chica,* so I can keep an eye on you."

"I feel safer already."

She headed for the elevator.

Forty seconds later, the doors slid open. As she walked into the third-floor corridor, she waved at the television camera mounted in a bracket just below the ceiling. Then she went directly to her office, turned on the lights, and looked down at the parking lot.

Rand was leaning against the SUV's front grille and staring up at her window. She waved. He waved back, then made a "spool-up" motion with his right index finger, telling her to hurry.

"Yeah yeah yeah," she muttered.

She dropped her purse on the desk, sat down at her chair, and booted up her computer.

It took forever.

The machine labored over the start-up page, then whirled and whirled before processing her log-in to the operations server.

Password Invalid

Her heart slammed.

Is there a special weekend access code?

She took a deep breath and logged in again. The computer accepted her with a welcoming bong.

Ten keystrokes later she was inside the Bertone account.

Holy holy hell!

Two hundred and fifty million dollars.

Her fingers shook over the keyboard. *Numbers, that's all. Just numbers in a column. Put it here. Put it there.*

No big deal.

Hell, the bank has deposits of more than twenty billion—that's bee-boy-billion—dollars.

Next to that number, Bertone's working fortune was lite beer.

But it could buy a lot of misery just the same. It could take apart a weak African nation, murder every citizen who objected, rape every natural resource, and leave behind starvation, disease, and ruin.

Her fingers were poised over the keys.

Trembling.

Here goes nothing. Well, not quite nothing. More like a quarter of a billion dollars.

She keyed in instructions that shifted the contents of the Bertone account to a Bank of America account in Tucson, punched enter, and waited. Seconds later, the screen confirmed that the money was now in her late grandmother's account a hundred miles away.

Grinning, she pushed back from her workstation and stood up, turning toward the door.

And right into Steve Foley's silver-plated pistol.

58

Phoenix
Sunday
1:25 P.M. MST

"What are you doing here?" Foley demanded.

Kayla stared at the shiny pistol and thought of the trophies he had in glass cases in his office.

Games, that's all. Paper targets or tin cans or bowling pins.

"Answer me!"

Fear slammed through Kayla. Fight or flee, and she couldn't flee. Her inner bitch rose up and snarled. "It's my office. What are *you* doing here?"

"Listen, bitch—" he began.

"Watch the sexist stuff," she cut in, forcing her voice not to tremble. "The company manual is real clear on that."

"Shut up or I'll shoot you where you stand. What are you doing here?"

"Looking at you."

His knuckles whitened on his pistol hand. "If Andre didn't want you alive . . ."

"But he does," Kayla said. *And she sure hoped he didn't change his mind before St. Kilda found her.* "So don't do anything stupid."

"Killing you wouldn't be stupid. It's your fingerprints all over Bertone's account. You're alone in the world. I could bury you in the desert and play dumb. The bank and the FBI would look for a long time and finally decide you're living in Venezuela or Brazil."

Carefully Kayla raised her trembling hands and backed around her desk, away from Foley.

Toward the window.

"Stop!" Foley said.

She looked at the black circle aimed right between her eyes.

She stopped.

"Bertone is a bad enemy," she said quietly. "If you kill me, he'll kill you."

"There's a lot I can do that won't kill you. You'll wish it had. And what I can't think of, Bertone will."

No argument there, so she waited.

Rand, I need you.

Now would be a good time to bring on Plan C.

But Rand was in the parking lot, fifty yards and a world away.

"Sit at your desk," Foley said sharply. "Hands in front of you."

Kayla put a leash on her inner bitch and her fear. She sat with her hands in plain sight. Foley's eyes were too wide, almost wild. She didn't want to get him so mad he forgot he needed her alive.

But being angry felt so much better than the icy fear coiled in her gut.

He kept the pistol trained on her and walked to the window. A brief glance was all it took. "Couldn't get your stud past the lobby guard, huh?" Impatiently he yanked the cord that closed the blinds.

Like the computer, it wasn't something he was used to doing for himself. The blinds jammed partially open.

"He knows I'm here," Kayla said. "He's expecting me in about three minutes. He knows everything I know. It's over, Steve. Put down the gun. I have friends who can help you. You won't even go to jail. It's Bertone they want, not you."

"You went to the feds? I'll kill both of you!"

"Kill me, and you're a dead man. The only question is who gets to you first, the man in the parking lot or Bertone."

"You just don't get it, do you?" Foley backed away from the window. "Andre Bertone is one of the most powerful men on the planet. You'll be a smashed gnat on his windshield."

"So will you."

Foley looked at the gun in his hand and smiled. "I can take care of myself."

"You've shot a lot of paper targets. You've got a lot of trophies. Any of them have blood on them?"

Foley flinched. "You really are a bitch, aren't you? And here I believed your girly-girl act."

"Shit happens. People change." *And a whole lot of shit has come down on me lately. Stand tight or run.*

Can't run.

So she would do the best job of standing she could.

"Call up Andre's account for me." He pulled out a notebook with the account numbers Bertone had given him. Not once did the muzzle waver from the space between Kayla's eyes. "I need to make some transfers."

Too late, she thought with fierce triumph.

But she did what he asked.

"It's up," she said.

"Show me."

She pivoted the screen so that he could see it. His glance flicked down to the bottom line. Widened.

"You've got the wrong account," he said flatly.

She switched the screen back and made a show of looking at numbers. "No, this is Andre Bertone's new account."

"It can't be. There's nothing in it!"

"Yeah." *When in doubt, brazen it out.* "I guess you're not the only bank employee he bought."

"What do you mean?"

"Simple," she said, lying through her straight white teeth. "When I checked the account just before you came in, it was empty. Bertone must have bought someone else in our bank to do his account juggling."

Foley was too shaken to question her words. He was staring at the screen and seeing his own death.

Kayla tensed to spin in her chair, hoping to knock the gun out of his hand, but Foley stepped back suddenly. He kept the silver pistol aimed between her eyes.

"Where's the money!" he demanded.

"I told you. It was gone when I got here a few minutes ago."

Foley's face went red, then white. His hand jerked, but he didn't pull the trigger. Instead, he backhanded her so hard that his signet ring left a bloody line across her cheek.

"Bitch. I don't believe you."

She blinked against the tears that wanted to come. Not fear or hurt.

Pure bitch fury.

"Feel better now?" she asked.

He lifted his hand again, then saw that she was ready to spring.

"On your knees," he said.

She thought about refusing. The sheen of his eyes didn't encourage her. She slid out of her chair onto her knees.

Foley exchanged his notebook for a cell phone and hit speed dial. "Andre? Your account is empty."

59

Phoenix
Sunday
1:31 P.M. MST

Rand McCree looked at his watch—*six minutes to go*—then shifted his focus from the front entrance to the windows of Kayla's office.

The blinds were mostly drawn.

Is it a signal?

The habit of a woman working alone?

Are the blinds on a sun/temperature sensor?

Watching the window, he walked to the far end of the business block that held the bank headquarters. Nothing changed. Nothing showed. No shadows moved in the small openings between the blinds.

And the lights were still on.

"Spool up, beautiful," he muttered. "We're on a short clock."

Five minutes to sign in and get to her desk was generous. She'd said transferring the money would take no more than a few keystrokes.

So where the hell is she?

He paced back to the car, then glared at the window again.

Nothing new.

Except the back of his neck felt like fire ants were crawling there. He hadn't been this jumpy since Camgeria.

Rand jerked his phone off its belt clip and dialed.

"Faroe."

"We're at the bank," Rand said. "I couldn't get past the lobby guard. Kayla's upstairs. She has five more minutes, but she should have been back by now."

"Bad feeling?"

"Real bad. I need some men to cover the exits, in case someone tries to sneak in. Or out."

"I'll see who's loose."

"I'll try to slide past the guard, but Kayla says they're off-duty Phoenix PD."

"Good luck."

"I'll need it," Rand said. "At least I might find out if there's anybody else in the building. Call and let me know how many bodies you're sending."

"Bodies. Sounds grim."

"Manpower, how's that?"

"Personpower. Grace would like that better."

"She Who Must Be Obeyed."

Faroe laughed. "Get used to it. You're next."

The fire ants crawling on Rand's neck disagreed. He cut the connection and headed for the lobby door.

Four minutes left.

60

Castillo del Cielo
Sunday
1:33 P.M. MST

Elena watched Bertone's face go from laughing to murderous seconds after he picked up the phone. When he looked like that, she feared for her children.

"Come, Miranda," Elena said quickly. She scooped up the little girl and retreated beyond Bertone's reach. "Poppa's busy."

A torrent of gutter Russian spilled out of Bertone.

"But he said he'd—" began Miranda.

"Later, sweet," Elena cut in. She kissed her daughter's pouting lips. "You can teach Momma your game now."

"You know how to play."

"But I don't know how to beat you at it."

Miranda's dark eyes brightened. "Won't teach you."

"I'll tickle you until you do."

Miranda giggled and snuggled against her mother. "You smell good."

Elena nuzzled the girl's hair as she carried her to the door. "You're wearing the same perfume."

"I smell good, too."

"The best," Elena said, carrying her out of the room. "The best-smelling little girl ever."

Bertone shut the door behind Elena.

And locked it.

"Again," Bertone said into the phone. "Tell me how you lost a quarter of a billion dollars."

61

Phoenix
Sunday
1:34 P.M. MST

Kayla was tired of being on her knees. She made a show of meekly staring at the floor, but she was listening to Foley's end of the cell phone conversation. Whatever Bertone was saying to Foley, he didn't like. He was pale, greasy.

He stank of nervous sweat and fear.

She was sure she did, too.

"I told you," Foley said to the cell phone. "The fucker is empty. No money. No funds. Nothing! You sure you didn't have someone else trans—"

Kayla couldn't hear Bertone's answer, but the roar of sound told her that he was throwing a fit.

Poor Elena. Does he beat her when things go wrong?

If he did, he never left a mark on her perfect face.

"Okay, okay, I hear you," Foley said. "I didn't move a penny, you didn't move a penny, and that leaves Kayla, who got here about a minute before me. That's hardly enough time to log in, much less—" He stopped talking and listened. "She told me, that's how. Wait. Let me check something."

More sound and fury poured out of the cell phone when Foley set it down. Then silence. He put the muzzle of the pistol in Kayla's mouth.

"If you make a sound," he said, "I'll kill you and take my chances with Bertone."

Kayla understood that Foley was under the kind of pressure that made people crack apart like a dropped egg. She held herself very still, breathing around the pistol muzzle, tasting metal and something darker. Fear and the rage of a cornered animal fought for control of her mind. Neither won. Or lost.

Foley wiped his forehead, picked up the office line, and punched in three digits.

"Yeah, this is Henning up in Operations," Foley said. "I was supposed to meet Kayla Shaw at her office a few minutes ago, but she's not here. Can you tell me whether she logged in and when?"

He listened, nodded, and glared at Kayla. "Okay, thanks. She must be around here somewhere." He started to hang up when the lobby guard asked him a question. "Oh, yeah, I came in from the executive garage," Foley said easily. "Used the card lock on the service elevator." He listened, then rolled his eyes. "Yeah, yeah, I know I was supposed to log in with you. I'll stop by in a few minutes, soon as I finish with Kayla."

He hung up.

Kayla watched the floor.

"You're a real lying piece of ass, aren't you?" Foley said, leaning on the pistol until she gagged.

Instead of killing her the way he wanted to, Foley yanked the muzzle out of her mouth and picked up the cell phone again.

"She's been here for almost fifteen minutes, more than enough time to kick the transfer out." He flinched, watched Kayla over the barrel of his silver pistol, and listened. "No, I can't reconstruct the transfer. Maybe some ass-wipe geek in IT could, but I'm a big-picture man." More listening. He glared at Kayla, set down the cell phone, and with no warning backhanded her again.

Kayla lifted her hands to block another blow, but instead of hitting her, Foley grabbed a handful of her hair and twisted.

"What did you do with the money?" he demanded.

She lashed at him with her left hand, curling her fingers over her thumb the way she had been taught by her dad, aiming for Foley's throat as she surged up off the floor. He managed to block the blow, but had to let go of her to do it.

"Nothing, you bastard," she said in a raw voice. "You get nothing from me."

"I'll kill—"

"Yada yada yada," she cut in savagely. "I'm the only one who knows where the money is. Kill me and Bertone is broke. Is that what he wants?"

Foley stared at Kayla. He wanted to kill her so badly that he could taste blood. He made a fist, but picked up the cell phone instead. Killing her was Bertone's privilege. He'd made that real clear.

"She's done something to the money," he said to Bertone, "but it will take a guy like Gabriel to get it out of her." He listened, nodded. "Good plan. See you." He punched out.

Kayla stood with a defiance that came from temper and fear. Fear, mostly. The more Foley talked to Bertone, the meaner her boss became.

"On your knees, bitch. Or do you want me to kick your feet out from under you?"

Slowly she sank to her knees again.

Foley stepped behind her.

She tensed against the blow she was sure was coming.

Cold steel slammed around her wrists, clicked, locked.

Handcuffs.

Her heart turned over. She fought not to throw up, to keep her head, to think.

“Stand up,” he said.

When she didn’t move fast enough, he yanked on the cuffs, wrenching her arms, pulling her to her feet. A hard shove between the shoulder blades sent her staggering toward the door.

“Open it. If you scream, I’ll kill whoever hears it. And I’ll hurt you real bad. I’d enjoy that. A lot.”

Kayla took a deep breath and opened the door. No one in sight. No elevator doors opening or closing.

No point in screaming.

“Where are we going?” she asked.

A shove between the shoulder blades was her only answer. She staggered, straightened, and looked at the wall clock.

Time’s up.

62

Phoenix
Sunday
1:35 P.M. MST

As Rand reached the bank's front door, he composed his features into the open, casual expression of an ordinary guy looking for his ordinary gal. He knew that cops and security guards made their livings by drawing lines in the sand. Respect their lines and make a friend.

Challenge those lines and go to jail.

"Hey, Officer," he said as he pushed through the door. "Did you see a good-looking girl called Kayla Shaw come through here about fifteen minutes ago? We're way late for our lunch."

The guard smiled. "Everybody in the world is looking for that girl. And I can see why. Hoo-yah, what legs!"

Rand forced an answering smile. "Hoo-yah is right. Where'd she go?"

"I signed her in to the third floor. She said she'd be right back down."

Rand crossed the lobby to the guard desk and leaned against it casually, glancing down at the log book that was still turned toward him. Kayla's name was the only one on the page with a sign-in time but no sign-out.

"Don't suppose you'd let me go up and drag her out, caveman style," Rand said.

"Not unless you've got employee ID from American Southwest Bank," the guard said.

"Hell. We're going to miss our reservations."

"Sorry. But she ought to be along shortly. Somebody from Operations just called down and said he was looking for her, too. Apparently they had a meeting laid on, but he said it wouldn't be long."

The fire ants on Rand's neck went into overdrive. "Well, damn. She didn't say anything about meeting somebody else."

"Maybe she's seeing somebody on the side," the guard suggested with a grin.

Rand pointed at the log. "I don't see anybody else signed in."

"Yeah, well, you know how these high-powered executives are. He came in through the card lock from the garage. They're supposed to come by and sign in with me. He said he would when he and your girl were finished."

"Did you get a name?" Rand asked.

The guard stiffened. He was used to asking questions, not answering them. "I always get names."

Rand took off his sunglasses, letting the guard see his eyes clearly. It was a gesture designed to win trust. The fact that the guard's eyes narrowed told Rand that he wasn't looking warm and fuzzy.

"And you don't want to tell me the name," Rand said.

"It's not my job."

"Right. Your job is to protect employees, as well as the bank itself."

The guard stared at him.

"So if a good-looking young female banker got hassled or worse on your watch, your ass would be in a crack," Rand said.

"Where are you going with this?"

"Kayla told me that she's been having trouble with a bank employee, a supervisor. She hasn't complained to Human Resources because she didn't want to get the grabby dude in trouble. Frankly, I'm worried that he might be up there right now, stalking her."

"What's the man's name?"

"Foley."

The guard shook his head. "Wrong name."

"Is it? Or did he give you a bogus one?"

The guard reached for a spiral-bound book on the desk in front of him and thumbed through the roster of employees. He found H, examined every name, and looked up. "The son of a bitch lied to me."

Rand started for the elevators.

The guard blocked the way. His hand was on the butt of his pistol. "Ease back, mister. For all I know, you and Kayla and this other dude are running some kind of scam."

Rand fought an urgent need to dump the guard on his ass. "Call her office. If she answers, tell her to lock the door until you get there and not let anybody in."

The guard took Kayla's extension from the registration log. He listened to it ring five times.

"She's not answering, but that doesn't mean she's in trouble," the guard said, meeting Rand's hard eyes. "Right now, mister, I want you to go back outside while I get some help in here."

"Use me."

"Can't. Against the rules. Move it. Longer you stand here, the longer it'll take me to sort this out."

With a silent curse, Rand spun and strode toward the front door. As he opened the heavy glass panel, a

Mini Cooper convertible darted into the parking space beside Kayla's car.

Rand jogged down to the car as Faroe stood in the driver's seat and stepped out without opening the door.

"She's inside," Rand said. "So is somebody who logged in through a card lock."

"Bertone?" Faroe asked immediately.

"More likely Foley. I'm assuming he's armed."

"Given what we've found out about him, that's a good assumption," Faroe said. "He's got a thing for guns."

Beside the Mini, another St. Kilda vehicle braked to a halt. Two streetwise operators in T-shirts and shorts piled out. Each wore a belly pack big enough to carry a pistol.

"The lobby guard won't let us in, but we can block all the exits," Rand said. "You two guys get around the corner. Foley came in through the executive garage. Likely he'll go out that way."

"He drives a black Range Rover," Faroe said.

"I'll do a walk-through of the garage," one of the operators said. He pulled a worn dog leash out of his belly pack. "You know, 'Here, Muffin, come to Daddy, you wretched little shit.' "

"Good," Rand said. "But don't crowd the security guys. I told the lobby guard that Kayla was being stalked. He's off-duty Phoenix PD. I wouldn't be surprised if he calls in real badges. He looked worried enough."

The two operators nodded and set off toward the garage at a lope.

"I'll take the other direction," Faroe said. "There can't be more than two or three exits on the south and west sides. I've got another crew coming in from Scottsdale north. So relax, Rand. We've got her covered."

"If it was Grace at risk?"

Faroe didn't answer. He just set off at a run to cover the exits opposite the garage.

63

Phoenix
Sunday
1:41 P.M. MST

The corridor was empty. Foley crowded Kayla down the hallway to his own office, keyed in, and locked behind him. It took less than twenty seconds. She hoped the guard had seen her on the corridor camera, but she wasn't counting on it.

Foley shoved her into a chair.

"Move and I'll feed you this gun," he said.

Kayla didn't move. She was still tasting metal and gun oil in her mouth, and her throat was raw from being raked by the end of the pistol. She watched him go to his desk, unlock a file drawer, and pull out a stack of manila folders.

A grim smile changed his tan, closely shaved face into a death mask. He tapped the files on the desk, then slid them into his briefcase.

KYC files.

Kayla's stomach flipped. Obviously Foley didn't expect to come back. Those kind of files weren't supposed to leave the bank. Ever.

He looked at her. "Bet you wish you'd thought to take the bank references and corporate documents of every suspect private banking client with you."

"I don't have any suspect private clients. I turned down their business or bucked them up to you for refusal."

"Have I thanked you for those referrals? Profitable for the bank. Very profitable for me. I'm especially pleased with Jesus Del Santos and Ramon Herrera Parra. Did you know who they were when you bounced them up to me?"

"No."

"Del Santos was the lieutenant governor of Jalisco, and Herrera was chief of the *federales* in northwest Mexico. They both have eight-figure accounts in our bank now."

"How did you wash the blood off their money?"

"Power, babe, power and politics. Don't cry to me if you weren't smart enough to get them on your books."

Foley unlocked another file and pulled out a flat aluminum case that could have held cameras. He was undoing the catches on the lid when the phone on his desk began to ring. He glanced at the console.

"It's your line," he said. "Your boyfriend?"

Kayla stared blankly at Foley.

Foley glanced at his watch, then cocked his head, listening.

"They're going to start looking pretty soon," he said, more to himself than to her.

The phone rang.

He opened the case.

Kayla saw that it was lined with plastic foam that had been cut out to hold certain shapes.

The phone rang.

The pistol on the desk would have fit one of the empty cutouts. Next to it lay a black metal cylinder that she guessed was a silencer.

The phone rang.

Black on silver is out this season, she thought. But she didn't say it out loud. She didn't trust her voice.

The phone rang.

Foley fit the cylinder to the end of his pistol and spun it into place.

The phone rang.

He picked up a loaded magazine from the case and dropped it into the pocket of the dark wind shell he wore over his white silk T-shirt.

The phone rang.

Methodically he closed and relocked the drawers.

The phone didn't ring.

"You have got two choices," Foley said. He forced the cold bulb of the silencer between her lips. "You can come with me and keep your mouth shut or you can die here."

His expression told her that he meant it. He was coming apart in front of her eyes. There was only one thing he cared about right now.

Getting out.

"I'll go with you," she managed around the silencer.

Finger on the trigger, he stared at her for several long breaths. Then he shoved her away.

"We'll take the elevator. If we run into anybody—your boyfriend or a security guard or a maid—I'll kill them."

Kayla believed it. She could wait to make a break for it until he got her to the garage. Rand would be there. She was certain of it.

And he was no innocent bystander.

"Be quiet or their blood will be on your hands no matter who pulls the trigger," Foley said. "Got that?"

She nodded.

He picked up the briefcase and shoved her toward the door.

They walked swiftly down the long corridor, past the employee elevators. They turned the corner, heading for the executive elevator that served the parking structure. He reached for the button to call the elevator.

Around the corner behind them, the employee elevator chimed, announcing a car's arrival.

Foley slammed Kayla against the elevator door and held her there with the weight of his body and the silencer digging into her throat. They listened to the metallic jingle of a guard's key ring and the faint tread of shoes on the hallway floor. The guard knocked loudly on a door.

"Kayla! Kayla Shaw!" The guard's voice was achingly clear.

So close.

"You first," Foley whispered. "Then him."

So far away.

She heard the guard open the door to her office, enter, and call her name again. Then he came back in the hallway, shutting the door behind him. A radio crackled.

"Desk, this is Wapner. She's not in her office. No sign of trouble. Nobody in Foley's office, either. You want me to start going office-to-office here?"

There was a pop of static, then a voice came back over the guard's handheld radio.

"Negative. Check the Operations floor and secure it. We still don't know if this is a diversion or a genuine

incident. When backup gets here, we'll clear the building floor by floor."

"Affirm," Wapner said.

Foley and Kayla listened to the guard's jingling progress down the hallway. The elevator was waiting for him. Its doors closed with a sigh very like the one Kayla let out as the crisis passed.

As Foley pressed the executive elevator button, for the first time he realized how good she felt squeezed between the metal door and his body. He smiled and slid the pistol down between her breasts, circled one nipple with the silencer.

"Too bad you never let me in your pants," he said.

She swallowed against the vomit rising in her throat.

The door opened. She staggered backward, free for an instant.

He laughed and punched a floor button.

She couldn't stop a sound of dismay. He hadn't punched the button for the garage.

He was going to the roof.

She wasn't going to get away.

Be safe, Rand.

Whatever you do, be safe.

Kayla no longer believed that safety was a possibility for her. Compared to Foley's sweaty finger on the trigger, doing federal time was looking like paradise.

At least she would be alive.

64

Phoenix
Sunday
1:45 P.M. MST

When Rand came through the front door, the lobby guard was on the phone and the radio at the same time.

"I told you to stay the hell out of the way," the guard growled. "No, not you," he said to the phone, then held the receiver against his shoulder.

"Some friends of mine are outside," Rand said quickly. "Two of them are in shorts and T-shirts checking the executive parking structure. Another man is keeping an eye on the opposite exits. Some more friends are on the way. Don't shoot them by mistake."

The guard squinted at Rand for a few seconds. "Are you some kind of badge?"

"We're private. Kayla hired us to protect her."

"Looks like you fucked up."

"Let me upstairs."

The guard shook his head. "I don't care if you're a friggin' FBI undercover. Nobody goes inside. My boss chewed hard when he found out I'd called in the local police. Then I told him a girl was missing."

"She is."

"You'd better not be screwing me here, or I'll have your ass for kicking practice."

Rand grabbed what was left of his temper and held on. "We're staying on public property, but if we see Kayla in trouble, we're going to trespass the hell all over your shiny shoes. You don't like that, find her before we do!"

The guard pointed at the door with a long index finger. "We'll do a floor-by-floor as soon as the PD arrives. Now get the hell out of my face."

Rand glanced again at the elevators, but knew the guard was just looking for an excuse to take him down. With a ripe curse, Rand strode across the lobby and out the front door before he or the guard lost it. The front door opened.

Sunlight poured over Rand like fire.

A fourth car had arrived. The woman trotting toward him was trim and lithe, carrying two radios. She gave one to Rand.

"Jeff and Barney are in the garage," she said. "They found a Range Rover that comes back to your brunch date, Foley."

"Tell them to sit on it. Don't let it move."

"Already done. Faroe has the back covered. We'll find the woman."

"What we'll find is a hostage situation and a bunch of cops who will take five hours to get organized."

He spun and glared up at the shiny glass skin of the building, looking from pane to pane, hoping to see something better than his fear. The woman answered the radio phone. Faroe reported that the back side of the building was secure.

No one had seen Kayla.

Rand saw his brother's face, covered with blood, no more pain, no fear, just a slow sliding away into death.

Only it was Kayla's face, Kayla sliding away.

"Suck it up," the operator said to him, gripping his forearm with surprisingly strong fingers, "or get out of the way."

He stared into her serious brown eyes. "What's your name?"

"Mary. I'm a sniper."

"Where's your rifle?"

"I'm on vacation."

"Then what the hell are you doing here?"

"Trying to keep you from going ballistic."

He drew a deep breath and let it out slowly.

"The true warrior fights best when he reminds himself that he is already dead," Mary said.

"Faroe's favorite saying," Rand said bitterly. "But what does the warrior do when his fear is for someone else?"

There was no answer but the one Mary had already given him.

Suck it up.

He looked away from the building, trying to find something, anything, that would allow him to focus. There was a tree nearby, bare branches. A fiercely colored hummingbird dashed in and sat for a moment, looking right and left, searching for flowers or competitors or females. Sunlight flashed on the bird's green feathers and brilliant red gorget.

Anna's hummingbird. A species noted for pushing the edges of its territory, its limitations.

Good luck, bird. You'll need it.

The bird took off in a flash of color and intensity.

Rand blew out a breath. "Okay," he said to Mary. "I'm okay."

She looked at him intently, nodded.

Then he heard the helicopter.

"No way," Mary said, grabbing his forearm again.

"Why not? Bertone owns more than fifty aircraft."

"In Africa."

"Not all of them."

The sound of the chopper was loud, but still low and far enough away that Rand couldn't see it. He turned and looked at the bank building. There was room for a good pilot to set down on the front lawn.

Mary followed his glance. "We'd still have her covered." She touched the belly pack at her waist. "If the pilot lands, I can put ten in the turbine."

Rand stared at the building. Certainty washed over him in an icy wave. "Not if he lands on the roof."

He ran for the front door while Mary punched the radio and started giving staccato updates.

An instant later the helicopter dropped down onto the roof and landed, still under full power. The cargo door of the aircraft slid back.

Rand reached the lobby just as the helicopter took off. It banked steeply and sped off to the east. The pilot was lean and blond.

Not Bertone.

Just before the cargo door slid closed, Rand saw two figures inside the bay. One was lying flat. The other flipped a bird at him.

Then there was nothing but the fading sound of rotors.

"*Shit.* If I'd had my rifle . . ." Mary said in a low voice. But all she had was a pistol and the radio was yammering. When Rand started toward the parking lot, her strong hand clamped down on his forearm, holding him. "Faroe wants to know what kind of helo, ID numbers, all of it," she said quickly.

"Hind, Mi-24. Russian. Bertone imports them for firefighting."

"Sweet."

"Oh, yeah, Bertone's a sweetheart."

And he's a dead man walking.

Rand wrenched his arm free and ran toward the rental SUV.

"Where are you going?" Mary called after him.

He didn't answer.

65

Phoenix
Sunday
1:50 P.M. MST

Rand fought Sunday-afternoon traffic on Scottsdale Road, cursing and wheeling from lane to lane until he almost overran a police cruiser and had to clean up his act. He wanted to smash his fist through the windshield. Instead, he concentrated on being a good citizen and courteous driver.

The cruiser finally turned onto the freeway.

Rand put the accelerator on the floor.

As he raced under the 101 Freeway, headed north toward Cave Creek and Pleasure Valley, his cell phone went off. He fished it out and punched up the speaker.

"What?" he demanded.

"What the hell are you doing?" Faroe shot back.

"Driving."

"Don't piss me off. Where are you going?"

"You don't want to know."

"Then I already know. Sky house, right?"

Rand didn't answer.

"Make sure you can do the time for any crime you commit," Faroe said.

"I'll bury it deep."

Faroe's end was silent for a moment. Then a low curse and "In your place I'd do the same. Let me know if I can help."

"Did the cops find anything at the bank?"

"Negative, so far. They're trying to trace the helicopter."

"They won't find a thing. The pilot wasn't Bertone."

"You sure? He used to fly helos before he could afford to hire someone else for the dirty jobs."

"Too lean. Long hair, wrong color."

"Damn. One of our guys works a regular job at the FAA regional center," Faroe said. "He may be able to get a line on the bird."

"They'll stay under the radar. If I see the helo at the house, I'll tell you, but I doubt that it's there."

"So why are you going?"

"Remember? You don't want to know."

"You met Mary. We're getting her the tools of her trade as I speak. Keep it in mind."

"I will."

Rand punched the call off and drove hard until he turned onto the county road that led to the gated entrance to Andre Bertone's house. He stopped on a high hilltop short of the gate and stared at the mansion on top of the mesa. From here he could see the garage and someone washing the bulletproof limo that drove Elena everywhere she and the kids wanted to go. He could also see the helipad.

Empty.

He wasn't surprised. Foley had left more wreckage behind than even Bertone's diplomatic passport would clean up.

But Elena was still there.

Maybe Bertone was, too.

Be there, you bastard.

He grabbed the cell phone and punched up Faroe's number.

"Where do you want Mary?" Faroe asked.

"Not yet. I need a helo. I'm going to test Kayla's certainty that Elena is a good mother."

"Huh." Faroe breathed out hard. "You want the helo open or stealth?"

"Bells and whistles all the way," Rand said. "Hell, bring in a news chopper."

"Okay."

"What?" Rand asked, confused.

"I told you yesterday."

"Tell me again."

"The camera crew from *The World in One Hour* put the squeeze on a local network affiliate for a weather and traffic chopper. They're doing background shots of Phoenix, the businesses Bertone owns, and as much of the Bertone house as they can legally get."

"Thank you, God," Rand said.

"You're welcome."

"You're going to hell."

"You know anyone who isn't?"

"No. I'm on a hilltop about a half mile south of the castle. If I can't get inside, is the helo pilot good enough to pick me up?"

"Ask Martin. You have his cell?"

Rand didn't bother to say good-bye. He just cut out, called Martin, and waited for the okay man to answer.

66

Over Phoenix
Sunday
1:54 P.M. MST

All Kayla could see was the shiny tops of Foley's loafers. All she could hear was the hammering noise of a helicopter in flight. She knew she was bruised and scraped from Foley's rough handling, but she couldn't feel anything except the adrenaline flooding her body. Her thoughts came with unnatural speed and clarity.

Can't run now.

Foley is the weak link.

Bertone is the stone killer.

Work on Foley.

She groaned and pushed away from the gun barrel jolting against her skull. Even Foley was smart enough not to shoot in a moving helicopter.

"Hold still, bitch!" he yelled.

The pilot winced and yanked off his headphones.

Kayla pulled her hair free of Foley's grasping fingers and shouldered herself into a sitting position against the helicopter's side. Behind her back, handcuffs wrapped her wrists like obscene bracelets.

No weapons within reach.

No purse.

No cell phone.

Not even a nail file.

The flat tract houses of Phoenix raced by in giddy beige curves as the pilot maneuvered to avoid power poles, telephone lines, and freeway overpasses. He was flying so low the skids nearly clipped roof tiles.

She wondered what Bertone would do if she died in a crash.

At least it would be quick. Maybe I should get my hands in front, do a Flight 93, and bring down this bird.

Or maybe not.

There's still a chance to get out alive after we land. Small, but still a chance. That's more than Flight 93 had.

Foley unhooked his harness and started to go after his prisoner.

The pilot grabbed his shoulder, shoved, and said, "*Nyet!*" loud enough to be heard over the engine noise.

The helicopter swayed and shimmied.

Foley sat down hard.

Kayla leaned her head against the vibrating metal of the helicopter and thought hard.

What is Foley's weakness? Greed?

Hell, yes.

Stupidity?

Depends.

Would he believe I'd be his sex slave in order to survive?

In my place, would he do it?

Hell, yes.

Then he'll believe it when I do.

With feral eyes, Kayla watched the men and waited for a chance to knee Foley in the balls and break his nose with her forehead. Her dad had taught her to fight only as a last resort—and then to fight hard, mean, and dirty.

All she wanted was a chance.

Just one.

67

Phoenix
Sunday
2:10 P.M. MST

The gate guards had been changed. Bertone was obviously digging deep for people with no previous loyalties or ties—except to him. The man on duty looked Uzbek, was sweating like a turkey on a spit, and smelled like a crowded Paris bus in summer. His hand was on the butt of his pistol, a Tokarev that looked as tough and hard-used as the guard himself.

Rand rolled the window down.

"Your business?" the guard demanded in heavily accented English.

"I'm here at Mrs. Bertone's invitation. I won the art contest last night. She said she wanted to talk to me about some other paintings."

"Wait."

The guard retreated, called the house, spoke, listened, and hung up. When he walked back to the car, his hands were at his side.

"You need appointment," he said. "Mrs. Bertone too busy with the United States senator to talk some painter. Come tomorrow."

"Huh."

The guard stared at Rand blankly. "Leave."

"Well, hell, could you just open up the gate so I can pull through and turn around?" Rand asked.

The guard narrowed his eyes. "Use road there." He pointed to the curbed semicircle in front of the shack that would allow vehicles to reverse direction.

"Oh. Got it."

Rand glanced across at the exit from the estate, which had no gate. It was protected by a strip of tire shredders. He reversed, keeping an eye on the guard, then started into the turnaround.

The guard walked back toward the shack to get out of the desert's brutal sun.

Rand cramped the wheels hard right, hopped the curb, and accelerated quickly toward the tire shredders.

At the last second he found a gap between two ranks of the shredders and swung the left-side tires into it. The tires on both right wheels blew out. The SUV lurched hard to the right. He yanked the steering wheel, fought the pull, and straightened out the vehicle.

With a grind of steel on pavement, he accelerated up the hill. As he rounded the first curve in the long driveway, he heard the hard metal slap of a bullet hitting the tailgate just below the SUV's rear window.

Then he was out of range and out of sight.

At the garage he crammed the nose of the SUV into the passageway that led to the house. Inside the garage, a driver was leaning on a Cadillac with congressional plates, chatting with the man outside washing the limo. The big black Humvee Bertone loved to drive wasn't there.

Both men stared when Rand bailed out of the rental SUV and raced toward the house.

Outside the servants' entrance to the kitchen, he nearly knocked over a round-faced maid in a classic black dress and white apron. She was emptying trash.

"Mr. Bertone," he said curtly. "Take me to him."

The maid's eyes got big. She was so startled she forgot to speak English. *"No es aqui."*

Rand wanted to doubt her, but she was too off-balance, too frightened, to tell anything but the truth.

He'd settle for second best.

"Mrs. Bertone," he said curtly. "Where is she?"

"En la casa." She pointed toward the glass wall of the great room that looked out on Pleasure Valley and the Valley of the Sun. *"Con* Senator Rogers."

Rand sprinted past her to the front door. Unlocked. He shoved it open, turned left in the atrium, and palmed his phone on the belt clip. Without looking he hit number one on the speed dial and came to a stop just outside the great room.

"Faroe here."

"Send in the helo," Rand said.

He punched out without waiting for confirmation. When he strode into the great room, Elena was facing toward the atrium. She looked puzzled for a moment before she recognized him. The handsome white-haired man sitting on the couch with her turned to see what had caught her attention. He looked more annoyed at the interruption than she was.

"Mr. McCree, I think it was," Elena said, a touch of disdain in her voice.

Rand nodded.

"I was not expecting you," she said. "The senator and I are in the midst of a tête-à-tête, a private conversation."

"What I have to say to you tête-à-tête is more important to your children than whatever bullshit you're trading with the politician."

"Who is this man?" The senator stood up and faced the intruder as he walked farther into the room.

The politician would have been more impressive if he hadn't been in shorts and a pink golf shirt.

Elena didn't rise. "He's a struggling artist who thinks winning a prize gives him the right to be rude to me. He will regret the impertinence."

"How did he get past the guard?" the senator asked.

"I have no idea. I'll call security and have him removed." She reached for a white telephone on a table at her end of the couch.

The pulse beating in the open throat of her silk shirt put the lie to her cool voice. Some things even a good actress couldn't hide.

"Don't bother," Rand said. "Your guards are scrambling right now."

He stepped in front of the senator and looked out the tall glass wall toward the south. A brightly painted helicopter was closing in at high speed. Already he could see the camera blister on its nose.

"But," Rand said, turning back with a feral smile, "you might tell your men to keep their guns out of sight. That kind of publicity will undercut all the social climbing you've done up to now."

"Guns—my children—" She leaped to her feet.

"Your children are fine," Rand said. "If you want them to stay that way, shut up and listen to me."

White-faced, Elena sank back onto the couch.

"Now see here, young man," the senator began.

"No, *you* see," Rand said to the senator. "Her husband kidnapped my fiancée. If Elena wants her kids to avoid the shit storm that's coming down, she'll listen to me."

"You're nuts," the politician said, reaching past Elena for the phone.

"How would you act if you were on camera, Senator?" Rand asked. "Think about it, because a news chopper is coming in right now. Elena can be gracious about it and help me, or she can look like a gangster's moll on the six o'clock news." He turned on Elena. "How would your children like that, Mrs. Bertone?"

She put a hand on her neck to cover the telltale hammering of her pulse. "Whatever you want. Just keep my children out of it."

"That's up to you," Rand said.

The sound of a helicopter's big blades beat through the windows. The craft was close enough that everyone could see the network logo on its red, yellow, and blue side. The pilot flared and took up station fifty yards off the pool, his camera aimed directly at the front of the house. Technically, he wasn't violating anybody's airspace.

Yet.

"I don't understand," she said in a strained voice.

"That's a good story," Rand said. "You stick with it when the reporters start screaming, asking what you think about the thousands of people who were slaughtered so that you could sit on your pampered ass in the sky castle you designed."

Her eyes widened. She hugged herself and made a low sound.

Rand kept pushing. He didn't like it, but it was the least of what he would do to get to Bertone while Kayla was still alive.

"It's over," he said flatly. "Your husband's a gunrunner. *The World in One Hour* can prove it. Bertone is going down. Hard. Your only choice is whether you and the children go down with him."

"What the hell is going on?" the senator demanded as he backed away from the windows like they were on fire.

Rand gave him a sideways look. "Senator, you better get the hell out of here. The good citizens of your district won't like finding out how you were caught in a tête-à-tête with an international gunrunner's arm candy. Blood, money, and sex make great headlines."

"This is outrageous!" the senator said.

"No," Rand shot back. "What's outrageous is that Kayla Shaw was kidnapped by Andre Bertone, who will torture her to get the magic word that will unlock a quarter of a billion dollars and start a war to overthrow a duly elected government half a world away."

"Elena?" the senator asked.

"Please go, Senator," Elena said. "Please. It is not good for you to be . . . here, now."

"All I'm doing here is talking about donations and campaign strategy." The senator gave Rand a cold look. "And if you imply anything else to the media, I'll have your balls." He switched his glare to Elena. "Where is Andre? He'll cut through this bullshit."

Elena looked blankly at the senator. "Andre is not here."

"Well, get him here." The senator glared at the helicopter. "Get him on the phone!"

The chopper's rotor wash whipped up waves on the lap pool. The engine roar made the panes of glass in the wall vibrate.

Suddenly Elena leaped up off the couch and dashed to the sliding glass door, throwing it open with such force that it nearly jumped the track.

A cameraman hung out the side door of the news chopper, baseball cap on backward, zooming his lens in on the angry woman in the doorway.

"Get out of here!" she screamed. "Get out! You have no right to be here. You are ruining everything. I will sue you. My husband will ki—" Abruptly she realized that she was truly on film.

She turned away and shut her mouth.

The senator had noticed the camera before Elena did. He made doubly sure he wasn't in the camera's sight before he pulled a cell phone out of his back pocket and hit a number. Without a glance at his hostess, he hurried out of the great room. His voice trailed away into the distance as he disappeared in the direction of the kitchen and the servants' entrance. "Listen, we've got a huge problem. Get hold of our contacts inside the local TV network. Find out what the hell is . . ."

Rand was on his own cell phone, talking to Faroe. "Tell the helo to swing around and cover the parking area."

"Somebody leaving?"

"Only the rats. One of them is a United States senator driving a big black Caddy SUV. They'll love a shot of that back in Manhattan, home of unrapid transit."

He closed the phone on Faroe's hard laughter.

When the helicopter lifted up and over the house, Elena was still standing like an angry statue with her back to the glass doorway. The aircraft's clatter and racket shook the roof, then faded slightly as it circled around to line up a shot of the car park.

Finally she looked at Rand.

He was waiting with the patience of a true predator.

"Why?" she asked.

"You were home. Decide, Elena. Now. Your kids or your husband. Which will it be?"

68

Phoenix
Sunday
2:14 P.M. MST

Kayla braced herself with a foot against the passenger seat and tried to pull down the T-shirt Rand had given her. The blue cotton proclaimed that "Life Is Good." Though the soft cloth was smudged with dirt, grease, and blood from her cut lip, and her hands were cuffed behind her, she agreed with the sentiment.

It certainly was better than the alternative.

And she really wanted to live long enough to watch Steve Foley eat the fancy gun he kept shoving in her mouth.

So think of that while you're trying to seduce the slimy son of a bitch. Maybe then you'll smile rather than hurling all over his Italian shoes.

She watched Foley through slitted eyes. He was jumpy, sweaty, pumped full of adrenaline.

But his hand never relaxed its grip on the pistol.

If he puts that gun in my mouth again, he'll be close enough for me to hurt him. Bad.

Much as she'd rather grab the gun and shoot him with it, she knew she'd have a better chance to survive playing scared and eager to please.

It was half true. As long as Foley didn't figure out which half, she'd have a chance.

Just one.

It had to be enough.

69

Phoenix
Sunday
2:14 P.M. MST

"I can't help you," Elena insisted again, looking out the window.

She hadn't looked at Rand since the senator had retreated, leaving her alone to face whatever came.

Don't smack her, Rand told himself. *It won't do any good.*

He silently repeated the mantra that was the only thing keeping him from trying force on the stubborn beauty queen. She'd come from the gutters of São Paulo. Her ability to take pain probably exceeded his ability to give it to her.

It wasn't something he wanted to test.

His hand shot out, fastened on the hinge points of her jaw, pressed hard enough to feel bone flex.

"Look at me," he said.

Her eyes turned toward him, large and tragic, swimming with tears that never quite fell.

He felt like shoving an Oscar down her perfect throat.

"You're going to jail with Bertone," Rand said. "Your children are going to Social Services. They'll be separated and fostered out to families who make less than your maid."

"Lawyers," Elena said through clenched teeth, all that she could manage through the iron grip of his hand.

But whatever she saw in his eyes made her flinch.

"Lawyers take money," Rand said. "Your husband is broke."

That shocked Elena more than anything Rand had said or done. She tried to jerk away, but his grip was too strong.

"There was a quarter of a billion dollars in the account Bertone set up through Kayla," Rand said. "She moved it to a place Bertone can't reach. You. Are. Dead. Broke."

Her skin turned the color of ashes. "No. No! He only has half that much money."

Rand smiled. "Then he'll have some really pissed-off partners. If you help me, I'll help you keep your children and enough money to live well in Brazil."

"My friends—"

"Will read about you in tomorrow's paper," Rand cut in ruthlessly. " 'Elena Bertone, wife of an international gunrunner, was arrested with her husband for plotting to overthrow the lawful government of Camgeria and reap billions in oil revenues through the immoral use of illegal arms.' "

"I'm innocent!"

Rand doubted it, and didn't care. "If you don't help me get Kayla back, I'll cover your reputation in the blood of all the innocent children who died in Africa to enrich you and Andre Bertone. Your own children can visit you in jail—if they remember your name. Your choice, Elena. It's the only choice you have left."

The television helicopter reappeared over the front of the house. It circled, grabbing footage from a variety of angles.

Elena clapped her hands over her ears to muffle the roaring sound of the engine. "Make them go away. The noise. I can't think!"

"Try being in a war zone. That helo is a songbird compared to the Russian gunships that Andre sells."

Miranda came running into the great room and threw her arms around Elena. "Mama, Mama, what is that noise?"

Rand released Elena's jaw.

Holding her daughter, Elena looked at Rand, really looked at him. She shuddered and gave up. She couldn't bear Miranda's fear, so like her own when she'd been young. "Yes. Yes. Whatever I can do."

He hit the speed dial on his cell phone.

"Faroe here."

"Tell the helo to pull back. She's cooperating."

"Roger," Faroe said, "but they'll stay in clear view."

Rand punched off. After a few moments the pilot banked right and darted away, taking up a position where his engine could still be heard as a dull roar rather than a howling scream.

"Where is your husband?" Rand asked.

Real tears ran down Elena's face and mingled with those of the child she was comforting. She drew a deep, breaking breath.

"The club," she said in a low voice.

"What club?"

"The Arizona Territorial Gun Club."

"Is it open now?" Rand asked.

"No. Andre keeps it closed on Sunday, except for special groups. The holy day, you understand?"

"Yeah. I understand. Irony is his middle name. How can I get in?"

"You can't. Andre has the only keys. A chain-link fence surrounds the thirty acres."

Rand hit the speed dial again.

Faroe didn't answer on the first ring.

Or the second.

Or the third.

Jesus, Joe, now isn't the time to take a coffee break.

"Faroe here." His voice was soft, almost secretive.

"Bertone's at the Arizona Territorial Gun Club. The helo was headed in that direction."

"Indian land," Faroe said. "The Hokams. Small, but mighty in the law."

"That leaves out the local cops. How about the feds?"

"They probably could bootstrap some jurisdiction, but St. Kilda can't help you right now. Everybody in Phoenix suspected of associating with St. Kilda has been rounded up and detained by the local police."

Rand hissed something beneath his breath.

"The badges are being nice about it," Faroe said. "Grace is doing a professional job of educating a sharp but still fairly confused watch commander."

"Bottom line?"

"Right now we can't move without getting our asses thrown in the slammer."

"Mother of all fuckups," Rand said.

"It'll do."

"Tell the news helo to pick me up. If someone with a badge cares, I can provide probable cause for any search warrant any kind of police agency wants to run past a judge." Rand looked at Elena. "I'm sure Elena Bertone will be willing to discuss the matter with whichever state or federal judge the cops decide to wake up from his Sunday-afternoon nap."

Elena nodded agreement and rocked her daughter, comforting both of them.

"If anyone with a badge and a gun wants to come and play at Tire City," Rand said, "Kayla and I will be the ones in blue jeans. Don't shoot us."

"Roger."

Rand punched out and turned to Elena. "Where does Bertone keep his guns?"

70

Over Phoenix
Sunday
2:20 P.M. MST

Abruptly beige suburbs gave way to beige desert. Paved roads became dirt tracks. Power lines strode on silver legs across the sand and creosote. The helicopter dropped, slid under the lines, and popped up again.

The pilot's grin told Kayla that he liked flying on the edge.

The sweat on Foley's face told her that he didn't.

She didn't like it either, but anything that happened now had to be better than what would come when Bertone got his hands on her.

Don't think about that.

When the moment is right, I'll crawl through the cuffs and . . .

Whatever it takes.

She kept repeating it silently, a mantra of fear and determination.

The helicopter swung to the right, then to the left, hard arcs that turned Foley's skin a nasty shade of green. The pilot either didn't notice or didn't care. He kept playing tag with the desert, skids brushing the tops of the taller bushes, rotor sending out billows of grit, skating on the edge of disaster with a wide smile.

Keep it up, flyboy. Foley will hurl all over your windshield.

The idea made her lips curl in a grim smile.

The pilot made a tight arc around a rumple of dry, rocky hills. A paved road appeared below. The helicopter followed it, then dropped eight feet to a butterfly-soft landing in an asphalt parking lot.

The front doors of the Arizona Territorial Gun Club rose in a dark rectangle from the side of a hill. Wide concrete steps climbed to it like a shrine.

Kayla surged to her feet, turned her back on the cargo door, and fumbled it open. She half fell, half rolled out, twisted, and somehow managed to hit the asphalt feetfirst. She took off, running as fast as she could with her hands cuffed behind her. Even if she didn't get free, she'd buy some time.

A black Humvee shot up the private road toward the club.

She spun and raced toward what looked like an obstacle course, chewing up as much time as she could.

Anytime now, St. Kilda.

Plan C is looking real good.

71

Over Phoenix
Sunday
2:22 P.M. MST

Martin handed Rand a headset, plugged it into a junction box, and made room for him on the jump seat.

"What's up?" the producer asked.

"Foley kidnapped Kayla," Rand said. Two pistols dug into his back when he sat down. He'd hoped for something with more firepower, but he'd had to settle for the Bertones' bedside artillery. "He's headed to Bertone's gun club. The man himself is either there or will be soon."

"Where to?" the news pilot asked.

Rand looked at the name sewed to the pilot's pocket. Lopez. "Know where the Hokam Reservation is?"

"Sure. Little vest-pocket holding to the east. Casino, failed dog track, and some kind of fortress."

"Get us to the fortress as fast as you can. Life or death."

"Roger."

The helo leaped up from the estate's helipad, banked hard, and headed flat out to the east. The pilot talked to Phoenix Air Control. A few seconds later the bird went up like a bullet, then leveled. Rooftops and streets raced by several hundred feet below. The pilot's face and hands were relaxed, steady, and his eyes never stopped checking gauges and airspace.

"Where'd you learn to fly a bird?" Rand asked Lopez.

"California and Afghanistan."

"Then you know how to shoot, too."

"Yeah," Lopez said, reading dials.

"Got a piece?"

"This is Arizona. What do you think?"

"Keep it handy," Rand said.

"Always do."

Rand's phone rang. "Yeah?"

"This is Steele. Do you have a computer with an uplink?"

Rand looked at Martin, who had a laptop with a satellite connection. "I can use someone's."

"I e-mailed you a URL for the gun club and satellite photos of the area. There is only one road, one entrance. The perimeter is chain-link fencing with razor wire. It looks like a military installation."

Without a word, Rand took Martin's computer and called up his St. Kilda e-mail number. "Got it."

Rand zoomed in on the sat photos. Steele was right. The gun club could have been a military bunker.

"Anything else needed?" Steele asked.

"A few warrants and cooperative badges."

"We're working on that."

"Then how about a miracle," Rand muttered.

"They're back-ordered."

The connection ended.

Rand studied the Arizona Territorial Gun Club's web page. It showed outdoor pistol courses and the roofless tactical shooting house nestled against some barren desert hills. Beyond the outside shooting areas, two huge doors led into the hill itself. He studied the interior photos of the club, orienting himself to the layout of indoor firing lanes, a firearms and souvenir store, and a lounge for members interested in shooting bull as well as live ammo.

It was called the Brass Club.

The web page mentioned an exclusive set of private tactical shooting areas attached to the club room, but showed no photos.

That's where Bertone will take her. Nice and quiet, with heavy soundproofed walls and plenty of privacy for an old-fashioned round of torture.

The thought made his gut lurch. Kayla was smart and quick thinking. Bertone was merciless.

He would peel her like a ripe banana.

"How long?" Rand asked the pilot harshly.

Lopez held up two fingers.

Rand called up the aerial maps and photos again. He located the perimeter fence and the guard shack that blocked the road into the club. Tracing recognizable landforms, he looked forward through the windscreen. The facade of the clubhouse rose several miles away, straight-lined and glistening, out of place in the dusty, unruly Arizona desert.

"There's a dry wash with steep sides about two hundred yards south of the clubhouse, at the bottom of the slope," Rand said to the pilot. "See it?"

The pilot gave a thumbs-up.

"Drop me there," Rand said. "Then haul ass back upstairs and fall back to one mile."

"We can't get good coverage from a mile away," Martin protested. "Faroe said there might be some great bang-bang footage."

"You stay in range and you'll get more bang-bang than you want," the pilot said. "This helo isn't armor-plated."

"Hey," the cameraman cut in, "no biggie. I was in Fallujah. After that, this is a piece of cake."

The pilot shot him a *you dumb fuck* look and shook his head. When it came to bullets and death, there was no such thing as a piece of cake.

"That club has more firepower in its vaults than the whole Iraqi insurgency," Rand said. "Hang back until the cops and agents come pouring in. It shouldn't be long." *I hope.* "Then you can come in close and get all the footage you need."

The pilot went into a sharp descent and stayed low, approaching from the west and then swinging around the hill, keeping well out of rifle range.

Martin leaned forward, lifting field glasses to scan the club.

Rand grabbed the glasses.

"What the—" began Martin. A look at Rand's eyes stopped the producer's protest. "Okay. Okay. They're yours. Enjoy them."

The field glasses brought everything close. The Russian-made helicopter that had snatched Kayla and Foley from the roof of the bank building had set down in the empty parking lot. The only other vehicle was a black Humvee.

Bertone.

Rand raked the ground with the glasses. Suddenly Kayla leaped into focus, running hard into the desert away from either helicopter. Handcuffed, she was no match for the long-haired man closing in on her, his arms pumping, swinging free as his legs ate up the ground. An AK-47 was slung across his back. He grabbed her, slapped her hard, and began dragging her back to the club at a trot.

"Can you cut them off?" Rand asked the pilot, pointing. He knew the answer but he had to ask anyway.

"Not before he could bring us down with that AK-47 or kill her or both."

Shit.

"After you drop me, keep an eye on their helo," Rand said curtly. "If it takes off, follow. Get on the emergency frequency and tell the cops."

"What about you?" asked the pilot. "Want me to pick you up before we tail them?"

"If they get airborne, I'm already dead."

The pilot leaned on the stick and adjusted the cyclic control. The helicopter dropped, flared, and settled into a sand-bottomed wash that was twenty yards across.

"Luck, man," the pilot said as Rand stepped out onto the skid.

The instant Rand's feet hit soft sand, the overhead rotor churned up a blinding boil of dust. He crouched and fought through the grit while the helicopter lifted off and spun in midair, using the walls of the wash as cover for its retreat.

He was running before the dust settled. He figured he had less than a minute.

72

Arizona Territorial Gun Club
Sunday
2:24 P.M. MST

Kayla lashed out with her heel at the pilot's kneecap. Her soft shoes muffled the blow, but the man still staggered, swore, and hit her with the butt of his AK-47 hard enough to make darkness spin around her. He drew the butt back to hit her again, harder.

A big hand slapped the weapon away. "Enough," Bertone said. "She has to be able to talk."

Bertone bent, put his shoulder in Kayla's stomach, and stood easily, taking her weight. With one arm clamped around her thighs, he ran toward the club's double-story front doors like he was carrying no more than an AK-47 over his shoulder.

Kayla's head bounced against Bertone's back while he trotted up the broad fan of steps leading to the club. At first she thought the roaring in her ears was blood returning to her head. Then she realized the sound came from a helicopter she couldn't see; she could only hear the rotors slicing air and the engine howling, going away.

Bertone unlocked the club's big doors, kicked them open, and rushed inside before a stray shot could kill Kayla.

Or an intentional one.

It's what he would have done if he wanted to keep her from giving away a quarter of a billion dollars.

The sound of the helicopter faded.

"Take my Humvee," Bertone told the pilot. "Kill whoever they left."

The pilot set off at a run for the parking lot, slapping his pockets, reassuring himself that he had extra ammo.

Behind him, the front door of the fortress slammed shut.

73

Arizona Territorial Gun Club
Sunday
2:27 P.M. MST

Rand hugged the dirt bank of the ravine until he found a break in its wall. He scrambled out through the dry, crumbling wash and onto the slope below the clubhouse. Crouching in the lacy shadow of a bush, he scanned the area for movement.

The scattered boulders on the slope were covered with dark desert varnish and traces of lichen. A spring bloom of desert wildflowers was already fading.

Nothing moved but a breeze.

He pulled one of the pistols from his waistband and automatically checked the magazine. Eight bright cartridges gleamed in the sunlight, with one more already in the chamber. He replaced it and pulled out the other pistol. Same count. A total of eighteen bullets against Arizona Territorial Gun Club's arsenal.

He'd get better odds in a state lottery.

Eyes narrowed, he studied the slope, picking out the best cover. Then he was moving again, keeping low, running hard. He paused behind shoulder-high rocks to check the ridgeline for anything alive.

Where the hell are they?

They had to hear the helo land and take off. They had to send someone after me.

Or are they torturing Kayla right now, figuring to get what they need out of her before anyone can stop them?

Ice twisted in his gut.

He sprinted toward the next bit of cover. A bullet screamed off a rock to his left, showering him with chips and grit. Instantly he dodged, ducked behind a different rock, and looked in the direction the bullet had come.

A white man with long, wild hair reared up from his cover behind a boulder and savagely hammered on the action of an AK-47. The usually reliable weapon obviously had a problem.

Next time, clean it better, Rand thought grimly.

It was a lesson he'd learned in Africa. Grit buggered up the works faster than water.

He stepped out of cover and took careful aim with the pistol. The range was fifty yards, uphill. Under those conditions, shooting with an unfamiliar gun, he'd be lucky to scare the man. He let out his breath and poured shots up the hill. Bullets whined and screamed as they hit the rock near the gunman.

Suddenly the man's arms flew open. He fell backward without a sound. The assault rifle clattered against the rock and slid to the ground.

Rand waited, listened.

Nothing moved toward the gunman.

No more shots came.

Rand didn't have time to wait around and be certain.

Wishing Reed was there to cover his back, Rand dropped the empty pistol, pulled out the second gun, and zigzagged up the hill. No one fired at him. When he reached the fallen man, he was groaning and jerking, covering himself in dirt. His face was a scarlet sheet of blood pouring from a jagged wound that had parted his hair just off center, parallel to his forehead.

A ricochet rather than a direct hit.

Works for me.

Rand shoved the pistol in his belt, grabbed the assault rifle off the ground, cleared the jam, and swiftly checked the surrounding area.

No one near.

The man thrashed and muttered in Russian.

Rand bent and rapped the man on his cheekbone with the assault rifle. "How many men inside?"

The Russian's eyes opened, glazed and wary. He didn't say a word.

"How many?" Rand raked the muzzle over the scalp wound.

The man bucked and tried to get away.

Rand put the rifle muzzle in the Russian's crotch. "How many men? Where are they in the building?"

Sweat broke out on the man's face.

"The first shot goes to your balls," Rand said calmly. "Then I'll take out your knees."

The Russian looked at Rand's eyes and started talking.

"Two," the man said hoarsely. "Bertone and some nancy redhead. And the girl."

Rand reached under the Russian, found no weapons in the small of his back, and began patting pockets. No car keys. No ID. But he did find a curved magazine. He pulled it out, hefted it, and smiled. "A full thirty. Thanks."

The Russian looked away.

Rand stood, pocketed the magazine, and slung the AK-47 into carrying position at his front. "This is your lucky day. If you can make the road, you might get away before the cops come. Now get the hell out of my sight."

While Rand backed away warily, the Russian sat up, then stood and staggered a few steps down the slope. He stopped, bending at the waist like he was going to throw up.

Rand started running toward the top of the hill.

Not good, bro. One of us dead is enough.

He spun around just in time to see the Russian yank a small pistol from his boot. Rand pulled out his own pistol and shot quickly, precisely. The Russian fell hard and didn't move again.

Rand had seen death before. It had nothing new to teach him.

He turned and ran toward the gun club.

74

Arizona Territorial Gun Club
Sunday
2:30 P.M. MST

Bertone stood at the front door, waiting to hear the AK-47 speak again. He listened intently. And listened.

Silence.

Apparently the pistol had had the last word.

With a curse for the incompetents he was surrounded by, Bertone turned back toward the lobby of the gun club. Foley stood ten feet away. His pistol was pressed hard against Kayla's neck. Her skin was pale, the pulse in her neck was hammering, and her eyes open, watching, always watching. She had been a great deal of trouble to Bertone, slowing him down, wasting time, mocking him with her silence. He was looking forward to killing her.

After he got the password.

"What happened?" Foley asked nervously.

"Obviously the fool got in the way of some bullets."

Kayla's smile was a mean curve in her dirty, bruised face.

"Now what?" Foley asked.

Kayla eased away from the pistol muzzle digging into her neck.

Bertone shrugged. "I can fly the helicopter better than he can."

"But—" Foley began.

"Shut it."

Foley flinched and shut up.

Bertone sorted through probabilities, possibilities, and miracles with the speed of the highly intelligent gambler he was. The odds of getting himself and an unwilling Kayla to the helicopter out front without being picked off were smaller than the odds of taking out whoever had killed the pilot when he came after Kayla.

Then Bertone would fly the helicopter to Mexico and work on Kayla at his leisure.

Without a word, he strode out of the lobby. A few moments later he was back with an M-16.

"You take the front," he said to Foley, handing him the weapon. "It's on full automatic." He put one hand in Kayla's hair, twisted hard, yanked. "She comes with me."

75

Arizona Territorial Gun Club
Sunday
2:32 P.M. MST

Rand found Bertone's black Humvee parked at the top of the slope, a hundred yards from the front of the gun club. Everything between the Humvee and the club was scraped level and cleared of brush and boulders.

A perfect kill zone.

And Bertone was a good shot with just about anything he could get his hands on, including a sniper's rifle.

Rand's skin prickled, waiting for the bullet that could strike before he even heard the sound of the shot.

Using the heavy body of the vehicle as a shield, he opened the driver's door.

The key was in the ignition.

The big engine turned over and caught, revved slightly, then settled into a healthy growl. Rand backed up, turned, and pointed the vehicle toward the club. He kicked the accelerator hard, wanting to see what the Humvee had under the hood.

It had enough. Dirt, grit, and sand showered from beneath the big tires.

Suddenly a tiny starburst bloomed in the windshield a few inches in front of Rand's face. Instinctively he flinched and sank down behind the wheel. Another bullet ricocheted off the heavy, angled glass, leaving barely a pockmark.

He laughed. "Thanks, Bertone. I should have guessed you'd bulletproof your favorite ride."

Driving hard, he plowed through the soft, sandy dirt. Then he popped up onto the asphalt parking lot. He accelerated toward the helicopter, then spun the wheel at the last instant. The butt of the Humvee smashed into the pilot's seat. One skid collapsed.

Let's see you fly that, Bertone.

Fifty yards in front of Rand, something red flashed. A man's hair.

Foley.

Using some landscape shrubs as a blind, he was firing a long gun with a telescopic sight. It looked like an American M-16.

High velocity, small caliber. Hope this glass is as good as Bertone is paranoid.

Foley poured bullets into the Humvee's windshield. Lead smacked and whined and skipped off the tough glass.

Then came silence except for the roar of the engine.

Now, do you have an extra magazine? Rand thought grimly.

Foley threw the M-16 to the ground and yanked a heavy revolver from the belt holster at his waist.

Rand put the accelerator on the floor.

Two bullets hammered, cracking the windshield.

Rand pointed the Humvee toward Foley and shielded his eyes against flying glass in case the windshield gave way.

No more bullets came.

Rand risked a quick look. Foley was running toward the big glass doors of the clubhouse.

Bulletproof, no doubt, Rand thought. *Let's see how they hold up to a battering ram.*

The doors slammed shut behind Foley.

One-handed, Rand took a folding knife from his pocket and flicked open the serrated blade. He didn't want to get pinned in the seat if the airbag deployed and then didn't deflate fast enough.

The stately parade of steps up to the club's impressive entrance slowed the Humvee's charge. It was making less than fifteen miles per hour when the armored radiator smashed through the glass-and-aluminum doors of the club. The airbag deployed with an explosive sound. Within seconds it began to deflate, its job done. A slash from Rand's blade speeded the process.

As he pocketed the knife again, he caught a glimpse of Foley scrambling behind the heavy concrete fountain in the center of the lobby. From there, the banker ran until he could launch himself up and over a long, waist-high counter where shooters registered for courses and arms.

The Humvee had enough momentum to climb the lip of the fountain before it crunched to a halt.

For a few seconds the only sound was the trickling of the fountain. Then the lobby exploded with the deafening chatter of a big machine gun.

The Humvee's bulletproof glass wasn't designed to withstand that kind of close, heavy fire. As Rand dove to the floor and kicked open the driver's door, the windshield exploded. He rolled out onto the lobby's tile floor, dragging the AK-47 with him. A heavy burst of machine-gun fire rattled off the Humvee's body as he crab-walked forward and hunkered down behind the concrete fountain.

Judging by the angle of the bullets, they were coming from somewhere behind the waist-high reception counter. Rand ducked back down. Lead thudded into the black Humvee, chewed chunks of concrete out of the fountain's pedestal, and ricocheted crazily.

Rand stayed down. He wasn't facing some handy, portable, rapid-fire weapon. This machine gun was the kind trucks and go-fast raiding boats used on fixed mounts.

Does the bastard have a machine-gun emplacement behind the counter?

Rand grabbed another quick look over the concrete rim of the fountain. He caught a glimpse of Bertone standing, firing a heavy M-60 machine gun from the hip. It was a feat that took strength, skill, and balls.

Another burst of bullets rattled and ricocheted through the clubhouse lobby, leaving behind a ringing kind of silence.

Rand heard a snarl of Russian curses, followed by the sound of retreating footsteps.

Ran out of ammo.

He sprang to his feet, AK-47 nestled against his shoulder, ready, willing, and quite able to kill Bertone.

Kayla screamed from somewhere just in front of Bertone, telling Rand that she was alive and somewhere in the private quarters behind the desk and down the hall. He kept his finger loose on the trigger, afraid of hitting her with a ricochet or having a bullet go clean through Bertone into her.

Foley sprang from behind a tile-covered concrete pillar and leveled his heavy revolver. The weapon went off with a roar. The impact of the bullet flung Rand against the front fender of the Humvee. The gun roared again as he slid limply down the vehicle and into the shelter of the front wheel. The AK-47 clattered to the tile.

Everything faded into the sound of a woman screaming in rage and fear, calling Rand's name, once, twice.

Silence.

"I got him! I shot him!" Foley yelled. "I got his ass!"

"How many times did you hit him?" Bertone's voice came from the hallway.

"Once for sure. Maybe twice. He went down hard. Nobody beats a .44 Magnum."

"Be certain," Bertone said.

Foley stared toward the fountain.

Nothing moved. But he couldn't see the downed man, either. He was on the opposite side of the fountain, maybe behind the Humvee.

"I'm certain." Foley laughed. "Damn, I'm good!"

That's it, asshole, Rand thought through a haze of pain. *Don't move and fire, move and fire. Just stand there congratulating your miserable self.*

Silently Rand rolled onto his injured right side, gritting his teeth against the pulsing, radiating pain. The AK-47 lay where it had fallen, between him and the black tire of the Humvee.

Inches out of reach.

"Make sure of it," Bertone said. "Put a shot in the bastard's head. Then we'll question the woman."

"You've got a better angle," Foley said roughly. "Just stand up behind the counter and let him have it from a distance."

"Do it close in, or I'll shoot you, then him."

In the shadow of the wheel, Rand lay still, clenching his teeth against waves of pain. Body armor was good, but not getting hit by a .44 would have been a lot better. He had at least two bad ribs and his right arm—his shooting arm—was half numb. His right hand felt weak.

Biting back groans and curses, he forced himself to reach out until he could curl his left index finger around the trigger of the heavy AK-47.

Foley's Italian loafers and eight inches of his legs showed beneath the Humvee. He was walking forward, flat-footed and slow, a man used to shooting at things that couldn't shoot back.

Rand's vision dimmed and the world started to spin. He bit into his tongue, creating enough pain to distract from the damage left behind by the hammer blow of a .44. Slowly the world settled into patterns of pain he could work with. He shifted the gun until its muzzle was aimed a few inches above the tile floor. Squinting through the iron sights, he moved the muzzle until it covered Foley's feet.

The fire-selection lever grated on the tile, just enough noise to freeze Foley for an instant.

It was more than Rand needed.

A short burst of fire chattered and echoed in the lobby, followed instantly by Foley's scream. Even as Rand lifted his finger from the trigger, shifted position, and aimed again, Foley went down like a dynamited building. As he hit the floor, the AK spit fire and death.

Three more bullets caught Foley in the torso. The force flung his body backward, sliding and skidding into the glittering, shattered glass that had exploded from the front doors.

Silence.

Then the liquid sounds of the fountain.

76

Arizona Territorial Gun Club
Sunday
2:35 P.M. MST

Kayla forced herself to be still, not to scream or cry or try to run to the place Rand had fallen.

He's not dead.

Wounded, okay, but not dead.

Not dying.

If she didn't believe that, she'd shatter into more pieces than the glass front doors. And with every piece, she'd try to cut Bertone's throat.

"Call out to him," Bertone said, twisting the hand in her hair until she was forced to her knees.

"Foley?" she asked through clenched teeth.

He wrenched her head. “He’s dead. The other one. Your lover. Call to him. Tell him I want to talk.”

It was something she wanted to do. “Rand,” she called. “Bertone wants to talk.”

Rand took a slow breath, then another, easing toward the waist-high counter. He wasn’t worried about being caught in the open. In order to shoot him, Bertone would have to reveal himself first.

The thought made Rand smile.

“I can hear Bertone just fine from here,” Rand called back.

His voice was changed, roughened by adrenaline and pain, but Kayla was so glad to hear him that she swayed in relief.

Get a grip, she told herself savagely. *We’re a long way from home free. Foley’s weapon is out of reach, and I can’t even lift that monster Bertone was carrying.*

She could try for the ugly handgun he had now, but only when all other chances were gone.

Rand glanced several times at Foley, then didn’t bother again. None of the torso wounds were bleeding. The shattered ankle bones should have had him screaming in agony.

Instead there was the silence of death.

“Throw down your arms or I’ll kill Kayla,” Bertone said.

Rand's laughter was as rough as his voice had been, and colder. "She's worth too much to you alive."

Silence. Then Bertone asked, "What do you want?"

Rand bit back the words he wanted to say—*Kayla free, unharmed*—and said what a man like Bertone would understand. "Your death."

Kayla shuddered and waited for the bullet that would kill her.

It didn't come.

Bertone really needed her alive.

"Why?" Bertone asked, trying to find a weakness in the man who hunted him.

"You killed my identical twin."

Bertone frowned and sighed. Vengeance was a stronger drive than love or greed. Much stronger.

And like all emotions, it could be manipulated.

"When?" Bertone asked. "Where?"

"Five years ago. Africa."

Bertone smiled. The beauty of emotion was that it could make a man hot when he should be cold.

"I killed many men in Africa," he said. "Be more specific."

"You were flying arms to the rebels in Camgeria."

"Ah, you were the photographer."

Rand didn't trust himself to answer. He just kept duckwalking toward the counter, silently cursing the pain in his shoulder and ribs that made it nearly impossible to breathe.

"I can only imagine the agony of watching an identical twin die," Bertone said, laughter curling beneath the words, "the gasping breaths, the bloody—"

Kayla shoved hard against Bertone, afraid that he would goad Rand into doing something stupid.

Bertone looked at her like she was a fly. He swatted her back the same way, casually.

When Rand heard her muffled cry, he was at the counter. His eyes and the muzzle of the AK-47 cleared the granite top at the same instant.

The hallway behind the counter was empty.

He thought he could hear sounds from the room at the far end of the hall, but the pulsing pain and the rush of blood in his own were disorienting. He dropped down and forced himself to remember what he'd seen of the club's layout on Martin's computer.

Anteroom at the end of the hall.

Private shooting rooms open out from there.

He checked the AK-47. Maybe ten rounds left, plus the second pistol Elena had given him, which was still stuffed in his waistband.

He tried to think back over how many shots he had fired from the rifle. He couldn't.

Faroe would have a fit. The man's a bear for counting shots.

Not that it mattered. However many shots Rand had, Bertone had a lot more, a whole shooting house full of ammo. Rand's best call was to wait for more men with guns to come and help him.

But as soon as Bertone figured out what his stalker was doing, Kayla would have his full attention.

Not good.

Rand staggered to his feet and covered the hallway with the AK's muzzle. He had to pin Bertone down, then cut him down. It was a job for several special weapons teams, but he didn't have any in his hip pocket.

He took a calculated risk by rolling up and over the reception counter and falling on his knees in the corner near the hall. From there he could control the corridor.

And fight the waves of blackness that were right behind the bright red pulses of pain.

Bertone circled Kayla's throat with his left arm. Using her as a shield, he leaned forward and sighted down the blunt action of his Glock.

The hall was empty but for a tiny bit of the AK-47's muzzle showing from the corner behind the service desk. He shot quickly, more a reflex than an aim.

Rand jerked back as plaster exploded, dusting the barrel of his weapon. He waited, hoping Bertone would come closer, would poke his head around the corner.

And get it blown off.

Bertone was too smart for that. He tightened his grip on Kayla and dragged her backward into the darkness beyond the far door, where the private shooting rooms waited. There he would get the only thing he needed from her.

Moments later Kayla's scream shattered the silence.

77

Arizona Territorial Gun Club
Sunday
2:38 P.M. MST

Rand forced himself to think when all he wanted to do was run down the hall and stop Bertone.

Suck it up.

Think.

The scream had been too far away to come from the hall itself or the anteroom beyond it.

He grabbed a handful of spiral notebooks from behind the reception counter and threw them down the corridor.

No one fired at the movement.

Time to buck the odds.

Riding a wave of adrenaline, he came to his feet and raced down the hall, weapon in firing position. The locked door at the back of the anteroom flashed a red warning light. Below that was a sign:

TACTICAL SHOOTING HOUSE

LIVE FIRE IN PROGRESS

Rand blew out the lock with a short burst of fire. The door slammed inward. He dove low through the opening, rolled behind the first cover he saw, and ignored the pain that was shutting down his vision.

The quick look he'd gotten as he dove through the door told him that the shooting house was the size of a basketball court. No windows. No ceiling for the maze of hallways and rooms. Light level so low that he had to let his eyes adjust.

Kayla's scream was louder this time.

Rand clenched his teeth. *I'm sorry, Kayla.*

God, I'm sorry.

Breathing as quietly as possible, he lay behind a concrete pillar, trying to pinpoint the direction of the scream that was echoing around the room. Somewhere to his left, down a hallway without ceilings and behind a closed door, he heard the ring of a brass cartridge hitting and rolling across hard concrete.

A piece of shooting debris kicked by a careless foot.

Or a distraction created in the opposite direction of the real threat.

"Kayla!" Rand yelled, and rolled behind another pillar.

She answered with a choked-off scream, all she could manage before Bertone clamped steel fingers across her mouth.

The sound came from Rand's right, down a narrow corridor formed by two eight-foot-high Kevlar "walls" designed to catch bullets sprayed by wild shooters. He examined the hallway. Thirty feet from his position, doors faced each other across the corridor.

It was intended to simulate a standard business-building arrangement, a place where a weapons team could practice tactics to use against a man who had gone postal.

Fifty-fifty.

I storm the hallway and take one door, only to find the shooter is waiting behind the other.

Rand didn't move. It wasn't like Bertone to settle for even odds.

The attack will come from the far end of the corridor while I'm busy shooting at empty doorways.

He circled to his right and came at the shooting maze from the other end. It was the only way he had a hope of surprising Bertone. With each quick step, he tensed against hearing Kayla's scream.

Nothing but silence.

Way too much silence.

But at least he'd distracted Bertone from Kayla.

Three more steps.

A leather sole squeaked on the smooth concrete ahead and on the other side of a wall.

Rand had run ten feet when sound exploded, a shattering burst from the M-60 machine gun. Apparently Bertone had found more ammo for his heavy iron. Slugs chewed through the Kevlar partition where Rand had been. The sound was more shocking than the bullets that ripped through the wall.

Rand couldn't hear his own breath, which meant that Bertone was also deafened for a time. Moving fast, Rand turned the corner of the shooting maze.

There was another long, dimly lit corridor with a series of facing doors and a side hall that cut away. At the far end of the corridor, a steel stairway climbed halfway up to the open ceiling and then cut back on itself.

Perfect ambush.

Tactical nightmare.

A defender could hide at the cutback point and fire down the corridor or wait at the second-floor landing and fire down on his attacker.

Rand focused on a Mylar dome hanging from the ceiling halfway down the hall. He'd seen gear like it in high-security installations all over the world. Closed-circuit TV cameras lived behind the Mylar. Other similar installations covered the rest of the shooting rooms.

Son of a bitch. Bertone can monitor every step I take.

Rand stepped into the center of the corridor and lifted the AK with his left hand, forcing his right arm to support the barrel. The fingers had feeling again, but his right shoulder wasn't worth shit. He fired three shots.

The closest plastic dome exploded in a shower of sparks as Rand raced back to cover.

The hard black snout of a machine-gun muzzle poked out of a seam in the corridor wall. A hail of bullets screamed and whined off the concrete floor. Bertone had turned jacketed slugs into a shotgun blast of shrapnel that shredded the wall three feet from where Rand was hiding.

Cute. If I'd stopped to admire my work like Foley, I'd be bloody rags on the floor.

Like Foley.

Breathing softly, listening hard, Rand wondered what Bertone's next trick would be.

78

Arizona Territorial Gun Club
Sunday
2:40 P.M. MST

Kayla pulled and twisted against the duct tape covering her mouth, scrubbing it against the rough console in the control room. High up on her thighs, flesh burned and bled where Bertone had cut her. She noticed it only because the blood got in her way when she tried to rub off her duct-tape gag on her jeans. Blood trickled down over the duct tape binding her ankles.

God, Rand, Bertone can see everything you do.

Can you hear me?

I'm screaming it!

But nothing useful got past the duct tape.

Breathing hard through her nose, she was forced to slow down for lack of air. She managed to roll up against the wall and look around. The first thing she saw was the ugly pistol Bertone had left on a metal table near one of the huge, silent monitors.

It was a better chance than she'd hoped for.

She began to work at getting cuffed hands in front of her, rather than behind. As she did, she watched the monitors.

One section was blank.

The section next to it showed Bertone lying in wait.

Rand was soft-footing it along a different corridor, a pistol in his hand. In front, across his chest, a wicked-looking weapon waited to be used.

Heart pounding, body struggling, Kayla watched the two men play a lethal kind of hide-and-seek.

Obviously Rand had figured out where Bertone was waiting behind a wall. Instead of continuing down the shredded corridor, Rand had retreated and reentered the maze from the front.

Kayla watched, worked, and tried to breathe through the duct tape as Rand ghosted up the metal stairs. Half-way to the top, he looked up. He ran up the rest of the way, grabbed a handful of wires, and ripped.

Another camera went out.

No shots followed.

Sweating, terrified, she wrestled with the cuffs and watched as Rand disappeared from the monitors. She looked overhead at the network of catwalks and observation platforms for the action below.

There was no cover.

And no cameras to track him.

Watching, raking her gag against the rough console as she struggled, Kayla saw Rand move down the catwalk one slow, gliding step at a time, scanning the maze below for movement. She could tell when he spotted her in the control room in the center of the maze.

Rand shifted the weapon from his chest to his back and eeled toward the control room on his belly.

Bertone was nowhere in sight.

Kayla gave up on her cuffs for the moment and struggled toward a bank of monitors, pointing with her bound feet, clearly wanting Rand to look at the TVs.

Two rooms away, he watched the big screens that were still working. Each was being fed in rotation by several cameras, perhaps as many as a dozen cameras covering the tactical course. The right-hand screen rotated through a blank monitor every four or five seconds, one of the holes he'd left in the coverage.

Kayla breathed hard through her nose and watched the screens like a bird watching a snake. Rand watched with her through several cycles.

A flash of movement.

Bertone was sneaking back across the corridor near the end of the maze, still carrying the heavy M-60 like it was an assault rifle. He was sweating but not breathing hard.

Damn, that's one strong bastard, Rand thought. *It will take a lot of lead to bring him down.*

And he was closing in on Kayla.

On the monitor she saw Bertone head for a concealed door in the control room. She slumped back against the console just before Bertone walked in.

She forced herself not to look at the ceiling catwalk.

Bertone gave her an amused look. The blood on the floor told its own story about her useless struggles. He focused on the monitors.

Motionless, Rand hugged the catwalk and sweated. He could hear his own breathing again; the deafness from the blast of the M-60 had faded. That meant Bertone's hearing was back online, too. Moving on the metal catwalk to get closer to Bertone would be difficult, but the range was too great for Rand to be accurate with a borrowed pistol.

Kayla was too close to the target.

Bertone studied each of the monitors through a complete sequence. Nothing moved. He shifted the M-60 and cat-footed it back to his peephole overlooking the corridor.

Kayla rolled as far as she could from Bertone's position, wanting to give Rand as much of a firing field as possible. Watching slugs ricochet off the stone lobby floor had been an education.

Am I making enough noise? she asked Rand silently.

She threw in some shoe scrapes and muffled thumps. She balanced on the tightrope of helping Rand cover his approach, yet not making so much noise that Bertone knocked her out—which he'd done before he found the duct tape.

Rand used Kayla's sound as cover, closing in on the control room. Now he could see a Glock pistol with an extended magazine lying on a narrow table beside one of the screens. A Glock tricked out like that was a mini machine gun, twenty shots on semi- or full automatic.

Using Kayla's muffled thrashing, Rand eeled to the place where another catwalk cut across the shooting house. Bertone hadn't moved from his ambush spot.

Now, Kayla thought. *Time to see if those yoga classes live up to their ads.*

It was her last chance. If Bertone found her, she would die. But then, he was planning to kill her anyway.

After he made her scream some more.

She shifted and wiggled and strained until she fell over. She glanced at the screen and saw that Bertone hadn't moved. She forced her cuffed hands over her butt, down her legs, then fought her ankles and feet through.

Her blood helped to grease the way.

When she was finished, she was sweating, her chest was heaving, and she felt like she'd strained every muscle in her arms. She was still cuffed, but at least her hands were in front of her.

She peeled down enough of the gag to breathe more easily, then dragged herself over to the ugly pistol Bertone had left behind. Her shoulders ached in time to the rapid beat of her heart.

She watched the screen.

Bertone hadn't moved.

She pushed herself to her knees and grabbed the gun. It wasn't as heavy as it looked, but she guessed it would have a hard recoil. She knew enough to recognize the safety. It wasn't on. Very carefully she set the pistol next to her on the floor. Watching the screen, she started clawing at the duct tape around her ankles. This time the blood got in her way, making her fingers slip. An inch at a time, she managed to peel the sticky stuff off.

She glanced up at the catwalks as she pulled the tape free.

Rand was grinning like a pirate. He gestured with one hand, sweeping her back out of the line of fire he would have to use if Bertone came back into the room.

She glanced at the screen again.

It was empty.

79

Arizona Territorial Gun Club
Sunday
2:44 P.M. MST

Bertone moved with incredible speed for a man of his bulk. By the time Kayla caught the motion on another screen, he was in the hallway just outside, his heavy gun pointed at the catwalk.

Rand saw him before Kayla did. He threw himself to the side and tried to pull the AK-47 into firing position. Something hung up on the catwalk. Suddenly the gun spun off and fell down into the opening below. He lunged for a narrow steel observation platform as he grabbed his pistol.

The sound of the M-60 deafened him all over again.

The hail of heavy slugs punched and clanged and sang around him as he wriggled on his stomach to the edge of the steel platform. A fragment of metal ricocheted so close that he felt a burning line drawn across one eyebrow. Pistol ready, he leaned over the edge just enough to see Bertone.

Too far for a pistol.

But not too far for the machine gun.

Bullets punched and exploded around Rand. Bertone was chewing the observation platform into ragged steel lace.

Rand rolled over and over. It was suicide for him to stay on the platform and certain death if he went back to the catwalk. Ignoring the blood dripping down his face, he took a new position, leaned over the edge, and fired two times, the shots a bare instant apart.

Bertone jerked and swung the machine gun. Rand kept firing as he watched the muzzle brake of the M-60 turn into a tunnel of death looking for him.

Finding him.

He kept pouring bullets into Bertone. He might as well have been pumping bullets into a tree for all the good it was doing. At this range, the little bedside pistol just wasn't getting the job done.

Or Bertone was wearing body armor.

Kayla stepped out of the control room and closed in until she couldn't miss Bertone. Eyes open, jaw clenched, she aimed at the back of his head and held the trigger down. Bullets and fire came in a continuous stream until the magazine was empty and the slide locked back.

With a violent shudder she flung the gun away and turned her back on the twitching Bertone. She had taken all she could, and then she had taken more.

She was done.

Distantly she heard sirens screaming and Rand talking to her. His arms held her.

"Easy, love, easy," he said. "It's over."

She closed her eyes and sagged against him. "You sure?"

He looked at what had once been Andre Bertone. "Yeah, I'm sure. Body armor only protects what it covers."

Leaning on each other, they walked slowly out of the bloody shooting house, toward the sound of sirens pouring in through the shattered front doors.

80

Phoenix
May

Kayla stood close to Rand and watched a lone hummingbird dip and drink, dip and drink, a tiny feathered pump sucking nectar from a feeder dangling above her apartment balcony. When the bird leaped back, hovered, and darted off into the velvet dusk, Kayla sighed and straightened.

"Okay," she said, "I'm ready now."

"You don't have to."

"I need to."

He didn't argue. He knew what some of her dreams were like. He'd held her through them.

She'd held him through his.

He shut the patio door, threaded his way through the painting gear that had taken over the living room, and went to the TV. An unmarked DVD stuck out like a silver tongue from the slot.

As he bent to shove the disc into place, she asked automatically, "How are your ribs?"

"Ask me next week, when we get to the cold, wet Pacific Northwest."

"Do you want to stay here?"

"Not unless you do."

She shook her head. "I've always wanted to see Washington's San Juan Islands."

He picked up the controller and sat next to her on the couch. "If you'd kept your grandmother's bank account, you could own those islands."

"I didn't even like taking the St. Kilda bonus."

"It didn't come from Bertone's money," Rand said. *Not directly. Hell, in today's world, clean money is a joke.* "And you earned every last penny of your percentage. Did I say thank you for saving my life?"

"Same back at you, and yes, every time you look at me and smile."

Smiling, he ran his fingertips down her face. She had a faint scar from Foley's ring. There were other marks, high on her legs. At first seeing the scars had enraged Rand. Then he'd accepted them for what they were—a warrior's mark of courage, more beautiful than perfection would have been.

Just as he had finally accepted that he had lived and Reed hadn't.

He pushed the button on the controller. Brent Thomas's handsome face smiled out at them from the screen. The backdrop was a Camgerian village.

"Thank you for joining me. I'm in Camgeria, Africa. Many of you will remember our March show, which featured the rise and fall of international gunrunner Andre Bertone. Much of the graphic footage of starvation and disease in that hour was filmed in the village behind me."

Kayla wanted to look away as the camera reprised the village's brutal past, but she didn't. She had learned the hard way the truth that lay at St. Kilda Consulting's core: when civilized people were too sensitive to face evil, then evil would bring down civilization.

"Today, I have the rare pleasure of sharing with you a miracle of rebirth. Villages all over Camgeria are being transformed, thanks to the outpouring of viewers like you."

"Plus St. Kilda's gift of two hundred million and change," Rand said, taking her hand. "And the courage of a certain unnamed banker lady."

"Don't forget the unlikely artist."

"Who?"

"You."

"What's unlikely about—"

"Shhh. I can't hear," Kayla interrupted.

"*—clinic opened today. There will be free exams and treatments for everyone in the village. Thanks to our viewers' generosity, the school has more supplies than they can use, so staff from* The World in One Hour *has been supplying schools in neighboring villages. The biggest blessing is the village well. With it, the waterborne diseases that have plagued these people in the past will be eradicated.*"

The view shifted to laughing children playing a local version of tag while their mothers lined up with buckets for a turn at the astonishing, ever-flowing silver water.

The scene shifted again, more angles on the difference a few hundred thousand dollars had made in a village that had known only poverty, violence, and despair.

When Thomas signed off, Kayla took the controller and killed the TV. "Amazing what one little old television program can do all by its little old self."

"Hey, Okay Martin begged you to—"

"Sell my soul for a few minutes of fame before the bruises healed," she cut in. "No thanks. I understand why St. Kilda shuns the spotlight."

"Public theater is necessary for society."

"So are public sewers."

Rand gave up, laughed, and pulled her into his lap. "Speaking of things that float, do you suppose Elena watched the show?"

"I doubt it was televised in Brazil."

He nuzzled against her hair. After all of it, she still smelled like cinnamon and vanilla. "Last time I talked to Joe, he was still wondering how you conned Grace and Steele into letting Elena get a slice of Bertone's pie."

"It was a very small slice. Microscopic, actually."

"It was a big pie."

"Her kids no more deserved poverty and privation than the kids in Camgeria. And there was no way to punish Elena without punishing them."

Kayla leaned against Rand, remembered his injury, and straightened.

He pulled her back against his chest.

"Your ribs—"

"Are healed," he said. "Cracked, not smashed, thanks to Joe's body armor. I owe him a new set."

Kayla savored the warmth of being close to Rand. After a few minutes she stirred and kissed his neck. "Are you going to do it?"

"Buy Joe body armor?"

"Keep working for St. Kilda."

"I don't know. But whatever happens, I've got a lot of painting to do for me. And for Reed."

"I wish I'd known him," Kayla said.

"He'd have loved you the same as I do."

"We talking three-in-one-bed kind of love?"

"Hadn't thought of that."

"Well, don't. One of you is all I can take."

He laughed and held her while they watched twilight deepen into night.

"Rand?"

"Hmm?"

"If we have a boy, I want to call him Reed."

Rand went still, then held her even closer. "We'd like that."